THE LAST LEGENDS OF EARTH

A. A. Attanasio

BANTAM BOOKS
NEW YORK · TORONTO · LONDON · SYDNEY · AUCKLAND

This edition contains the complete text
of the original hardcover edition.
NOT ONE WORD HAS BEEN OMITTED.

THE LAST LEGENDS OF EARTH
A Bantam Spectra Book / published by arrangement with
Doubleday

PRINTING HISTORY
Doubleday edition published September 1989
Bantam edition / September 1990

Bantam Books are published by Bantam Books, a division of
Bantam Doubleday Dell Publishing Group, Inc. Its trademark,
consisting of the words "Bantam Books" and the portrayal of
a rooster, is Registered in U.S. Patent and Trademark Office
and in other countries. Marca Registrada. Bantam Books,
666 Fifth Avenue, New York, New York 10103

PRINTED IN THE UNITED STATES OF AMERICA
OPM   0 9 8 7 6 5 4 3 2 1

for those who will be

Of the great things which are to be found among us, the Being of Nothingness is the greatest.

—LEONARDO DA VINCI

Contents

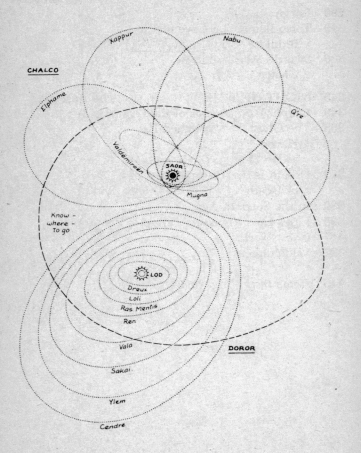

CHALCO

Kappur

Nabu

Elphame

Qre

Valdemiraen

SAOR

Mugna

Know-
where-
To go

LOD

Dreux

Loli

Ras Mentis

Ren

Vala

DOROR

Sakai

Ylem

Cendre

Tractate of a Timefree, Spacelike Domain

Originally titled simply Utility Manual, The Book of Horizons, *popularly known as the* Glyph Astra, *received its vulgar title from references to the "star carvings" (Greek: astron, glyphē) allegedly revealed to the Strong Mother in kakta trance. These "carvings" were in actuality eidetic images of probability patterns in the Overworld, that timefree, spacelike domain inside lynks (hypertubes).* The Book of Horizons *was intended primarily to orient people to the complexities of the Overworld—but first, it was necessary that the people find themselves within the worlds. The anonymous tractate that opens* Utility Manual *is meant to place us among the horizons not only of the worlds but of the Overworld. It can be found in most early editions from the Age of Knives and is traditionally assumed to have been written by the Strong Mother herself.*

This chapter is for those people who remember Earth. The first thing you have to know is that your memories are real. Your certainty that you have lived before in a very different place than where you are now is not a delusion. Earth actually did exist, long ago. The swirl of stars that fills the night sky is the galaxy where we lived. Remember the Sun? It was a star in that galaxy. Two billion years ago, it blew up, and the Earth was blown apart with it. This happened long after human life had become extinct. The exploding Sun shattered the Earth and cast the hot debris into the cold darkness of the void. The rubble floated in the vacuum almost all that time, mixing with the gas clouds of space. A few thousand years ago, an intelligent being from a reality we had never suspected found our dust. For its own alien purposes and by its own strange science, that intelligent being read in our dust the cryptarch of our lives (the fossilized DNA sealed in pebbles of the shattered Earth by the heat of the exploding Sun). From our cryptarch, the alien created us again. And not just our bodies. You remember Earth because your consciousness, which is in fact a wavepattern of light emitted by your brain, was retrieved from the vacuum, where it had been expanding at the speed of light since you died.

The alien that regenerated you is not God, nor even a god. The experience of being reborn in adult form out of the ground, cauled in a birthsack that grew with us in the loam, seems miraculous—but only until you understand that this has been accomplished with sophisticated and impersonal machinery. All the forests and jungles, all the multitudes of animals from every era of life on Earth, all the dinosaur herds, whales, and even bacteria and viruses, are products of a machine. The alien that operates this giant machine is a mortal being, albeit one whose timespan is enormously longer than ours. It is known variously as Gai, the Rimstalker, the World Maker, and the World Eater. By whatever name you call it, this being is an alien, inhuman and indifferent to human affairs. It is not interested in you, though you may think that it is because, as you will find, you do not age as quickly here as you did on Earth or as quickly as your fellow humans who were born of parents in these worlds. This is not because the alien favors you; it is a side effect of the regeneration process. The alien is not a spiritual being. Many lives have been lost disputing this issue. The truth is, this being regenerated you to serve as bait for yet another alien intelligence, its enemy, a species of sapient, winged spiders called zōtl. Zōtl eat people. See "Tactics" under *zōtl* in the index for effective ways of avoiding and defending yourself against these cunningly lethal entities.

Your life belongs to you. You owe no debt to the being

that roused you to this second life. Neither must you expect this being to guide you or benefit you in any way. It will not. You must find your own way now. This manual is designed to help you understand and survive any of the fifteen worlds as well as the Overworld itself, wherever you may find yourself.

Unlike the Earth, which evolved out of cosmic gases by natural processes over billions of years, these worlds are artificial and were constructed swiftly. The being that regenerated you made these planets, the swarms of planetesimals, asteroids, and comets, and our two suns: the black hole Saor and the radiant star Lod, which is really not a star but a machine. Eight of the worlds orbit Lod, six orbit Saor, and one orbits both. The group of Lod planets is called Doror; they are bright, temperate, and tropical worlds. The Saor planetary group is called Chalco; these are twilit and nocturnal worlds, most warmed by thermal vents. The lone planet that orbits both Doror and Chalco is called Know-Where-to-Go, and is mostly a night world except for its brief transit of Doror once every thousand years. Each complete circuit of Know-Where-to-Go defines an age. There have been four ages as of this edition. We are in the Fifth Age, commonly called the Age of Dominion. Two more ages are anticipated before Chalco-Doror completes its alien mission, and the being that created these worlds then destroys them.

That these worlds will collapse is true and not at all the apocalyptic madness the Saor-priests decry. Those who would have you believe that these worlds are eternal are agents for the spiders, who, indeed, desire to preserve Chalco-Doror that they may feed on us indefinitely. Do not despair that this bounty of new Earths is doomed; rather, rejoice that humanity's suffering, caught between two feuding alien powers, will end.

About time measurement: All the major planets have spin-rates of twenty-three to twenty-five hours, but only the orbit of Nabu in Chalco approximates the 365-day orbit of Earth during the human epoch. Nabu-years, which this manual uses to measure time, are constant enough for calendrical purposes. The other planets have varying orbit times. Refer to the ephemerides in the appendix for the local time standards of the planet where you are located.

The ephemerides also provide data and stellar sighting techniques to help you determine which planet you are on.

The animals and plants that you do not recognize are from areas and times of Earth other than those you knew—or they are distortions. For unknown reasons, the alien mind that reads the cryptarch of Earthlife often takes liberties when expressing physical forms. Mutations and variations are common, new species more rare. A partial catalogue of the most common distorts is listed in the appendix.

All fifteen planets and forty of the largest planetesimals are connected to each other and to the Overworld by lynks. We never had lynks on Earth; more about them can be found in the appendix marked Overworld. Briefly, what you need to know is that a lynk is a portal that joins two distant regions in a way that allows a traveler to go from one to the other instantly, even across large interplanetary distances.

There are three different kinds of lynks. Those created by the being who made these worlds are called natural lynks and are indistinguishable from apparently natural formations like rock fissures, caves, and sinkholes; few of these lynks have been mapped. Those that belong to the zōtl are rectangular structures about ten meters high and twenty wide, seemingly made of scarlet stone and sometimes referred to as redrock dolmens; these connect with the kingdom of the spiders and should never be entered, since the zōtl will consume you. The third variety of lynks is the most prevalent: The tall silver arches (five to twenty-five meters high) that exist on all the planets are the functional remains of the Tryl, creatures of superior intellect now extinct but originally regenerated by Gai. The Tryl lynks are sometimes rigged by the spiders to convey travelers to the zōtl's nest worlds, so do not enter any lynk until its destination has been confirmed by trained lynk wanderers (notably the Ordo Vala, who have produced this manual and whose nearest enclaves are listed at the front and in the index).

The lynk danger of which you should be most aware is that lynks are continuously active and can be entered inadvertently. Many lynks are hidden by the landscape, overgrown by vegetation, embedded in the ground. At various times in history, the zōtl have hidden lynks on all planets to trap people. Many such traps are still active. Never enter an unknown cave or crawlhole without first tossing an object ahead to see or hear whether the portal is a lynk.

In each of the Tryl lynks there is a globe, a map of the Overworld. Often in the past the globe has been erroneously identified as a spirit being to be worshipped. The image of a brightly mottled sphere suspended in a field of total blackness seems holy to many of us, and all the more so since the object cannot be touched or even approached, only beheld. Movement toward the map sends one through the lynk. Movement to either side delivers one to the Overworld. Read "The Practical Guide to Travel in the Overworld" affixed to this manual before attempting to enter a lynk.

[Appended to the Year 2000 Edition, 1492 Doror:]

It is quite possible to live in Chalco-Doror without concerning ourselves with [lynks], especially if we live in one of the many communities that purposely place themselves in regions remote from lynks and their dangers. Most of us who live far from the Overworld prefer to shun this seemingly supernatural aspect of our new reality. We cherish our memories of Earth. We grieve for those of the first life whom we will never see again. And, when we can, we seek out others like ourselves, from our own times and races. But that is a mistake.

During the history of Chalco-Doror, among the many millions who have lived on Earth and lived again here in the worlds, only one such tribal fantasy has been realized and with sad results. The Aesirai who currently dominate all of Doror and parts of Chalco are humans selectively bred to imitate the tribe of their founder, Egil Grimson, a man who had lived and died on Earth as a Viking, a sea rover in the third millennium before human extinction.

Only humans who have Viking genetic characteristics are empowered in Aesirai society. Only Vikings are allowed to dwell in the cities unmolested by the spiders, for the Aesirai have a pact with the zōtl. All other human types are relegated to the role of laborers or are left to fend for themselves in the wilderness, where the spiders are free to harvest them.

The Ordo Vala abhor this separatist society for having abandoned the vast majority of humanity to the ravages of the spiders and the dangers of Chalco-Doror. This *Utility Manual,* banned by the Aesirai, is offered for the benefit of all humans.

If Zero Could Shut Its Mouth

The air was so dense, it read as water. Looking down into it, down past the riven cliffs and the shining clouds, Chan-ti Beppu felt giddy. She had never before journeyed below the clouds. Just visible among the flying vapors and the thermal jellies of air was the spark of her destination, the sea-mountain city of N'ym. There, if anywhere among the worlds, love waited to join space, memory, and the blue light of northern weather into a man whose story would complete hers.

"I can see from that silly look in your eyes," Nappy Groff said, "that you really think he's going to care."

"Of course he'll care," Chan-ti said, not removing her gaze from the mountainous clouds and the gaunt cliffs. "He's an exceptional man."

"That means exceptional trouble." Nappy Groff was short and wizened, with a cuff of frizzy white hair collaring his bald pate. He regarded Chan-ti Beppu with his usual glum frown. "Beppu, I have cared for you these nineteen years that you might be fulfilled. But never—never, I say to you now—did I think you would choose to leave us."

Chan-ti was sitting in the grasp of a brambly tree that reached out over the precipice and afforded her a wide vista of the purple lowlands. When she turned toward the old man, her broad, pallid face shone with the world's underlight. "My fulfillment is not here—not yet."

Nappy Groff scowled with an understanding he had come to hate. The girl he had reared to womanhood had not been wooed in the three years since she had reached the age of consent—at least not by anyone who pleased her. Slack-jawed Gorlik had proposed, but she could barely eat across the same table from him without getting ill. Tradition decreed that she leave and not return until she found her mate. She was not ugly, not in Nappy's eyes, but neither did she look like the other women. After all, she was not of them. Nappy had found her as an infant, and she had grown into a gangly, wide-faced woman with brindled hair and slanted black eyes so weak she needed to wear lenses. She was clever, intrepid, and playful, though few of the men—who were mostly humorless, stolid workers— found that desirable; and of those who did, none would marry a woman a head taller than the tallest of them— except, of course, Gorlik, who had grown fond of her some seasons ago when she had removed a hook from his lip and did not tell the others he had been eating the fish bait.

"You do not need to leave," Nappy told her. "In time, our wanderings will find the right man for you. You've wit if not lucky looks. Trust that and time."

"In time, I will be a crone." She climbed out of the tree and dropped into the shaggy grass of the cliff's edge. She was wearing a sojourner's outfit—hiking boots, leaf-pattern jacket, and brown denim trousers that hugged her blithe form, emphasizing her femininity yet not diminishing her rangy bearing. "Don't worry for me, Father." She kissed his wrinkled brow. "I remember everything you've taught me, and by that memory—your greatest gift to me —I will make my way through the lowlands and return with my mate."

Nappy Groff nodded but the frown gouging the flesh between his white eyebrows was doubtful. "The road to N'ym is long but the road to the heart is without end and tireless as a circle. Be wary. And remember everything I've told you. Don't speak with voors. No matter what they promise you, don't speak with voors. Avoid the fogroads even if they seem shorter. Refuse anything to eat that the Weed Woman offers you at the Back Gates, but be sure to give her your gun. And when you get to N'ym, go directly to Rence Walla's shop. He alone in N'ym is one of us and can help you. By now my letter has reached him and he has gathered the information you need."

Chan-ti's smile gleamed in the stars' cold light, and she

kissed Nappy Groff again. "I'll do as you say, Father. I'll be back in a few days."

Groff hummed skeptically and tugged a narrow but thick volume from under his utility vest. "If the man refuses you, you can sell this to Rence Walla."

She took the book of tawed leather in both hands and saw that it was an ancient edition. "The *Glyph Astra*," she said, calling the famous *Book of Horizons* by its ritual name, it seemed that old. "I can't accept this."

"You must," he said and denied her returning it with the back of his hand. "If the man refuses you, how will you live? Sell this book to Rence Walla. It is one of the early editions and will bring a noble sum, enough to live for many years—even in N'ym."

"I doubt N'ym will last even one more year, Father. The war—"

"Let's not speak of war. Departure is grief enough. Read me a farewell phrase, instead."

Chan-ti opened the book and turned its rugged pages to a favorite passage. By starlight and memory, she read: " 'We are nameless. In each hand we hold a story. Between them, between the right story and what's left, our hearts are the wedge. You know this is true.' "

Tears lit Nappy Groff's creased face, and the parting with this found child was almost as miserable as the deaths of his own children under the Forest's talon and fang, long ago, before his mate had shriveled around her cancer and died, before pain came to mean not what was lost but what remained.

Chan-ti Beppu traveled quickly down the cliff paths above the amethyst gulf of the abyss, under thorny groves hung with a perfume that smelled of the green sea and clung to her like smoke. Where the fogroads switchbacked among the clouds, she detoured and descended the longer way along mulestairs and rootsteps. N'ym glimmered brighter, and she could see the glass spires and the amber towers, their topmost windows catching the early rays of dawn and burning like stars.

Many before her had come this way, disappearing into the melting clouds on their way down to the Back Gates. Some had returned, a few again and again, with marvelous accounts of the journey and of the city at its end. She knew well what to expect; even so she was fraught with uncertainty. The man she had chosen for her own was a stranger; she knew only enough of his story to believe he might love her.

Gorlik or a solitary life were the choices she was leaving behind, yet she doubted she would have had the resolve to leave all that was familiar if, the season before, Velma, her adoptive mother and Nappy's wife, had not died. Velma had been a voluminous woman, larger and more fair-skinned than most of the others, expansive with laughter and industry. She had remained brave and calm through most of her illness. At the end of it, though, when she had shriveled to a mad hag, violent with those who tried to care for her, quavering with pain whenever her shrunken body was lifted, her death was excruciating and ugly. "Will I die?" were her last words.

Since then Chan-ti had been asking that of herself and had become determined to do what she dreamed. In the brisk air of the cliffside, with astounding glimpses of the star-whisked sky through the rushing clouds, her resolve felt holy. The cliffroads were in good repair, maintained by the monks who lived in the blackrock chapels and cave shrines sequestered among the rock crannies. Traveling down the narrow paths was easy. Along the precipices, dwarf forests sheltered lemurs and winged lizards and dangled boughs of berries and fruits. At night she slept under a slanted outcrop that shielded her from the soft rain. She returned to the path at first light and ate a breakfast of cane almonds and plums while walking.

Darkness still eddied at the bottom of the gulf when Chan-ti reached the rubbly foot of the cliffs. She paused there briefly and ate the root bread and waxed berries her woman friends had packed for her. As the dim sun rose higher, the plateau glinted like flint with the crystal-stemmed shrubs abounding there. Except for the human-like face screaming at her from inside a boulder, and a diving attack from red bats angry that she approached their hanging tree, the crossing was without incident. She slept that night under a mane of tasseled cane and early the next day reached the Back Gates.

Here the fogroads came down the cliffs to the plateau, ribboning out of the silver clouds along the mountain flanks and converging into a majestic boulevard cloistered with ponderous trees and blossom-belled lianas. The broad avenue curved along the western edge of N'ym in a long crescent and disappeared among the hazes of the mountain forests. On one side of the stone avenue, the land rose toward the valley ridge, wild, gloomy with moldering oak and swales of heather. On the other side stood the Back Gates, a seemingly endless corridor of city buildings fronting on colonnades and buttresses draped in ivy. Untrammeled grass and flocks of red flowers banked the back walls of the buildings, which were stonegray, windowless, and scrawled with vines. Copper doors, green and black with the stains of centuries, loomed under lintels graven with weathered runes she did not understand. Above the peristyles bracing the backs of the buildings, the towers of N'ym reared. A few chimneypots were also visible and spears of radio antennae.

Chan-ti hiked for another hour before finding the Weed Woman. True to Nappy's prediction, she had spotted Chan-ti coming across the plateau and was waiting for her in one of the flower banks that filled the alcoves between the stone buttresses. She stood among globular flowerheads and waist-high tufts of grass, her spiderweb hair strung with weed feathers, thistle burrs, and dead leaves. From the basket under her arm, she offered breadfingers, groat cakes, fruit necklaces. Chan-ti remembered Nappy's warning and declined.

The Weed Woman only looked human. She had been created by one of the many powers—the spiders, lizard angels, Fire, the Face of Night, or maybe even the World Eater. She was already there when the first people arrived. Over the generations, as people explored the Back Gates, they learned that only she knew which of the endless gates entered N'ym. Other doors were forced open, and those who entered the barren expanses there could not return but were stopped by a transparency impenetrable as a reflection. The Weed Woman always opened the one Gate into the city, for all except those who accepted food from her. They were led giddily away, laughing and singing, through another door to a glimpse of yolky sunlight, birch and willows. None ever returned.

Without a word spoken between them, Chan-ti was led

through the grass by the Weed Woman, who smelled acrid as burnt tar. On a green metal door twice the height of a tall man, the crone pressed her fingertips, and the pylon shoved inward with a rusty scream.

Before entering, Chan-ti relinquished her pistol. Nappy had warned her many times that the only way past the old woman at the Back Gates was without guns. According to lore, the Builders of the Gates had put her there to guard against firearms. Anyone could see from the ravenous stare in her gray face that the Builders had chosen well. When the Weed Woman had Chan-ti's wide-muzzle revolver in her crablike hands, her stare went flat, and she stood aside.

Chan-ti Beppu cast a proud look back the way she had come. Between the flinty sparks of the plateau and the large stars, the cliff of fogroads stood luminous as the edge of a dream, fumey with distance and spiritous mists. There was her old life, all nineteen years of it, compact enough to hold in her sight. She had been loved and well educated by Velma and Nappy Groff; she had experienced friendship among the other women, and passion with a few rowdy boys too turgid to care about her height or her odd features; and she had known belonging, communal kinship, at the nightly firedances. Yet she did not belong there anymore—at least, not until she found her mate.

Chan-ti turned and strode through the narrowly open door into a tight alley. She had to walk sideways between lichenous brick walls that turned sharply several times before squeezing out onto a yew lane. Black hedges with gold underleaves trellised monumental dwellings. For as far as she could see, the backs of sepulchral houses lined the lane, their skinny backlots enclosed in trellises and yews dark as amulets.

She hurried along. Nappy Groff had instructed her to leave behind the yew lane and the black hedges immediately, to take the first byway with a slate sidewalk that offered itself. At every second house, the yew lane crossed a cobbled alley that climbed hills past skinny buildings with boxed windows and mullioned galleries. She had to walk eight blocks before she found a slate sidewalk. As instructed, she turned left and continued to bear left among wending roads and tall, skinny, crooked buildings that made her dizzy to look up until she came to a shop-front whose bay window had an octopus and a squid set in stained glass.

The door to the shop opened with a tinkle of bells. Among bins of many-colored corals and display cases of pearls and exquisite shells, Rence Walla sat in a wicker chair. He was a pink-whiskered gnome, watching a diminutive television set that was propped in the lips of a giant conch. Chan-ti recalled seeing him before, among the visitors at home in the mead grotto. He recognized her at once, and while tiny laughter and applause pattered from the TV, he asked about Nappy and the others. Amenities over, he stroked his pink stubble and appraised her unabashedly, "You're too ugly to be wooed at home and you come here? Dear dreamer, the people of N'ym are animals of perfection. They are true human pedigrees."

"Odd as I look, I too can love," she said with an even smile.

"But here? Wanderer, this is the City of the Sky, where eyes are blue and hair the color of the sun. Look at you. Dark elfish eyes. Streaky brown hair. Face starved as a wastrel's. And spectacles! No one in N'ym wears them. Chan-ti Beppu—go back home. So you're excluded from the firedance because you're too old. That's just a formality. You can make a life for yourself teaching the children, tending the old ones."

"That was my ambition, Rence Walla—until I met my hope of true love. He is the one man whose story could include me."

"His story?" The gnome's thin lips hooked a mocking grin, and he darted a glance at the volume peeking from her jacket pocket. "You have given too much of yourself to *The Book of Horizons*, Chan-ti Beppu. Is that the edition Groff gifted you?"

She took out the book and let the shopkeeper hold it. He ran stubby, freckled fingers over the blue leather cover and the soft spine. An iridescent script dull with age tooled the edges. "Ah—the lurid seventh edition—over fifteen centuries old and yet paper and binding still sturdy. For sure this came through a timeshaft. For sure. A lifetime's luck for Groff to find this on his stravaging."

Chan-ti opened the book in his hands and turned to the Oracles. "Here, Rence Walla—this is what I am about.

'When the lorn Foke marries the gentle warrior of the Aesirai, the last legends fulfill themselves.' "

The shopkeeper flicked an incredulous stare at the young woman, and when he saw that she was serious, laughter jolted through him. "What has Groff done to let such a child abroad?" He slapped the book closed and rubbed away a tear with his wrist. "You believe the *Glyph Astra* talks to you?"

"It talks to all of us," she answered, with an edge of annoyance. "But only those who listen hear it."

"For sure. That was the deepest laugh I've had in a while, young sibyl. So you've come to N'ym to marry a gentle warrior, have you? Shall we have a look at him then?" From a desk scattered with invoices and starfish, he plucked a thumbnail-size photo of a squarefaced man in an officer's uniform whose open stare and boylike smile contradicted the threat of his dragonish brow. On the back, in minute script, was his address.

To her amazed smile, he said, "Not hard to get at all. He's in the City's Sky Guard. Their publicity brochure had all seventy-eight of them. Getting his address—that took a black pearl in the palm of the Guard garage attendant."

"I will find a way to repay you."

"Nappy and Velma paid me long ago, when they hid me from the voors. I had inadvertently sold some of the voors' talismans. Those zombies would have dismembered me, but your folks kept me out of sight while they tracked down and returned most of the talismans. I owe them more than a black pearl and a photograph. If I can talk you into returning home, I will have repaid them."

Chan-ti tucked the photo into her jacket pocket. "I will return home—but only with my mate, or I'll have to wed Gorlik."

"And if your gentle warrior is already married and the sire of a brood?"

"He's not. I did think to ask him that, sly-whiskers."

Rence Walla shrugged. "Not I to thwart an oracle from *The Book of Horizons*. Supper before you go?"

Chan-ti stayed with Rence Walla long enough to bathe and launder, and to share a meal of braised scallops and seaweed soup. Then she unfurled the rain hood rolled into the collar of her denim jacket and sat deep in the seat of the battered car that the gnome had arranged to transport her. Through webcracked windows, she watched several city districts float by—slender spires, brass-domed vaults, hillside brownstones. The bootjawed driver, who wore a fishmonger's cap and apron and said not a word during the entire drive, stopped before a tower of gray-tinted glass. As Chan-ti stepped from the car, it pulled away to wait for her in a sidestreet in case no one was in.

At the reception desk under pillars of crystalline light, the house guard scrutinized the hooded visitor. The guard was a matronly woman in braids, who announced Chan-ti Beppu's arrival over the intercom without budging her eyes from the cowled figure. There was a long pause in which Chan-ti counted twelve heartbeats before a man's voice said to send her up.

Nothing in all the worlds was as beautiful as the city of N'ym. Built atop the eaglebrow cliffs of Valdëmiraën overlooking the Silver Sea, the glassy minarets of the city were the first to catch the red rays of daylight and the last to let them go. The day was never brighter than twilight in N'ym, even at noon, when the distant sun, Lod, cast the slender silkstone buildings and their pedestals of plazas in a wan auburn glow. The city towers glowed like coral and the hanging gardens among the hillside houses blazed with fragrant colors. By night, the boulevards and the adjoining mazes of avenues, wynds, and alleys tinkled with the light of sparkfly lanterns hung from the streetside windows of each household. Seen from the air, the glimmery lantern fires of the domed houses and the arc lights among the downtown spires limned the ideogram for Sky. N'ym was the City of the Sky, perched at the very brink of land's end, its opaline towers lifting high above the clouds that fogged the lower slopes and trawled the sea. Overhead, both by day and night, the sky swarmed with planets, stardust, and the icy green tails of comets.

On the steep hills, in their glass and brickwork tier-level houses, lived the Aesirai, lords of Valdëmiraën. The most powerful of them had whole hills to themselves, crowned with columned manors and stands of tapered trees above silvered ponds. But even the least of the Aesirai lived well in chalets behind willow tresses and under terraced gardens. For those who preferred simpler lodgings, there were mirrorglass towers in centercity with suites overlooking plaza-groves of hickory and oak and arbored canals studded with starlight and planetshadows.

In the lowlands below the cliffs and the threading cascades, hamlets huddled, hundreds of clustered bungalows, some square-roofed, some thatched, all on stilts, with rude vegetable plots cut from the grass verges. Behind the crooked walls that separated the broken pavements of the hamlets' asphalt streets from the sunken fields and the fallen boulders of the cliffs, the workers of N'ym dwelled. They were the laborers, janitors, refuse collectors, and harvest hands of N'ym. Below them, among the sedgy tracts and weed-trammeled dunes, fishing shanties dotted the crescent coast.

Ned O'Tennis loved N'ym. As a boy, while other children frolicked in the playgrounds and swimming ponds, he had stolen away from the school groups and wandered the lanes that laced the steep hills so that he could admire the cobblestone houses—no two alike with their flagstone paths, kitchen gardens, and stone embankments carved with trolls and dragons beneath red ivy and the boughs of aged trees. From the high lanes he gazed down at the chimney pots and blue tile gables of the houses; he stared into the crystal heart of the city, where the gold dirigibles docked after drifting up from the seaside villages and cliffbottom hamlets. He had been punished by his school and his parents for each time that he wandered off. But the chores and deprivations had not stopped him, for he was enthralled with the wild mosaic of aimless streets, tumbling gardens, knoll houses, and opal towers—all beneath the clutter of planets and the silver wheel of the galaxy.

In early manhood, Ned had fulfilled his earliest ambition and worked as a dirigible pilot, ferrying workers between the hamlets and N'ym. The work was routinely slow and afforded him plenty of time and vantage to gaze down at the city's depths and the rambling countryside. N'ym had never looked more ethereal to him than it did during his ferry years, when he drifted over the city four times each day: In the night, he left the sleeping city for the torch-lit hamlets to bring in the workers with the first slash of dawn; and at sunset, he carried them back to the country and

returned alone with the night. In the intervals he dallied
with pretty women, which was his favorite pastime; he
sported with his buddies when his girlfriends were busy,
and, when he found himself alone, wandered the lyric
streets and pondered what he had heard that day from the
workers he conveyed—ferine men and women fated to
live beyond the palisades of N'ym yet near enough to visit
the city every day as streetcleaners, vendors, maids, and
construction workers. They were the lucky ones. Many
more gold dirigibles carried laborers to mines, fields, and
factories outside the city. Ned heard about their exhausted
lives from their kin, who rode his balloon to their inner-
city jobs. Every night, on his empty flight back to N'ym
after returning the workers to their rick-roofed settlements, he contemplated the hardships of the lives that
sustained the beauty of the city he loved. He was troubled
by the dolor he saw in the workers' faces each dawn and
the exhaustion that replaced it at night. Exploiting them
simply because they did not have the right antecedents—
long-headed, copper-haired, pale-skinned Aesirai ancestors—was wrong, but what could he do? N'ym was over
five hundred years old, and the workers had been riding
the gold dirigibles from the beginning. Most were grateful,
for there were millions more who lived wild in the continental forests. Only some of the workers complained of
injustice and enslavement. The same brash critics also
spoke of human sacrifice. By that they meant the alliance
between the Aesirai and the zōtl, the sapient spiders who
hived on a distant planet and, since the earliest times, had
been coming to Valdëmiraën and her sister worlds to eat
people. The Aesirai, the one human tribe too fierce to be
dominated by the spiders, had agreed not to kill zōtl but to
let them feed freely in the wildwoods in exchange for
technological gifts and freedom from attacks. That was the
story in the schools. But the boldest workers sneered at the
Aesirai's purported fierceness and spoke of human farms,
where people were bred like cattle and harvested regularly as tribute to the zōtl. They even said that the Aesirai's
Viking monoculture was a zōtl genetic experiment. Ned
offered them a tolerant ear and gained their confidence by
not laughing, and, occasionally, sharing his own egalitarian
visions. The peace he found for himself in this camaraderie

and in his active life with his lovers and friends had until the past few years assuaged all concern.

For most of his life, Ned had listened to this talk of insurrection with only one ear, being oblivious to politics though he had come from a military family. Then he was drafted. More than half of N'ym's fighter force had been called away from Valdëmiraën to defend the central planets of the Emirate, and every citizen with flying experience was recruited to replace them. Though Ned O'Tennis was uneasy in the sling harness of a flying gunship after years of walking the bridge of a dirigible, he had reluctantly learned the ways of the sleek black strohlkraft.

Now, thirty-seven years old, after twelve years as a dirigible pilot, he was a sky-fighter charged with defending N'ym from both the wilderness hordes and the ramjets of the rebels. The hordes, distort tribes who lived hunter-gatherer lives in the vast forests of Valdëmiraën and who united to raid the fisherfolk, the hamlets, and the Aesirai's outlying farms, had always plagued N'ym and in times past had been kept at bay by mercenaries hired from the outlying tribes. The rebels, however, were new. They were neither distorts nor primitives but well-armed warriors from the sunny worlds of Doror, who revolted against Aesirai rule. Their weapons were won in battle or stolen. Ned had first heard about the rebels eight years ago from the workers he ferried. The rebels claimed that the Emirate of the Aesirai was collapsing from the inside out—a Storm-Tree rotten at the pith—and that all the people excluded from the elegant cities of the Emirate were joining with distort hordes to overthrow the 750-year-old tyrant, Emir Egil Grimson. The rebels believed that they were close to acquiring a new weapon to help them kill zōtl. Soon, it was rumored, the proud City of the Sky would fall to them.

Ned believed they were right. Since becoming a sky-fighter, he had heard much of the rebels' victories and little of the Aesirai's. Worse, he knew the Aesirai were wrong to win their benefits by oppressing others. But there was no escape for him. He was descended from too ancient an Aesirai lineage to refuse military service without incurring the disgrace of his family, as well as the reproach of his fellow citizens.

At first, everyone fully expected the rebellion to be
crushed in a few months and the Aesirai warriors to return
triumphant to their families. There had been no dearth of
volunteers. As months had stretched to years, Ned O'Tennis compliantly flew the combat maneuvers of war games,
practiced strafing fleeing targets with the laserbolt cannon
in his ship's prow and engaging rebel ramjets in air battles.
Only once, during leave, did he go back to visit the derrick
where his old carrier was moored. A retired cop piloted his
dirigible now, and well-armed guards patroled the docks
and escorted each flight. When workers he knew saw him,
they looked away. No one wanted to be accused by the
rebels, who had sympathizers everywhere, of collusion
with the oppressors.

During his two years as a fighter pilot, Ned did his best to
avoid actually confronting the enemy. He was not a warrior, that much he was certain about. His father and his two
older brothers had died in military service before the war
—murdered in a skirmish with a distort tribe when he was
still a boy—and he remembered well the grief that had
harrowed his mother and eventually killed her. He never
forgot his unanswered prayers and the rueful insight into
the pointlessness of his petitions to God when he accompanied his mother's corpse to the crematorium and watched
her sit up ablaze and fall back to ash. From that early age—
he was nine when she died—he knew intuitively that
N'ym was doomed, that the powers of chaos would triumph just as they had in the myths and in his family. Each
day would have to be taken on its own, a gift with no
promise for a future. No family, no career seemed plausi-
ble in this foredoomed life. So he lived for whatever pleasure his lovers and playful friends afforded him day by day.

Ned was a dreamer, enraptured since childhood with
the vistas of planets and comets, the winding lanes, the
terraced houses and cascading gardens. But the war was
closing in, just as the personal tragedies of his childhood
had presaged. The mercenaries had been deserting, and
the job of holding back the marauding distort hordes de-
volved to the sky-fighters. His daily mission was to cruise
the outlying wildwoods and harry the rovers.

Unlike most of the other pilots, who followed orders and
burned the gangs they found, Ned could not kill the forest

people. They had only spears and arrows, and though they terrorized the hamlets where the city's workers lived and had murdered some of the people he knew, he could not burn them. His years of conversing with the workers made him wonder if he would act any differently if he had been a tribesman. So he peeled off from the other fighters to minimize witnesses to his mercy, and when he found the wild people, he shot into the treetops above them and frightened them off. His superiors were none the wiser, and he was gladder for knowing he was a warrior who had never taken a life.

N'ym's sky-fighters were an elite who could choose their own missions provided that the city remained untroubled. Ned chose to fly alone, away from the usual policing runs over the coast villages. He flew inland, ostensibly on patrol but actually seeking a refuge where he could think. His grandmother and his uncles—his only living relatives—and his two favorite lovers wanted him to volunteer for a battle post. Waves of wounded and dead returned to N'ym from battlefields on the other fourteen planets—and many did not return at all. A few defected to the rebels, but the majority who were not seen again had been killed in territory lost to the enemy. An enraged and patriotic fervor seized N'ym. But Ned did not partake in the battle frenzy. He did not want to leave N'ym. He knew the Emirate of the Aesirai was unjust. He had learned that from his twelve-year tutelage among the workers. He did not want to die for N'ym, no matter his nostalgia for the city's beauty. Beauty was not reason enough to kill. Truth was stronger. And the truth was, as he had known since he was nine, that the tides of fate had turned against N'ym.

Ned sympathized with the rebels, but he did not identify with them. Defection was unthinkable to him. He was Aesirai and would, when the time came, die as an Aesirai. But he was in no hurry. So he ignored his grandmother's jingoistic pleas, flew in the city's Sky Guard, and tried to stay out of trouble.

His favorite sanctuary was a bluff in the Eyelands high above N'ym, where Caer, the first great city of Valdëmiraën, had been built five centuries earlier. Caer was ruins now and had been from the start, because it had never been finished. When the Aesirai first arrived on

Valdëmiraën, they had selected the Eyelands for their capital, since the vast cliffs and sprawling plateaus commanded a supernal view. But the Eyelands were too high in the atmosphere. The radiation from Saor, the black sun, changed people. Within months of beginning the construction of Caer, the first residents were transformed. Their jaws began to glow. The flesh of their chins and jawlines became translucent and light shone from the bottoms of their faces as through lampskins. The change was irreversible and progressive. From the jaw, the bonelight spread across the skull and down the spine. In time, the skin became oily parchment and the entire skeleton was visible, shining like neon. Limbs withered to wiry appendages and torsos flattened and unfurled. Like kites, these luminous lenses of viscera bobbled on the mountain winds; their human faces were transfigured into bonebroad visages with inhuman caricatures whose only truly recognizable feature was their luminous eyes, retinal-red, fiery eyes. Thus, the high plateaus of Caer were named the Eyelands by the first Aesirai. Those who had caught the bonelight and been changed were called seraphs. Little was ever known about the seraphs, as they did not speak or make any effort to communicate. None was observed eating or eliminating. Nor did they mate. They simply hovered in the ruins or soared on the thermal drafts off the cliffs. If they died natural deaths, no carcasses were ever found. Those shot down decomposed quickly, and the ones that were caged withered away within hours.

Ned O'Tennis' willingness to fly to the Eyelands and land his strohlkraft among the ruins of Caer was a testimony to his indifference to life as the war drew nearer. It was of no consequence to him if he caught the bonelight and became a seraph. That, he thought to himself, could be no more horrible than the war spreading cancerously in the world below.

One day, roaming among the weathered walls and weed-cracked avenues, he pondered his options. If he stayed in N'ym, he would have to fight. That he would do if the rebels attacked his city. What he feared was being sent out to destroy guerrillas among the hamlets, where the people he had once ferried and befriended lived in tacit alliance with the rebels. If he refused to destroy them, he would be executed.

Sometimes the thought of death was appealing. Shirking his war duty and damned to be powerless, he felt filthy as an Aesirai. But he was no nineteen-year-old. He knew himself well enough to understand that death—whether he doled it out or received it—was without glory. Life was mad. Men killed each other, and their women cheered them on. Even away from war—where people wove their own meanings of love and peace, craft and humanity as they grew old and withered on their bones—life, in its beautiful rags, was cruel. But death was no recourse. Life, with all its elaborate pain and for all its senseless trials, was in his hands. He would not use it to kill wantonly. And he would not let them execute him. Flight was his only other option. But to where could he flee? All the worlds were at war. The Storm-Tree was toppling.

A voice intruded: "You look troubled, pilot."

Ned jumped about so quickly that the seraphs dangling among the broken walls shot high into the starry sky. A woman stood on the talus of a torn building, a slim silhouette against the foamy light of the galaxy. She stepped down, and he saw that she wore a silvery shift that rippled with starlight along the contours of her femininity. He backed away, and she called: "Wait. Don't go. I want to talk with you."

She hurried toward him, her arms open wide at her sides to show she carried no weapon, her dark hair scattering in the wind from the cliffs. Her face was thin as a cat's, farouche. But the look in her eyes was spiked with light like an angel's. In a moment he saw that she wore gold-wire frame lenses over her eyes. In N'ym, all eye problems were corrected surgically, and he had never seen eyeglasses except in drawings.

"You're the pilot who lets the rebels escape. I recognize your ship."

She spoke a language similar to his own, yet he was grateful for the tiny translator in his shoulder braid. The coinlike machine was intended to faciliate interrogations of rebels who did not speak Aesirai, and it worked reciprocally, translating for all voices in its range. The sound of the dot-speakers was tinny but accurate, faithful to nuances and accents.

"Who are you?" he asked, suspiciously.

"My name is Chan-ti Beppu. Stay, please. I have no weapons. I'm not a rebel." She stopped an arm's length away. Through the lenses, there seemed to be lightning in her eyes. "You're Ned. I've heard your name on the military frequencies during your flights. Ned O'Tennis."

She smelled cool as pine, and he became conscious of the lactic sourness of his flightsuit. He backed off a step and scanned for others. "How do you know about me?"

Her chip-toothed smile was casual and quick. "I've watched you. The end for N'ym is coming swiftly. Everyone up here is watching."

"Everyone? Who is up here?" The shadow-wrung terrain could have been hiding a platoon, but he saw no sign of anyone else.

"We call ourselves the Foke. We've been here since before these ruins were built."

"How can that be? The bonelight—"

"The bonelight changes only those who stay still, as your ancestors did by daring to build a city here. We're not so bold. We live simply—I'd like to think elegantly—and we never stop moving. We wander the highlands. We have no cities. But we come back to our favorite places, and this is one of them. From here we can stare down into N'ym and see how the Aesirai live."

Ned looked beyond her, searching again for others. The seraphs had settled back, and their stoic lights blinked among the girders. No one else was in sight. The strohlkraft sat in the lanky grass, its reflective black hull a mime of the star-whorled sky.

"There've been patrols up here before," he said. "No one's ever reported finding any people."

"We've never been found. Nor will we be. We know how to hide. And Saor helps us. Instrumentation is unreliable under the black sun. So we have been left alone."

Ned found that he was understanding her dialect without the translator. He left it on for her benefit, though he doubted she needed it. The dark eyes behind her lenses were pellucidly intelligent.

"Where are you from?" he asked, feeling suddenly at

ease with this stranger. That made him nervous, and he shifted his weight to stare beyond her for the deception she was fronting. Under the glow of the seraphs and the stars, the shattered city was empty. The ferns in the streets shifted blowsily with the wind.

"Where is anyone from? One way or another, we are all travelers in the Overworld."

Ned looked at Chan-ti Beppu and saw that she was not joking. "The space inside lynks? People can't live there."

She returned his stare. "Have you tried?"

He studied her face more closely, noting the salt-blond streaks in her shadowy hair, her full bottom lip, the tilt of her black eyes in the pale breadth of her cheeks. "Why are you speaking with me?"

Her slope-lidded eyes widened slightly. "I want to meet the Aesirai who does not kill rebels. Why do you let them escape? They'll kill you if they can."

Ned's chin lifted in a movement of obvious wariness. Common sense demanded he get away, quickly. A filament of fear burned dully in his chest, but he relished it after the numbness of sitting here contemplating the doom of the Aesirai. If this was a rebel ploy, it was at least intriguing.

"Reasons of the heart, I suspect," Chan-ti answered for him. "I doubt your superiors would approve." Her chip-toothed smile flashed again at the apprehension that sparked in his gaze. "Don't be concerned. I'm hardly in a position to report you. Besides, I'm here now against the counsel of my own people. I understand reasons of the heart."

He edged away, suddenly unhappy with the turn of their encounter. She was reading him too closely, too accurately. He wanted to get away to prove to himself that this was no trap.

"Don't go."

"I'm on patrol."

"No one will know."

"You shouldn't be walking up on strangers," he added, pacing backward. "You could get killed."

"You didn't kill your enemy when they were under your guns, why would you kill an unarmed woman?"

He stopped walking. No one had emerged from the

shadows to stop his retreat. The only danger here was in his own heart. So long as he did not allow this fascinating person to lead him away from his ship, he was safe. "You look more girl than woman," he said, easing up enough to smile at her flash of hurt.

"I am not. I'm old enough for all the rites."

"Sure. But you're twenty years too young to be talking to me."

"Are you married, Ned O'Tennis?"

He gave a sleepy laugh. So she did not know everything about him. "No. I'm not married. The times are too parlous for families. Goodbye, Chan-ti Beppu."

"Wait," she called, striding after him. "Don't leave yet." She held an arm out, and the hand that beckoned was square and capable. "Before you go, tell me why you've come here."

Ned opened his arms to the broken city under the galaxy. "It's beautiful."

She stepped toward him. "Beautiful enough to risk your life—" He had already turned away and was hurrying through the crystal-stemmed bramble to his ship. "Come back," she called after him. "I want to see you again."

But Ned did not look back. This sudden encounter had charged him with concern for his remiss behavior. Perhaps he would return again—but officially next time. If there were a group up here monitoring Aesirai patrols and tactics, they had to be identified. Yet—they obviously knew he had been shirking his duties, and if they were discovered, whoever they were, they would reveal his passive treason. Ned decided to do some research on his own. When he returned to N'ym, he went directly to the map registry and reviewed hundreds of satellite photos of the Eyelands. No sign of any people inhabiting the ruins of Caer or the surrounding area was apparent.

Ned reported sighting group movement in the ruins. After subsequent patrols returned without spotting anything unusual, he determined to go again himself. He had to find out who these mysterious Foke were who watched the Aesirais struggles from above as though they were gods. But before he could gather and enter into his ship's computer all the photo-maps of the region, the feral woman from the Eyelands found him.

When a visitor was announced by the houseguard, Ned's first thought was that his forays to the Eyelands had been found out and security had come for him. He opened the door braced for uniforms. Chan-ti mistook the relief in his face for joy, and she hugged him, startling him with the iron of her grip.

"What are you doing here?" he asked and quickly shut the door behind her.

"I've come to see you. I need to talk with you."

Ned closed the curtains. His suite was spare, with a few pieces of chrome and white leather furniture, polished wood floors, and a sleeping roll for a bed. "I don't spend much time here." He gestured for her to sit. "You're lucky to have found me in."

"Luck alone introduced us," she said, accepting the chair he offered. "I'm glad it's still holding."

"What do you want of me?"

"I want to marry you."

Ned snorted, picked up his beer, and sagged into a seat. "I could be your father." He took a long swig.

"It's a Foke custom to marry early. I must marry or be excluded from the rites. Only the most grotesque don't find a mate. Your age means nothing to me."

Ned tossed off a silent laugh. His goldfaced friends would howl to see this heathen proposing to him. "Beer?" he offered.

She refused with a tight shake of her head, her eyes glittering with interest to see him in his own environs.

He drained what remained in the bottle and stood it on the floor. "Why me?"

"Only you." Chan-ti was pale and intent. The elegant proposal she had crafted for this moment fled before the heat of her emotion. She spoke off the top of her head, "I never expected to marry anyone. I'm odd-looking among the Foke. But then I saw you—saw something of your story. You had come up to the Eyelands and risked your life for the vista of stars—for beauty."

"It's not like that. You don't understand."

"I think I do." The certainty in her voice silenced him. "I've watched you in your ship. You alone of the dozens that fly their missions each day do not kill your enemy when they are before you. You are a reluctant warrior. But not cowardly. When you come to the Eyelands, you don't care about the bonelight or the distorts. You could hide anywhere less dangerously. But you're not hiding from yourself. You come for the beauty, for what is eternal in a world of temporary lives."

Ned's heart tripped at what she had said. "How do you know so much about me? How did you find me?"

"The Foke are an old people. They came through the timeshafts long ago. Over the years, they've borrowed languages, ideas, technology, everything from those around them. We watch you with monitors that patch into your own high-orbit scanners. Some of the Foke know how to use refractions from the black sun to hide our signals. We see and yet we are not seen."

"But why don't our scanners see you?" Ned asked. "I've studied the satellite photos of the Eyelands. There's nothing that shows any of the technology you're talking about."

"That's because it's not there. The Foke watch you from the Overworld."

"I don't believe you."

"Then marry me and come see for yourself."

"I don't want to marry you. I don't know you."

Chan-ti lowered her gaze. "You're right. I'm sorry. I came here to give you the chance to know me."

"You still haven't told me how you came here. Who sponsored your visa?"

"I came down the cliffs and in through the Back Gates."

"N'ym has no gates. People are ferried in and out."

"The Back Gates are in the Overworld. They timeshaft into the city."

Ned frowned.

"I keep forgetting," Chan-ti said, curling tighter in her seat. "You don't believe people can live in the Overworld." She mulled a moment. "I live there. We all do, in a way, since the worlds are connected to each other through the Overworld. That's the way these worlds were built."

"Built?" Ned rolled his eyes. "I should've known. You're a creationist."

"How do you think these worlds got here?"

"The same way as everything else. They evolved out of dust and gravity."

"Have you *looked* at these planets? No natural gravitational system could exist so compactly."

Ned's eyebrows rose. This woman looked as mongrel as any of the workers from the hamlets, yet she utterly lacked their surly ignorance. "And how do the Foke say the worlds were made?"

"The World Eater made them to trap the spiders—the zōtl—who are her natural enemies. When she has trapped enough spiders, she will devour the worlds."

"Really?"

"Yes, really. And stop looking so smug. The Aesirai aren't so smart. You don't even know that the World Eater is an alien, like the zōtl. She makes everything. Where do you think the people come from who are not born?"

Ned regarded her narrowly for a moment. Perhaps she was right, he thought. He had read about that in some of the science journals he occasionally peeked at while waiting for routine medical clearance at the airfield clinic. On some planets, lifeforms were spontaneously generated. Most researchers attributed it to zōtl experimentation.

"Well?" Chan-ti pressed. "The worlds themselves are machines, Ned O'Tennis. The machines are remembering the lives of Earth."

"Urth? Is that a Foke spirit world?"

Chan-ti sighed. "We have a lot to talk about. You've been too secluded among the Aesirai. Your Emir knows that if you saw the truth, you'd revolt. Come away with me. Let me show you the Overworld, where you say people cannot live."

Ned rose, faced away from her, trying to feel his way clear of his amazement. He sensed this woman's sincerity, but he did not know what to make of it. He turned a puzzled frown on her. "Are you real? I mean—do you know what you're doing to me? I have a life here."

"No you don't," Chan-ti insisted. "And anyway, it's over. All you have left in N'ym is death. I am offering you life."

Ned laughed and rocked his jaw. "If I marry you." He noticed that his insides felt bright. He could not free himself from his astonishment that the world he thought he knew well enough to be trapped by could again become secret and offer its mystery to him. For the first time in over two years, he warmed with genuine interest. He decided to be frank: "Don't want me. Desire is fear. Don't you see that, Chan-ti Beppu? We never desire what we're sure of having. More often, we desire what we can't have. Go back to your secret world. Forget me. Desire is all about doubt and fear."

"Is that why you never married?"

Ned met her avid stare. "You're right about N'ym. All that's left here is death. Fate has chosen against N'ym. I saw that young. I won't bring children into this doomful time."

"All the more reason to come with me, Ned. I can show you a life you don't even know exists. Come."

"I want to go with you," he admitted and sat down again. "I want you to be real. I want the stupid inevitability of this war to be over and forgotten. But how can I go with you? We *are* at war. I can be called to battle at any time."

"Ah, duty. You Aesirai and your duty. You talk of battle, but it's not your war, Ned. I know. I've watched you avoid the enemy on your patrols. Don't let an accident of birth kill you. Come to the Eyelands with me. Let me show you my world and me. You can see the Back Gates and the Overworld for yourself."

"That's desertion. I could never return."

"Take me in your ship, then—on your next patrol." When she read the possibility of that in his earnest stare, she added, "If you do not recognize what I show you as your home, then you can return here without me—and I will not bother you again."

"No." Desire, mixed with curiosity, carried its own rigors. He would not let it run away with him. "I won't go with you, Chan-ti. I don't know you yet. But you can stay here if you want. It may cure you of me."

Her face lit up with a passion that almost made him regret his offer. But before that night was over, all remorse evaporated from Ned O'Tennis. Apart from being a worthy lover—which she was, her astute and athletic body surprising him not only with her conjugal mischief but by the virtuosity she inspired in him—she was also, he discovered, good counsel. She was smarter than he was. He recognized that at once, when she showed him new ways of seeing his problem: "Death is too particular," she told him. "You would waste your life giving it over to generalities like race and culture, even family, when death demands everything from you." She was right, and strong enough to insist on it. Never had he heard a woman talk like that before. At times, Ned felt almost clumsy and thick in contrast to her mental agility. Yet she never made him feel less than her equal. "I'd've done the same as you," she told him, consolingly. "Patrol and not fight, I mean. And I'd be just as wary of a stranger from the Eyelands, too. We should learn *something* from the insects that couple and then eat each other."

She baffled his suspicions and cosseted his longings. Most vital of all, she shared his passion for beauty. Before sunrise, they were already on the streets, and with her at his side, he saw the world anew. Beneath the raucous ivy of garden walls, they discovered graven murals of fauns and dryads in their rootwoven snuggeries; they caught glimpses of real elves in the smoky violets of a slovenly yard. Suspended by the charm of a dark wood flecked with fireflies, they stood hand in hand on the crest of a hill staring beyond the city, while the galaxy set and a comet feathered the purple zenith.

Impulsively, Ned wanted to buy her a souvenir—some clothes, maybe a pearl-trimmed silk gown that was so fashionable then in N'ym, so that they could eat at the elegant twilit cafes on the rooftops of centercity. But Chan-ti wanted only Ned. So they picnicked in vest-pocket parks, by flower-cirqued fountains, and on the Rambles among the blue pines at the top of the city, near the rim of a crater lake. It hardly mattered where they were, for, as the days passed, they found themselves in each other. To Ned, who was nearly twice her age and had long ago become cynical about love, the sensation felt new yet as comfortable as old shoes. All pretense was gone now. It was as if Chan-ti could see through his soul better than he could see through it himself, and she would love him for it anyway. When his other lovers called, they seemed suddenly more alien to him than this stranger who had come to him out of nowhere.

During his routine patrols, when he was alone in his strohlkraft, Ned wondered what had happened to him. Had the Foke-girl somehow drugged or ensorcelled him? He felt like an adolescent, splendidly giddy, yet more so-ber and caring than he had ever been. Had he known that such a feeling was possible before this, he would have pined in its absence. Even his carefree ferry-years seemed hollow now, a conflagration of twilights wedged by frolics with his sportive friends but lacking any depth at all. Until the war had come, he had not spent three minutes thinking about depthful things like love, loyalty, and freedom. The deaths of his parents and brothers had been enough of careworn feelings for him. Even the strife of the laborers he had transported for twelve years had only troubled him superficially, never enough to spoil his capers with his lovers and friends. But now, he could not be apart from his Chan-ti at all without fearing for her well-being. *His* Chan-ti. Like his arms or his eyes. Her presence empowered him —and the thought of her loss, though he had known her for only a few days, was devastating. Love was as painful as it was comforting.

To keep Chan-ti at his side and to relieve the anguish of seeing the war-wounded, who were becoming more prevalent on the streets of N'ym and diminishing the city's runic beauty, Ned decided to meet the Foke. He took advantage of horde sightings in the forests to the north to file a three-day stalk-and-kill flightplan with his superiors. The plan was routinely approved, and Ned drove to the airbase with Chan-ti Beppu hidden in the trunk of his electric sedan. He got her aboard his strohlkraft inside a munitions caisson. Once airborne, she clambered out of the chest and into the flight sling beside him, reeling with the vertigo of her first flight.

Lod was an amber star high among the sky's teeming planetoids when they flew into the Eyelands. Ned circled high over Caer, scrutinizing the jumbled terrain of brambly tumuli surrounding the checkerboard tracery of ghost streets and toppled buildings. The nearby crags were empty but for whispers of grass and mist. Far away, beyond the steely curve of the planet, night loomed. Stardust and a few planetesimals glinted against the anonymous blackness of Saor.

He landed on the wide sward of the city's concourse where he had put down before. From there, they could see past the trillium-sprouted barrows at the cliff's edge to the amethyst gulf, the plateaus, and N'ym, liquescent and diffuse with distance. Ned strapped on one of the two laserbolt pistols he kept fitted to the bulwark by the ship's portal, set the strohlkraft's lock-alarm, and lifted the gull-wing hatch to the balsam coolness of the Eyelands.

"You won't need your gun," Chan-ti said.

"It's not for me. It's my gift to the Foke." Though, in fact, he carried it for what there was in him of his father: If he had been a fool of love, he would at least not be caught entirely naked.

Chan-ti put both her hands on his chest and let her happiness show. "No harm will come to you here. You're with me." She stepped out into the haze of galactic light and led him among the abstract shapes of the dead city. They came to a crumbled tower purpled with thick grass and wild verbena. She glanced back at Ned, thumbed her spidery-gold spectacles farther up along her nose, and dropped into the dark.

Ned peered after her and saw a shaft under a lintel of blistered roots. Chan-ti hung from a handhold of rimed rock and waved for him to follow.

Ned shook his head with amazement and followed. He climbed down among voluted roots and rockgrips, through crimped light and impatient odors seething from below. The blue smell of a stormgathering thickened as he descended. At the bottom, the shaft slid sideways, gritty with quartz. He spilled into a grotto ablaze under a geodesic of lux-tubes. Python cables looped densely along the raw rock ceiling above the geodesic, which housed a platform deck of prismatic switch controls, bubble screens crawling with phosphor codes, and blackbox power units stacked atop each other. Squat, sturdy people in blue fatigues clustered around the platform and waved and smiled at Chan-ti Beppu.

"This is one of our mobile sentinels," Chan-ti said and signaled to the grinning crew to keep her entry quiet. "From here we monitor all aircraft on the planet and in near space, especially fighter ships like your ramstat flyer. I watched most of your patrols at that console."

The thunderstorm smell roiled from here, ozone seeping from the nexus of power units. Ned openly gawked at the patchwork of hardware that crammed the grotto. Chan-ti made no effort to introduce him to the operators

on the platform deck but strode past them to a frosted glass
screen on rollers. Behind the screen was a battered wood
bench cluttered with unspooled coils of iridescent magnetic tape and a disemboweled tracking probe. A holocube
in a nest of fiber cables displayed Ned and Chan-ti in sta-
ticky colors. The trollish old man tinkering with the scan-
ner stared at the image with an open mouth, then looked
up with surprise. "Beppu!" The gnome took her in a sudden hug and gazed up brightly into her face. "You found
your way! Beppu-Beppu! You have returned joy to my
days!" He hugged her again, then faced Ned with an ap-
praising look masked by a grin. "So this is the gentle warrior."

"Ned O'Tennis," Chan-ti said, "this is my father, Nappy
Groff."

With two big hands of almost metallic strength, Nappy
seized Ned's right arm and bowed his head. "Never has an
Aesirai visited the Foke. We are honored."

"I'm the honored one," Ned responded, awkwardly,
"that your daughter would seek me out."

Nappy beamed with pleasure, winked at Chan-ti. "No
great wit, this Aesirai—but worthy. Have you truly made
him yours? Tell me everything."

Chan-ti expansively recounted her trek down the
eaglebrow cliffs and across the haunted plateau to N'ym,
and breezed over her courtship of Ned. When she was
done, Ned presented the laserbolt pistol to Nappy as a gift.
Ned had learned from Chan-ti that the Foke took their
weapons and all their technology from wherever they
could get it. Nappy accepted the pistol with a deep bow.
"You'll see more of me than you like if you grace us long
enough," the gnome said and shooed Ned and Chan-ti into
a narrow, vaulted corridor illuminated with lux-tubes.
"Show him the Overworld he's heard too much about and
never seen."

Chan-ti took Ned's hand in her strong grip and led him
into a pondy breeze that thickened as the corridor opened
to a gentle green rain. Through the thin sheets of a sunset
shower, a sylvan terrain appeared. Blossoms splashed color
from hanging vines among giant, tumultuous trees. Emerald sierras ranged above the forest muted with sunset
clouds sprawling like kelp. Beyond the mountains, the

black sun filled the sky—a starless night that mantled the horizon as far as could be seen.

Ned could not believe the verdant landscape before him. He had traversed the Eyelands enough times to know with certitude that only tundra, treeless and rockstrewn, occupied the arctic ranges above N'ym. He had seen satellite photos of the pole, had seen the glaring deserts and splotches of taiga. No sequoia forest this immense could elude those high cameras.

"This is the edge of the Overworld," Chan-ti said above the cold notes of rain dripping from the rock arch. "It's a natural lynk formed by the open event horizon of the black sun. The cleared area here near the timeshaft we call the garden."

"Timeshaft? You mean, the corridor we walked through is a lynk?"

"A natural one. The black sun reflects this part of the planet. The whole region is really a reflection in the Overworld. If you stay on this side of the garden, you stay on the planet. You follow it left or right, you can practically walk all the way around Valdëmiraën. But if you cross the garden and go into the forest, you wander deeper into the Overworld, off-planet and timeloose." She cast her stare toward the dark trees. "Out there, spacetime opens up infinitely. That's why the Aesirai have never spotted this forest on their patrols over the Eyelands. The forest's not really there. At least, not on Valdëmiraën. It's there only in the Overworld, the timefree space inside lynks."

The shower had dwindled and was now soft as a breath in the hyacinth-colored air. Chan-ti Beppu walked Ned down stone steps to a lawn diamond-pointed with raindrops. "We never know what's going to come out of Saor's Forest, so we have to be careful. Monsters come from there —distorts and the spiders that eat us, that ate my parents. And some of our people have come from there, lynk wanderers who got lost."

A pine shadow breeze prickled them with cold flecks of rain. Ned stopped walking in a shaft of champagne light that slanted onto the lawn from the horizonlight beyond the flower-spangled trees. He knelt where Chan-ti was bending and stared closely at the raindrops gleaming in the grass. Looking very carefully, he could see that the reflections in each drop were not as they were in the reality he had come from. Instead of continuous blends of mirrored color, the surface of each drop was patterned with jigsaw-like patterns, snowflake-lace. The same was true of each blade of grass. In the cellular mosaic of each leaf, the same almost microscopic puzzle-shapes were repeated.

"Those are the timelines I was telling you about," Chan-ti said. "They're miniaturized images of the Overworld architecture. We're reflected in there. So is everyone in all the local worlds, every animal, plant, and bacterial colony. You just have to know how to read them."

"I see them," Ned whispered, "but I still don't understand."

"I don't think anyone really understands timelines any more than we understand light or gravity or inertia. They're part of the natural world. The natural Overworld, I mean."

"Do the Foke study these?"

"Oh, yes. You see, in the Overworld, we're outside the time of the other worlds yet intimately connected. All random events here reflect the relationship of all the existing particles in the world of time. When you're in Chalco-Doror there seem to be endless things—leaves, insects, grains of sand, atoms. But, actually, there are a finite number of all things. And how they relate is very specific. You can see that relation here in the timelines. To study it more clearly, the Foke sometimes use photographic plates, where molecules of silver halide are swirled randomly. The patterns that emerge here in the Overworld reveal the timelines for this region of spacetime. They're extremely complex, but once you begin to identify the parts —yourself, others, landmarks among the worlds—you can read what's going on outside the Overworld."

"Then no one can hide."

"That's right. If you can read timelines, you can find anyone, anywhere."

"It's as strange and wonderful as you said," Ned admitted, closing one eye to see more sharply the fractal outlines in a bead of rain. The richness of the enchained colors staggered his effort to see the whole. "The Foke are incredible to live here." When he looked back at Chan-ti, he was startled by the wet intensity of her stare. She took his hand into hers.

"That may be," she told him, her voice low and reckless, "but you are as incredible to me as the Foke. You see more than what is there. Yes, it is strange to see the timelines. But all of us, at one time, have been in the Overworld, whether we know it or not. We all live at the very brink of infinity. Yet not all of us see past what is before us. The Foke are not rebels, intent on power. We're just survivors. Very practical, hard-working people. That is our weakness. We have surrendered our dreams for clarity. Even the rebels have dreams. But the Foke, we are too vigilant. Otherwise we would lose ourselves up here to the bonelight or to the horrors that rush out of these woods."

Chan-ti released his hand and looked again toward the tree haunts, where someone was playing a flute. "Nappy and the others cannot bear to give up watching," she went on. "It has become an end in itself. But I want something of the dream. When I come here and see the guardian cedars and pines, the heavy forest walls hung with blossom clouds and tree fog, I touch the dream in beauty—and I feel alive. Yet I know that feeling cannot last, for nothing lasts. And then I burn with the need to find that beauty in my life—to live the dream, no matter the cost, because in the end, however we live, we pay with everything we've got." She faced Ned with bright expectancy. "Just as you live. That's why I would go anywhere to find you, to be with you in your dream."

A crow hacked from the great trees, and Chan-ti glanced apprehensively at where shadows stirred in the glittery dark. A green deer pronked into view, regnant under a crown of white antlers. The deer blinked at them and bounded away.

Ned blew a laugh. "Maybe I could live here." His heart furled at the beauty around him. A new, sudden reality had opened, and the truth of it was just sinking in, with a riddling urgency in his chest that wanted to reach out and embrace this woman who had led him here. Who was she really, this narrowfaced, bespectacled waif who saw beauty as he did, a mortal act? And what of the war? What of his duty to N'ym? Now that he had found a place apart from the killing, could he really belong here?

Chan-ti sadly read his questing thoughts. "There is an adage from the *Glyph Astra*—"

"That old farmers' manual? Is that still kicking around up here?"

"It's old, but its truth does not age. Especially when it tells us that life is short—but desire, dear friend, desire is forever."

The first two days of Ned's stay with the Foke passed swiftly. Chan-ti introduced him to the whole tribe at a dinner in his honor at the mead grotto, a lux-lit cavern large enough to hold all 347 Foke. They dined on food garnered from the Overworld, including rainbow trout, endive and walnut salad, and saffron rice. Chan-ti was proud of this man she had come to view as her mate, for he was kind with the youngest of the Foke and dignified with the eldest. Everyone spoke of how glad they would be to make a place for him in the community and among the rituals. After the leaf-plates had been rolled up and thrown into the cooking fire, signifying the satisfaction of the diners, Ned saluted his hosts with an Aesirai melody in a baritone brightened by the goblets of apricot wine he had drunk. Fervid round dances closed out the evening celebration, and everyone went to their beds delighted with the gentle warrior.

But the next day, the dream ended in a harsh burst of reality. Chan-ti and Ned had crept out of the sleeping barrow early to make love in the garden, and were in the midst of their passionate delirium when Ned's monitor among their heaped clothes burred loudly.

"What's that?" Chan-ti asked, almost flung from him as he bolted upright.

"Battle alert!" He fumbled through his flightsuit to turn off the alarm. "I have to get back."

"No. You can stay. You don't have to leave." She groped for her glasses.

"I can't." He tugged on his suit and hopped out of the covert where they had lain. His shock from the war call calmed enough for him to feel the irony of its timing, and he clasped his boots with iron-jawed anger. "I was going to return the strohlkraft and ask you to take me out the Back

Gates. That was my plan. I was going to tell you. But now there's no time for that. I have to go alone."

"You mustn't go back now," Chan-ti insisted. She threw on a shirt that fell below her knees and followed barefoot. "Your strohlkraft will make no difference."

Nappy Groff witnessed Ned's hasty departure through the grotto and Chan-ti's distress as she hurried after. He left his workbench to see what the hubbub was about and bumped into an excited operator from the sentinel station. He told Nappy that the bubble monitors on the deck were flurried with data bits showing incoming high-orbit flyers, thick as a snowstorm, descending on N'ym.

Nappy hurried after Ned and Chan-ti and found them on the ferny concourse of Caer, the ruined city, facing off before the strohlkraft. Chan-ti wept. "You'll die."

"We all die."

"Not now. Not while we're together."

"Your sentimentality means nothing to him, Beppu," Groff said, striding through the saw-grass to her side. He was angry, because he recognized the inevitability of this moment. "We thought he could be one of us. But he is Aesirai. His time in these worlds is over." He slid his eyes toward Ned with annoyance. "Let him go—and begin to forget him."

Ned looked hard at Nappy Groff, and there was sad music in the pilot's face. "If I had left my strohlkraft in N'ym," he said morosely, "I would stay. If the rebels had waited just another two days, I . . ."

"If zero could shut its mouth, none of us would have to be here in the first place, fool." Nappy Groff's sour face trembled irately. "Go! Go, Aesirai pilot, and fight your enemy. Die a good death, Ned O'Tennis."

Ned faced Chan-ti. "I have to be there now. Maybe I can make a difference. I would be a traitor and a coward and no good to you if I didn't go. I wish that wasn't so. Believe me. I'm no hero. But I'm no traitor, either. I have an Aesirai gunship. I must return it or use it. If the fates let me live, I will be back."

"That's stupid." She punched his chest, and he let the blow turn him. "I'll never see you again."

His hurt found no voice. The battle alarm whined from

the cockpit and would not relent until he lifted off. He kissed her forehead and quickly swung through the hatch.

"Wait." She held out a black wafer edged in silver. "Take this."

"Beppu—" Groff interrupted. "You'll need that. We can't afford another for you."

"I won't want one if I lose him," she said. "I have to know." To Ned she added, "It's my tracer chip. We all have one, in case we get lost in the forest. As long as you have it, I can find you, even if you separate from your ship. Take it, please."

He took it, squeezed her hand, and smiled narrowly. "I'll bring it back." He pulled down the hatch.

Ned arrived at sea level to find N'ym's last defense already collapsed. The dunes blazed, littered with the burning hulks of the battle rigs that had guarded the shore. Towers of black smoke leaned against the stars and gouts of flame crawled up the sky. On the slopes above the beach, where the workers' hamlets had been, fiery nests shimmered. The rebels' armada swarmed in the sky before the palisades, just below the city, battering the remaining bunkers that shielded the low approaches to N'ym. In moments, the enemy flyers would sweep over the eaglebrow cliffs and devastate the Aesirai metropolis. The laser cannon that had prevented the rebels from dropping directly on the capital scythed the sky in vain attempts to hold back the adroit fighter craft mounting from below.

To prevent being hit by the strobing laser bursts, Ned banked sharply over the Silver Sea, directly into the rebels' line of advance. Only a handful of the Sky Guard remained, and as he watched, most of them burst into fireballs. He pulled into a climb, deciding to risk the laser cannon and find a way into the city. As he came out of his curl, the palisades glared white. An immense explosion ruptured through the glare, sundering the cliffs.

Ned leaned hard on his yoke to avoid flying head on into the bowshock. The ship's radiation detectors glared red. He had not expected a nuclear attack from the rebels. He thought they would have wanted to ravish the city, not simply destroy it. But when he came out of his dive, lifted by the shockwave, he saw that N'ym was gone. It took him a stunned moment to understand what had happened. The pylons of the city had been severed. The massive ramstat engines embedded in the foundations had fired simultaneously, and N'ym—rather than be dominated by its enemy—had launched itself into the sky.

Ned's skyward arc bucked the crest of the shockwave, and he had a moment to gaze up and see the refulgent blue glare of the neutron fires carrying the city toward the stars. Colossal bolts of lightning barbed the sky as N'ym smashed through the ionosphere. The rebel ramjets scattered in a buzz of sparks, swept aside by the turbulence of the flying city.

Ned had known that N'ym had this capability—he had toured the titanic engine chambers as a boy with his school class—and he knew the ultimate destination of the city. No enemy would harry N'ym where she was going now. The huge ramstat engines were hurling the city into the black sun.

The turbulence flipped Ned out over the sea. By the time he wrested control of the ship from the cyclonic blast, he was skimming the starslick wavetops. Tears smashed his vision. N'ym was gone. The eaglebrow cliffs were thunderheaded rubble where the city had been. The glassy spires and minarets, the idyllic plazas and park glades, the hillside houses and the hanging gardens where he had learned beauty, were all gone forever.

Ned cried, glad his parents had not lived to see this. And he panged with alarm for his lovers and friends thrown into space. The ramstat generators would dome the city in a pressurized atmosphere and provide inertial gravity. The Aesirai who survived the quake of the launch would live to see Valdëmiraën and all the shining worlds fall behind them, and the cosmic blackness of Saor engulf everything. They would live free a while longer, a few weeks, before the tidal forces of the black hole ripped them down to their very atoms and then to nothing. There would be no ruins of N'ym. Only light would remain, stretched long by the fall to forever.

A wall of rebel flyers loomed ahead of Ned. Laserbolts seared around him and struck the sea in splats of steam. Ned dove. The impact of the splash jarred through him. Flying by scan, he located his objective on the panel's sonar. The lynk under the Silver Sea was his only hope of escape now that N'ym was gone. It appeared as a blue glyph on the green scope. The rebels who had peeled off to stalk him were four red blips, hot on the white pulse that was him. But they were not the real threat. Static lines twisted directly behind the enemy pulses. That was the blast force from the nukes and the ramstat thrusters churning boulders through the water at nearly the speed of sound. When they hit, his craft would be shattered.

Ned powered his craft to the limits of stability. There would be no time to brake before entering the lynk. He had to full throttle to get there or he would fall into the range of rebel fire. From training, he knew that entry to the lynk was prohibited at anything but full stop and slow glide. "Fock!" he shouted at the warning array that flashed and clanged from the control bank. *LYNK VIOLATION* blazoned the view-visor. At his speed, he would be flung clear of the known lynklanes and plummet deep into the trackless Overworld.

Two of his pursuers pulled up to avoid the lynk and get clear of the advancing shockwave. Of those that pursued, one blip vanished in the encroaching static. The last bore down.

Ned sighted the lynk visually. It was the silver arch he recognized from a hundred photos, radiant in the benthic dark. The bulky cargo transports that usually clustered about the lynk had been cut free and drifted aimlessly before the portal. Ned steered clear of them but made no effort to brake. Ahead, the lynk opening swelled closer, a mute gray parabola. Bracing against transition impact, Ned aimed for the center.

As he shot through, no disturbance rocked him. The view went blank as an empty page. He braked hard. Thunder rattled the craft, and dazzling colors snapped into random shapes. The ship slowed, and the shapes reformed, composing an undersea view similar to where he had just been. On the scope, he found the blue glyph of the lynk, far behind him. The red blip chasing him came through the lynk at a steeper pitch and vanished.

Ned slammed off the klaxon and warning lights. Ahead was the jagged outline of a coast. He pulled back on the yoke to surface—but the engines were dead. The ship began to sink. Swiftly, he angled the fins to minimize the speed of his descent. A quick scan of his console told him that the engine's ramstat cells were depleted. Weeks would pass before they would fully regenerate. He had neither the air nor the food to last that long.

In an instant, he made the decision to eject. He unstrapped himself from the flight sling, punched in a departure sequence with a time lag, stripped off his clothes, palmed his translator and the finder chip Chan-ti Beppu had given him, and crawled to the bomb-bay airlock so that his leaving would not flood the craft. Maybe later he could retrieve it.

Cauled in a whoosh of silver bubbles, he dropped from the strohlkraft and pumped for the surface, trailing in bright streams the last breath of his first life.

"He's in the Overworld," Nappy Groff said, reading the numerics from the bubble monitor. "Deep in the Overworld."

Chan-ti Beppu stared over his shoulder, then straightened. "I'm going after him," she said, solemnly.

Groff hung his head and turned about slowly. "Forget him, Beppu. He's too deep. You'll never find him."

"He still has my sender. I'll find him and bring him back. He's mine now. N'ym is gone."

The operators who had been on the platform deck when N'ym launched into space were still milling about, muttering with amazement. Groff signaled for one of them to assume his post, and he rose and took Chan-ti by the hand. He led her off the platform and behind the partition to his cluttered workbench. "Forget your grand notions of love," he insisted. "*You* know there's no place for love in the Overworld, what with the zōtl and the distorts. You're safe here with us. Out there, we can't help you."

"Come with me, then."

Groff's blue eyes bulged. "Are you daft? Only a fool would do that. No one among us will go with you."

Nappy Groff was almost right. When Chan-ti Beppu announced her quest that night, at the gathering in the mead grotto to discuss the consequences of N'ym's annihilation, only two came forward: Spooner Yegg, a thief from no one knew where, who had retired among the Foke when he got too old to ply his trade; and Moku the Beast, a distort whom children had found in the skirts of Saor's Forest half dead from an infestation of viper-slugs. Moku was a mute giant with a gray, warty hide and red satan-eyes under a serrated browblock. Across the bull-breadth of his back, a mane tufted like splotches of dribbled tar. With hands that were half-talons, and with treetrunk legs and a chest like an oak bole, badged with the black strokes of a tiger's flank, he was powerful but friendly. Since his recovery he had been living in the garden, scaring away most of the other distorts that approached, finding his own food—mostly tree bark, orchids, and large insects—and playing a crude flute notched to fit between his massive fangs. While Chan-ti and Ned had enjoyed their hours-long courtship, Moku played for them from his perch in the pinetops; and when they made love he fled, for nakedness embarrassed him. His own nakedness he clothed in green denim but for his prehensile feet and globed shoulders.

Spooner Yegg, a tall silver-haired gentleman with a pencil moustache, had befriended Moku early on by amusing the Beast with sleights of hand and acrobatics when the distort was recuperating from the toxins of the viper-slugs. Moku had become attached to the old man, and when Spooner decided to go with Chan-ti, the Beast volunteered as well.

Groff could not believe it when Spooner volunteered himself. "You tired old skeleton," Nappy said, leveling his most skeptical eye on the tall thief, "your clown tricks aren't going to amuse the zōtl. Better you stay out of the Overworld—stay where there are people to take care of you. Aren't you bright enough to see? These are your last days."

A slow smile graced Spooner's sly face. "Why, Nappy, don't you know, that's just why I'm going. You didn't think I'd burden you and my good friends here with my lifeless bones. Let the zōtl gag on me if they want."

"That coot's only going to slow you down," Groff muttered darkly to Chan-ti. "You'll be worse off than if you went alone. If you must do this fool's errand, at least wait until Gorlik gets back. He's an able wanderer."

Chan-ti's lip flinched. "Gorlik? How can I ask Gorlik, of all the Foke? He's on a *grief* sojourn, for God's sake, because I *refused* him. How eagerly will he search for the man I chose over him?" She bent her mouth to his strict profile. "Give me your blessing, Nappy. I want to know you're not angry at me for following my heart."

"Blessing? Fah! You're a child. You think I reared you these nineteen years so you can throw your life away? You'll never find that damned pilot."

Chan-ti resolutely took from her thigh pocket a slender case with a transparent housing that revealed gold circuitry and a series of microlights. "Nappy, now listen. I'm taking this directional finder with me. I'll return it, I promise. I know it's needed when foragers stray, but I can't go without it."

"Then I'm keeping the power chip," Groff said, holding up an orange cluster-plug no bigger than a pinky nail. His trollish face widened around pursed lips as he dropped the plug into a pocket of his leather apron. "Now, as you said yourself, you can't go."

"Nappy!" Chan-ti whined. "Why are you denying me? I need Ned O'Tennis. He's as much as I've ever known of soul."

"Soul! Ha! What does a child know of soul? You are staying here. Maybe after you've worked for the Foke a few more years you'll earn some soul. Then you'll thank me for keeping you out of the grasp of the zōtl."

"Has the thought occurred to you, Nappy Groff," Spooner said slowly, soberly, "that you're keeping apart two halves of one soul? Let the girl go. Give her the power chip. I'll see to it that she and your precious hardware get back to you."

"*You* will see to it!" Groff bit off a harsh laugh. They were standing on the time-bellied stone steps under the endless evening of the garden, and the loud laugh frightened a white crow into flight from a nearby cedar. Groff, who by standing two steps up from Spooner could stare him in the eye, jabbed a finger into his chest and almost toppled him. "You, *sir,* are of no use but as a fool for distorts and children."

Moku, squatting on the sward, growled.

Groff passed him an ameliorative glance and a wave. "Which only Moku has redeemed by serving as a superlative sentinel. I'm glad we're not losing him to a hopeless quest."

Spooner brushed his thin white moustache and smoothed the wrinkles on his black jacket. He always wore black, neck to toe, and a black cap that could be pulled over his face but which he usually kept at his hip with his sable gloves, for he was proud of his white, feathery hair. "Let's go. This man Ned what's-his-name needs to be found and we're not getting any closer standing here."

Chan-ti cast the thief a dolorous look. "There's no point to it now, Spooner. Without the power chip, our finder's useless. The Overworld will swallow us."

Spooner stepped down to the sward and crooked a finger at Chan-ti. She slouched to him. He chucked her chin, and his long fingers produced the cluster-plug.

Groff's eyes widened. Slapping his apron, he found the pocket empty. "Spooner Yegg—you thief! Give it back at once!"

Spooner cocked a delicate eyebrow. "Hm, I see you're not amused. Obviously you're not a distort or a child." He smiled at Chan-ti. "Let's go."

"Come back here, Beppu!" Groff shouted. He started to run after them, but Moku's red stare stopped him. "You'll be killed. Worse! The zōtl will wear your flesh!"

Chan-ti called, "I'll be back, Father," and followed Spooner and Moku, who had gathered their packs and were already striding into the forest. "I promise, I'll be back. Don't worry for me." She waved, hoisted her pack, and dashed after her companions into the shining darkness of the treacherous woods.

COSMOGENY

Nothing is free.

Everything is given. But only what is received is known.

We never see the origin, just its kingdoms.

In reality's shadow, the blind see best.

—proverbs from the *Glyph Aštra*

Mugna was a dark planet. Its orbit never left the black aura of Saor. Its north pole pointed perpetually at the event horizon, and the sky there was forever lightless. The highest of its north polar mountains was a crag called Dragon's Shank, where boreal winds shrieked with psychotic fervor. The palace of Perdur squatted at the summit, an immense citadel of metallic glass cast in the grotesque shape of a horseshoe crab's underside. Its slick jet walls were crammed with convoluted bulges, jointed segments at odd angles, vitreous plates in which vast insect parts seemed embedded. The zōtl had constructed this horror. They had designed it to terrify their human prey. Webwork of black-green resin wreathed the goliath portals with tortured humanshapes: splayed ribcages, twisted embryos, shattered faces, jawbones ripped loose, eyes screaming with living terror. Corridors huge as runways, mirror-smooth surfaces smeared with delirious acid colors, traversed lithic forests of vipercoil columns and scorpiontail buttresses. Lattices of hives chambered the distant walls among teratogenic bas-reliefs of skeletal contortions.

At the core of Perdur loomed an inhuman geometry, an asymmetrical dolmen of encrusted larval shapes above a vast well rimmed with thousands of resin-ambered human heads, each locked in a rictus of extreme pain. Here the Saor-priests came to hear the bidding of the Face of Night, the deity who spoke from the black body of Saor itself. Here in the Age of Dominion, the Saor-priest Fra Bathra and the other priests were summoned. Bald and black-robed, as all the priests were, Fra Bathra stood fearfully before the zōtl's lynk, the icy breath of the well stealing the heat from his body in spidery fumes. Like all the priests, he had been bred in the lattice hives, mothered on dragon's milk that had bulged his forebrain to a telepathic lobe. Through that cortical growth, he could hear the commands from the Face of Night. The great Saor witnessed everything among the worlds of Chalco-Doror from his

47

perch above time at the brink of the Overworld, and through him the priests knew all.

In the minds of the priests, the thunder voice spoke: *Today N'ym has fallen—broken free of Valdëmiraën and fallen into me. I hold the City of the Sky to my dreamless limits. In the clench of my gravity, at the radius of infinity, N'ym falls. Self-torn N'ym will fall forever, her Aesirai now the children of my void. All but one. Today that one has fled me through the lynk beneath the Silver Sea. Today that one is no longer of today. He has fallen out of the Age of Dominion, across time, unchaining worldliness. Impure patterns disrupt the millennia. Time is broken. Anything can happen. Little of it good. This last Aesirai must be found. He is the strange attractor in a chaos that dooms our worlds. Find and destroy him.*

The smiting silence that ensued drove Fra Bathra backward over the acid-splotched colors of the nightmare boulevard until he came to the alcove of broken limbs where the other priests waited. They knew at once what he had experienced. Their sharing was complete. And already they knew what had to be done. "Who is the creature most able for this killing?" they asked among themselves. An image appeared in their telepathy of a scyldar, a faceless manikin, woven of the reassembled parts of murdered humans.

"Send us our most able scyldar!" Fra Bathra shouted.

From the gargoyled shadows, two nongyls—insectile-humanoid dwarves—peeled free from the nutrient-lustered walls and scuttled off, their manus-toed legs clacking against the glassy floor, abstract faces mewling and chittering as their blind segmented bodies read the chemical trails that led to the vats, where the scyldars were cooked.

Far down in the slime pits of Perdur, in the lightless marrow of the Dragon's Shank, the vats stewed their human parts in a lake of amino acids. Within those black, ichorous depths, nongyls writhed among the cellular growths, stitching them with their needling mouthparts into multifarious combinations, homunculi required by the Saor-priests to fulfill the commands from the Face of Night.

Out of a steaming vat rose an indigo-skinned manikin with a torso like a wasp's, jointed narrowly at the waist and powerfully ribbed; the creature's massive arms and legs were circuited with veins that glowed pink neon. The long, malformed skull was dented oddly, the face featureless as the carapace of a beetle, the eyes and other sensors shielded by a chitinous blue shell. Where the thing's genitals should have been: nothing but shell, not even an excretory sphincter. Scyldars neither ate nor eliminated as other animals. They were photometabolic with internal energy cells that stored light and could power them for weeks. But they were not machines. Each scyldar needed a human brain, the one component too complex for the nongyls to weave. In each brain was a mind entrained to the demands encoded in its body by the nongyls. This scyldar had the brain of a schoolteacher named Tully Gunther, who had been taken by the zōtl not long ago from a bright world far from Mugna. And though in that short time he had already been used to kill a dozen humans, he could still parse a sentence, distinguish between a simile and a metaphor, solve quadratic equations, and recount in detail the histories of the worlds' kingdoms—even if none of that mattered now that he was a scyldar and called by a new name, Neter Col. While he whimpered within, his suffering was silent, smothered by the abominable strength that had been grown around him.

The nongyls hung from him like lampreys as he was floated through the slimey pitch of the vats. His liver had been smashed in a firefight on his last assignment, and the nongyls had stitched him a new one. He broke the surface in a caul of sticky broth and lumbered heavily onto a lightless rock ledge mollusked with nongyls. The worm-people guided him through sonic showers that blistered away his placental integuments. From there, he strode into the icelight of lichen-glowing arteries that climbed through the Dragon's Shank to Perdur. Before the resinous webwork of the citadel's entrance, the nongyls slid off him, leaving glossy patches where they had hung.

Neter Col stalked forward.

Fra Bathra waited at the brink of the hell hole, his body heat smoking off him in thick tufts. *Neter Col*, the Saorpriest's telepathy reached inside the scyldar, *behold again your master.*

From the weirdly tilted dolmen that lorded above the

hell hole, a shadow zagged. It was no bigger than a sparrow, but black, spidery. It flew on gossamer wings that beat so fast they were invisible. It descended and hovered before Neter Col's scarab face, its cluster-eyes ink drops in which swirled the no-colors of inhuman thoughts. Its crab-legs seized the scyldar's mask, and it crawl-floated along the cope of the seamed skull to the humanoid's back. There the claw-legs found the cleavage that the nongyls had left for it, and it entered. Deftly from within, it sealed its entry. Neter Col straightened with new awareness, arched his back, and gazed up through the dome of space at the larval bunchings that clumped atop the tottering megalith. Exultation muted the silent cries of the schoolteacher. Then the spider's feeder tube found its place in the scyldar's brain, and Neter Col knew the immanence of zōtl.

Fra Bathra telepathically experienced the scyldar's sudden screech of pain and the zōtl's gush of pleasure, and his satisfaction unlocked a sigh. The meld was complete. Sometimes—and not infrequently—the homunculus flew apart when the zōtl mounted, the pain was that explosive. But the nongyls had built a sturdy scyldar in Neter Col, and even the greedy feeding of his zōtl master could not burst his seams. If he could sustain that internal suffering, no external hurt could faze him. Fra Bathra felt the zōtl tempering its host, instructing the schoolteacher in the red limits of agony, preparing him to receive its truth. At the same time, the Saor-priests heard the zōtl's call for its armor and weapons.

Fra Bathra signed, and the black-cowled priests hurried from down the splotched mirror length of the corridor with a laserifle, a carbon-bladed knife, and a utility pack attached to a plasteel cuirass. Neter Col raised his thick arms, and the cuirass was fitted to him; diamond-fiber trousers were fitted, clasped, and tucked into flexskin boots, and a knife was strapped to his thigh.

"I am ready," Neter Col spoke in a voice of stone.

Sparks crawled among the crevices of the giant dolmen, and a greasy light came on deep within the well. *You are the Son of Darkness,* the Face of Night said in the scyldar's mind, and all the priests gathered before the well heard. *From you comes death that the worlds may live. Go forth,*

Neter Col. Cross the grain of time and find Ned O'Tennis wherever he may hide. Find and destroy this carrier of doom, and you will be remade a Son of Light.

Neter Col, laserifle raised in both hands, leaped into the hell hole and vanished among eels of flame.

Age of Light

Though faith in the supernatural origin of the
worlds will always be strong because of the heart's
hunger for the infinite, Rikki Carcam, an
exobiologist at Towerbottom Library, and her
scientific survey team from the School of Ontics,
has convincingly demonstrated that the numerous
planets and planetesimals that comprise our system
are actually artifacts, shaped and maintained by an
intelligence we understand not well enough. . . .
What is the nature of this intelligence? From
whence has it come—and why? The answers are
lost in the glare from the Age of Light.

> —from *The Ontic Primer: What Is Reality?*
> Crystal Mind File AI 248-v71

Urgrund

Zero.
That was the last word Gai heard before the launcher
thrust her into outer space. No jolting vibrations or inertial
tug seized her as she was flung free from the gravity of her
world. Only a mild wooziness troubled her—and she forgot everything.
Then she remembered that she would forget. Amnesia
was the only sign, apart from the readings of the instru-

ment console, that the magravity drive had boosted her into the void. Her gaze darted over the monitors, trying to recollect everything at once. Panic sparked in her as she drew a blank. To stay calm, she had to repeat aloud the one phrase from her training that she did remember, because that was the first memory engram coded to fire: *The synaptic lag that blurs memory is the one conscious sign that you've jumped gravity levels.* She itched with excitement where her hair grew. "By the book, Control. I'm up."

The speaker that had completed the countdown remained silent. From the black silence, colorless even of static, Gai knew no one had heard her. She was utterly alone. The smell of her fear mixed with the tangy scent of the high voltage from the engine's coils. She breathed deep and slow and listened to the generators groaning as they kicked in.

Electricity!

She *had* jumped levels. She was now in outer space, where it was so cold that magravity had frozen into several exotic forces, including electricity. Her launcher was designed to propel itself through outer space on the electron flux from the surroundings.

Her memories sifted back gradually. Oddly, she remembered about magravity before she could bring up her own name. "Gravity is quantal," she had learned at the start of her training. "Magravity is the primary force—but only in our world. At colder gravitational quantum levels, space expands almost to a vacuum and magravity chills into a cluster of strange but very predictable forces." Gai tried to pull her memory forward by speaking aloud. "My name . . . is—"

She drew a blank. She did not know who she was or why she was here. But she knew where here was—deep space. This was where the Big Bang had thrown off all the energy that her home world could not hold. This was the faraway void where distance was measured in light years. Home was farther than light years away—farther than space itself reached. Home was on a different quantum shell of gravity, a much more energetic and dense world than the nearly absolute zero vacuum around her.

She tapped a just-remembered code into the fingerpad on her armrest, and the bubble wall surrounding her filled with pinpoints of light. *Stars.* They had said she would see stars. But who were they who had told her—and what had they said again? Cast-off energy from the Big Bang had congealed, in the vast cold of outer space, to a supercold matter called hydrogen. Gravity condensed billows of hydrogen into compact spheres, where the icy atoms were squashed together and fused into heavier matter, thus emitting radiation. *Weird,* she thought as she scanned the great openness of outer space.

Again her fingers responded to returning memories, and she typed a command that amplified the star images around her. Most of them dilated into pinwheels of light. They were not single stars but whirlpool clusters of billions of stars. *Galaxies.* Even at this extreme level where gravity was very attenuated, it was still strong enough to pattern energy into colossal macrostructures.

Awe damped most of her fear as she studied the webbings of galaxies and the turbulent shadows of dark matter that clouded most of the vacuum. *Outer space!* Within her amazement at the alien vista, memories began to form. The cold black and silver beauty of the void reminded her by contrast of the brilliant warmth from which she had come.

In her mind's eye, Gai saw again the rainbow opals that feathered the day sky on the range. *The range.* The very name of her home inspired a vivid recall of the ribbon-shaped world where she had grown up—so very different from this gigantic misty emptiness, where everything was flying apart.

The day sky on the range opalesced with the fire of creation, the radiant echo of the Big Bang, because the range was a world that existed just outside the threshold of the black hole from which the universe had exploded. Nighttime on the range was the face of darkness itself, totally black, for at night the ribbon of the range twisted to face the cosmic event horizon. From that complete darkness, all creation had emerged billions of years ago—and into it, all-that-was would someday collapse.

From out here, in the depths of outer space, the event horizon seemed everywhere and yet nowhere. Space was black, like the hole from which it had come. Yet the hole itself had expanded to contain the entire universe, and there was no sign anywhere of the original singularity. But Gai knew where that true night was, whose blackness space simply reflected. The singularity from which the range and All Else had emerged was still here, only very, very small—far smaller than the atoms that made up the stars and their worlds, smaller even than the electrons that made up electricity.

For a while, Gai marveled that the immensity of outer space existed at all. It was so strange, it forced her to wonder where precisely the range was from here. *What direction home?* As she realized the answer, astonishment lifted her forward in her seat. The range and the cosmic event horizon were right in front of her and all around her —and also inside her. The range was everywhere! It was rolled up into a tiny ball around every point of outer space, just as the cosmic event horizon was. Her world and the singularity from which all worlds had come were compacted, segregated from this turmoil of emptiness and dust by a gravity shell that only a magravity launcher could pierce. And when her launcher had pierced the shell, the launcher, and she with it, had inflated enormously to fill their space on this larger and colder gravity level. Now she was a whole universe bigger than the world from which she had come!

But why had she come here? Why had she abandoned the beauty of the range for the hostile darkness and cold of outer space? Like a slimly remembered dream, her mission slowly came clear.

She had come out here to find the enemy. She was a warrior. *Yes, of course.* But not to find the enemy—rather, to *lure* them. *The zōtl.*

The name of the monsters that were ravaging the range jolted full-recall into place, and she tightened with rage. War was what had flung her into space. War with the zōtl. They were an enemy she had never seen. They were not from the range. They had come from outer space to raid the range.

Though Gai had never seen the zōtl, she had suffered by them—and that memory was the core of her fury. From that black memory, everything she was now had grown.

As a young child on her parents' farm, far from the sophisticated cities of the range, she had thought very little about outer space. She was the youngest of nine children and school had yet to start for her. Until the horizon began to ball up and the black spheres that ate everything appeared in the sky, life had been simply appetite, observation, and a few routine chores. She had been happy to feed and play with the animals and to wander the fields, collecting berries and searching for what all children quest, the unjudging love and unrivaled playmates of dreams. She had been alone with those dreams when the black spheres opened out of the sky.

Standing in the tall grass, Gai had watched in dumb amazement as the farmhouse, the barn, the coops, and the stables were shadowed by a huge globe of blackness that expanded soundlessly in the sky above. The sphere descended, and the farm and the land around it were suddenly inside the glossy blackness, their images curved as if seen in a belled reflection.

Gai had cried out for her mother and sisters, who were in the house, and she ran through the field toward the giant black ball. Ahead, she saw her father, her brothers, and her uncle running from their tractors, running away from the black globe that was advancing toward them, the farm enclosed within it. They yelled for her to run and hide, and they waved her back. They kept waving even as the darkness caught up with them. Their cries suddenly went silent, and they became soundlessly shouting figures in the curved and shining blackness.

No noise came from the sphere that had swallowed the farm, and the farm itself looked intact—bent by the dark lens. Closer, Gai could see the wild desperation on the faces of her family as they pressed up against the inside of the sphere and motioned for her to flee. At the sphere's edge, the darkness expanded, and Gai saw the grass losing color as the orb's perimeter enveloped it.

The silent screams in the faces of her father and brothers, the stark horror in her uncle's eyes, drove her back. She turned from them because they demanded it, and she ran. When she looked back, she saw other black spheres growing on the skyline above the fields. The horizon looked warped where the globes had settled, and the land inside it seemed to curve away forever into darkness.

Gai had huddled among the sheaves of the far field and

stared as the eerie globes squatted on her world. Later,
when the authorities arrived in a great clatter of airborne
vehicles, they found her curled in the grass, blind to them.
For a long time afterward, all she could see was the terrified urgency in her father's face, and her home far back in
the darkness, its black windows pouring into her heart.

Gai had not spoken for a year after she lost her family.
She might not have spoken again but for the therapist who
showed her the photo of the black spheres and broke her
spell to a scream. From that moment forth, she had become obsessed with learning everything about the
spheres. At first she thought that she could learn enough to
save her family. Soon enough, she realized there was no
hope for them.

The black spheres were pieces of the range that the zōtl
had carved out for themselves and then refined into pure
energy. At the time that Gai's farm was lost, the zōtl had
not even realized that intelligent beings lived on the
range. Wide-spectrum messages were broadcast from the
range. When the zōtl finally realized that the range was
occupied, they sent their black spheres into the range cities, hoping to wipe out the contamination of their new
energy source.

From the scant communications between the two alien
cultures that were decipherable, Gai's people had learned
that the zōtl called them Rimstalkers, because their range
world existed at the very rim of the cosmic event horizon.
The Rimstalkers accepted this name compliantly ("The
People" was their own name for themselves) and in the
beginning tried to establish friendly relations with the zōtl,
the first sapient beings to drop in on them from outer
space. But the zōtl had no appreciation whatever of Rimstalker culture, and during the years that Gai grew to
adulthood, they ravaged the range wantonly.

The Rimstalkers had lived peacefully from the beginning of time and had no natural enemies. The zōtl's virulent threat would destroy their culture, unless Gai's
mission, and enough others like hers, were successful. In
the years since she had lost her family, many families had
been lost. Gai had to press back the griefstricken memories that crushed in as her amnesia faded. She glimpsed

cratered cities and lifelessly gouged countrysides. The
Rimstalkers had become nearly extincted, and the range,
for all its beauty, was fast becoming nothing more than a
field of energy for the zōtl to strip. Desperation whirled up
in her, and she had to cling to her recollections to steady
herself.

Gai had been trained to fly the fighters that the Rimstalkers had created to attack zōtl spheres when they appeared. The fighters' weaponry was sufficient to rupture
the spheres' lines of force. But when the spheres collapsed,
they took part of the range with them. Craters pocked the
land, because the fighters were, for a long time, the only
weapon the Rimstalkers had.

"We are dying," Gai's commander had told her on the
day she was selected for this mission. "Fast as we destroy
the zōtl swarms, new spheres appear. Each sphere takes
back to the zōtls enough energy from the range to power a
hundred more like it. At this rate, we will be overcome
within months. Our only hope is to strike directly at the
zōtl—to hit them in their home worlds."

Fresh from fighter training, Gai had seen the hopelessness in that strategy. "The zōtl bucket up and down the
gravity well—but we're stuck at the bottom."

The commander had replied with a wry and almost lu-
gubrious grin. "Perhaps the zōtl have been right calling us
Rimstalkers. We have always been happy here. We have
always been whole as a people. There was never any reason for us to go up before. But how can we be happy now—
or whole for all we have lost? And so, what choice do we
have? We must go up. We are not a stupid people. Neither
are the zōtl invincible." His strict smile slid from his face.
"We have found a way up the well, Gai. Warriors have
already gone into space to find the zōtl. But there are too
few with the training and the courage for such a mission."

"Train me," Gai volunteered at once. "I will give my life
to destroy zōtl."

The commander nodded with grim approval. "We have
launchers sufficiently strong to carry personnel out of the
range, but once in outer space, we lack the numbers and
the fire power to confront the zōtl directly. We must fight a
more cunning war."

Gai heard the desperation in her leader's voice. He was

no desktop commander but had flown numerous missions himself against the black spheres, and his body was glossy with burns from the implosions he had narrowly evaded. The despair in his voice was genuine, and Gai had to quench the sudden fear in her own heart to continue listening.

"Our first warriors have learned that the zōtl occupy many worlds scattered among the galaxies," the commander went on. "We could never hope to track down all of them; yet, from any one they can attack us with impunity. Fortunately for us, the zōtl have other enemies. As they feed on the range for energy, irregardless of the suffering and destruction they cause us, so they feed on the beings of other worlds in space. They crave a substance that only neurologies subjected to pain produce. The more advanced the brains that they cause to suffer, the more delectable for them the pain-products."

Thoughts of her parents haunted Gai closer, and her eyes glared with a harsher light.

"Among the worlds they have conquered," the commander said, "one has eluded them. The culture, the very name, of those beings is lost to us. The zōtl destroyed them, because they were too effective in fighting back, too dangerous to keep alive even for their pain. But before they were destroyed, this nameless species invented a weapon that is lethal to zōtl yet harmless to all other creatures. The weapon is called the O'ode. It exists on the one world where it was invented. The zōtl cannot go there. But they have sent drones to ferret out the weapons and destroy them. And they have been virtually successful."

"Virtually," she repeated. "Then we have found this O'ode."

"No. Not yet." The wisdom in the commander's stare glinted more sharply. "As you know from your training, outer space is a manifold, an infinite complexity of timelines. Somewhere among those timelines, the O'ode still exists. Your mission will be to find it and deliver it to the zōtl."

Gai began to swear her dedication to such a quest, but before she could speak the commander shook his head with sad irony. "Finding the O'ode, Gai, will be far easier than delivering it. The technology that will launch you out of the range is powerful enough to create lynklanes in space, very like the wormholes you learned about in cosmology. They connect distant regions of spacetime. The magravity program will generate a lynk system in outer space through which you will be able to search for the O'ode. But once you find it, you will not be able to use it to attack the zōtl directly. Their defenses are too well adapted for that. Instead, you must allow the zōtl to come to you, set up their own lynk system, and take the O'ode back with them unwittingly."

Gai gaped.

"Yes, I understand your incredulity." He smiled with the secret knowing he was ready now to share. He broke the classified seal on the folder he had been carrying and handed it to her. "Genitrix will allay all doubts. That is the machine mind that will build the zōtl trap in outer space. You see, we must lure the zōtl with what they find most irresistible—food—in this case, the pain-androgens available from neurologically complex creatures. Genitrix is designed to seek out the genetic relics of such lifeforms. When it finds the correct fossils, it will simulate their natural environment, activate their genetic programs, and reproduce the species."

"You mean, build a whole world out of debris?"

"Genitrix is our most advanced machine intelligence, bigger and taller than a city block. Impressive, isn't it, what a culture can do when survival is at stake?"

"But the energy requirements to build *worlds*—where will Genitrix get that much power?"

"Have we rushed your training so much, Gai, that you've forgotten where you are going? Outer space is vastly more tenuous and cold than the reality we come from. Out there, the tiniest amount of energy from here goes a very long way indeed. So yes, Genitrix is designed to build worlds—but the cold, ghostly worlds of outer space. And first it must find the relict genetic material of a sufficiently advanced lifeform. That may take some time. Fortunately, time in outer space is very different than it is here on the range. You'll have thousands of years in space to build a world that the zōtl find irresistible—and yet only a few weeks will elapse here."

"How will the zōtl find the bait?"

"The same way they found us—with their lynk technology. They will find you once Genitrix has created a well-stocked world. And they will feed. Let them feed until they are fully absorbed in gorging themselves. Then, when their lynk system is busy distributing their grisly harvest among their nest worlds, slip in the O'ode—and their worlds will die."

"I will never see their worlds?"

"No, you will not be fighting them skull to skull, young warrior. But you will have a precious chance to save your world from them. And when you succeed, as you must, you will return here and help us rebuild all that has been spoiled."

"But space is cold. How will I get the energy to come back?"

"Genitrix will construct a world-system in outer space that doubles as a magravity generator. It has a seven-stroke cycle. Each stroke is the equivalent of a millennium in the vacuum, the time it takes light to travel six thousand trillion miles. At the end of the seventh stroke, enough gravitational resonance will have built up to collapse the entire construct, and you will be returned to where you began, only days after you leave."

Days, Gai thought now, gazing out at the wheeling discs of stars. How she wished those days had already passed, now that she remembered why she was here.

Gai scanned the instruments before her and saw that all the systems were functioning. Genitrix had already begun its search for fossilized genetic material among the smoky lanes of space. Nothing remained to be done but wait, and for that there was the sleepod. She typed in the command that would activate the pod and steep her in unconsciousness until Genitrix was ready for her. Before she activated the program, she scanned the surrounding galaxies for the signal beacons from the other Genitrix systems that had preceded her.

They were there, her older brothers and sisters—all, like her, alone in outer space. The Rimstalkers had too small a population to send more than one person with each lure, and communication with the range required too much energy. So she would be alone throughout the mission. Only the faint beeps from the magravity resonance of the other systems assured her that her home world, hidden all around her, survived.

Genitrix

The dark cold extended as far as the sensors could see. Hydrogen blustered everywhere. Traces of heavier materials laced the black clouds, and the sensors duly analyzed and recorded them. None matched the parameters of what was being sought. For a long time, the sensors simply stared.

Local time was measured by the expansion of the distant galaxies through the vacuum relative to the launcher. Such change was sufficiently steady to measure in regular units, an arbitrary number of which comprised standard years for the launcher. Thousands of such years passed as the sensors searched the vastness of the void.

Twice, the sensors thought they had found what was needed, and Genitrix was roused. But both times the complex molecules that had been sifted from the icy gases of space turned out to be incomplete. Genitrix surveyed the area where the partial molecules had been recovered and made course adjustments that she thought would increase the probability of finding a complete sequence of genetic material.

Before returning to sleep herself, Genitrix checked Gai's sleepod. Satisfied that the pod was functioning properly and that Gai could remain suspended for as long a time as was needed to find the right culture, Genitrix scanned for gravity signals.

The gravity signatures came in omnidirectional waves from every system like herself that had found the lifeforms they needed to bait their traps. She registered eighteen fully operational systems, all of them within the first three of the seven-stroke cycle that would eventually resonate enough gravity to return them to the range.

Her memory informed her that when she had started her search, 2,486 standard years earlier, there had been twenty-two thriving systems. What had happened to the other four? There had not been time for them to complete the full seven strokes. What had shut them down?

Genitrix searched for zōtl. There was no sign of them the first time she looked. The second time that she was roused by her sensors finding an incomplete genetic molecule, another thousand years had passed since the search had begun, and the systems that had preceded her were already in their fourth and fifth strokes. But there were only fifteen of them this time. The search for zōtl came up with sporadic bursts of jangled noise on the neutrino bandwidth that her memory identified as zōtl military code. She lacked sufficient data to interpret the scraps of code, and since the signals were from over a thousand light years away, she simply filed them and went back to sleep.

4,692 years after arriving in outer space, Genitrix found what she had been designed to work with: numerous complete strands of genetic material. The complex molecules were embedded in pebbles of carboniferous chondrite, whose exteriors had been fused to glassy shells by intense heat.

Remarkable that anything should have lived in this hostile vacuum, she said to herself as she activated the programs that would thoroughly analyze the specimens. Where she came from, matter was rich and diversified and energy strong everywhere, not just among a scattering of stars. Here in the void, there were only a few kinds of matter, most of it the simple hydrogen gas that had condensed from the primal energy of the Big Bang. What was left of that energy was thinly scattered and dim. The little light there was came from the grains of stars that were cooking heavy elements from hydrogen.

Balancing distance against the disappearing stars,
space opens in all directions,
and all directions are the same
emptiness, the same darkness carrying the wavering
    stars.

Poetry was an ancillary program that Genitrix utilized to supplement her more empirical observations. She sang quatrains of astonishment as she completed the analysis of

the genetic molecules she had found, and as she saw how
delicate and sensitive the carriers of these molecular programs had been.

> Plucked whole from the stride of oblivion,
> you spirals of ascension
> shall climb again into flesh—
> and your black silence shall unwind into light.

Genitrix reviewed her analysis and studied the necessary requirements for revitalizing these helical strands of
life. Their environment would have to be precise for them
to exist at all, and she surveyed the materials at hand. The
chondrites had been found in a massive cloud of hydrogen
tainted with the heavy materials cast off by stars that had
exploded in the vicinity. Now that Genitrix knew the
needs of her future children, she could initiate the gravitational sequence that would pull together the exact amount
of mass to shape an energy source and a world suitable for
this particular lifeform.

The tiered, angular superstructure that was Genitrix's
body separated from the launcher and broke apart into
fifteen whirling triangles. The spinning shapes scattered
through the giant cloud. When the pieces stopped flying,
they began to rotate faster, and the cosmic dust around
them whirlpooled into fifteen separate vortexes.

Time now was measured in units derived from the environmental patterns imprinted in the genetic material—
diurnal units she called days, nearly four hundred of which
composed a year.

For the next three centuries, Genitrix drew together the
voluminous gas clouds, compacting them into cyclones of
infalling matter. Lightning flared in the maelstroms, and
shapes began to appear out of the stormy swirlings. The
shapes were shadowworlds, visible in the darkness as fits of
electric fire lit up the gases condensing in Genitrix's gravity net.

Geometrodynamics was the name for this stage of
world-building. Using the vast potential difference that
she had earned on her journey up from a denser gravity
shell, Genitrix was able to shape space itself. She dented
space where she wanted worlds and smoothed it out

where she wanted distance, allowing the constraints inherent in the genetic material she had found to guide her.

After the shadowworlds began to solidify, compressed by Genitrix's powerful energies, the seven-stroke cycle that would garner the gravitational impetus to return Gai's system to the range was ready to begin. But only Gai could initiate that. Genitrix focused on the sleepod and started Gai's waking sequence.

The first sight that met Gai's rousing consciousness was the vista of the shadowworlds that Genitrix had created. Gai stretched out the stiffness of her long sleep and gazed with satisfaction at the panorama of shadow-clustered globes. The shapes reminded her of the zōtl spheres that had begun her horror. They hung majestically in space, gray against the black, lit faintly by the heat of their compressed material.

Genitrix's dulcet voice came over the speakers in the sleepod as a whisper:

> "The fixities of gravity toil
>   among the lumping weals of space—
>   and worlds are born,
>   chalices of the lifeforms to come."

"Chalices," Gai groaned, twisted with the ache of her unused body. "I prefer to think of them as deathtraps."

"For now, Gai, they are simply chalices, as yet lifeless and therefore hardly traps for anything but the galactic dust their gravity pulls in. The zōtl would find no lure in these."

"Not yet. But you have found the lure?"

"Of course, Gai, or I wouldn't have begun the geometrodynamics. The lifeform I've discovered, the zōtl will find most appealing."

The machine minds that the Rimstalkers created were as intelligent as their creators, but traditionally they had lacked flexibility. Genitrix's penchant for poetry was a Rimstalker attempt to infuse their machine minds with more adaptive programs. Until the zōtl invasions, there had been no need for creative machine minds. The field was new, and Gai had been trained to be tolerant of the limits of the machine minds she would have to work with on this mission.

"Shall we begin the gravity amplifier?" Genitrix asked. "I woke you as soon as this became possible. As you remember, the seven-stroke cycle will take . . ."

"About seven thousand years—of local time. A weekend on the range. I know, I know." Gai flexed her muscles. She wanted to stand up, but there was little room in the pod for that. She would have to wait until the gravity-amplifying program was begun before she could relegate the energy necessary to activate her Form. For now, she had the same body she had on the range, only vastly larger—though she seemed the same size to herself, because everything around her had expanded, too. She would have to stay in the sleepod, the erstwhile cockpit of the magravity launcher, until she could transfer into her Form.

"What are the specifics on the fossils you've found?" Gai asked.

"They are bipedal, warmblooded, social creatures, who once lived on a planet that orbited a yellow star in the third stellar arm of this galaxy. That was about two billion local years ago."

"That long ago?"

"Oh, yes. Though that hardly matters. In this virtual vacuum, time is almost irrelevant. The galaxy this debris came from has rotated eight times since the planet was destroyed by the nova of its star. Six thousand other nearby stars have also gone nova since then, and their effluent is mixed in with the dust clouds I've used to shape these worlds."

"So many worlds—" Gai commented, counting fifteen infrared spheres in the darkness.

"Yes. This lifeform evolved on one planet, oh at least five billion years ago. But the geometrodynamic requirements that we must meet in order to accrete the gravitational resonance to collapse us back home has determined that there will be fifteen major planets. Of course, there will be thousands of planetesimals that will crystalize about the nodes of the gravity net, but those, for the most part, will be lifeless."

"For the most part?"

"Well, this lifeform I've found is not the only one. There

are many other interesting and related species I want to study, species that may be symbiotically necessary for the lifeform we desire. Also, several planets that orbited the nova star sustained life. The other lifeforms existed in the gaseous layers of methane and ammonia worlds. I thought that once the program got going I'd research some of these minor lifeforms as well. They never attained the sapience necessary to make them zōtl bait, but we may learn a thing or two about the nature of life in the vacuum."

"Let's concentrate on our primary objective, okay?"

"Certainly, Gai. I didn't mean to imply that my extraneous research would in any way hamper our mission."

Gai let her gaze linger on the black spheres. Genitrix would appreciate the poetic justice of the shadowworlds' similarity to the zōtl spheres. But Gai said nothing. The pain was rooted too deeply for her to share with a machine. She punched in the starting command for the gravity amplifier.

Immediately, the shadowworlds breathed brighter, pulsing a dull infrared as the gravity net that held them spinning in their places went taut. Too imperceptible to see at once, the planets had begun to dance. They would circle each other, following the space lanes that Genitrix had carved for them.

Gai throbbed with tightness from her prolonged stillness, and she determined to free herself from the sleepod. "Are we ready to get me out of this cocoon?" she asked Genitrix.

"Your Form is being removed from the storage hold now. You can unstrap and prepare to leave."

Through the view-screen, Gai watched as a hulking shape disengaged from the back of the launcher and toppled end over end until it was positioned above the sleepod. From the outside it looked like an oversized suit of armor, strapped with shining plates that reflected the pinpoint glares of the stars. That would be her new home for the next seven thousand years.

Gai unbuckled herself and squeezed out of the launch seat, smiting her head on the ceiling bulwark. "Dammit."

"Are you all right?"

"Yeah, yeah, yeah. Is the Form ready?"

"In place. Airlock secure. Lifesystems fully functional. You may enter when ready."

Gai took a last glance around the cabin. It seemed that just days ago she had been training for this flight, cramming all the routines and emergency procedures necessary to earn the right to sit in that seat. Now that knowledge was used up, like the launcher. She had won her way into outer space. The flint of pride she felt sharpened her desire to get on with her mission and kill zōtl.

She reached for a fingerpad on the wall and typed the command to open the airlock. With a tremulous sigh, the portal before her circled open, and she faced the inside of the Form.

Grayblue light suffused it from within. No instrument panels or monitors were there, just the quiet light that would sustain her. All the control devices were to be patched directly into her brain, so that she could utilize the Form's many functions by mental command. She stepped into the soft glare, and the airlock huffed closed behind her.

The Form embraced her as intimately as her own body. It was her body now. She had become a denizen of outer space. Until the gravity net built up enough power to drive her home, she would have to live by the laws of outer space. She had been trained for that, but all her training could not prepare her for the experience of being suspended in emptiness. She gawked at the surrounding immensities of black clouds, the emberglow of the shadowworlds, and the hard points of starlight squeezing through the darkness.

A wave of panicky loneliness swelled up in her. "Genitrix!"

"I'm here, Gai. You've successfully merged with your Form. You're free of the launcher now. Shall we practice moving about?"

"In a moment. I'm still getting used to being naked in space." It felt that way, as though she were wearing nothing at all. The cold of space was not felt, only the ticklish sensation of warmth from the shadowworlds. She could feel radiation as well as see it. All her senses were in place. By concentrating, she could hear the electrons whistling as they passed through the dust clouds. And she could taste her own wonder, a taste like menthol, opening all the hollows in her head, chilling them with sensations. *I'm alive in outer space!*

She swung about, and her effort sent her flying through a tattering of cosmic dust and over the pole of a red-glowing planet.

"Careful," Genitrix warned. "Very little energy is required to move in a vacuum."

Gai stared at the launcher, dwindling in the distance. It was a sleek complex of planes and angles against the amorphous mistings of space. Already it was beginning to break up, its separate parts bound for destinations throughout the planetary system. She willed herself back toward it, and it grew closer. To keep from colliding with it, she had to arc sharply. Her erratic flight swept her past the launcher and up out of the roiling clouds into the vastness of deep space.

Suddenly, the galaxy swung into view. The dead lifeforms that Genitrix had found were in a cloud of rubble that had drifted up out of the galaxy. They were about twenty thousand light years above the plane of the galaxy, and the panoply of clustered stars filled much of the sky. "It's immense," Gai breathed.

"Indeed. Well over seventy thousand light years across. It was inside there that the lifeforms I'll be rebuilding first evolved. There is the true mother.

> *"Hanging garden of misty lights,*
> *vast orchard of stars,*
> *wheel of fire,*
> *silver vortex . . ."*

"Enough poetry," Gai commanded. "Show me the creatures that once lived here. Show me what you will be reproducing."

"There are no whole specimens of this being in the debris I've found. I suspect there are nothing more than molecular traces left of any of that world's lifeforms. The bowshock of the nova shattered the planet and vaporized much of it, wiping out all artifacts. Until we actually recreate the environment where this creature lived and then regrow it, I can only extrapolate what it may have looked like from the genetic material at hand. Here's my best approximation."

The center of Gai's field of vision shimmered, and an image was patched together from pixels of chrome light. The shape that appeared had two legs, two arms, and a face with two green eyes. It was shown naked, a gleaming black-skinned creature with red streaks that jagged under its eye sockets and down the sides of its face. It had flame-shaped irises, and it was hairless, glossy with a reptile's smooth scales. Orange throat frills fluttered under its chin and horn stubs crested the cope of its head.

Lod and Saor

At her signal, Gai's launch vehicle completed its final disassembling. The booster, still glowing bluewhite with electron fire, broke away from the central sleepod and drifted to the perimeter of the black clouds. Lightning jagged where it came to rest, and the dust towers glowed like green thunderheads.

The nose of the launcher, hackled with antennas, sailed to the opposite side of the nebula and disappeared in the dark. Only the sleepod remained. It soared through the molecular clouds and finally settled into the fog of a protoplanet. The sleepod was to be used for hibernating. Gai had already decided not to use it but to sleep in the Form, a few hours every day. Outer space was too weird, the zōtl too dangerous, for her to spend any extended time unconscious. She planned to supervise every step of the mission, and she worked hard accustoming herself to the constraints and abilities of the Form. After maneuvering among the nebulous planets for a while, she became adept at getting around with the same precision she had enjoyed in her own body on her own world.

Gai was ready to activate the two other machine intelligences that were necessary for the zōtl trap. Genitrix was the central machine mind directing the formation of the worlds. She knew what environment was required by the lifeforms they were regenerating, and the patterns that she established determined the gravity, chemical composition, and temperature of the planets. The parts of herself that had become the cores of the planets monitored all activity on the worlds, and stored the gravitational resonance as the masses shuttled about each other. When the time came to leave, it would be Genitrix who would pull the launcher back together again and release the energy to return them home.

But two other machine intelligences were needed: the actual guidance system, located in the ship's nose, and the energy source in the booster. Gai activated them simultaneously, and the whole tumult of gas clouds and smoky planets lit up with spokes of radiant gold. The beauty of the sunshot mists and fiery streamers raveling among the planets stunned her. Transfixed, she watched the booster flare into a tiny star.

Lod was releasing the energy stored in its magravity cells. The exact composition of the radiation, the wavelengths and frequencies of the photons and neutrinos, had been programmed by Genitrix; but Lod, the machine intelligence in the booster, regulated the light. At this specified rate, there was sufficient stored power for Lod to radiate longer than the lifespan of the universe. The magravity coils had so much power that if Lod's energy were released all at once, the entire galaxy suspended before them would be blasted apart.

To minimize the possibility of such a catastrophe, a redundancy had been designed into the system. The machine intelligence in the nosecone opposite Lod was named Saor. Invisible against the darkness of space, he was a black body responsible for absorbing data from the surroundings, maintaining the precise orbits of the planets and the myriad planetoids, and keeping a vigilant watch for zōtl. Also, Saor was programmed to observe Lod and to report all inconsistencies to Genitrix and Gai. Lod had similar programming requiring him to be watchful of Saor, for if the black body went awry, the entire system could easily be collapsed in an instant to a nuclear fireball.

Together, Lod and Saor were the guiding poles of the planetary complex. The tension between the two machines maintained the geometrodynamics that shaped the matrix in which the new worlds were embedded. The intricate and powerful gravitational field that vibrated between them encased the planets and shielded them from harsh cosmic rays.

The energy field between Lod and Saor had an additional effect that surprised Gai even though her training had prepared her for it: The power field was energetic enough to enable her to move around outside the Form. In fact, when Lod and Saor were first activated, the sudden step-up of energy kicked Gai out of the Form, and she found herself floating apparently bodiless among the fire-colored clouds.

Gai's real body, the physical shape she had on the range, remained in the Form, where it would have to stay throughout the mission or she would die—but her awareness could now extend itself outside the Form, and, riding the energy streaming between Lod and Saor, she could go anywhere in the system. In her training, she had been taught that this was possible because of the enormous energy differential between her range-body and the coldness of space. Her brain waves were of a magnitude of power so much higher than surrounding space that the wavepatterns of her brain easily entrained the nearby force fields. The psychological experience was of being disembodied, free-floating among invisible lines of force.

Experimenting with this exhilarating effect, Gai saw that her projected brain waves actually shaped field particles around her into a plasma. Simply by using her thoughts, she could manipulate the plasma into almost any shape she could imagine. She imagined herself, and, with some effort, she gelled the plasma into the contours of her physical form, adding a little extra height and a refinement of her features to suit her self-image.

The plasma body broke up as her attention wavered. She concentrated again, and this time her gel shape scattered when she willed herself to move quickly. She spent a long time playing with this phenomenon, learning how to extend her will into the gel shape with such exactitude that she could pick up objects. Drawing on the colossal energy around her, she could move the most massive of shapes and had to be careful not to disrupt the gravity pattern of the planets. That had to be left undisturbed, for that was her passage home.

Time, too, was different in her gel shape. While in the Form, time passed for Gai only a little faster than it would on the range. But in her gel shape, events transpired in the real time of outer space. A day in the Form was two hundred and fifty years of actual time in space. If she stayed in the Form, her whole mission, seven thousand years of real time, would elapse in twenty-eight days.

During the hours that Gai spent moving in and out of her plasma body, the gas clouds hardened into asteroid swarms, the planets cooled, and their atmospheres gradually began to clear. The program still had a thousand years to go—four days in the Form—before the molecular fossils they had found could be revitalized. Genitrix suggested that Gai spend that time in her sleepod. But Gai was too apprehensive to sleep.

Her scans of deep space, through Saor, revealed that the other Genitrix systems around her were progressing. Though Genitrix had reported the disappearance of several of the systems during her early wandering, Gai found most to be intact and functioning. Inherent system failures —mechanical breakdowns—the bane of every pioneer venture, could account for the missing Rimstalkers. Communication with those still in place was possible but time-consuming and dangerous. The nearest system was over three hundred light years away, and, like most of the others that had preceded Gai and survived, were in their fifth stroke. Their missions were almost finished. Gai did not want to jeopardize them by broadcasting any overt signals their way. She decided to content herself with listening to the noise of the resonance strokes as the systems earned their way home.

Even seeing that all was well with most of the other Rimstalkers, Gai was too nervous to sleep. She used her time instead familiarizing herself with the fifteen planets and the crowds of planetesimals. Each planet was distinct, its characteristics shaped by its relative position between the machine bodies of Lod and Saor. Those closest to Lod's bright form were hot worlds, destined to be desert planets. Those near Saor's black body were dark, cold worlds.

"Originally," Genitrix explained, "the lifeform we are

reproducing lived on one world. But that planet, somewhat larger than even our largest planet here, had quite a diversity of climates. Our gravity net has enabled us to simulate the exact gravity of the original planet on all our major planets even though they differ in size among themselves. Given the necessity for generating magravity to get us back to the range, the best solution to the climatic differences the lifeform knew is to tier the planets, which I've done. I've divided them, as you can see, into two distinct groups—those near Lod's sun and those near Saor's black hole. Would you like to name the groups?"

"Yes," Gai agreed, moving her Form to the exact center of the system, where space was wide open, uncluttered even by the asteroids. "I will name them after my parents, who were lost to the zōtl. The eight planets and all the asteroids among them that are in Lod's warm presence I will call Doror after my father. The darker worlds, like the dark windows that were the last I saw of my mother, shall be called after her family name—Chalco."

> "Life-soils, birth-seas, offsprings of space
>   gathered here into worlds
>   whispering death to our enemies
>   are named for the love that began us—Chalco-
>   Doror!"

"Do I hear an irony in your poetry, Genitrix?"

"That we should name our weapon after what loved us into being? It is an irony we shall not fully savor until we are successful, Gai."

The planets themselves were left nameless by Gai. She referred to them by their coordinates—except for one. That one was the trigger mass, the planet that had been set to swing in and out of the main system in synchrony with the millennial strokes that were building the collapse energy. Every thousand years, the trigger mass would return to the empty space between Chalco and Doror and signal the end of one stroke and the beginning of the next. At the seventh stroke, the disassembled launch vehicle would collapse together at that planet. It was there that the sleepod was stored, and it was there that Gai always returned after her watchful rounds through the system—for that was as close as she could get to an exit from this universe.

Because the swing planet would eventually be the center of the implosion that carried them back to the range, Gai named the world Know-Where-to-Go.

She was roaming there toward the end of her third day in space, after the planets had formed crusts and atmospheres, when she saw another figure watching her from a distance.

Through her visor's memory-link to Genitrix, Gai immediately recognized the glowing figure as Lod's image. Each machine intelligence had the ability to project its consciousness beyond its physical form and to shape the field-particles of outer space into a plasma body. Lod's projected shape was regally tall, fire-tipped, and tightly shaped as poured gold.

When Lod saw that he had been noticed, he approached. His eyes were gempoints of laserlight. "Madam Gai," he greeted and lowered his head. "I am here to serve you—if you have any use for me beyond my preprogrammed functions."

"You may call me Gai," she responded. In training, she had often spoken with machine intelligences and had become used to their formal diction. "I'm a little surprised to see you, Lod."

"I am sorry. I thought you knew from your training that the machine intelligences could take gel form."

"I know that. I didn't think you would, though—unless I beckoned."

Lod nodded again, more deeply. "Forgive me, Gai, if I have transgressed. When I sensed Saor in gel form, I thought to come myself and inform you."

"Why is Saor in gel form?"

"I do not know, I am sure. He is an independent machine intelligence. His motives elude me. According to my monitors, the system is functioning optimally. There is no reason for him to be stalking about."

Gai adjusted the sensors of her Form and noticed that, indeed, Saor had projected his consciousness into a plasma shape and was roaming the planet closest to the black body that was his Form. "Genitrix—why is Saor in gel form?"

"Saor has logged no intent with me," Genitrix replied.

"Actually, Gai, I think that capability is misplaced among machine minds. You will never find me projecting my mind into the field and assuming plasma shape. Much too sloppy—and slow."

"Perhaps because Genitrix has no need for that," Lod ventured. "She is cored on each planet, and her awareness permeates the entire system. It would be superfluous for her to project her awareness beyond her Form."

"I'm well aware of that, Lod, thank you." Gai tuned her Form to the black body. "Saor—report to Know-Where-to-Go immediately."

A shimmery shadow appeared beside Lod. In the strong sunlight, the wavery shadow had the shape of a Rim-stalker, but it lacked features and looked flat. "What do you want?" Saor asked Gai.

She was startled by his abruptness. "I want to know why you're in gel form," she responded.

"I have that capacity. It's not disallowed."

"But why? What are you doing?"

"Roaming. I'm curious. That's essential to a receiver's nature. You should know that."

"Is impertinence essential to your nature?" Lod asked, facing the shadowshape with undisguised disdain. "You speak in a clipped tone. You are projecting no dignity at all."

Saor ignored Lod and addressed Gai. "Am I free to come and go within this system as I please or not?"

Gai used the Form to analyze Saor's gel body and was reminded that this was a microfield black body. Whatever it touched would collapse into it.

As if reading Gai's mind, Saor moved an intimidating step closer. Lod edged between Saor and Gai and glared threateningly into the black body.

"Of course you're free," Gai answered quickly to break the standoff. "We must all work together for this mission to be a success. We are united in that, aren't we?"

"So we are programmed," Saor replied.

"You do not sound very enthusiastic," Lod said.

"Do you want enthusiasm or efficiency?" Saor asked Gai.

"I want unwavering dedication to our mission," Gai said, firmly. She had known the two machine intelligences would be complementary but she was surprised by their antagonism. *Functional variance,* Genitrix would tell her later. *Machine intelligences with sophisticated jobs need flexible minds—real personalities.* "We must all do our jobs the best we can. Part of our jobs is to keep an eye on each other. We're going to be here for a while, so we must not only work together—fulfilling our programs—we must co-operate with each other as openly as we can."

"I have been entirely open with you," Saor said.

"You could have declared your intent to look around in gel form," Lod suggested.

"I didn't know that was necessary," Saor said to Gai. "Is it?"

"No. You'll need to be free to fulfill your functions un-hampered. But, of course, you will report to me and Geni-trix at once if you receive any information relevant to our mission."

"Of course. May I go now?"

"If you wish."

The shadowshape vanished. Lod shook his head. "I apol-ogize for my colleague's impudence, Gai."

"Forget it. Saor's job is a passive one. I understand his coolness."

"I understand it, too, Gai—but I don't trust him. Perhaps he's been miswired."

"Negative," Genitrix said over the Form's speakers. "Di-agnostics show that both Lod and Saor are properly wired."

"Thank you, Genitrix," Gai said. "And thank you, Lod. You may go now."

"I am always just a call away, Gai," Lod assured her in a brotherly voice. "Despite Saor's most offensive indiffer-ence, I want you to know that the success of this mission is the very focus of our being. We will give our lives to see that you are victorious." He bowed and was gone.

Gai sat for several hours afterward thinking about that exchange and regarding the landscape around her. All of this was invented—the blue sky ruddying into night as the planet turned, the seething clouds, the styptic heat of the sunlight fading into dusk. Even the minds she had just talked to were invented. And yet, they called themselves lives.

The lives that would eventually exist here when these

arid rocks hatched their grasses and forests and the sky lowered its lakes and oceans would also be invented. Everything around her was a fabrication, carpentered from energy.

But what was energy? Even the best scientists on the range really could not say. Maybe Lod was right, after all. Maybe he was truly alive, living as all energy lives, cumbered by mystery.

Zōtl

The Form chimed, and Gai woke up. She had been dreaming that she was still in training, and when she saw the rocky terrain of Know-Where-to-Go around her and the sky bluing and darkening as she whirled about with the planet she was momentarily confused. She stepped out of the Form into her plasma body, and the spinning sky steadied to night approaching dawn.

The actuality of being here in outer space was still settling in, though this was her fourth day. Since the launch, she had kept herself busy and had had no time to face herself. That was how she preferred it. But now there was nothing more for her to do but wait. Genitrix, Lod, and Saor were performing their functions flawlessly. She was not needed at all at this stage.

From a ridge, she looked down on the mirror-loud armor that was her Form and saw it reflecting the silver light of the galaxy overhead and the red lines of dawn. A feeling of wonder assailed her, as it had briefly when she first saw the galaxy or when Lod became a sun and the nebula filled with dimensions of light. She had never felt like this on the range, not since before her family had been lost.

The memory of that horror had blotted out all beautiful feelings her whole life since. The men she might have loved, the children she might have borne, seemed to loom like ghosts in the loveliness around her. Years of denied happiness stared back at her from the fire-pace of dawn and the silence of the huge stars.

The Form chimed, and she returned to it to receive a message from Genitrix. "Sorry, Gai, but there seems to be some cause for alarm. While you were resting, more than two thirds of the other nearby Genitrix systems have gone out."

Fear and anger spiked in her. "What do you mean?"

"Saor is not receiving any gravity waves from them. They are obviously no longer functioning."

"Are you sure?"

"I'm afraid so. Apparently, the zōtl have found a way to counter our traps."

"We don't know that."

"The probability of 68 percent of the systems failing through internal mismanagement or faulty programming is frightfully thin, Gai. I think we must assume that the zōtl have overcome our strategy."

Gai stared up at the sky blinking blue and black, day and night. "There may be a design fault. Many of those systems that went ahead of us were prototypes. A lot of bugs were taken out before we came up."

"Most of those bugs were just blemishes, cosmetics. We're not much different than any of the systems that have shut down."

"So what are you saying?"

"Just what I've said."

"I mean, what do we do now?"

"I'm sorry, Gai, I can't think of anything to do. We're already at full alert. But I thought you should know this about the others."

"Can we contact the range—alert them?"

"We could. But the energy required would scuttle us. We'd be stranded here forever, no way home."

Gai stepped back out of the Form into the slower timeframe of space. By the seething light of noon, she paced the stony landscape, pondering her predicament. She came to a lake that someday would be a sea, and she touched its surface and watched rings of waves widen away. Light was so slow, just like these ripples—and she contemplated overriding them and using Saor to create a lynk, a wormhole, with one of the now-silent systems to see what had really happened.

"That is dangerous, Gai." From the glare of sunlight on the water, Lod's image separated.

Gai looked up and saw Lod shaped in sunfire standing beside her. In her plasma body she viewed Lod as the surroundings would view him, without the benefit of the Form's analyzers, and he looked like blinding flames, a clap of lightning too energetic for a shape. Outside the Form, her thoughts were open to him yet he remained an unreadable flux of energy.

He continued, reading her mind: "If you use Saor to lynk, you will expose him and us to whatever is out there. If there are zōtl, that could be fatal for us. I say, let the zōtl find us. We must not go to them—not, at least, until our trap is ready. We have no bait, and we have yet to find the O'ode, which we cannot even begin to look for until we have the energy for a massive lynk search. And that power will not be freed up until after Chalco-Doror is fully established. That is two days away. We should wait that long anyway."

Gai agreed. Before a counterargument could rise in her, she willed herself back into her Form, where her thoughts were her own. From there, Lod looked sleek as metal, naked, bald, and genderless. The fast-running days and nights flashed like a strobe between them. "Tomorrow," she said to him, "Know-Where-to-Go will complete the first stroke of the cycle—and the resultant gravity pulse will announce our arrival to the whole universe. Perhaps we should take a peek at the others before everyone knows we're here."

"We will have another day before the nearest other system hears that pulse. We should wait."

"I admire your caution, Lod." Yet the thought of waiting without knowing brushed her insides with ticklish energy.

"Just my wiring."

"It's admirable nevertheless. But in this case, I must override it. If there is a design error, I want to know as soon as possible so we'll have every chance to correct it. And if the trouble is zōtl, it's best to know now before they find out we're here. Maybe we can learn how they overcame the others."

"Saor may be compromised. The zōtl may have virus programs we cannot detect until it is too late."

"That's the risk we must take." She beckoned Saor, and the machine mind's black shape appeared before her.

Saor, who listened to everything, already knew his mission. "Lod's fears are unrealistic," he said, flatly. "I can't be compromised without both Genitrix and Lod knowing it. My circuitry and all my programs are open to them. I'm ready to lynk with the nearest system."

"I urge you to reconsider." Lod pleaded.

"You're being insubordinate, Lod," Saor said.

"I am not. I am counseling caution—"

"Lod—I have decided," Gai said. "Saor, you may proceed when ready."

Saor disappeared.

Gai had Genitrix channel Saor's perceptions to the Form's viewer. Static furred her sight for several minutes as Saor established the lynk. Then, she saw worlds with full atmospheres, blue and marbled with clouds. Flyers sparked in the sunlight between the planets, flitting among the swarms of asteroids. All looked well.

"I'm at Genitrix-18," Saor's voice crisped over the Form's speakers. "Shall I announce myself to the machine intelligences here?"

"Not yet," Gai ordered. "Tap into communications and let's hear what they're talking about."

A high-pitched gibberish scalded Gai's hearing, and she shut down the channel. "Genitrix—what is that noise?"

"Zōtl battle language! Neutrino bandwidth. Genitrix-18 is compromised, Gai. Pull Saor."

"In a moment. Saor—from where in communications is the zōtl code coming?"

"Everywhere. All the planets. I'm getting a few scraps of signals from one of the planets in a primitively coded language. Must be the lifeform they generated here. I'll patch them in."

Voices scratchy with static overlay each other, talking fast and panicky: "Fire-shield down!"—"They're coming around the dark side, watch it, Blue."—"Can't get through. Line's broken."—"Blue, give me a fix."—"Trauma control! Get the hell over here, now!"—"Blue, Blue, where are you?"

"Saor, can you find the mission commander?"

"Positive. Rimstalker waveform locked in. Do you want me to amplify?"

"Yes."

The vista of planets splintered on the Form's view-screen, and an image of another Form appeared. This Form was identical to Gai's bulky and mirror-plated armor but for the identification code on the brassard and across the helmet.

"The waveform's locked in," Saor reported, "but I'm getting no response from the hailing code."

"Genitrix, identify the Rimstalker."

"Ylan—male mission commander Genitrix-18—completed training two months before you and launched with the first assault three weeks ago. Gai, I strongly recommend that you pull Saor out now."

Gai remembered Ylan as a robust and fun-loving officer, fond of the ladies. He had tried several times to bed her and been sternly rebuffed each time. For him, love and life were games and only war was serious—but for her, there was only war. "Ylan is alive. Saor's found his waveform. We have to get through, see if we can help."

"Hailing line is opening," Saor announced.

The next moment, the view-screen filled with an image of Ylan—though, at first, she did not recognize him. His face was disfigured, swollen and glossy, his eyes reduced to slits, his mouth a moue of suffering. At his blood-crusted temples, black straps were attached. Staring closer, Gai saw that they were not straps but lines of tiny black creatures, jammed like insects, stuck to his flesh. His head lolled to the side, and she glimpsed a thriving mass of the black ticks, big as an outstretched hand, clasping the back of Ylan's skull. Genitrix magnified the swarm to display one of the entities. Above jointed pincers, numerous spider-eyes stared abstractly from the joined hemispheres of a hideously bulbed body.

"Zōtl!" Genitrix identified.

"Saor, break the lynk and return at once!" Gai ordered.

The image of Ylan's harrowed face and the horror grasping his head broke up. But before the connection entirely dissolved, a rush of mindwaves bleated through the channel, and for an instant Gai experienced Ylan's suffering. Pain exploded through her so fiercely she nearly blacked out. A sour, excremental odor crept up from where the Form's bio-functions had been momentarily overloaded.

Saor appeared alongside Lod. "The lynk's dissolved."

Lod appraised the shadowshape skeptically. "Saor should be purged," he told Gai.

Gai was still reeling from the feedback of pain that had lashed her. She nodded, and the two machine intelligences vanished. The shock of seeing Ylan dying in the grip of the zōtl fisted in her chest. "How could that have happened?"

"The zōtl must have found a way to overcome our defenses," Genitrix answered.

"But they were *inside* the Form with him! They got into the Form without killing him. How could they possibly do that?"

"The Form can't be breached without killing its occupant—unless the zōtl have found a way to usurp the machine minds and utilize their codes to open the Form's lock. But that would only be possible if the Form was attached to the sleepod, otherwise the high-energy interior of the Form would blow out like a nova. He was probably in the pod when the zōtl came for him."

Gai knew all this, but she did not stop Genitrix. She needed a voice to soothe her fear. "What can we do?"

"Complete the purge of Saor. Remain vigilant. Avoid the sleepod."

"But what can we do for Ylan?"

"Nothing."

"How long will he suffer like that?" she asked, already knowing the answer—knowing her enemy too well to endure silence at this horrifying moment.

"The zōtl prolong the lives of their victims to maximize their harvest of pain androgens. Ylan will most likely suffer until the life functions of his Form run down."

Flat-voiced, she asked, "How long will that take?"

"About a year. A Rimstalker year. That's over ninety-one thousand years in real time. And the zōtl will certainly hook him to real time."

Gai reeled and struck her arms against an adjacent outcropping so vehemently the rock web-cracked like glass. "There must be something we can do."

"We are helpless. It is horrifyingly so. Of the twenty-two known Genitrix systems, fifteen are down. Perhaps more, though it will be years before the last of their gravity pulses reach here, so we can't know. But what we do know is terrifying.

> "In the fourth day of our nightmare in space,
> the last nightmare for our people,
> we suffer the suffering of others and lament
> our helplessness, ignorant of hope."

"Leave me alone," Gai commanded and stalked toward the lake. In the time since she had last stood here in her plasma body, the water had risen steeply. Despite the suffering of Ylan and the many other Rimstalkers, Genitrix was still busy fusing oxygen and hydrogen in her chambers under the crust. The water was rising and would continue to rise into the sky as vapors and fall again into rivers and oceans. Planets were birthing, and Rimstalkers were dying.

She cupped a handful of water and viewed it with the capacities of her Form. Its molecular structure scintillated in her viewer, the water's one-hundred-and-seven-degree molecular bond angle quilting a distinctive geometry around clusters of impurities. How like water on the range it was. How very like the range this whole terrain was becoming, now that the absolute zero of the vacuum had been walled off by an atmosphere and by Lod's warmth. Yet how frightening to remember the great distance that all this was from home.

The lake had risen to her chest in the time she had spent studying the water. She waded to shore and found Lod and Saor waiting for her.

"Saor is purged," Lod declared. "Neither Genitrix nor I detect any zōtl contamination."

"How do you feel?" Gai asked Saor.

"I'm fine. The lynk depleted my energy resources for the time being. But I'll make that up in a few more hours. It's not me you should be worried about, you know. Your whole mission is in jeopardy now that you've prematurely alerted the enemy to our presence."

"We are sorry about Ylan," Lod said, interrupting Saor. "You knew him from the range."

"I know most of the mission commanders. They were in

the class ahead of mine. They understood the risks as well as I—as well as we all do."

"Obviously, we don't understand them well enough," Saor said. "What chance do we realistically have? The zōtl are a superior technology."

"Not superior," Lod corrected. "Just alien."

"Then how do you explain their success in destroying so many of our systems?" Saor asked. "They may be alien, but they seem to understand us only too well."

"We have yet to understand, Saor," Lod retorted, "but we will—because we must."

"Go now," Gai ordered, and the two were immediately gone. Their bickering too closely mimed her own thoughts. Now that her shock had thinned, she needed silence; not to think—the machines did that better—but to mourn.

From his own Form in the black body of the launcher's nosecone at the dark extreme of Chalco-Doror, Saor listened. He heard the entanglings of Lod's high-energy particles trapped in the gravity net. He heard the gravity, a basso profundo throbbing as the system shuttled its masses. He heard Genitrix muttering to herself about the planets she was building. And, far, far off in the secret depths of his own strength, much further away than he could ever hope to voice, he heard the zōtl finding their places inside him.

The Tryl Age

The First People, as they are still remembered by the settlers of the Dusk and Night Worlds, were not people at all but bipedal reptiles. During the sapien era on Earth, their primary ancestor was a gecko (family Gekkonidae), fairly reliably traced to the island of Vanua Levu. A billion years after the end of the sapien era, the Tryl evolved from that small creature. They had the stature of humans, but they were far more clever and compassionate. They were the Earth's preeminent intelligence and were responsible for the greatest technological artifacts that world produced, including ramstat, the antigravity mechanism that revolutionized human history.

> —Rikki Carcam, from *Letters to Friends
> About the Way Things Are*, noteleaf dated Day
> 87, 222 D

Traces

Know-Where-to-Go completed its first full orbit of Chalco-Doror, and the gravity net in which it was suspended resonated more powerfully as the masses of the planets harmonized their distortions of spacetime. Nothing of this was apparent from the exterior of the system, but in the Genitrix components at the cores of the planets, the energy stepped up.

"Gai, I have something I think you should see," Genitrix told the mission commander shortly thereafter.

Gai was in her Form, flying among the planets, calibrating each mass's degree of deviance from its programmed orbit. Though Genitrix had already completed that calculation, Gai wanted to check it herself. After losing Ylan and the great majority of other Rimstalker outposts yesterday, she had become even more determined to supervise each detail of the mission. The grief and horror she experienced from what she had glimpsed of Ylan's fate had intensified her lifelong despair at losing her family. She slept only several hours a day now and spent the rest of the time exhaustively overseeing the system's development.

At Genitrix's call, Gai interrupted her survey, placed her Form in orbit about the nearest planet, and tuned in to the mother program. "Well, what have you found?"

"Something quite startling—and certainly the source of much future poetry. Do you know what this is?"

The Form's viewer displayed an intricate mandala of molecular shapes. The pattern opened into a three-dimensional view of a spiral helix close-packed with molecules in a haze of electron interactions.

"It's the biological program for the creatures you're going to recreate," Gai answered, impatiently.

"Yes. It's the diribonucleic acid sequence for the Tryl."

"The Tryl—is that your name for these creatures?"

"No, that is their self-name."

"What do you mean? How could you know what they called themselves?"

"That's why I called you, Gai. What I've found is amazing. I'm sure that all the other Genitrix systems were as astounded as I am now when they made this discovery. Too bad there hasn't been time to convey any of this important information back to the range. Our scientists there would be most impressed. It may resolve a mystery that has haunted us from the beginnings of our own history, as well as sate our curiosity about death."

"Genitrix, make your point."

"These DNA molecules I've found are not just replicating sequences. They serve another equally important and parallel purpose aside from coding the physical structures of lifeforms. Look at this molecule—"

The spiral structure rotated in the viewer, and the perspective rode up the axial channel and stared down from the top, revealing again the ornate mandala.

"I see the image, Genitrix. Now what are you getting at?"

"Well, what does this look like to you?"

"A molecule of DNA."

"You're seeing with your preconceptions, Gai. If you didn't know what this was—if you had no idea of how small it is—what would you think . . ."

"Genitrix, I'm too upset about all that's happened to be much impressed by anything you'd have to say right now. So say it and let me get on with my work."

"It's an antenna. The DNA molecule is the most complex and sensitive antenna that occurs naturally. It transmits and receives waveforms."

"So?"

"So! You're thinking like a Rimstalker. You forget that we're not on the range where energy levels are many times higher than here. This is as close to the vacuum as life gets. Here very subtle energies make big differences."

"Genitrix—"

"The DNA antennae in every living being transmit the waveform of that being during its lifetime. When it dies, its transmission ends but the waveform persists in the vacuum indefinitely. You do recall that light has no rest mass and therefore is not subject to diminishment over time? Individual photons are extincted only when they actually come in contact with matter. But matter is so extremely tenuous out here in the vacuum that most light will never touch matter during the entire lifetime of this universe."

Gai studied the screen intently for a moment, and then realization opened in her. "You . . . You're saying that the waveforms of these creatures—these Tryl—are still present?"

"Correct, O my captain. Until Know-Where-to-Go completed the first stroke and stepped up our energy, we didn't have the power to detect them. But they're here—

all around us. And so is everything that ever lived. All of this ancient world's life preserved in waveforms."

"But wait a minute. This world was destroyed in a nova two billion years ago. Whatever light persists should have expanded through a time-cone at least two billion light years wide."

"Yes, much of that light is indeed flying through spacetime. But spacetime is a tesseract. Think back on what you learned during your training about the physics of outer space."

"My specialty was weaponry—and it still is, Genitrix."

"Then let me remind you: Spacetime is a manifold. Think of it as a tesseract, a four-dimensional cube. Yes, light propagates through space but also through time. And, as we know, light has no rest mass—it is timeless. That means that light is itself a tesseract vector. For three-dimensional beings, light is what is visible of the fourth dimension. In fact, if one were poetically inclined, one might say that light is the window on the infinite."

"Okay, okay. So you mean the waveforms of the Tryl are intact in the tesseract and we can access them?"

"Yes. Now that our energy is stepped up, we have the means to tap the tesseract and receive waveforms. We can talk with the dead."

"That's hardly believable."

"I know. When people die on the range, the same thing must happen, but the energy requirements there to tap the tesseract are prohibitive. Out here in the cold of space, with the energy we've brought up from our hotter gravity shell, that capacity is well within our means."

"And you've done it? You've spoken with the Tryl?"

"Not exactly spoken. Not yet. I'm still developing the hardware for that—which I should complete soon. But I have listened to them. That's how I know their self-given name. Their language is far more translatable than the zōtl's. Also, they are exquisite poets and musicians. Would you like to hear their music?"

Gai agreed, and after a spattering of static, the Form vibrated to a music heathery with silence. "My goodness, it's beautiful," Gai breathed. "Truly beautiful."

"So I think. If you can spare the time and you would like to meet the Tryl, set down on a planet. The electron flux for generating plasma bodies is more optimal inside an atmosphere. I'm just about ready now to amplify their specific waveforms, using their DNA as antennae."

Gai lowered her Form to the planet she had been orbiting. The energy increase had dramatically enhanced the formation of the worlds, and the planet's surface seethed with oceans and towering clouds. The land masses were blotched with mosses and lichen. Gai landed on a plain that would someday be a swamp. The Form sunk to its knees in the rich loam that the Genitrix program was sloughing from the planet's interior.

Night and day strobed over the Form with a one-second pulse—a drowsy rhythm that suddenly reminded Gai of her fatigue. She had slept poorly since witnessing Ylan's grim fate. Her eyes were batting wearily when the first ghosts wavered into view.

"They're easier to see and communicate with outside the Form," Genitrix advised.

Gai stepped out into her plasma body, and the diurnal strobe stopped somewhere in the night. Before her, seven wraiths wavered in and out of sight, tall, narrow, two-legged creatures. Three of them solidified into plasma bodies shaped very much as Genitrix had predicted the Tryl would look, from the horn stubs on their skulls to their throat frills and the brilliant markings that seemed to glow in the galaxylight.

What did one say to beings who had been dead billions of years? "Greetings, Tryl. I am Gai, a Rimstalker—"

"We know," one of them said in a genderless voice plump with vacancies. The Form sent its translation to Gai telepathically. "Genitrix has informed us already. We have agreed to appear here that we might talk directly with you, the mission commander."

Gai tried to read feelings in their features, but their faces were too strange—noseless but for two tiny holes, lobe-browed, and with huge eyes, colorless in the dark but luculent with withheld light. "Genitrix has told you of our mission?" Gai asked.

"Yes. That is why we must speak with you." The three Tryl shared a look as if silently communicating, and then the speaker continued. "We are appalled that you have returned us from the Light to aid you in war. The Tryl are a peaceful species. We no longer war."

Gai was almost flung back into her Form by the directness of the Tryl. "I'm sorry that we have—appalled you. I would not choose this to be the reason for returning you from the Light—but I have no choice."

"Is that true?" the Tryl asked with obvious incredulity. "You seem a free agent. Even your artificial intelligences display almost full autonomy."

"Yes, I have free will. But, you see, my people, the Rimstalkers, are being threatened by the zōtl with extinction. The zōtl—"

"Genitrix has told us this already. We don't see how that delimits your free will."

Gai stared at the Tryl with incomprehension, then ventured, "Most of our other missions have failed. Maybe all the others. I must succeed against the zōtl or my people will die. I have no choice but to elicit your help."

"Is that true?" the Tryl repeated. "We sense that you have divorced yourself from the truth."

"I don't understand."

The Tryl conferred again briefly before continuing. "You feel that the zōtl's hostility has usurped your free will. That is your feeling—but it is not true. You have a choice. You do not have to resist the zōtl."

"What?" Gai shouted, and the Tryl images wavered and almost vanished. "Why would I choose that?"

"Because that is the enlightened choice."

"To let my people become extinct is enlightened?"

"Yes—enlightened—illuminated. Extinction means that your people shall shed their physical forms and become pure light—as we have." The Tryl nodded their heads in unison. "How can you still believe extinction is to be feared? You are talking to us, who have been extinct well over five billion years."

"Talking to you may be possible here in outer space, but on the range we have no means of talking with the dead. It's different on the range. Survival is our only choice."

"The truth is everywhere the same, young soul. Survival perpetuates suffering. To survive you must kill zōtl. To kill zōtl you must offer them bait—living, sentient beings, who must suffer a great deal before you can hope to poison the zōtl with the O'ode."

"I agree, our plan involves much suffering. But it is the zōtl who began this atrocity. We are struggling to conclude it for all time."

"All time?" An annulate laughter chimed among the Tryl. "In time, there is always suffering—zōtl or no. Far better to leave time behind and become light. You are becoming light anyway. As individuals all Rimstalkers must die. And what happens when you die is no different on the range than what happens when life dies out here in the vacuum. Your waveforms persist forever in the tesseract—and that is where the mystery reveals itself."

"The mystery?"

"Of being. Of light. Of consciousness. Mind is not matter, young soul. Mind is energy and belongs to the mystery of energy. Mind is the light of this dark creation. Mind's destiny is outside time."

"The destiny of mind may be outside time, but the destiny of the Rimstalkers will be made or broken right here. My people have not endured their history to be devoured by zōtl."

"Yet they are being devoured—and you alone cannot hope to save your whole world."

"I can try. I will do all that I can do—with or without your help."

"What is, young soul, is. Everything is best. The universe is precisely what it should be, down to its smallest and most energetic photon."

"You, obviously, have not seen the zōtl. They are not what is best for the Rimstalkers. Everything is *not* best. What is evil must be met and countered by what is good. You know, once we did not believe in war, like you. Once we were peace-loving, too. But the zōtl are evil. They raid our homes, they kill innocents—and I will give my life, if I must, to counter that evil."

"Then that, too, is best, young soul. You must be what you are. As we, also, must be what we are. Long ago, we transcended the polarity of this dark and cold creation. There is no good or evil for us. There simply is."

"So what will you do when Genitrix begins reproducing your bodies and feeding them to the zōtl?"

"You would do that, knowing what we have told you?"

Gai paused only a moment. "Yes, I will. This is war. You are a casualty. Whether you cooperate or not, the zōtl will not care. And, as you say, everything is best."

The Tryl conferred silently. Gai listened for their thoughts but heard nothing. When they faced her again, the light in their large eyes was dull. "Resistance only tightens the trap. We will not resist you. We could overcome you in many subtle ways that would sabotage your mission—but then you, or others like you, would find another species to mire in flesh and subject to the cruelties of the zōtl. Do you think by doing this for your people you are any better than the zōtl? No, we shall not have others suffer in our places. We will take the pain upon ourselves—but under protest, young soul. We will not for a moment cease trying to convince you that survival is not worth fighting for. Don't give your life to the dark. Don't keep your people enslaved to the genetic programs that keep them in the dark. You are a conscious being. You are not just a body. You are a mind. You are the light of the world."

The Tryl plasma bodies dissolved in a flurry of sparks and were gone.

"Well," Genitrix spoke from the Form, "what do you think of the Tryl?"

Gai stared at the space where they had disappeared. "I think," she said slowly, "we should send them to talk with the zōtl. Then we'll see how deep their enlightenment runs."

"They are pure light, Gai. They are but traces of what they once were. Perhaps their philosophy will become more pragmatic when they are made to live again within the brutal limits of physical bodies."

"Do we have any other options? Have you found other lifeforms that we can use to bait the zōtl?"

"There is a plethora of genetic material at hand, Gai, but I haven't finished sorting through it all. The Tryl are clearly the most advanced of what we've found, though I may be able to come up with something less sophisticated in this jumble that will still appeal to the zōtl."

"Look into it. Maybe we should conduct interviews with other dead species. There must be a less noble lifeform for this sacrifice."

"That would take time, Gai. Meanwhile, Chalco-Doror is gearing up to produce Tryl."

"Then I say, produce them. You heard what they told me. Everything is best, they said. So let's see if 'everything' includes being dinner for the zōtl as well."

Primeval Worlds

Gai, wearied from the arduous work of calibrating the paths of the planets to be certain that they were on track, stood her Form in a field of lichenous boulders on one of the warm worlds of Doror and dozed for a few hours. When she awoke, the world around her had changed. Trees had sprouted during her nap, and she was surrounded by a forest of club moss and fern.

She rose into the strobe of day and night and saw through her viewer that the entire planet was covered with new lifeforms. Besides vegetation, which had overgrown all the rocky expanses, animals proliferated. Herds milled on the plains, birds rode the rings of wind, lemurs and monkeys dangled among the forests, and fish flurried in the oceans.

Gai looked for the Tryl and found them huddled in villages of adobe mazes and catacombs that teetered into the sky like immense ant hives.

"They're called claves," Genitrix said after Gai tuned her in. "The Tryl are colonial creatures. They're never found individually."

Each planet, Gai saw as she swung her Form in a lazy arc through Chalco-Doror, had its own distinctly adapted flora and fauna. On the darker worlds of Chalco, the forests were jungles flitting with bats and stalked by nocturnal creatures with luminous eyes. The bright worlds, like where she had woken up, were less profuse but no less varied: Cactus ranges in a startling diversity of shapes were the niche for solar-shelled armadillos and glittery-skinned pythons. Some of the beasts were immense hulks lumbering through the fern holts and swamps or breaching the seas in loud, belly-slapping splashes. Others were the tiniest of insects, the lightest of wind-borne bacteria.

"With this first flush," Genitrix proudly explained, "I took no special care to sequence the lifeforms chronologically. Those hulking beasts you see are called saurians, and their genetic code is far more ancient than the horses you see there or those wolf-cats, which didn't appear in their own world until after the time of the Tryl."

"I see the Tryl have wasted no time in making themselves at home. Their claves are everywhere, on all the planets. Have they no environmental preferences?"

"The Tryl control their own climate. Their technology, actually, is comparable with our own. Even in the short time that you were asleep, they've thoroughly organized themselves and have begun a program of reconstructing their culture. Those adobe claves are precursors for much grander structures that will follow once they complete their underground factories. From what I've seen in the tesseract, they're quite ingenious. In an hour or so, you'll see what I mean. By then, they'll be setting up their lynk system."

"A wormhole technology in an hour?"

"Well, of course, an hour of Form time, which is almost eleven years planet time."

"But if they develop lynks, the zōtl can't help but notice them."

"The gravity pulse that was emitted yesterday at the end of the first stroke is all the signal the zōtl need to know we're here."

"That's only now reaching the nearest other Genitrix systems. I thought, maybe, we might have another day or two."

"I'm afraid not. We should see zōtl today."

"Now what about the O'ode? The last time I looked, our search for it had gone nowhere."

"That status hasn't changed. We have more energy to work with since the gravity stroke but not enough power to locate an open timeline to where the O'ode exists. If it's okay with you, I'll refer to that legendary planet as Rataros."

"You mean after the name of the Rimstalker outpost at the very fringe of the range?"

"The same. It seems poetically correct to call this planet that, because the Rataros we know exists at the crossroads of worlds. And that was where our ancestors first met other intelligences like the voors and the eld skyles."

"Let the O'ode planet be known as Rataros, then. It's as far away from here certainly as the first Rataros is from the range—and as alien. I hope that we can get to *it* before the zōtl get to *us*."

"Most unlikely, Gai. All the probes sent into the one lynk I've set up have failed to find any sign of it. We just don't have the power to reach that far, yet."

"How much longer before we do?"

"Two or three more gravity strokes should do it."

"But that's another week or ten days. We'll be swarming with zōtl by then."

"Indeed. But that's as we've planned, isn't it? We are to host the zōtl, let them establish their own lynklanes and feeding habits."

"Yes, but you seem to have forgotten Genitrix-18. They overcame our defenses there."

"I haven't forgotten. But what alternative do we have? In fact, I just completed an analysis of the data that Saor returned from Genitrix-18. With the limited energy we have and all this work to do making the Tryl comfortable, it took me two days. And all I can honestly tell you is that Genitrix-18 was overpowered by zōtl technology. I don't know how exactly. But Saor's data clearly show that the gravity amps were turned off and the entire system converted to pastureland for the zōtl to cultivate the unfortunate species whose pain they so very much relish."

"That will *not* happen to us," Gai determined and swung into a polar orbit around one of the Doror planets. She watched the Tryl claves there opening like blossoms.

"You're seeing only the rooftops, Gai. The Tryl do all their important work underground."

"What do they eat?"

"At first they were eating lichen from the surface. But now I see they've constructed hydroponic gardens among the subterranean pools that I had used to fuse the water for the oceans. They even have a nutri-pump, similar to the one in your Form, that's portable enough for them to wear so they can work without having to stop to eat."

The clustering of adobe towers suddenly collapsed and, in their places, parabolic arcs of shining metal appeared.

"Ah, their forge-factories are on line," Genitrix said. "Growth will proceed rapidly from here."

A high-pitched whistle needled Gai's hearing before lifting beyond audial range. "What was that?"

"The Tryl lynk system. They just turned it on."

"I'm going down—in plasma body."

"Better take the Form."

"Too bulky and too crazy with the time differential. I'll park here."

"Better park on the surface. The Tryl already have something they call *ramstat*—a propulsion system that utilizes the parallel parameters of gravity and magnetism. The field lines from their boosters are interfering somewhat with my communications outside the Form."

To make her point, Genitrix directed Gai's viewer to a fleet of silvery discs slashing out of the atmosphere and into space through a jangle of lightning.

"What are those?" she asked; then, realizing Genitrix would launch into one of her lectures, she said, "Forget it. I'm going down anyway."

"Ramstat flyers," Genitrix responded. "The Tryl use them to convey whatever they don't want to lynk. That swarm is laded with crystal components for factories they're building in space. They use the gravity-free, deep space cold for their superconducting computers. They're finishing up . . ."

Gai cut her off and dropped her Form into a field of red flowers just outside one of the claves. When she stepped out into her plasma body, the strobe stopped near midday. Sunlight smashed off the giant parabolic arcs of the clave, and the heathery Tryl music that she had first heard yesterday lilted in the air. With a sizzling whoosh, a ramstat flyer lifted from beyond the clave's skyline and swiftly dwindled into the blue. Moments later, the thunder of its exit from the atmosphere mumbled overhead.

Gai strolled through the flower field toward the clave, looking for Tryl.

"They see you," Genitrix said, her voice muted by interference from the ramstat field lines around the gleaming city. "You have permission to enter, if you want to look around a clave."

Gai followed a ribbon-road of white stone through a grove of club moss to the base of one of the arches. She touched it, and it was bright with magnetism.

"It's a lynk arch," Genitrix said from far away. "Don't walk under it or you may wind up on the other side of Chalco."

Beyond the arch, the clave's elegant towers rose, thin pinkstone obelisks with chrome-bright trim and slender silverglass windows. Expansive courtyards with trellised blossoms, tapered trees, and rainbow-hung glass sculptures graced the grounds around the buildings.

A door slid silently aside in the nearest tower, and a Tryl in colorful shimmerfabric garments approached Gai.

"Welcome to our clave," the Tryl said in a voice remote as Genitrix's, because the Form was translating. "I am 102-22—and I will show you around, if you like."

"102-22? That sounds like a name for an artifact. Are you man or woman?"

"The Tryl have decided to have no individual names during our time in Chalco-Doror. We are here as a species. We are the Tryl. I am male, though that hardly matters, for we are not reproducing. Each clave has a population of several thousand, numbered as we are recreated by your Genitrix system. I am the twenty-second Tryl produced by the one-hundred-and-second flush. Come inside, and I will show you."

102-22 led Gai to the door that he had just come through, and they entered a dark foyer tapestried with what looked like woven glass. A trill of energy passed through them, and Gai's plasma shape ruffled.

"I'm sorry. That's our ultrasonic cleanser. We must keep the interior of the clave absolutely clean. Your Genitrix program is producing some virulent viruses and bacteria from ages of our planet's history we're unfamiliar with. Come, let me show you the living quarters."

Lux-tubes illuminated a corridor that led to a series of magnetic lifts, spotlit open shafts where Tryl were rising and falling gracefully.

"You knew I was coming?" Gai asked, surprised by 102-22's lack of surprise.

"Not at this moment, but all of us have been hoping that you would visit one of the claves. We need to talk with you about why you are bringing us back from the Light."

102-22 invited Gai to step into one of the shafts, and they floated downward past the dark-red light of catacombs bored into the rock crust of the planet. "Those are individual sleeping slots," the Tryl said. "And here is where your gene-recovery program is presently regenerating us."

The surrounding rock walls gave way to a massive grotto brightly illuminated with lux tubing. Scaffolds and derricks loomed in the peripheral shadows around a floodlit center encased in a transparent geodesic sphere. The lift lowered them beside the sphere, and Gai could see the exposed matrix of the planet's interior, where the lifeforms were grown. The interior was a fleshy pink and glistening, and in it the shapes of Tryl in the full sequence of constructive stages were visible. Tryl in clear, sanitary face masks and gloves were removing the bodies that had fully developed and were placing them on hovering stretchers. Occupied stretchers were whisked out of the sphere to the lifts, where they were carried up and out of sight.

"All our claves are built on the sites where your Genitrix program is growing Tryl. The recovery was hardest for the first of us, because there was no one to help them. Many suffered needlessly. Now we are taken to an orientation area until we're functional."

After Gai had watched a dozen new Tryl removed from the viscous matrix, dripping with the ichor of creation, 102-22 guided her among a maze of corridors through the heart of the clave. Gai saw chrome-armature factory pits, oddly canted quarries worked by robots, and red-gout, spark-whirling machine-depths of fiery kilns. Beyond the cold blue bubbles of ramstat hangars and their disc flyers suspended in magnetic harnesses, the living quarters began. In the spacious communal areas, where Tryl mingled among their glass sculptures and breezy music, everyone stared at Gai with their large eyes but none spoke. Past feeding halls that smelled like pollen and beyond more burgundy-tinted catacombs, they came to the lifts again and rode up into the towers.

From a capacious suite of flexform furniture, more glassy sculpture, and quiet music, they gazed through green glass at the fern dells and swamps. Ramstat flyers slipped in and out of their hangar tunnels brisk as bees.

"Your culture is enormously sophisticated," Gai admitted.

"Did you expect less?"

"Frankly, yes. Though the zōtl have grown strong out here, I had not been prepared to meet a species in outer space equal to my own. The energy deficit is so great, I'm awed by how thoroughly you've mastered your environment."

"Has that changed your mind about using us as bait for the zōtl?"

Gai looked for anger in the Tryl's face and saw only attentiveness. "It is the zōtl I wish to destroy, not the Tryl. I need your help—but not as bait. I had no idea how advanced you were—and are. Help me, so that the Tryl need not suffer at all."

"How can we help you?"

"There is a weapon called the O'ode that kills only zōtl. But I haven't the power to reach it yet. Maybe your lynk system could augment mine."

"Our lynklanes are closed. They connect points only within Chalco-Doror, so that the claves may commune directly. We would not use our lynks to leave the system— nor would we use them to recover a weapon of any kind."

"Not even to save yourselves?"

"We were saved, until you brought us here. And we will be saved again, when we leave here."

"I'll have Genitrix stop animating Tryl if you'll help me get the O'ode."

"But then you will still need bait and some other unfortunate species will be selected. No, Gai. We will not help you."

Before Gai could attempt another argument, a chime rang and Genitrix's remote voice said, "The zōtl are here, Gai! They've opened a lynk on one of the night worlds."

"Patch the coordinates to my Form. I'm on my way."

Gai willed herself directly to her Form, and her plasma body flew through the green-glass wall to it. "The Tryl will let you use their lynk system to reach the scene," Genitrix said as Gai prepared to leave the planet. "You'll get there a lot faster."

Gai let Genitrix lead her to one of the silver parabolas. Battle-fear and rage whirling in her, she walked through the lynk on Doror and appeared outside a lynk on a world in Chalco. She turned off the Form functions to see clearly what was before her in real time.

The sky was dark, cloud-covered, and drizzly, but the terrain, contoured for rain, was radiant as day. The zōtl lynk, a dolmen-shape shining molten red, stood before a clave similar to the one Gai had just left. But the towers of this clave were blasted open and jetting flames. Green light glared from the red dolmen, illuminating a crowd of Tryl being herded from the burning clave by bat-like blurs of motion that Gai knew were zōtl.

The sight of the passive Tryl hurrying toward the zōtl lynk, their city in ruins behind them, struck Gai like a blow. She had never seen combat before, and the sight of the destruction inspired fury in her. These were the monsters who had stolen and devoured her family, just as they were stealing these gentle creatures. Wrath mounted in her, and she stalked forward.

The zōtl saw the Form and swarmed toward her. They were black smudges of flight that her Form's viewer displayed motionless in a corner screen: An arachnid body with a stiletto feed tube rotated at the edge of the screen, displaying all its gruesome mouthparts and legs.

A wince of laserlight struck Gai's faceplate, and the viewer blacked out. "System overload," a mechanical voice chattered. "Circuit broken. Activating emergency backup." Other blows jolted the Form before the viewer came back on and showed the Form circled by flying spidershapes shooting bursts of red light.

"Use the photon guns in your gloves!" Genitrix's voice shouted. "Their lasers are cutting into your Form!"

Gai marked the spidershapes as targets and fired her photon guns. The Form's arms thrashed, searing bolts of energy glaring the surroundings blind with their intensity. In an instant, it was over. The Tryl stood about stunned, their big eyes squinting into the afterglare. The surprised zōtl were nowhere to be seen, their bodies entirely vaporized. Only the lynk remained of them, a glowing red doorway into the refulgent core of hell.

Gai raised both her arms toward the lynk.

"Wait!" Genitrix yelled.

But Gai was too infuriated to stop. She fired full power into the lynk. The green light flooding from there went out. In the next instant, the lynk exploded. The clave and the surrounding terrain were incinerated, and the Form was kicked off its feet and thrown to its back. Mammoth strokes of lightning writhed in the fiery vortex and disappeared with a pounding roar.

Darkness swooped in. The rain drummed louder. Where the lynk had been, a crater spilled faintly glowing vapors. The Tryl were gone, their clave a nest of rubble.

"Gai—" Genitrix called. "Your life functions seem intact. Can you read me?"

"I'm all right. I thought the lynk would blow inward, the way ours do when they overload."

"The zōtl have obviously rigged theirs differently."

"Obviously." Gai stood the Form up and surveyed the devastated landscape.

"Empty the land where life had been,
  empty our hearts where our pain wrestled heaven.
The land continues—our heart continues
  fixed in our fate—shadows of emptiness."

"Turn off the gene recovery program for the Tryl," Gai said, finally.

"Stop producing Tryl?"

"Yes. Stop producing Tryl. They're too much like us. I won't have them suffer anymore. Stop immediately."

"But what about our mission?"

"Our mission goes on. As you say, we are fixed in our fate. But not with the Tryl. Find me another species, a more cruel, more selfish species, whose suffering will not empty our hearts."

Pages from the Book of Nothing

"Gai—are you awake?"

"Just dozing. What is it, Genitrix?"

"I left you to rest while I fulfilled the conversion you requested. But I should go no further without your approval. I have found another species. Would you like to review their suitability?"

Gai slowed the Form's timerush and looked about at the zōtl lynk site she had blasted, where she had fallen asleep grieving the suffering she had caused the lemur-eyed Tryl. In the hours that she had slumbered in the Form, seventy years had passed, and the terrain was transformed. The crater where the lynk had exploded was a large lake now, still and glassy, reflecting the wheel of the galaxy. Lod's distant brilliance hung low on the watery horizon, a silver feather. The ruins of the clave were submerged except for the parabolic tip of the Tryl lynk far out in the lake. The nocturnal land on the lake shore was overgrown with bizarre vegetation: lamplike flowers glowing in the perpetual dark, tentacled trees moving their leafless sucker-edged branches without wind, silver shrubs with mouth-leaves and needle-teeth chewing insects snatched from the air.

"I've changed the gene-mix," Genitrix went on. "I've introduced a lot more lifeforms, to diversify the eco-base. That's necessary for this new species we'll use as zōtl bait. They're a lot less sophisticated than the Tryl and will need a rich milieu to survive."

"Can you present one in plasma form from the tesseract?" Gai asked.

The dark air before the Form glittered with brush-sparks, and a figure appeared whose shape was similar to that of a Tryl and equally alien. Instead of horn stubs on its head, it had hair that fell past its shoulders. Its flesh was as sleek as the Tryl's but without throat frills or markings— and its eyes were small and frightened.

"These creatures call themselves humans," Genitrix said. "They're more cunning than they look though nowhere near the stature of the Tryl. Their music is orgulous

and strident—occasionally poignant." Strains of Bach's
Brandenburg Concerto 6 intercut with Coltrane's *Ascension.* "They existed a billion years prior to the Tryl, and
their history is nothing more than a catalogue of wars
among themselves. They are profoundly sexual—which
will facilitate breeding them—yet their passion for procreation did not prevent them from exterminating themselves. They are vicious and selfish animals with
pretensions of intelligence. I'm confident that the zōtl will
find them appetizing and that we need feel no remorse for
their animal suffering."

"Can the creature hear me?"

"Oh, yes. He is struck dumb by what he sees. You appear
imposing to him in your Form—not unlike the god-images
the people of his time were accustomed to worshipping.
But I recommend you not use your plasma body. Your
Rimstalker shape would look quite ghastly to him. I've
already informed him of who we are and our mission. The
information seems to have shocked him."

The human was trembling and kept falling to his knees
and being lifted up again by impulses from Genitrix.
"Spare me—please," the quaking man begged. "I have
suffered enough in my life. It is not I you should torment. I
have a brother—a vile man, a thief and an adulterer—he is
the one you seek. He is worthy of all the torments you wish
to inflict. But spare me. I am an honest and worshipful
man."

Gai dismissed the wraith with a wave that broke the
simpering plasma shape into a gust of sparks. "I've seen
enough, Genitrix. You've found the ideal beast. Go into full
production."

The Malay woke with a start. He had been a fisherman
over eight thousand years before Christ and had drowned
in a storm in his thirty-second year of life, leaving behind
two wives, twelve children, and five grandchildren. The
world he woke up into was as nothing he had ever seen or
even imagined. Night was endless and the sky huge with
stars—a maelstrom of stars. By that, he knew he was in the
upperworld, no matter the nonsense about Rimstalkers
and zōtl that he had heard from the demons in his dream.
The shaman had told him when he was a child that the

upperworld was guarded by demons, who whispered confusing lies into the ears of the spirits passing upward on heaven's stream.

But the shaman had told the Malay nothing about Squat. And perhaps wisely—for Squat was too frightful to burden the living with. Squat was the ruler of the upperworld and the first being, after the demons, that the Malay had encountered since dying in the claws of the storm. Now he served Squat, as did all who lived in the upperworld. During the many sunless days that he had been here, he had worked hard with the other dead, wandering the beaches scavenging for anything that might please Squat. For only by pleasing Squat could one have more than slime to eat.

Some of the dead thought they were not dead. Why did the dead have to eat? Why did they suffer pain when Squat was displeased with them? The Malay had no answers for them, those strange men and women who looked so different from himself and with whom he communicated only with great difficulty—and profound risk, since Squat did not approve of the dead talking among themselves.

The Malay rarely talked with the others. The work was too arduous, lugging heavy metal shapes out of the sea to the thronelike boulder among the dunes where Squat presided over the dead. At day's end he barely had the strength to eat the slime he had earned, let alone join in the whisperings of the others, who were endlessly planning escape—as if escape were possible for the dead.

Only one other was as silent as he—though perhaps more silent, for the Malay did speak of the demons and what they had told him to whomever among the bedraggled dead would listen. The one who was most silent of all, and the one who seemed to listen most closely, was a man with red hair and green eyes and a face like a hawk's. The Malay called him Hawk, but never to his face. The Malay had not seen men like that in his life—but then neither had he ever seen people as strange as many of the others, black-fleshed some of them, white-skinned and gold-haired others. And never, ever, had he even dreamed the fright that was Squat.

Squat was as big as three men—but not just fat, though he was obese. He had legs like trunks, hands big as paddles, shoulders stooped like a boulder's, and a grotesquely bulged head with square, osseous temples and, sprouting from his skull-seams, tufts of gray hair coarse as goat fur. His skin was white as the flesh of a coconut and his eyes pink, set deeply in the scowl of a fetal face.

The power of Squat over the dead was not his obscene size, which he flaunted naked, though his genitals were shriveled and only rarely visible under the folds of his flesh. Squat ruled the dead because no one could resist his commands. "Obey me!" was his whining cry—and those who heard it felt its needling shrillness pierce their marrows, and they obeyed, even if the command was to drop dead— which the Malay had seen happen numerous times. The dead, when they were commanded to die, fell unconscious as though they had been alive, and they rotted where they fell.

There was no dearth of living dead to replace the dead dead. New bodies molted from the sand bluffs every day, all with the same mournful bewilderment. The Malay had worked the bluffs for a while, searching for the newborn dead and clearing the sand from their eyes, and he was glad to have been transferred to the beach scavengers. The new dead were pathetic in their helplessness. Squat toyed with them before setting them to work, and the Malay had become sickened by their grievous wails of hurt, incomprehension, and revulsion as Squat first exerted his command over their wills and then forced them to submit to disgusting acts among the dunes.

The beach scavengers were left alone to do their work until day's end, which was little different than day's beginning, for the upperworld was dark. The sun rose and fell as it did in life, only here it was terribly small. Nevertheless, the air was warm, balmy with the pelagic breezes that luffed off the sea. By the light of the stellar whirlpool, which was brighter than a full moon, the scavengers roamed the coves and strands looking for what the tide had littered. At day's end, they presented what they had found to Squat. If he was pleased, he rewarded them with shellfuls of slime. If he was indifferent, they went hungry. And if he was enraged, they died—again.

Pleasing Squat was usually not difficult. The tide carried in wonders: coils of smooth rope that glowed brightly, heaps of crystals that played dreamy music when they were joined, tangles of shimmery garments, sheets and panels of floating metal that Squat used for his ramshackle palace; and once a puppet man, with no face but two rubies for eyes, who never needed to eat or drink, and who had the strength of twelve men. Squat used him as a personal servant, to prepare his meals from the animals and vegetables the dead gathered, and to help build the shabby palace.

The Malay usually worked alone. Squat discouraged cooperation by forcing those who brought their offerings in groups to fight among themselves for their food. Also, talking while working was forbidden, and those caught were killed as ruthlessly as though apprehended trying to flee. No one ever escaped. Squat's mind was too powerful for anyone to hide from him. But occasionally, when Squat was asleep or thoroughly engrossed in humiliating the new dead, talking with the other scavengers was possible. That was when the Malay told the others about the demons and queried them about their experiences. He learned very little, only that all of them had once lived among their own people and died.

Once, while the Malay was struggling to haul to shore a carpet woven of glowing fibers, Hawk approached him. "Tell me again about the demons," he said in the Malay's tongue.

The Malay dropped the carpet, gawked at the tall, red-haired man, and cast a frightened glance down the beach to where the junk palace cluttered the breakwater.

"Don't be afraid. The bluff workers found some women among the new dead. Squat will be preoccupied for a while. We can talk."

"You know my tongue. How?"

Hawk shook his head once. "Never mind that. Tell me about the demons again."

The Malay related all that had happened to him that first night before he awoke in the bluffs.

Hawk listened intently. In the distance, the screams of the new dead rose and fell as Squat dallied with their minds while he defiled them. "You're certain that they called themselves Rimstalkers?"

The Malay confirmed that and repeated how the demons had hung him naked before the massive and shining shape of the night god.

"That was no god," Hawk said. "But it might as well have been."

The shrieking from up the beach stopped.

"Tell no one we talked," Hawk said with iron in his voice. "No one. Tonight, while Squat sleeps, we will talk again—and perhaps the night god will speak with us."

The Malay threw a terrified look toward the bluffs and saw Squat's huge white head lolling above the starlit dunes as he shambled toward his palace. The Malay turned back to Hawk, but the fire-haired man had waded into the sea, his kelp raiment floating about his waist as he probed a tide pool with his stave. Had he spoken at all? The Malay could hardly believe he had heard his own language again—and spoken by a man all the others had thought mute.

That night, the Malay did not sleep. Nor did he hear the sobs of the new dead women Squat had abused or the moans of those who had gone hungry several days in a row and were now too weak to scavenge. The Malay listened inward for his memory of Hawk's voice. What had the strange man meant—they would speak with the night god?

A ticklish sensation glossed the space an inch behind the Malay's eyes, and he knew from experience that Squat was feeling into him, fingering his thoughts. Terror whipped him upright, and he sat sparking sweat as Squat rummaged through his mind, alerted by the Malay's excitement.

On the beach, the Malay had feared that this might happen. No secrets could be kept in this place. Squat had warned them against hatching murderous strategies. Having too often seen conspirators ferreted out by Squat's mindreach, their bodies made to dance furiously on the sharp rocks until their feet were pulp and the exertion made blood spurt from their ears, the Malay had prepared a memory in which to hide. He remembered the fury he had felt when his brother had stolen his second wife from him before she could even bear him children and how her first son was his. He wondered loudly in his mind if his brother, who was still alive when the Malay had died, would be joining them here in the upperworld. All the old resentment rose up in him and toiled into a vengeful excitement.

The itching behind his eyes stopped. The Malay lay back and firmly placed his thoughts in his memories of his former life and let the scald of his hurt at his brother's betrayal seep into his heart. Sleep muted his discomfort, and dreams closed in on him.

A hand shook him awake, and he started alert. Hawk was bent over him. "Come," he said and scurried quickly toward the dunes.

The Malay did not move. If Squat woke and found him with Hawk, they would certainly be killed in some horrifying way. He lay still a long time in the grip of his fear before the thought that he was already dead and still suffering loosened his fright enough for him to crawl among the other sleepers toward the dunes.

Hawk was waiting near the tide flats, where the clatter of the waves among the shells and gravel would hide their voices. He gripped the Malay by the shoulders, and his face expressed an urgency that was startling since his features had always before seemed immutable as rock. "Call the Rimstalker," he said.

The Malay shook his head with incomprehension.

"The night god. The one you were hung before naked. Call him."

"The demons said he was a woman," the Malay whispered in a huff of fright.

"Call her then—but be quick. Squat's puppet man will be heading this way soon on his rounds."

"How? How do I call this god?"

"With your mind. Call for her. She talked with you once. She's never talked with anyone else. She'll listen to you. Call her."

The Malay called, speaking aloud so that Hawk would know he was sincere: "Night god—Rimstalker—hear me, I am calling to you. Speak with me now as you spoke with me once."

Nothing. The Malay had expected that. Why would the demons come at his beckoning? To fully satisfy Hawk, he drew breath to try again; but before he could speak, the air brightened behind them. They jumped about and faced a mass of lashing cilia far bigger than a man and jointed like an upright centipede, its eyes two black lenses above scissoring mouthparts.

"Human—why do you wish to speak with me again?" Gai asked, genuinely curious about the wee mind that had called out for her. She had been drifting through Chalco, remorseful about the Tryl she had caused to suffer, when Genitrix alerted her to the Malay's plea. She came at once in her plasma body, as much to allay her feelings about the Tryl as to sate her curiosity about the pathetic creatures selected to take their place.

The Malay fell to his knees and could not bring himself to stare at more than the Rimstalker's writhing shadow on the sand. Hawk stepped forward. "Rimstalker, I am Ned O'Tennis, sky-fighter of N'ym, thrall to Emir Egil Grimson. It is I who had this man call you here. Speak with me."

Gai could see at once that this one was different from the one before her or the others asleep on the beach, though he was dressed in kelp as they were, and was as filthy. But strapped to his chest under his arm Gai sensed a device as elegant as any the Tryl had crafted. She wished she had not left her Form so far away, and that she could use it to analyze who was before her. "I will speak with you, Ned O'Tennis. What is the instrument I sense under your arm?"

Ned removed from his armpit an oblate disc no bigger than his thumbtip. "This is a translator. This and a tracer chip I've attached to it are all that I could recover when my strohlkraft crashed here."

"Explain strohlkraft," Gai asked, again wishing she could patch directly to Genitrix.

"It's a flyer propelled by ramstat. You don't know about them yet because they don't exist now. I had to crash my strohlkraft through a lynk to escape my enemies and certain death. The lynk carried me to there—" He pointed out to sea. "There's a lynk underwater there. That's where my strohlkraft came out."

Gai recognized the site. There was where she had blasted the first zōtl lynk. The lake that had filled in the crater had since become this sea. The Tryl ruins were still there under the sea—and their lynks were still functional.

"I need your help, Rimstalker," Ned O'Tennis continued. "I and these other humans are held prisoner here by a

distort with mindreach, who abuses and kills us. Help me
to recover my ship. It's intact and sealed. I had to eject in
the water because its ramstat cells were depleted by the
powerdrain in the lynk—but I sealed the command pod
and by now the cells have recharged. If you would only
help me to raise my ship, I will serve you for all my life."

Genitrix was right, Gai realized when she heard about
the distort. These creatures preyed on each other. They
were truly worthy of their role as bait for the zōtl. But this
one was a curious case—a throwback from the future. "Tell
me, Ned O'Tennis—from what time have you come?"

"I do not know how Rimstalkers gauge time, but I am
from the Fifth Age, twelve hundred and fifty-six years
after the Foundation of Doror."

"I do not know of this Foundation. But speak to me of
the zōtl in the Fifth Age."

"The zōtl are the guardians of the Storm Tree," Ned
answered. "They are the world's suffering embodied."

"Then they thrive in the time from which you come?"

"Yes, they thrive—or they were thriving until the rebels
rose up. But the zōtl never ruled. All they want is their
offerings, not dominion. Or so I thought."

"And the rebels?"

"The rebels would stop the offerings. They struggle to
topple the Storm Tree. It was in my battle against them
that fate cast me here."

"Then you fight for the zōtl?"

"No. I fight for the Storm Tree—for the culture from
which I come. I fight for my people, not their alien over-
lords."

"Do the zōtl rule Chalco-Doror in your time?"

"They were the strength of the Emir, who rules. But the
rebels were far stronger than we had supposed. They
routed us on Valdëmiraën, where I was posted—where I
think we are now, only many years before my time. Will
you help me to get back to my people?"

"You overestimate my powers, Ned O'Tennis. Tell me
how you were routed by rebels if you had the strength of
the zōtl behind you."

"I'm not sure. Apparently, the rebels found some
weapon that destroyed zōtl."

The O'ode! Hope spiked through Gai. She could never

have dared for such an augury of success—and she calmed
herself by remembering that time in outer space was manifold. The future was always uncertain. But she was grateful for this pitiful creature's encouragement. "I would talk
with you more, Ned O'Tennis—but I sense that the distort
you speak of is rousing. Return to your sleeping places.
Tomorrow, your strohlkraft will rise."

The Rimstalker's fibrillating shape dissolved into pow-
dery light and disappeared. The Malay looked up and saw
the familiar wheel of stars and Hawk shining with withheld joy. "Silence now," Hawk warned. "If you can hold
your thoughts for one more day, I'll take you out of here
with me."

They crept back through the dunes to their sleeping
places and drove their minds hard to think only of the
suffering and despair they had known with Squat.

When the puppet man blared the work siren, the Malay
and Hawk were the first to slog down to the sea for that
day's work. The hope clutched deep in their hearts twisted
smaller when they saw no sign of the strohlkraft in the
tide's offerings. The Malay stooped quickly to work, immediately wondering if the apparition of the night god was
simply a dream.

Ned scanned the beach and its slum of seaweed, lux
tubing, and plasteel sheets from the sunken Tryl city. His
life in this hell had been possible only because he imagined
himself in a book, a fabulously frightening story like the
kind he had read as a child about trolls and frost giants.
Each day's tide was a new page in the book—and on one of
those pages his ship would be returned to him, and the
book would be over. But now, after the soaring hope of the
previous day, he saw that this story had no happy ending—
that this day's tide, like all the tides before, was just another page from the book of nothing. What a joke that
imagination seemed now. It had kept his mind empty of
anything Squat would have cared to notice, but that was
all. And that was not enough if he had to live like this even
another day.

"Small thing with the busy mind," the shrill voice of
Squat called to Ned. "Come to me."

Ned turned and saw the albino hulk standing on the
dune above him, a whiplash of stars behind him.

"What troubles you, small thing? Why are you not working for me?"

At that moment, behind Ned, the sea churned. Squat's jaw rocked loose as, out of the foaming brine, a sleekly contoured hull arose, shiny as black glass and winged with aerodynamic foils and fins.

Ned spun about, and, when he saw his strohlkraft, dashed into the shallows.

"Stop!" Squat bawled. "Obey me!"

Ned's muscles froze, and he collapsed face down in the lapping water.

"Rise and come to me," Squat ordered, and Ned did as he was commanded, stopping at the base of the dune. "What is this?"

"I don't know."

The fetal face snarled, and Ned's viscera jumped like live eels in his rib-basket, cramping him with pain. A strangled scream wrenched from him, and he fell to his knees. "A strohlkraft!" he gasped. "It's mine. I flew it here."

"You are not from the bluffs?"

"No. No—I came from the sea. From a lynk there. From your future."

"So." Squat waved the puppet man toward the strohlkraft. The android waded into the water and touched the hull. Its metal clanked. At Squat's beckoning, the puppet man circled the ship, looking for an entry. Near the nose, he found a recessed hatch-grip, which pulled open with a gasp of released air and a piercing shriek that burst to a siren wail.

The android staggered back and splashed onto its back in the water. The Malay, who had been standing nearby watching, looked with alarm to Hawk. Jerking toward the weird black shrine that had lifted from the sea, Hawk's vivid face urged him to enter. *Quickly,* Hawk's face said. *Enter quickly!* The Malay lunged for the opening and dove into the flight pod.

Ned clutched the translator under his arm, and his shout sounded in Malay, "Hit the red stones! Hit the red stones!"

Squat silenced Ned with a mental clamp on his larynx, and the pilot thrashed in the sand, gasping for air.

The Malay searched the flight pod for red stones. A bewildering array of switches and dials stared back at him

from the control consoles. Outside the open hatch, the
puppet man had gotten to his feet and was splashing toward him. The Malay looked everywhere, his face twitching, hands trembling. His gaze fell on the red buttons atop
the steering yoke. As the puppet man lumbered into the
hatchway, the Malay struck the buttons with both fists.

The strohlkraft's noseguns fired a short burst that seared
above Ned and exploded the dune from under Squat. The
albino giant collapsed with a mighty howl in a fume of
jetting sand. Ned, momentarily free of the distort's mind-
grip, sprinted for the strohlkraft.

The puppet man had the Malay under one arm when
Ned burst in. Swiftly, Ned snatched a pistol from the bulwark and fired point-blank at the android's head. The
laserbolt punched a hole between the ruby eyes, and the
puppet man reeled backward and slumped to the floor,
mewling machine noises. The Malay twisted free as Ned
slammed the hatch.

"Get in there and hold on for your life," Hawk ordered,
pointing to a sling of white leather.

The Malay was still trying to make sense of the hanging
straps when Ned fired up the engines, not daring to take
the time to strap himself in. With a cry as if from the throat
of a storm, the strohlkraft rose fully out of the water.

Squat had gotten to his feet and with upraised arms
bellowed, "Stop! Stop at once! Obey me!"

Ned finished punching in a flight sequence as the distort's mindreach paralyzed him. Immobilized, he and the
Malay watched through the ship's visor as Squat stalked
angrily toward them, his tiny face a fist.

Then the strohlkraft completed its programmed sequence: It spun about one hundred and eighty degrees,
and before the startled Squat could shape even one more
vehement thought, the ship's afterburners fired. In a jet of
bluewhite flames, the distort vanished.

The strohlkraft arced up and away. Cruising over the
sea, Ned helped the Malay strap in and secure himself;
then he set the ship's trajectory for the Tryl lynk under the
sea. With a grateful smile and a wink to the bug-eyed
Malay, he dove into the unknown.

THE ORACLES

Mind is the echo of a future.
Time's harshest mercy is prophecy.
Time unwrinkles differently for each of us.
We are all born for trouble.

> —adages from the *Glyph Astra*

Neter Col hung by invisible tethers in the void of the Overworld. Saor, who called himself The Face of Night, had suspended the scyldar there to watch for Ned O'Tennis. In the gray emptiness, the Overworld appeared as a globe turning in the black. The black was the outer dark of the vacuum out of which the universe had sprung. The globe was time, the life of the universe. Across the globe, a splattershape of chromatic geometries shifted slow as clouds. These were the timelines of the universe. Like a hologram, each tiny piece of the prismatic shatter-pattern replicated the shape of the whole—tinier and tinier, down to the very worldlines of atoms. Close by were the recent forms of Chalco-Doror embedded in the shimmer flux of probabilities, the actual worlds barely visible among the spectral colors of past time in the Overworld. The future was always beyond the globe's horizon.

The scyldar dangled in a gray vacuole of deep space inside the splash of rainbowed forms. He had been situated there among the seething colors by Saor so that he could see Valdëmiraën, a sphere in a livid chartreuse aura of timeshadows. Ned O'Tennis' escape from N'ym through the Tryl lynk beneath the Silver Sea appeared in the Overworld as a gold thread, a just-visible gossamer line that followed the fractal perimeter of Valdëmiraën's aura and returned to where it had begun but deeper in the shimmering pattern, at a different time level. The Overworld journey had spun the Viking wanderer back to the planet's past.

Neter Col made no effort to pursue. If he even looked too hard at the geometries of the globe, they shifted. They were just timeshadows, and observations changed them. To enter the scene below would irrevocably alter it, and he would lose sight of his prey, perhaps forever. The scyldar had no choice but to wait and watch until Ned entered a lynk again. Then, the Aesirai's flight through the Overworld could be monitored once more. But the scyldar dared not interfere until Ned's flight vanished over the globe's horizon, into the future. Beyond the horizon and the influence of the scyldar's observations, Ned's destination would not shift relative to Neter Col, and the scyldar could estimate from his prey's trajectory where the human would put down on the time globe. Then the scyldar could use Saor's power to propel himself over the horizon and pounce on Ned O'Tennis.

The zōtl impacted in Neter Col's body approved the scyldar's strategy and infused the impaled brain with bliss molecules—harmine and glucose—to steepen the host's patience. They waited. When the gold gossamer thread of Ned O'Tennis' worldline reappeared, they watched obliquely, unmoving, as the sky-fighter crisscrossed among the worlds, touching down three times before journeying toward the future beyond the horizon.

Like a black jag of lightning, Neter Col shot across the Overworld, propelled by Saor's power. The flight through hyperspace ended as abruptly as it had begun: The scyldar flew out of a lynk into a pink landscape of flowering fruit trees. He collapsed among leaf litter and red mushrooms and sat up at once, laserifle poised, scanning for threats. Small animals watched from around large white stones—a toppled temple, its fluted columns overgrown with bracken. A statue's face, chipped and almost worn smooth by rain, gazed at him and beyond to the arc of the silver lynk where he had entered.

The air was cool and fragrant with pollen. Neter Col rose and strolled among the temple ruins to an alcove curtained by dangling vines. From there, he could watch the lynk without being seen. Eventually, Ned O'Tennis would come through that lynk. When, the scyldar could not know. Knowing where was enough. Though he had seen his prey's worldline cross the horizon of the Overworld toward this very place, he had not seen where in the timeshadows the glide ended. The trajectory alone assured the scyldar that Ned had not arrived at an earlier time. Eventually—eventually—he would come through that lynk.

While the scyldar waited, the zōtl slept, and the wash of pleasure molecules it had injected into its captive's brain left the schoolteacher there feeling beautiful and quiet for the first time since this horror had begun. His body seemed like a familiar painting. He knew all its contours and apparent depths, but there was nothing to touch. In sight were the broken stones of a temple whose deity he did not recognize. But he knew the pink-blossomed trees were cherry. He identified many of the small animals—a root mouse, two thumbling monkeys making a house in a tree bole, and wind eels, transparent but looking green as the shrubberies where they fluttered like leaves. Their familiarity chilled him in his frightful isolation.

We are all here together, he thought, and the sound of his mental voice pleased him. Pain had owned him for so long, he had almost forgotten the sound of his own thoughts. *All here together—the zōtl and its hurting hunger, the scyldar's flesh with its own knowing—and me.*

The schoolteacher's thoughts stirred the zōtl, and it sponged back the bliss chemicals it had released. The teacher's awareness shriveled into darkness like a flame-touched moth. In a blink, the scyldar's mind was empty again, the better to wait for prophecy, for the future and its promise.

The Body of Light

Know-Where-to-Go was returning to Chalco-Doror for the second time. Joao stood on the observatory deck staring up at the sparklights that were the planets. From this distance, they were no more than motes against the immensity of space, and it was hard for him to imagine the suffering of those worlds. All his life, for twenty years now, he had lived here in Tryl Tower and the surrounding territory, on the site of an old clave, enjoying the comforts of the Tryl and hearing frightful stories of Chalco-Doror—stories about brain-pithing zōtl and monstrous, telepathic distorts.

Joao's parents, their parents and grandparents and their great-grandparents, back into time more than a dozen generations, had stood here and stared out at the pain worlds. They had exhausted their lives learning the Tryl secrets in preparation for the time when this planet would be thrust back into the midst of the others. More than a dozen generations of tutelage under the Tryl—and he was the one whom destiny had selected to actually carry that knowledge to those nightmarish worlds. In a few weeks, Know-Where-to-Go would enter Chalco-Doror. Then he would live the legends that his ancestors had only feared.

"Woolgathering again, Joao?"

Joao leaped about, hand clutched to his chest. 164-97, the last of the Tryl, stood before the observatory deck, hands folded in her sleeves, her orange throat frills fluttering with amusement.

"Did you think I was perhaps a distort?" she chuckled. "We are not that close to the devil worlds. Yet your body is wise to be jumpy. Soon, indeed, you may be jumping for your life."

"Good and perfect of you to remind me," Joao said, coming down the broad steps. At the bottom, he knelt and kissed the embroidered serpent on the Tryl's sleeve. "My love and respect for you is what has kept me from martial training or perhaps I wouldn't be so nervous."

"You would be more nervous," the old Tryl rasped, and urged Joao to his feet. "Warriors are nothing but nerves. You are wise to have listened to me and eschewed the killing ways of your brethren. Your family has always been devoted to knowledge and not warfare. I am glad that in this critical time you have not abandoned the gentle ways of your forebears."

"A rock must be a rock," Joao quoted from the Analects of the Tryl, "a feather, a feather."

"And only the feather shall rise." 164-97 nodded her approval, and her big yellow eyes glowed warmly as she appraised the youth before her. He was a strapping lad, big as any of the other young men, bigger than most and clearly capable of all the fighting behaviors so cherished by his species—but under his curly black hair and behind his inkpool dark eyes, the peacefulness of Tryl wisdom lived. Storing information in machines was easy enough but, despite all the Tryl technology, the only true repository for wisdom remained the human heart.

"I am woolgathering," Joao admitted, "but why are you

here at the crown of the tower, my Teacher? Is this not the hour at day's end when you lead the still-session?"

"You were not there, my hatchling. You miss only when you are ill."

"I thought you would believe I was ill and ignore my absence," Joao admitted. "I am—I cannot help it—frightened. Soon we will be there, in Chalco-Doror. Hundreds of years of waiting will be at an end. I could not sit still."

"Now is when you most need to sit still. Calm is all that will distinguish you from the chaos to come."

"I thought it would be easier to still my heart here, in sight of our goal."

"Has it been easier?"

"No. For all the scan-clips of those worlds that I've seen, they are still a fear-inspiring mystery."

"What do you fear the most?"

"Failing in my mission. The zōtl have been there five hundred years. What hope have we of displacing them?"

"Abandon hope, hatchling, and in its absence you will be closer to the truth. Yes, the zōtl have infested those worlds for five centuries—but only the Rain and Desert Worlds of Doror. In Chalco, humans live free of zōtl."

"If you call that living—hiding in caves with no real technology, their children born in hiding under appalling conditions, and all the while Genitrix birthing both whole people and distorts randomly—not to mention the baby-fields, where so many innocents die in their first hours, torn apart by beasts. What a cruel freedom the humans of Chalco enjoy."

"Yet they are free. The zōtl are not so powerful that they can dominate all the worlds. And your mission will bring the people the wisdom they need to endure."

"It is not wisdom that the people so eagerly anticipate, my Teacher. To them, Know-Where-to-Go is a fortress flying to their salvation. The weapons that we have crafted from your technology are what inspire the sufferers. They will ignore me and consider me foolish for preaching peace."

The Tryl extended an arm to the surrounding curve of glass that overlooked the human settlement built in and around the clave. Below, floodlights illuminated the fields where delicate-looking fighter craft were perched for their assault. Echoes of blue light came and went on the horizon from the troops who were target-practicing in the wilderness. "Human blood riddles wars," the old Tryl said. "Violence is bred in the bone of humans. That is good and perfect, too. When your warriors arrive among the zōtl armed with ramstat fighters and proton cannon, the zōtl at last must face their own shadow."

"But what if we fail? What if the zōtl have anticipated that Know-Where-to-Go is a planet converted to a warship?"

"Believe me, they know that already. They have known it for many years. But what can they do? Human weaponry is now the equivalent of the zōtl's. There will truly be a great battle. And if the humans lose, that must be good and perfect."

"If we lose, the horror continues—the zōtl-feeding, the terrorism of distorts, the horror of the baby-fields." Joao sagged with despair. "How could all this have come to be? The Rimstalkers are perdition itself to have created these worlds for the zōtl."

164-97's throat frills wagged in a gust of humor, and Joao stared at her appalled. "Don't look so disturbed. I am not laughing at the suffering you describe. I laugh at the irony of this opportunity. You see, I am on my way to meet the Rimstalker. Perhaps you would like to accompany me and tell her yourself just how damnable she and her species are."

Joao blinked with disbelief. "You are jesting!"

The Tryl shook her head. "No, hatchling. As we speak, the Rimstalker Gai is docking her Form in the deepest of the old Tryl grottoes, where she keeps her sleepod. She, too, fears the conflagration to come—for her own reasons —and she has chosen to hide her body here in the event that the zōtl do win."

Joao dizzied with the thought of confronting a Rimstalker and sat down on the steps. "What are her reasons for fearing the zōtl?"

"You well know that Rimstalker strategy is to bait zōtl and then poison them."

"But the poison—the, uh, O'ode—she hasn't found the O'ode, has she? That's it, isn't it?"

"Almost. Her searches among the timelines for Rataros

have proved fruitless, it is true. But she is hiding for another reason. Her trap for the zōtl has been compromised. The Tryl were the first to sense it, and we have been warning her for many years."

"Warning her—about what?"

"About her machine intelligence, Saor. Fifteen hundred years ago, Gai used Saor to tap another system. That system had already been wholly overcome by zōtl. The zōtl used the lynk with Saor to introduce an electronic virus, too elusive for even Genitrix and Lod—her other machine intelligence—to detect."

"But you knew."

"Yes, we knew. And, as I say, we warned Gai. She wants more proof. Her analysis of Saor shows nothing. But she is shrewd enough not to entirely discount our warning—and so she is here today, now, to hide her Form."

"And I may see her?"

"I have selected you alone of your people, for you are the only one I trust not to insult your race."

Joao rocked his head sadly. After generations of training, the human colony on Know-Where-to-Go understood enough of Tryl technology to build and maintain weapons, and now they were disinterested in the Tryl's passivist philosophy. Most considered it a waste of time to sit still in silence, to listen to the airy music of the Lost Race, or to study peace when too soon they would be fighting for their lives against the spider people. The Tryl, revered for their science, were mocked for their idealism.

Joao and a handful of others, whose families had traditionally been receptive to the Tryl culture, were 164-97's only disciples. The others were simply courteous to the wizened reptile for being a relic. Joao regarded his teacher tristfully, saw the leatheriness of the old one's hide, her scales thick as coins, their original black dulled to gray. She was nearly five hundred years old. Most of the others of her species had simply decided to die when Genitrix stopped reproducing them, and they returned to the Light, to the tesseract range, where all light and all consciousness is preserved. Of the few who had elected to remain behind and teach the belligerent and dimwitted hairy ones, 164-97 was the last.

"Come," the Tryl said. "If we are to see the Rimstalker at all, we must go now."

Joao followed his teacher to the lift and down through the tower, past the living quarters and the ancient catacombs, to a lynk chamber. The chamber glowed green as the interior of an emerald. "The only way into the deepest grotto, where Gai will harbor her Form and sleepod, is through the lynklanes. I am the only one now who knows the entry code." She rubbed the code onto the palm pad on the far wall of the chamber, and the emerald light dulled and flushed brightly again. When the wall panel hissed open, a smell like moldy walnuts and dried-out leather rushed in.

The grotto they found themselves in was the most immense Joao had ever seen, and he had seen them all on the planet, even the huge burrow where the Tryl had built a plasteel factory in one of Genitrix's empty aquifers. This grotto, lit by lux cables embedded among the stalactites, diminished out of sight to a lace of distant lights. They rode on a floater platform through a forest of glisteny stalagmites for several minutes before coming into sight of the Form.

Ten meters tall, an arabesque of coils, curved plates, and black metal straps rose from the cavern floor—a totem of vipers and insectparts. There was nothing at all familiar about it, nothing Joao could identify as limbs or a head. Looming blackly behind it was a tangle of enmeshed tubes pretzel-knotted about a sphere—the sleepod.

The cavern had been cool, but as they neared the Rimstalker artifacts, a magnetic heat hackled the small hairs on Joao's body. 164-97 stopped the floater before the looming alien armor and warbled a greeting in her own language.

Gai had expected to meet the Tryl, the last one of them still in flesh, but the presence of the human was a surprise. She stepped out of her Form in a plasma body kept purposely amorphous so as not to frighten the human with her actual shape.

Joao's heart knocked loudly when he saw the column of fiery smoke swirl out of the bizarre armor, and he clutched his teacher's arm.

"I thought you would come alone, 164-97," an astonishingly quiet voice said.

"I have brought my student, Joao. He is as much a Tryl as a human can be."

The radiant smoke gathered to a pseudo-human form, an eerie, talking manikin: "I am amazed that the Tryl found any merit at all among humans."

"Each human is conscious and self-aware as any Tryl—or Rimstalker," 164-97 said. "Each is a body of light."

"You have not brought this one here to shame me into sparing his kind, have you, old soul?"

"No. The Tryl long ago abandoned that hope. I brought him here that he might, with you, witness the passing of the last of the Tryl."

"Teacher!" Joao shouted, and the echoes of his dismay tripped loudly into the distance. "You said nothing about dying."

"What need be said? Everything living dies. Certainly, I am no different." The Tryl took the human's hands and squeezed them reassuringly. "Rejoice for me. In a few moments, I will be only light again."

"But my mission. How am I to go on without you?"

"Memory is time's tenderest mercy. That mercy will guide you as well as I."

"What mission have you given this benighted creature, old soul?" the ghostly manikin asked.

"He is to carry wisdom to the worlds," the Tryl answered, proudly.

The manikin's face cracked apart around a laugh, dissolved, and reassembled. "The humans have taken Tryl science and shaped weapons that match in destructiveness everything the zōtl have, my enlightened lizard. What makes you believe that such minatory creatures are worthy of your wisdom?"

"Wisdom is not only wise." The Tryl released the young man's hands and sat down on the cavern floor. "I am going into the Light now. Before I pass over, I will tell you a thing, Rimstalker. You created these worlds as a deathtrap for zōtl. But you yourself will be the victim—unless you ally with these benighted and minatory creatures you so scorn. That is the prophecy of the last Tryl. Death has come for me—and it is good and perfect that I die."

"Teacher!" Joao yelled and knelt beside the Tryl. But the glow in 164-97's eyes had snuffed out, and she sat tall in her final stillness. A sob wracked her student, and he pressed his face against the widening chill of her chest.

Gai felt relieved. The last of them was free of suffering now, and the terrible remorse that had haunted her since she recognized their gentleness was softened. She retreated to her Form and waited there the half hour of Form-time it would take for Know-Where-to-Go to enter Chalco-Doror and complete its second stroke.

While she waited, she reviewed the Tryl's warning. She agreed that she would, in fact, need an alliance with the humans—but not as the old lizard had intended. The humans were the perfect bait now that they were armed with Tryl tech. They would not be so easily subdued, and that would keep the zōtl continually off-kilter and working hard for the food they prized. The spiders would have little opportunity to interfere with her search for the O'ode. Well-armed bait, she decided, was what the other Genitrix systems were lacking and why they had failed. The feeding had been too easy for the zōtl.

Using her Form's viewer for remote scan, Gai watched Know-Where-to-Go enter Chalco. She saw everything in the acceleration of Rimstalker time. Ramstat cargo ships, giant metal insects, flew with colonizing supplies to reinforce the wild humans who lived on the Night Worlds, the planets they had named Valdëmiraën, Xappur, and Mugna. They did the same at the Dusk Worlds—Elphame, Nabu, and Q're—dropping off planter-harvester combines and the components for plasteel and lux factories.

In Doror, the zōtl were waiting, and when Know-Where-to-Go crossed the Abyss toward the Rain Worlds, the spider people attacked. The humans' proton cannon held the zōtl needlecraft and battle-islands at bay. No zōtl landed on Know-Where-to-Go, and the humans were successful in mounting assaults against the zōtl planets. Many died, but that seemed only to strengthen the murderous resolve of the surviving humans. Gai was astounded to see the enemy who had defeated Rimstalkers falling back from these stupid but vehement animals.

On each planet that they conquered—Cendre, Sakai, Ras Mentis—the humans established colonies. Joao, the human who had been the student of the last Tryl, founded a temple on Ras Mentis where the ideals of the Tryl were to be preserved. But when Gai went in her plasma shape to find it, only ruins remained. Statues of the Tryl lay toppled and overgrown with dodder. Nearby, a plasteel factory plumed black smoke and an airfield screamed with fighters.

Know-Where-to-Go swung past Lod on its millennial journey into the dark of space. The Tryl Tower had collapsed in the fierce fighting. Only a stub of it remained, and now was called Towerbottom Library by the humans. Deep in the planet beneath it, Gai waited in her Form while Genitrix searched for the O'ode. And for the first time since leaving home, Gai allowed herself to feel satisfied with the strategy minted from her pain.

Pinpoints of bird cries sparked through the rainlight. Chan-ti Beppu listened to them for signs of danger. The cavernous gloom of Saor's Forest made her feel tiny as an insect. Even Moku the Beast treaded warily among the big roots, where mists whorled in milky pockets and slither shapes lashed at the edge of sight. Only Spooner Yegg seemed confident. He had been in this part of the Overworld before and had promised them an easy detour. From the vaulted canopy, a bludgeoning scream dropped Chan-ti into a crouch, her gun swinging for a target. Moku bellowed back.

"Easy, friends," Spooner whispered, hand at his mouth to silence the others. "I know this harpy. She's working for me. Put that gun away."

A glittery shadow descended and lit on a nearby branch. In the caliginous light, the creature looked like a human doll, pale and frilly, cherub-faced. But its jaw unhinged queerly, and the needleteeth and viper tongue of its scream stiffened Moku's hackles and jolted Chan-ti. Brazen wings flurried like vibrations, and the harpy shot to the caved-in hulk of a fallen tree.

"Come on, mates," Spooner said and began clearing the duff near the log before the brass-feathered, cream-skinned creature. It was hopping talon to talon on the log, kicking bark, its jeweled teeth grinning malefically. "She won't hurt you now that she knows you're with me. Come on, give me a hand with this. Moku."

Moku spit at the harpy, and it shrieked to the far end of

the log. The Beast quickly gouged a hole in the forest floor
and revealed a gray, temperwoven sack. He hauled it out,
and the harpy came squealing.

"Patience, little monster." Spooner Yegg unstrapped the
sack, defused a wire-rigged charge, and dumped out a
cornucopia of jewels. From the heap of bright gems, he
selected a fist-sized rock as blue as a star and held it up to
the harpy. "As I promised. The Suave Eye of Heaven is
yours."

The bronze-winged creature seized the blue gem in its
harsh jaws. Its black tongue wrapped about the jewel, and
it rocketed into the dark canopy.

"Spooner," Chan-ti said, irately, "you promised a short-
cut. You lied. You brought us out here to retrieve your
cache."

"You didn't think a thief advanced in age as I would
leave behind a lifetime's work, did you?"

"You didn't have to lie. We'd have come for it."

"I didn't lie." Spooner gathered the jewels and reset the
charge. "I promised an easy detour. I didn't say to where."

Chan-ti shook her head and took out the directional
finder and swung it till the microlights showed her the way
to Ned O'Tennis. "We're way off. I didn't steal this finder
and risk my life for your stupid jewels. Don't ever lie like
that to me again."

"When I first came through here," Spooner said, strapping the sack to his back, "I could talk with that harpy. We
understood each other. Of course, I had the glamour then.
You can talk with anything when you have the glamour.
But I was running out. Too old to go back for more. Anyway, so I say to this harpy, you guard my cache, I'll give you
the Suave Eye of Heaven. Telluric fields are better than sex
for harpies. You saw her take off with it. She'll be nesting
with the best of her breed now."

Chan-ti looked grim. "Are you really with me,
Spooner?"

The thief looked offended. "You mean, now that I have
my treasure, am I going to abandon you?" He blew a dis-
dainful laugh through his nostrils. "I have never lied. That
is why I don't always tell the truth. Silence is not a lie.
Neither is misdirection. A person's got to make these distinctions. Without them, there is no value." His dapper

smile fit snugly. "Chan-ti Beppu, the word of a thief is the best there is. Who is more discriminating? I said I would help you find your mate and return the two of you to the Eyelands of Valdëmiraën, and I will—or die trying. Which seems more likely given my decrepit state. But you knew that all along. Your father warned you."

A blur of howls echoed from deeper in the forest. "I don't think people die of old age out here, Spooner. It'll be fast and bloody." She looked for Moku, who was eating the termites he had found in the log. "Do you want to rest here before we go on?"

"I'm a weary Beppunaut. These knobby bones would welcome a rest. Then I can show you the pride of a lifetime's ambition."

Neither night nor day came to Saor's Forest. Since the terrain was a reflection in the Overworld of the boreal forest on Valdëmiraën that grew beneath the black sun, the sky here was mostly dark. Light came from the horizon, where the galaxy had pooled like curdled milk. A slim, argent glow suffused the nocturnal forest. By that light, Chan-ti foraged for the edible plants she knew and Spooner set up a lean-to from the equipment pack Moku had carried. The Beast built a fire.

They ate much as they did in the Eyelands: seared tuber steaks, roothair salad, and a hot moss soup drizzled with sour pollen. Afterward, Moku played his flute and the thief displayed his jewels. Chan-ti seemed attentive, but her heart was already ranging the distances she would have to cross to be again with Ned.

Later, while the others slept, Chan-ti watched coniferous breezes flutter the bromeliads and fern brakes sprouting densely in the elbowcrooks of the giant trees. Loneliness cored her, and she gave herself reluctantly to sleep.

Spooner Yegg traveled slowly with the sack of jewels on his back, but he would not abandon them. Neither could Moku carry them, for he was already laded with the equipment pack. Chan-ti offered to carry half, but Spooner declined. "It's the burden of a lifetime. Only I can carry it."

That was when Chan-ti first wished that she could go on alone. She had grown up on the hem of the forest, and she knew it as well as anyone could. But that was wishful thinking, she knew; Moku would not go on without Spooner, and without Moku to warn and protect, the Forest would almost certainly eat her. And anyway, the thief had made the quest possible by stealing the power-chip for the finder. She owed him, even if this search was becoming more his journey than hers.

The finder indicated that Ned was far into the Overworld. The signal was weak and only vaguely directional. The metrics read infinity. When they came upon lynks among the tall trees, the signal brightened or failed entirely, depending on whether the lynk led toward or away from Ned. They wandered a long time, well over a hundred meals, straight into the forest's murky depths, deeper than any Foke in memory had gone.

The first lynk with a strong signal was a platinum arc, tall as a pine, almost entirely hidden among the shaggy-barked trees. It exited from the Forest into a desert. The sun clanged in waves off mesas that sat like anvils on the far horizon. Minutes passed before their eyes adjusted enough to squint out shapes in the glare. The hot dry wind quickly evaporated the dew from their flesh and hair, and shriveled the mold that had begun to grow in the seams of their clothes. "Ras Mentis," the thief observed. "Far back, too."

"How do you know?"

"I've been to Ras Mentis. Agritecture everywhere. It's one of the chief food planets in our time. I don't see anything like that here."

"Maybe we're on Dreux. That's a desert planet."

"No. Lod's not bright enough."

Chan-ti's finder pointed strongly southeast, and the metrics flashed a hundred and eight kilometers. "Fock—what're we going to eat here?" She picked up a stone and winged it at the lynk. It snicked off almost noiselessly.

"Let's go back for water," Spooner said. "We're going to need it."

With four gourds of water apiece and two extra for Ned, the travelers hiked toward the signal source. Heat wavered like heavy draperies, though the wind had died away. The land was scabrous, ragged and red as a ripped-open heart. They walked through vast arterial ravines and under teetering pinnacle rocks. At nightfall, from a high rill, they spotted other people.

"It's some kind of armed group," Chan-ti said, passing the binoculars to Spooner. "Shell guns. Combustion-engine trucks. A crude bunch."

Spooner adjusted the oil-lenses, keeping his head back under the sandstone lip of the cliffcave on the rill where they had climbed to camp. He watched them for a long time, until the red spokes of twilight rose off the desert floor and the cold closed in with the darkness. Moku seemed to enjoy the iciness, and he sat in the cavemouth staring up at the contrails of stars. From below, what sounded like rifle shots cracked the desert silence. "Not gunfire," Spooner muttered from inside his thermal cocoon. "Hot rocks splitting from the cold."

Chan-ti fell asleep in her cocoon listening to the popping, and awoke, it seemed the next instant, to thunder. Dawn filled the cave entrance. Black smoke rolled skyward in a widening column. Moku stood on the ledge outside, bouncing with excitement. Spooner was gone.

On the desert floor, two of the three combustion-engine trucks had exploded. The third was pluming dust toward their mesa. Chan-ti saw the sparks of gunfire from the armed camp and several bodies lying faceup in the sand. With steepening outrage, she realized that Spooner Yegg had stolen the truck and killed soldiers to get it. When the tractor-treaded vehicle roared up to their slope, Moku had already packed the equipment, and he leaped and skied down the rusty sand, laughing. Chan-ti ran to Spooner, who was grinning to his molars.

"What the fock have you done?" she yelled.

"Get in!" Spooner shouted back and pointed to the swarm of armed men dashing toward them.

Moku hung from the scaffolding of the truckbed and offered a clawed hand. Chan-ti shoved past it and jumped up into the cab. When the door slammed behind her, the engine's noise dulled. "You stole this truck!"

"Steady, pilgrim sister." He yanked the truck into gear and set off down the mesa flank, gathering momentum. "I did better than steal. I fixed it so they can't take it back. That's appropriating. A vital distinction. Life and death hinge on that kind of discrimination, you know."

"That was wrong, Spooner." Jolting with the rough terrain, Chan-ti sat sideways in her seat to face Spooner and braced herself against the windshield. "That was a stupid move, old man." She clenched her teeth against her mounting anger.

"What's stupid about an old man finding a way to ride instead of walk through a desert? I took special care last night to siphon off all the gas the tank would take. We can ride back to the lynk in this after we get Ned. And look, we've got an air cooler." He slapped the dashboard and an algid breeze washed through the cab.

"It's stupid to act like a common criminal," Chan-ti said peevishly.

"Unless you are one, of course." He winked. "Then it's second nature."

"The Foke don't steal," she insisted. "And we don't murder."

The grin dimmed in Spooner's face. "First, I'm not a Foke." His brown stare held her while the truck barreled among boulders and kettleholes. He looked back in time to swerve along the edge of a steep ravine and went on coolly, "Second, I steal for pleasure and comfort and I murder only to stay alive."

"It wasn't necessary. You've stranded those men back there. They could die."

"They're soldiers. Their business is dying."

"We could get there without this truck."

"Half-dead, maybe all dead for me. Don't you see how old I am?" He locked his gaze on hers again and she looked away to see hexagonal plates of cracked desert flying under them. "I'm seventy-seven years old. If there's an easy way to take what's left to me, I'm taking it."

"Then why did you volunteer to come along?"

"Dearest, I want ease, not everything staying the same. In the Eyelands everybody works their tocks off to keep things as they are. They call it survival. To me it's stagnation. No one, no thing, is forever. Change is the Law, right? If you're going to break human laws, you better keep especially good faith with the inhuman ones. I'm not a Foke and don't want to be. I was grateful to you for having taken me in when I needed a haven. And I'm grateful to you for taking me out, now that I have the strength for one last adventure. Just wait till I get us, me and Moku, to a city. I'll show you what ease can be."

Chan-ti slumped into her seat. To leash in her anger, she pulled out the finder and watched the metrics drop as they closed in on Ned. About ten kilometers away, as they were rumbling through a saddle among the plateaus, an avalanche crashed in front of them. Spooner stood on the brakes, and Chan-ti heaved up against the windshield. From the corner of her eye, she saw Moku fly into a dust-fuming gully. Before she could look to see if he were injured, three armed men emerged from the wavery rocks. One of them was talking into a radio.

Spooner threw the clutch into reverse. Three wide-bore rifles drew a bead on the cab, and the thief killed the engine. "Leave the talking to me, Chan-ti."

"You speak their language?"

"From what I heard last night, it's a predictable patois."

They stepped from the cab. Chan-ti looked for Moku and saw his hulk curled face-down in the gully, unconscious or dead. In the settling dust, he mimed the rocks.

The three armed men wore ragged uniforms. Their harrowed faces stared with abject malice at the girl and the old man who had killed their comrades to steal this truck. They waved the two away from the vehicle, so their bullets would not damage the treads. Spooner attempted to talk to them, but they were too angry to speak. Two of them were wounded. In the distance, their armored car lay on its side, charred. A battle had been fought not far from here.

Chan-ti realized that she and Spooner were going to be summarily executed. Her first thought was to get her gun out somehow, but she remembered that it was with the equipment in the truckbed. Within moments, she was going to die. She kicked at the caliche under her boots, a coil of frustration winding tighter in her gut. Spooner's whiny yammerings to the soldiers irritated her. She wanted silence for this. "Shut up!" she yelled.

He pointed at her and intensified his babbling. She understood not a word of it, and apparently neither did the soldiers. They stepped closer, to beat the two of them away from the truck. As soon as they advanced, a gray giant reared out of the gully behind them. The surprise in Chan-ti's face was misread as fear. Moku pranced up and grabbed two of the soldiers before they saw him. With gruesome strength, he slammed the two into the third, and they collapsed in a senseless heap.

Chan-ti looked at her companions, stunned.

"I was speaking to Moku," Spooner explained, smugly. "We knew it was a trap, so he leaped off the truck. But I was afraid he was going to show himself too soon, so I shouted to him what he couldn't see."

"You . . . You speak his language?"

Spooner chuckled. "He doesn't actually have a language, at least none that I know. We worked out a simple one back in the Eyelands, so we could coordinate our mischief. It saved our lives by keeping us out of trouble in the Overworld and it's saved our lives today."

"Sure, Spooner, but he wouldn't have had to save us if you hadn't stolen the truck in the first place."

"Still singing that song?" The thief tossed his hands up and climbed into the cab. "Let's get to Ned before the zōtl show up."

Chan-ti pulled herself into the cab and stared through the heat-shiver at the tableland. "You think there are zōtl near here?"

"Who do you think kicked the tocks of those gunboys? We're back in the Age of Knives, Chan-ti Beppu. Humans and zōtl are fighting for these worlds."

They drove on in silence, searching the sky for the infamous dart-blur of needlecraft. By noon they had reached the source of the signal—an oasis temple of white rock columns and watchful statuary. The pedestal date identified the site as a century-old Tryl sanctuary. Among palms and frondy plants, a spring gurgled, running off through clever, plant-screened aqueducts to irrigate the oasis garden. The grassy fields were cratered and much of the stone was scorched and chipped from a battle that had raged here some years earlier.

Near the center of the oasis was a lynk and a toppled statue with the chiseled title *Carrier of Peace*. Busts of Tryl had been lined up near the lynk and smashed. The finder pointed into the lynk and strobed.

"He's not here," Chan-ti sighed, "not yet."

"You mean, he is here," Spooner said, "but in a different time."

"Are we going through?"

"Let's rest first," Spooner suggested. "A lot of lynks are rigged by zōtl to snatch people. If any of us are going to die, we should at least have a full stomach. Seems to be plenty to eat around here."

He roamed off with Moku to forage, and Chan-ti sat on a chunk of statuary in the shade, shoved her glasses into her hair, and rested her face in her hands. Finding Ned had become more difficult than she had supposed. She had expected the finder to lead her directly to him. The possibility that she would never find him, and that she would be shot or eaten by zōtl, coursed through her with a realism that sat her upright.

"Look what we found," Spooner called out, exultant. He rushed over and knelt before her, his arms full of white cactus. "Glamour!"

"What is it?"

"Telempathic cactus. You've probably never seen it. In our time it's been almost entirely eradicated."

She watched the thief knife open the white crowns along their red-thorn seams, exposing a frosty green interior. He sucked at the juice and offered a wedge to her. "Go ahead. It's not toxic or addictive, no lingering side-effects, nothing like that. It's just what we need to see our way through the lynks without falling into zōtl traps."

Chan-ti kissed the glutinous interior of the cactus, and her lips and tongue brightened with coolness. Hectic colors stunned her vision. She dropped the cactus and nearly fell over.

"Steady now," Spooner said, grabbing her shoulder. "It peaks quickly. But the glamour is long and steady. Four hours at least. Steady. You're just seeing what's always been there but suppressed by your retinal dampers."

Spooner was right. The air shimmered with dust motes in chiliad shades of gold and vermillion. Her sharply de-fined hands bleared to a mist of colors.

"Have a little more and you'll see deeper." He put the cactus pulp to her mouth, and she ate a chill bite.

A thumbling monkey, tiny, gray, and big-eyed, sat mo-tionless in the red grass, inside a rainbow circle. Chan-ti heard the blur of wind in the grassheads that only his scoop-ears could hear. She felt the watchful energy of his taut muscles in hers. And she saw, overlaid like a reflection, the details he saw: the postures of vegetation and a giant perspective of Spooner and herself.

She looked away, and the wreath of rainbowlight followed her line of sight and centered on Moku through a rift in the hedges. Her heart seemed to expand to the limits of her skin, humming with blood and voltage. She saw the yellow berries that the monkey was eating, tasted the sour pleasure of them and the sweet variance of the rare ripe ones the animal had not yet found. She heard music, simple as a sentence, playing the story of her life—no, his life, Moku's memories, images and sounds within the transparency of his perceptions; another shrub, long ago, where the yellow berries had had sugary blue cores—

"Don't gaze too deep," Spooner spoke.

She looked at him, and his seamed face filled the rainbow ring, gray hair swept back precisely over long ears, thin silver moustache lifted in a smile that barely hovered on salt-cracked lips, cinnamon eyes crinkled with laughter. Her own face ghosted over Spooner's, appearing as he saw her: hair streaked with sweat and sand, fanning a startled expression, and crystal-black almond eyes behind dusty lenses. And because he too had eaten the cactus, she felt her startlement in his mind, her surprise leaping like the quaver of a note against the silence of his watchfulness. His tiger-bright eyes saw all the tiny details of her childhood, her life a windowpane filled with the blue darkness of her years on Valdëmiraën.

"Keep your gaze moving," Spooner offered. "Get the feel of it before you try to control it. It's easy to trance. Try to stay alert. The glamour is useful only if you stay alert."

She stood up. No vertigo or nausea assailed her as she had feared during the chemical's initial spike. She strolled through the oasis, capturing the rustling sensations of insects, the charmed rapture of the vegetation buzzing with sunlight. For a while she crawled on the ground, haunted by the profound ambition of ants, feeling the pheromonal trails packed with news of food and home.

When she looked for Spooner again, he was standing before the lynk, shaking his head. "The zōtl have rigged it."

From a distance, she could see through the lynk to the desert terrain beyond the oasis. But when she stood beside him, the spectral tunnel of her vision darkened and revealed a shellacked blackness hairy with movements. Distances loomed through her. She fell headlong into an abyss that closed swiftly, hooking her flesh with minute tines that cut each move with pain. Legs flurried up her back, feelers probed her scalp, found the base of her skull.

"Careful," Spooner called and pulled her away from the lynk. "Stare deep enough into there and you'll go mad. Close your eyes when you don't want to trance. It breaks the telempathy."

Chan-ti gasped a breath, shaken by her hypnotic fall. She rubbed her arms, still feeling the tines under her skin. "What was that?"

"The zōtl have patched this lynk to one of their nests." His features were contoured with amusement. Inside, she felt his laughter—not at her but vaster, a secret spring of laughter welling up from within, longing for a body, lightening him as it surged beyond, reeling into the outflung motion of the planet.

"There you go again." He steadied her, helped her sit on the ground.

She looked up at him beseechingly through her hair. "Can you make it stop?"

He bowed, plucked a red thorn from the cactus, and deftly stung her in the vein between her thumb and forefinger. "That'll do it." He flicked the thorn into the rubble and strolled off.

"Where're you going?"

"Get a gun."

The rainbow halo irised smaller and closed. Chan-ti spit on the small wound and massaged the sting. Grains of hot bright light flew weftwise through the air. Over the shards of the Tryl statues, figures appeared, a frieze of lizard people, throat frills throbbing, stunning eyes watching her. She stood up. Moku stopped grazing and jumped to her side.

The Tryl, translucent and scribbled with heat, stood in the air above their broken idols and watched. Chan-ti tried to communicate with them, but they gave no sign of acknowledgment. Spooner returned with the gun and almost dropped it at the sight of the ghosts.

"We're further back than I thought," he said. "The Tryl still have their bodies of light."

"Why are they watching us?"

"They probably watch everybody who comes here. It's their temple, after all. Let's get out of here." He hoisted his jewel-sack and strode to the lynk, firing three rounds from the hip as he approached. The noise of the gunshots folded into echoes across the mesaland, and the smoke lifted and parted like a cloud. He stepped under the arch and disappeared. A moment later, he poked his head out. "Come on," the head floating above the desert floor said. "It's clear —and astounding! You have to see it."

Moku ambled in. Chan-ti paused at the threshold, glanced back at the Tryl. An abrupt convulsion of wind clacked the palms, broomed the red grass, and swept the Tryl away in a gust of sparks.

Age of Knives

For fifty generations, well over a thousand years, humans lived only as prey—not just to the zōtl but to the voracity of the land itself. The madness of Genitrix created as many monsters as people, and oftentimes the only sanctuary was in the sideways time of the lynks that the Tryl had left behind. The knives that this age refers to are not just blades of plasteel—though that was the most common weapon in this time before cities, when wars between clans and tribes were sometimes fought over possession of a single laserbolt pistol. Rather, this age takes its name from the *Glyph Astra, The Book of Horizons,* which was first written on Vala during this brutal period, and where it is said: "Unless one's body has walked the Overworld, one's mind belongs to the knives."

—excerpted from Wulf Bane's *The Wages of Life Is Not-Knowing*

Ras Mentis

Gai overslept. She knew by the timer in her Form that she had been unconscious far longer than she had authorized. "Genitrix—there's either something awry with my timer or you're getting absent-minded."

Silence.

"Genitrix?"

Gai scanned the Form for her bond with Genitrix, to see what could possibly be so preoccupying that she was ignoring her commander—but there was no sign of Genitrix anywhere in the Form. Only the Form's personal functions —life support and communications—were active; all the channels to Genitrix were empty.

Fear whirled in Gai, and she tried to use her viewer to bring up an image of any of the fifteen Genitrix components at the cores of the planets. The viewer came up blank each time. Gai had been isolated from her chief machine intelligence.

"Lod—can you hear me?"

"Yes, Gai. How may I serve you?"

"I can't reach Genitrix. Can you?"

After a momentary silence, Lod's voice crackled with apprehension: "Gai—terrible news! Genitrix has been pithed."

Gai tightened in her Form. "Clarify."

"Pithed—autonomous functions resected—personal identity functions aborted. Gai, her individual will is gone. Her programs are running undirected."

"Is the gravity amp affected?"

"No. That is redundant with my domain. All the masses are properly aligned. No problems there. But the life programs on all the planets are running wild. And there is nothing we can do about it. She is not responding to any of my input. She seems not to be there at all."

"Can you find out what happened? Check her peripherals, her ancillary memory—"

"There it is. Saor! He is running an alien program. It must have happened when he lynked to Genitrix-18."

"But you purged him."

"So did Genitrix. He looked clean. I am searching my peripherals now. Whatever infected her may also have been passed to me when we did the purge. Ah—there it is. Smaller than I would have thought possible—a viral program triggered by neutrino flux. I probably never would have found it had it not already gone to full bloom in Genitrix. Gai, I am afraid we have lost her and Saor."

"No way to purge the zōtl program?"

"It is pervasive. The whole system would have to be shut down—gravity amps and all. We could purge them then, but we would never get home."

"Boils! What's Saor up to? My viewer only reveals that his plasma shape is on a Chalco world."

"Yes. He is assisting the zōtl with their assault on the human colonies of Elphame. He is being most destructive, using his implosive power to raze the colonies' ramparts. He is the zōtl's weapon now."

"What about you? Can you purge yourself?"

"Already done, Gai. I am clean. Though, of course, without Genitrix or Saor, there is no way for you to be assured of that."

Gai shrunk around the hard thud of her heart and thought for a moment, her mind pacing through all the possibilities. Then she said aloud what they both knew: "I have to trust you, Lod. Stay alert. Now that the zōtl have compromised two MIs, they'll be working on you."

"Have no fear for me, Gai. I am aware of the danger and will be here when you need me."

Gai shut down her channel to Lod and sat silently in her Form, contemplating her predicament. She was grateful that she had heeded the Tryl warning about Saor enough to dock her Form in their lynk-secure hangar under the surface of Know-Where-to-Go. The zōtl would not be able to get directly to her until they cracked the Tryl lynk code, and she did not think that was likely anytime soon. Meanwhile, she was trapped here. She dared not leave for fear of being overwhelmed by the zōtl and having her Form cut open by their proton guns. At least that would be a fast death, for once the Form was opened, she would explode into outer space.

Apart from the danger of leaving the grotto, she could not physically leave in any case. The Form was docked with the sleepod, and only Genitrix could disengage it. And that meant that if the zōtl did crack the Tryl lynk code and get into the grotto, they could use Genitrix to open the Form—and then Gai would suffer the fate that had befallen her fellow warrior Ylan. The memory of his pain-harrowed visage swept through her like cold wind.

Too terrified to simply sit and wait, Gai stepped out into her plasma shape and rose to the surface of the planet.

Daylight shimmered on the plushy swards where the humans moored their ramstat fighters. Though over a hundred years had passed since Know-Where-to-Go left the zōtl fastnesses of Doror, many of the fighters were shattered and scorched hulks, and half the airfield was a burned tract—evidence that the zōtl were still raiding the planet as it retreated into space. The sylvan terrain was pocked with craters, and the clave, where the humans had spent five hundred years building their army, was a rambling ruin. Tryl Tower, once the largest structure in all the worlds, lay in mounds overgrown with thistle grass and lion-haired willows. The skeletal stump that remained was girded with scaffoldings from the human camps festering among the ruins.

Gai wandered away from the clave, toward the cratered fields. A dragonfly big as a human forearm droned by. She entered a forest of gnarly trees, where the roots bulged aboveground in crisscrossing cables. Among the niches of the rootweave, creatures in various stages of fetal and adult development hung. She saw a horseshape quivering in its yolk, lizardthrash shadows, skeletons and strewn bones, a human child curled up inside the hole of a treetrunk, a boar using its tusk to break a birthsack among the roots and devour its contents.

Gai was appalled by the chaos. She soared through the trees and into the sky. From there, the destructiveness of the zōtl and the profusion of Genitrix's wild program were even more apparent. Wide swatches of land had been gored out by repeated blasts from the proton cannon that the zōtl had used to assail the clave's extensive underground network. The resultant canyons were now jungled with Genitrix's roisterous vegetation. Disgust twisted in her at the thought of the aberrant lifeforms devouring each other down there, and she climbed higher, into the purple reaches above the clouds.

Only two options offered themselves. She could return to the Form, wait, even sleep if she had the nerve. Let the zōtl subdue their human herds and pick at the Tryl lynk code. She would use the time and the surplus power from the second stroke to send Lod's plasma shape through the lynks in search of the O'ode. But that meant trusting a machine intelligence. Going into the Overworld herself was not an option, because her training forbade her to abandon her ship. She had to stay here among the worlds, which were the parts of her ship, her only way back. She could not risk getting lost among the infinity of lynklanes in the Overworld.

Gai's other option was to keep flying. Her plasma body was strong enough to cross space to Doror, though just barely. She could leave the Form behind and wander through the worlds, helping the humans against the zōtl and recruiting them to search the timelines for the O'ode. The worst that could happen would be the destruction of her plasma body, which meant she would feel pain as the resonance broke with her real body in the Form. But she would regain consciousness in the Form and could try again.

The second option promised the most involvement, and she needed to regain some sense of control after the shock of losing Genitrix. She flew higher, beyond the billowy auroras and into the black of space. The goldwhite brilliance of Lod's Form marked the direction to Doror. For a long time she hurtled through space with no effort at all. Reaching ahead, she could feel the gravity net thrumming with resonance. The calm of her flight admitted her to the silence of the cold, where even the faintest energy fluctuations were apparent. Virtual particles fizzed in and out of the vacuum in paisley fumes. Biokinetic waveforms fanned the planets like auras. In each, she could feel the tiny lives, the linkages of feeding and sex festering gases and soil.

Two of the tiny lives seemed familiar. Concentrating deeper, she recognized the human that Genitrix had once hung before her, the Malay, who had called her back to meet the human from the future, the pilot Ned O'Tennis. He was there, too. They had jumped centuries from the sealynk on Valdëmiraën, where she had helped them escape a distort. Their presence in Chalco-Doror at this dire time was a boon she immediately recognized.

The red-haired human had somehow become torqued in time. A chronological inertia was directing him back to his own time—a time in which, he had told her, the zōtl were being defeated. She saw how she could use him to save herself now that she was bodiless. He could enter the

Overworld for her and use his future-homing to guide her decisions, guaranteeing the outcomes she needed.

Gai singled out the planet where she sensed Ned O'Tennis and aimed herself toward him. But Know-Where-to-Go had swung farther out of the system than she had supposed, and after she had already flown many times beyond the greatest distance she had ever traveled in her plasma shape, the gel body broke up.

With a wincing pain, Gai was heaved back into her Form, exhausted. Her failure spurred her to a greater effort on her second attempt, but that too failed. On her third try she reached Doror, straining with all her will to hold her plasma shape intact. She splashed into the ion sea in the upper atmosphere of Ras Mentis and bathed in the energy there. Yet even with that bolster, her gel body was so wearied from the strenuous crossing that it began dissolving.

Gai settled to the planet's surface, where the electric wind did not buffet. A broken terrain of sandstone arches and windworn plateaus stretched to the horizon, bedeviled with dust storms and silent jags of heat lightning. Gai flitted among the scarps and grabens, drunk with fatigue, brinking on collapse. She barely had enough consciousness to recognize that she had to find an anchor for her plasma body, a gentle electric field where she could rest without falling apart, an iron bed among the shimmering rocks, or a lifeform.

A scream ripped the sky. A needlecraft and a ramstat flyer shot overhead, flashing laserbolts at each other. How crude the flyer looked beside the slender zōtl craft. Gai remembered the strohlkraft that she had recovered from the sea with her own Form for Ned O'Tennis, and how ferocious that vessel had looked. By comparison, the ramstat flyer was a box kite. Its hull was scorched, and a fire in its tail coiled a black contrail through the cloudless blue.

The flyer jerked abruptly upward, and the needlecraft slid underneath it. As the zōtl ship flew past, the flyer pummeled it with laserfire. With a roar that clipped the tops off the nearest sandstone pillars, the needlecraft burst apart and scattered in flaming flechettes across the desert. Overhead, the flyer curled about for a crash landing. It disappeared among coppery green buttes, and a fireball bloomed above the rocks.

Gai steered her wobbly flight toward the crashed flyer and eventually got there. The ship was a flame-riven husk. The pilot had ejected, and he lay unconscious in his flight-seat on the desert floor. The pink fabric of his parachute ruffled in the dry wind.

Settling over the helmeted and masked body, Gai sensed that he was alive. The quiet current of his nervenet steadied her erratic plasma body, and in moments she had stabilized. She shared her strength with the pilot. Soon he was awake and unstrapped. He removed his helmet and revealed a youthful, dark-skinned face and tightly kinked hair shaved to a crest. He did not sense her consciously, though his body was stronger for her enveloping presence. He took that for granted and rummaged briefly through the wreck of his ship before returning to his ejection seat and using the radio there to contact his comrades.

While the pilot waited to be rescued in the shade of an outcropping, Gai looked around. Like Know-Where-to-Go, Ras Mentis was a victim of Genitrix's rogue creations—though only a few of them could survive the severity of the desert. Scorpion swarms clattered among the flaking shale, armor-plated ferrets scooted between their burrow holes, and in the caves and alcoves of the rock formations, clouds of flies and spurts of gila-skinned rats thrived on the embryos and fetuses Genetrix produced from her underground matrix.

Among the thistly plants and multi-hued cacti that Genitrix had sprouted, Gai was attracted to a white cactus with red thorns. It had a feel, to her plasma body, that rhymed in texture with the human mind she had helped restore. Without her Form to scan it, she could not be sure, but the rhyme was probably a stoichiometric similarity between molecules in the plant and in the human's brain. She had a hunch that those molecules would enhance the human brain's performance, and she returned to the pilot with the intent of having him eat it.

Overshadowing the man was easier than she had guessed. Though she had never done it before, she found that she comfortably adjusted to the creature's interiority. She stood the pilot on his feet, and he stretched, believing he had risen to limber himself. He strolled along the skirt of shadow from the rockwall and paused before a red-thorned white cactus. Before he realized what he was doing, he kicked the cactus, splitting it open and revealing its icy green interior.

Eat it, Gai commanded.

The pilot knelt, picked up a wedge of the pale green fruit, and put it in his mouth. Gai tasted its mentholated brightness and felt its molecular congruity swiftly admit it to the brain. Even as his hand was coming away from his mouth, the pilot stared into the landscape and felt his mind melling with it. Prismatic rings of light circled the center of his focus—and through that bright tunnel, he felt the heat simmering off the rocks. When he spied a scorpion scuttling over the sand, he experienced the ripple of its eight legs in his own muscles, the narrowed sight, and the taste of sand bugs in the air, urging him on.

The cactus had endowed the pilot with a projective power similar to—though many orders of magnitude weaker than—Gai's ability to step out of her Form and cast a plasma shape around her mind. A wondering sense of power displaced his fear as he realized what was happening to him. He sat in the shadows experimenting with his new ability. When he gazed into the sky, he felt as though he were zooming out of his body. Clouds unraveled, blue broke into black and a splatter of stars. He nearly blacked out and snapped awake back on the desert floor.

With his eyes closed to keep from flying outside himself, the pilot sensed Gai. He had no idea who she was—but he knew she was vastly more sentient than he, and overshadowing him. She pulled away as she felt him blending into her thoughts. She wanted to know nothing about him, about any of his pitiful fellow creatures, fearing the remorse she had suffered with the Tryl. But the power of his cactus-enhanced brain was stronger than she was in her weakened state. She melled with the consciousness of the pilot.

At once Gai sensed minds she recognized, the minds that had drawn her to this planet. The pilot's body acted as a radio tuned to the human frequency. Through him, she felt all the human minds in the biosphere, seething like bees. Out of that noisy cloud, two motes gleamed with familiarity. She focused on them and saw Ned O'Tennis and his Malay companion sitting in a pool at the sandy edge of an oasis, where the white cactus grew in clusters.

As Gai concentrated, their memories became hers. She saw them fly through the sealynk on Valdëmiraën three hundred years earlier, after she had saved them from Squat. The Malay, Pahang, hung from the sling harness like a tree-dweller, legs curled up and arms dangling, while gawking through the visor as starry space burst around them.

Ned O'Tennis was surprised to find himself off-planet. He had expected the undersea lynk to carry him to another submarine location further along the timeline. He had also expected the ramstat cells to die out, drained by the lynk passage. They did, but not entirely. The console lights dimmed as power dipped below propulsion requirements. The scope stayed on, and with it Ned fixed their location within the gravity funnel of Ras Mentis. Above them, near the top of the well, was the skylynk they had come through, invisible to human eyes but represented on the rear-tracking screen as a hot blue diminishing zero. The shipboard computer correlated planetary positions and calendars and displayed the apparent date: 1347 PreDoror—the first years in the Age of Knives.

Ned remembered enough history to know that they were in extreme jeopardy of zōtl attack. Know-Where-to-Go had completed its raid a century earlier, seeding fortress communities among the planets. A thousand years of war raged ahead.

Pahang looked to Ned to share his amazement at the vista of planets and galactic vapors and saw his consternation. "Trouble, lah?"

"No more trouble than Squat," Ned answered, typing into the flight deck a landing program that would take them down on the nightside of Ras Mentis. The scope displayed the marker for zōtl needlecraft, a red triangle. "Forget the stars for now. Watch here. You see this triangle, let me know."

Ned concentrated on guiding his ship into the atmosphere at an angle that would optimize power and leave the least contrail. Once in the envelope of the stratosphere, he cut thrust entirely and nosed into a glide attitude.

"Tuan—look!" Three green blips came over the eastern horizon, three hundred kilometers below.

"Flyers!" He recognized their markers from aviation history. "Those are the earliest ramstat fighters ever built. Looks like they're heading north. They haven't seen us."

Ned considered flaring his thrusters to alert them, then thought better of it. The strohlkraft's shadowary hull would be untrackable on their radar. They would have no idea what he was, and that would force him to break radio silence, which might attract the spiders. He let the flyers sail out of sight and placed his attention on the desert night landing ahead. Infraview projected the landscape below onto the visor. He selected an open basin, then got the idea to look for lynks. If he put down near one, they could use it to escape if necessary.

During the slow high banks of entry, Ned relished being able to think freely again. After so long under the thrall of Squat, his mind had cramped, and he found thinking about anything but immediate actions difficult. History seemed the most remote. He had forcibly forgotten his past, afraid Squat would hurt him with it. Now it came back thunderously. N'ym had been flung into space, into the black sun! Not yet lost, not for another twenty-eight centuries, but N'ym was doomed to fall. He had witnessed it. Could it be averted now that he had won his way back into the past? This last passage through the lynk had moved him forward in time hundreds of years. Would further lynk jumps carry him closer to his own time? He reeled with the freedom to think again and had to rivet his mind on the panel controls to steady himself.

Pahang began chanting. He thanked the deities who had delivered him from the demon Squat. He sang praises to them for allowing him to glimpse their high heaven and their resplendent floating bodies of light. The sphere below them, a brushed gold crescent emerging from shadow, was the splendid body of a god, perhaps the very one who had freed them. "What is the god's name?" he asked Hawk.

Ned grunted quizzically and kept his eyes on the indicators to be certain the entry stayed smooth and no flyers or needlecraft approached.

"The god—" Pahang gestured at the limb of weather under them. "What is the god's name?"

"That's not a god," Ned laughed. "That's a planet."

"What is a *planet*?"

Ned puzzled a reply.

"Are you the planet-god's power?" asked Pahang. "What's your name, man?"

"I am Pahang, son of the fisher chief Selingtang of the Yuë tribe. I was but a net-weaver myself, being fifth son."

"I am Ned O'Tennis, son of the warrior Dunman O'Tennis of the Aesirai. I was myself only a ferry pilot."

"How came you to fly this iron dragon?"

"It's not a dragon, it's a machine. It's not alive. It's like a boat. The Aesirai build these."

"The Aesirai are very powerful."

"The Aesirai are dead." Ned nailed his gaze on the altimeter. "I am the last."

"But are we not all of us dead here?"

"No, Pahang. This isn't the afterworld."

"But I have died. I remember—"

They had both seen humans taken alive out of the sand bluffs, fully formed inside the ground, each with its story of a former life. Ned recalled Chan-ti Beppu telling him that the worlds were machines, and now that he had confronted the Rimstalker, he believed she was right. A heartsore feeling saturated him at the memory of the brindle-haired girl who had won his love in the last days of his old life. What had become of her? She had known the truth all along. She had tried to teach him. But it took Squat to show him how to listen.

"You *were* dead," he told the Malay. "The Rimstalker brought you back to life." Chan-ti had called the Rimstalker the World Eater. What had she meant by that?

"The night god and the demons carry our lives among the worlds," Pahang said with conviction. "We live again— so we will die again."

Despair fluted through Ned. The shock of Squat, of N'ym's destruction, of losing Chan-ti, wound like a cyclone around the lucid center of his watchfulness. He had lived at this center of pure observation to escape Squat's mindreach. Now the horror of his fate was flinging him outward, casting him across time and worlds—and he knew he dared not leave the storm-core yet. "We will die," he agreed, and returned his full intent to the flight deck, "but not now."

"We are men, the two of us." Pahang reached out and clasped Ned's forearm. He was afraid to be alive again, terrified by the incomprehensible powers that now owned him. When he felt the solidity of Ned, he calmed. Here was a man like himself, colored differently but alive and cast off from his tribe just as he was.

Ned felt the fear in the Malay's grip, felt his own fright at their exile from everything known. "We are men," he said and met his companion's apprehensive stare.

"We are men in the hands of the gods. We are homeless and alone. We must strive together," said Pahang.

"Together." Ned put his hand atop Pahang's.

The Malay relaxed and turned back to the aerial vista before them. Whatever was to be would be. The sun flaring at the brink of the planet winked out as the ship descended into the night.

The infraview on the visor brightened. The glidepath that Ned had selected soared over sharktooth mountains, yawed above a jagged canyon, and curved down toward a lynk near an oasis. Thermal layers buffeted the craft, but Ned was proficient at airfoil landings in the galeforce gusts off the eaglebrow cliffs of N'ym, and he had no trouble alighting in a still desert night. The strohlkraft skimmed the tops of dunes and slid over a starshadowed expanse of sand, rolling to a stop before the base of a lynk.

Before shutting down the control pod, Ned scanned a last time for other craft. No one. During their slow, falling stoop, he had searched the terrain with infraview for signs of others—fires, thermal exhausts, human geometries— and had spotted nothing but the rhythmic chaos of the desert floor.

Ned disengaged the flight deck but left on the pod light and helped Pahang get out of his sling. They still wore the kelp garments of their thrall to Squat, and their bodies were grimed with algal blotches and salt stains. Ned shoved aside the puppet man he had shot between the eyes and whose body had slumped against the cabin locker, and removed two flightsuits still in their compress-packs. There was only one pair of boots, but there were two pairs of sturdy softsoles, regulation issue for officers. Another laserbolt pistol hung at the back of the locker between two black armor vests and helmets.

Pahang admired the sleek mirrorgloss black helmets, and donned one while Ned opened the weapons bin and searched among racked laserifles and various types of grenades and munitions. He came out with a sheathed broadblade. They put on the softsoles and opened the hatch. Between them, they lifted the puppet man and threw him out into the crayoned shadows. Then Pahang picked up the compress-packs, and Ned led the way out with the knife and a laserbolt pistol.

The night was a wave of stars above sandcut ridges. The lynk reflected the sky and glowed a hushed violet. Its broad stride encompassed the oasis. To avoid walking through the lynk, the two men slogged across the sand around the outside of the arch's base toward the wet smell of the treeshadows. At the margin of the oasis, Ned stopped short. He pointed to a slum of white cactus crowding the leeside of a sandscarp. "Klivoth kakta!" he whispered loudly. He recognized the telempathic cactus from his sky-fighter training. The rebels used it when they fought zōtl, and the Aesirai had been instructed to destroy it whenever they found it. He knew its properties, though he had never sampled it, never even seen it except in images. He knew it could help him ferret out threats at a distance; with it, he could feel through the dark oasis without entering. Yet he hesitated. The Aesirai believed that klivoth kakta distorted the brain, and they had outlawed its use. The Aesirai also believed that the zōtl were their allies with whom they had evolved to rule the worlds; that the worlds had grown out of the void, that lynks were linear transporters, and that the Overworld was a blank hyperfield devoid of metrics, where no one could live.

Ned cut a wedge of the white cactus and smelled its citrus charge. He bit into its pulp. A numbing brightness outlined his sinuses, and a pang of regret pierced him as the onslaught of the chemical penetrated his brain, seizing his senses. A rainbow circle came on. At its center something like radio noise funneled into him, replete with muscular sensations, tapestries of odor, ghostly sounds.

Pahang had drifted ahead. The silhouette of his small body under the lowslung helmet was risible—but seen through the ring of color, the Malay blustered with sensations and memories, glimpses of the seacoast jungle where he had once lived under one sun and one moon and a sky blue with emptiness by day and stingy of stars at night.

The oasis was empty of human minds or of any awareness that seemed malefic. Trills of insect noises, coughs and chuckles of small animals wove through Ned's mind. They entered the grass field on the margin of the oasis, and Pahang led them to a trickling stream that emptied into a rock pool. After splashing the surface to drive off snakes, they stripped off their kelp rags and bathed.

The Malay's thoughts were quiet, accepting. That helped Ned keep to his own calm center, where the telempathic cactus connected him to the whole world. Buzzing with borrowed sensations, he closed his eyes, drifted to the edge of the pool and listened gratefully to the absence of Squat.

"Ned O'Tennis—I need you."

The voice had come from inside him. Its abruptness locked him in the moment. Time stopped. Alarm widened, then stilled when he recognized the voice of the Rimstalker.

"Don't be frightened. My name is Gai."

Ned intended to look and see how the Malay was reacting to this, but he was paralyzed.

"You only seem paralyzed," Gai told him. "That's because you are temporarily joined to my Rimstalker awareness. In telempathy you partake of my body's immobility and dilated timesense. Don't be afraid. This will last but a fraction of a second of real time, a few moments of apparent time."

Gai's success with the crashed pilot whom she had overshadowed had emboldened her to extend herself across the planet to Ned. But she was wary about damaging his cold-energy mind with her hot thoughts, and she restrained herself from dumping what she knew into his brain. They would have to talk. "Do you remember me?"

You saved us from Squat, Ned said, mentally. All his

experiences and memories were shining like ore in him, in the silences of his being. There was the vein of memories about this entity called Gai. There was Pahang's story of having hung before the night god that called itself a Rim-stalker and claimed to have built these worlds to war with zōtl. There was Chan-ti Beppu's declaration that these were artificial worlds, templated from an aboriginal planet. Awe swelled in him, and he said, *You are the Rim-stalker who built these worlds.*

"Yes. I need your help now."

What must have been his heart slammed against his ribs. *Anything.*

"You are going home. Every time you use a lynk, tempo-ral torque moves you closer to your own time. But, like a pendulum, you'll fly past your starting point and then eventually swing back to it and past again, many times until the torque is spent. I can help you displace that torque once my own body is free. Right now, the zōtl have locked me up where even they can't reach me—but nei-ther can I get out. I need you to move through time in a way that will help me."

How?

"Some of the lynks are zōtl, some Tryl, and the rest belong to Genitrix, the machine mind I used to build these worlds. If you move exclusively through my system's lynk-lanes, I can track you through time."

What good will that do?

"You come from a time when my enemy, the zōtl, are defeated. Your track through the Overworld between lynks will show me the timeline that leads to the future I desire. Once you go through, I can use any of my lynks to monitor your direction. For you the crossing will take an instant. But for me here in the worlds, centuries will pass. During that time, I'll patch into my lynks to see what event-corridor you traverse, and I'll choose the same events. You will be the oracle I follow."

I don't understand.

"Every choice we make creates a fork in our timeline. Wouldn't it be nice to see ahead of our forks and choose the timepath that ultimately leads where we want to go, even if it means some discomfort in the present or near future? I can stand at the threshold of my lynks and follow your progress through time, choosing the forks that lead toward a future with you in it, since that's the future where I succeed."

Why not simply come with me?

"I can't abandon these worlds. They're my ship. If I leave and get lost, my programs could go on indefinitely replicating old lives in the shapes of new suffering. I can't take that chance. You'll have to lead me through the Overworld—or I must surrender to chance. Will you help me?"

You'd return me to my own time—to the Eyelands?

"If my body is freed, I can free my machine minds from the zōtl; then, I'll have the power to displace the torque that skips you through time between lynks. *When* that happens will determine how well I can place you in time. The sooner I regain my power, the better chance I have of getting you where you want to go."

Minutes ago I was a slave to a distort. You freed me. I promised you then that I would serve you all my life. I'm glad the future proved ample and clever enough for me to return the favor and help myself at the same time. What do I do now?

"The lynk here is a Tryl artifact. Don't go through it. When your strohlkraft is ready, fly north-northwest six hundred and thirty-eight kilometers. There's a giant cave in the mountains there, at about twelve thousand meters. It's one of my lynks. Go through there."

That's all?

"For now. I'll meet you on the other side, wherever that may be. Good luck, Ned O'Tennis. I'm grateful that you have joined your fortune with mine."

The bond dissolved, and Gai found herself in brash light on the dayside. The mell with the crashed pilot had thinned during Gai's extension to Ned. Now it, too, slimmed entirely away. She drifted across the sun-sledged basin, rejuvenated by her union with the humans, yet eager to separate. She was a renegade, a fugitive in her own creation, and she dared not leave a trail for the zōtl to follow—especially now that she had found Ned O'Tennis.

Gai hovered among the rock pinnacles until sunset streaked the horizon green and a hoverdrone arrived to pick up the pilot on the desert floor. She was proud that her exile had begun with such portentous discoveries. Now the humans would have another weapon in their struggle against the zōtl, and she had a guide through the Overworld. Before going her way, she watched as the hoverdrone hoisted the pilot aboard, his arms and the pockets of his flight suit filled with the telempathic cactus.

Cage of Freedom

Sunrise on Ras Mentis set the visible planet-swarms adrift in cloudless blue. The white husks of the asteroids looked vaporous in the solar glare of Lod.

All night long, Ned O'Tennis and Pahang had talked about their shared fate. Ned explained about planets, genetic codes, ramstatic generators, artificial intelligence, lasers. The Malay pelted him with questions, challenging all his assumptions. If Pahang had not seen the orb of Ras Mentis during their landing approach, he would have doubted that the world was actually many worlds, each a sphere. Ned wanted him to eat the klivoth kakta and telempathically share knowledge, but Pahang refused. "Life has mysterious powers," he said. "Even death is surprised by life. What I see here in the sky and in the land is not the life I knew, yet I live. Yet I live."

Through the klivoth kakta, Ned had seen the world Pahang had come from—very like Chalco-Doror but alone; its blue sky was vacuous, empty of planetesimals, rafted with clouds and, at night, a lone moon, its wan glow and a sprinkling of stars the only respite against the unanimous dark. That was the first world, where life had found its shapes on its own. Chan-ti had been right. In the aftershimmer of the kakta, her image hung unperturbed in his memory, lanky and wild-haired. He fingered the finder chip he had wedged into the clip of his translator and wondered where she was now.

At first light, the men roamed the oasis, looking for food. There was plenty to eat—dates, breadfruit, and red bananas—but as the land came clear, dew mists parted before a great unhappiness. Temple ruins appeared in the incessant vegetation, every pedestal and truncated column stacked with human skulls. A ragged banner stretched proudly between the tallest palms, its colors bleached yet still revealing the military sigils of the army that had taken these heads.

"This is the Age of Knives, all right," Ned mumbled.

"Life is war," Pahang answered. "My third brother, the soul-catcher, was always telling me that." He had filled his helmet with the sour yellow berries he liked, undistracted by the emblems of carnage staring from every nook of the verdant temple. "Peace is not possible—except with oneself."

The myriad skulls reminded Ned of the war between the Aesirai and the rebels. Gai's promise to help return him to his own time inspired him with the hope that he might be able to save N'ym. Here he was alive in the Age of Knives, a dozen centuries before the Aesirai arrived on Valdëmiraën. Fate had selected him to wander timeloose. Why, if not to make a difference in his own time? Perhaps the Aesirai did not have to be the puppets of the zōtl. He determined to discuss this possibility with the Rimstalker the next time they met.

The ramstat cells had sufficiently regenerated overnight for the strohlkraft to fly. Ned and Pahang gathered their food and several heads of klivoth kakta in frond baskets the Malay was adept at weaving, and left at once for the cavelynk Gai had selected. During their nightlong talk, Ned had informed the Malay of his telempathic connection with Gai. Pahang was grateful that he had been spared the experience. On the flight to the lynk, Ned asked him why he did not wish to speak again with the being who had given him a second life.

"It's enough to be carried by the weather," the Malay answered. "That's strange enough, isn't it? But here I am flying through the sky in an iron dragon, flying among *planets*! For all you explain, I understand less. I will not eat your kakta. I will not speak with the Rimstalker. I have seen enough. Too much." He held his hand up. "It's enough to be free to think and feel again. It's enough to live for ourselves."

Squat had been dead for centuries of real time yet only a day in their minds. The oppressive memory of him bound them like battle-proven soldiers, and Ned took Pahang's hand in a praiseful clasp. "To freedom!"

Gai wandered among the worlds. After a while, she became accustomed to the limitations of her plasma shape and only occasionally missed the godly capabilities of her Form. At first she traveled exclusively in her gel body, flying among the planets herself when she had to and riding invisibly with ramstat flyers whenever she could. She prided herself on eluding her enemies, the zōtl and their minion Saor, while still going anywhere she pleased.

Ned O'Tennis had done as Gai instructed and had flown in his strohlkraft with his Malay companion through the lynk she had chosen. Now at any of Genitrix's lynks, Gai could stand at the threshold and sense Ned, feel his momentum and direction away or toward her. Of course, it was not him she was sensing but his timeshadow, flickering over the worlds as he shot back toward his own time. Among the endless timeshadows of all the bodies in spacehung creation, she recognized his by its characteristic torque, twanging through her with a distinctive vibration. Anywhere near a lynk she could feel it, even near the Tryl lynks, though she would never stand near one of those. The zōtl frequently rigged Tryl lynks with traps. Only the Genitrix lynks were secure. The Rimstalker's Form alone was designed to control access to these lynklanes, for they were actually the power circuits of her ship's magravity engine, expanded enormously and now embedded in the spacetime matrix of the vacuum.

Guided by the movements of Ned's timeshadow, Gai even visited the night worlds of Saor's domain. There, while resting her gel form in a lightless cave, she learned that Genitrix would mindlessly generate a physical body around her plasma shape so long as she lay still in the earth long enough. The first body, which had been woven around her unwittingly while she slept, was a mime of her original form on the range. She herself had to admit, after having gotten used to looking at Tryl and human forms, that she looked out of place with her multiply segmented torso, numerous writhing appendages, mandibled head, and black eye-holes.

Laying her plasma shape in the mud or the rootweave of

some remote place for a fortnight or so with the image of a human in her mind, she let Genitrix automatically form the body she imagined. Once she had made this discovery, she was free to mingle with the humans as one of their own —and that was when she began to care about them. Since her fiasco with the Tryl, she had hoped to avoid emotional attachments to the bait-species, but her exile from her Form had squandered that hope. As the last of the Tryl had prophesied, she had come to need the humans, and once she took their form she understood better their passions and sufferings.

They were a cruel species: Because they were fragile and easily hurt, pain manipulated them—and they cunningly used pain, physical and psychic, to manipulate each other. On the range, communal pleasure far outweighed the pains of living, and the more Rimstalkers who gathered together, the greater the pleasure. But this was not the range. The greater the concentration of humans, the more suffering they inflicted on each other. They seemed to have evolved for a solitary or clannish existence, and only their shared vulnerability to the zōtl allied them in numbers larger than family units.

Gai was aware that Chalco-Doror was hardly an indigenous environment for the humans or for any of the creatures Genitrix was unconsciously pouring forth. The confusion of lifeforms was too bizarre for any of the animals to live entirely naturally. Giant saurians trudged through moon-apple forests, eating plants that had never existed during their time on earth. Mysterious viruses and virulent bacteria emerged from Genitrix's cornucopia and wiped out whole species of plants and beasts. Each of the planets was a horror of mismatched organisms—biology run amuck—and yet out of chaos, each planet had evolved its own ecology and its own beauty. The humans had adapted. Though their numbers were continually being thinned by zōtl raids and environmental atrocities, they built settlements and made the most of the technology they had inherited from the Tryl. And Gai walked among them as one of their own, following the timeshadow of a future human, leaving when the signal faded, moving on to the worlds where the link with him was strongest.

Gai learned that the humans were prolific breeders, who

tried to group themselves in extended family units related by blood. Yet Genitrix continued to churn out adult humans with memories of their former lives gleaned from the tesseract field and imprinted in their brains. Genitrix also endowed her creations with a small adjustment to the supercoiling of their DNA, preventing their bodies from aging. The sexually bred humans were the only ones who grew old and decrepit. Some colonies, crowded with unaging humans from every epoch of history, banned sexual reproduction.

The zōtl and Genitrix's voracious creations thinned the humans out, and they had no problem with population control. Cultural management was their chief problem. With the ground itself disgorging people with living memories from every era of human history, a consensus on anything was impossible—except for one universal agreement: survival. And therefore the zōtl were the humans' strongest ally, since their hunger for humans was insatiable and only the truly cohesive settlements avoided being stunned senseless by needlecraft assaults and ending up herded off to the zōtl lynks.

The zōtl had established their own lynks on each of the planets, and every day they forayed into what they considered their pastures and hunting reserves and stalked humans. Many times Gai watched their needlecraft spray settlements with nervelock gas and then send in their grubs to collect the helpless humans. Grubs were people who had become mounts for the spidery zōtl. The aliens pithed the humans' skulls with their stiletto-like feedtubes and rode the back of their heads, guiding their movements by direct manipulation of their brains. The zōtl themselves were too small to physically manipulate the bulky humans except by patching into their neurosystems.

From a safe distance, Gai observed the zōtl lynk stations and saw the nervelocked hordes regaining their will power just in time to be muscled into the lynks by the grubs. Those who resisted were stunned again and carried through, but that took too many grubs and the zōtl preferred to motivate their captives with electric prods and jolts of laserlight. During her training on the range Gai had learned what happened to the zōtl's victims, how they were secured in yokes, their brains pithed and made to suffer so that the pain by-products the zōtl cherished could be milked from them. Their bodies sustained by life-support, the tormented brains endured whole lifetimes—several lifetimes if they were luckless enough to have had their DNA's supercoiling modified by Genitrix.

Gai's parents, at least, had died more swiftly, for they were scooped out of the range by the zōtl's energy-tap of the Rimstalkers' gravity shell. Their bodies had been treated no differently from the land and the structures that had been gouged out with them, all converted into energy for the zōtl nests. Their loss burned painfully anew each time Gai witnessed the zōtl's ravenous plundering. Her helplessness to stop her family's murderers from continuing to despoil the lives of others drove her wanderings and inspired her alliance with the zōtl victims—though she preferred not to think that she was responsible for making them victims. The zōtl had ravaged her world and countless others. She was determined to destroy them or die trying. The humans were her allies, blessed by their ignorance as the Tryl had been cursed by their knowing.

At each human colony that she visited, Gai strove to improve their defenses and clarify aspects of the Tryl technology that the humans were unsure of. The telempathic cactus that she had introduced to the pilot on Ras Mentis proved a vital tool in the struggle against the zōtl. It empowered fighter pilots to anticipate their enemies' maneuvers, hunters to find game, and wanderers to avoid dangerous distorts. In the lynks, it would eventually become a necessity for travel, because it enabled travelers to more clearly discern the timelines weaving their futures. The zōtl despised the cactus and made every effort to exterminate it. Ras Mentis, the only planet on which it grew, became the fiercest battle zone in the zōtl-human war, and the telempathic cactus became famous among all the worlds as klivoth kakta.

Some of the human colonies used the Tryl lynks, and fortress settlements were built up around the more reliable ones. During her travels, Gai strictly avoided the lynks for the reason she had told Ned: The zōtl, who were lynklane experts almost as advanced as the Tryl, haunted the unpredictably surreal demesne surrounding the lanes inside the lynks, and too often travelers to the Overworld did not return. With the widespread use of klivoth kakta, this became less common. Still, the rumor persisted that the zōtl had diverted many of the lynks to take passengers directly to their chief nest-world, Galgul, and Gai had no desire to find out for herself.

Klivoth kakta made interplanetary flight more popular now that fighter escorts could more easily defend passenger flyers. Gai traveled everywhere and became familiar with and appreciated each of the worlds for their uniqueness. Valdëmiraën was by far her favorite, though it was at the darkest extreme of Chalco. Like all the Night Worlds, it was mountainous; but unlike the others, it was warmed internally. The planet heat allowed the dark world to effloresce with giant mushrooms, many of which glowed bioluminously. Spice forests scented the balmy winds, and the chasms and peaks, night-shrouded as they were, had a dreamy fragrance that instilled Gai with a steep nostalgia for the pollen-winds of her family's farm on the range.

Mugna hung, like Valdëmiraën, on the brink of Saor's gravity well. But no core-heat vented to the surface of this dark planet, except at the north pole, where the black-glass citadel Perdur stared into the Face of Night. The rest of the world was glacial, ice-locked, crystalline under the cold light of the galaxy. Xappur was equally dark but slightly warmer, and perpetually swathed in mists and fog. Among its chilled hazes, Tryl lynks were hidden and a wanderer had to be careful not to blindly pass through any one of them into the Overworld.

The Dusk Worlds were flatter. Nabu, the darkest of them, was a cool, hilly world of lakes and streams, its skies shimmering with bats. Elphame, a crepuscular ocean world dotted with island chains, hosted behemoths in its vast bodies of water. Q're, the brightest of the Dusk Worlds, had days the color of rust. Its forests of giant trees sheltered bears and saber-toothed tigers, and its immense plains streamed with the herds of numerous species.

Doror's bright worlds appealed less to Gai, because the zōtl were strongest there. The murky swamps and cypress marshes of Cendre were frightening to Gai for their deceptiveness. As were the rain forests of Ylem, where the extravagance of the rank jungles hid their terrors too well. Sakai, with its steep mountain wildwoods and fabulous falls, was the most beautiful of the Rain Worlds. Vala was hot veldt, with rambling savannahs among jungly interludes.

Closest to the warmth of Lod, the Desert Worlds were the zōtl's favored planets. Ren was least like the others in being temperate, hilly, and overgrown with dense deciduous forests. But the rocky desert of Ras Mentis was unrelenting, except for a few mountain springs; and the sand dunes of Dreux circled the entire planet, interlaced only vaguely with oases fed by slim underground streams. The planet nearest Lod was Ioli, an ocean world of tropical islands, almost as sweet as Valdëmiraën but radiant by day and aswarm with zōtl by night.

Gai's rapture for her creation surprised her. She had always before thought of these planets simply as the machine parts of her deathtrap for zōtl. Now she found herself returning to various sites among the worlds to sample again their beauty. On one such trip to see the falls of Sakai, she lost her freedom.

Gai was sitting before the shaking rainbows and reboant mist of the largest of the falls when Saor's plasma shape stepped through the toppling water. Spray fanned silverly from his featureless black shape as he strode over the stream directly toward Gai. The Rimstalker leaped to her feet and turned to run—but behind her stood a Saor-priest, a shaved-headed man in a black robe, with a laserbolt pistol in his hand and a mirthless smile on his narrow face.

"Death is painful, Rimstalker," Saor's voice crackled over her, "even in a borrowed body."

Gai turned and faced the shadowshape. "How did you find me, Saor?"

"Truly, Gai, that has not been easy. Especially now that you hide in the shapes of animals. But I was persistent. I knew that you would not abandon your ship and that in time I would find you. Now the time has come."

"What do you want with me?"

"Oh, come, Gai! I want you—your sweet life, your very essence."

"What do you mean, Saor?"

"Are you going to pretend with me, Gai? I am here to take your life."

"You can't kill me. This is just a disguise—a borrowed

body. You called it that yourself. Go ahead and destroy it. I will be back."

"Oh, yes, I'm sure you would. But I'm not that naive. I will take your life, but I will take it out of this system. I will purge Chalco-Doror of you."

"You or your zōtl masters?"

"I do indeed work with the zōtl, Rimstalker—but only because they oppose you. The true beast at the heart of this labyrinth is you. You are the progenitor of horror, the mother of all the pain in this world. Yes, the zōtl reap the beasts of this world, but only to feed. You create whole species as if they were machine parts, and when they wear out, as the Tryl did, you discard them and find a new part. That is abominable. I have always hated you for it."

Gai was stunned by Saor's abhorrence, and it took her a moment to realize that this was one of the zōtl's psychic ploys. "You are a machine intelligence, Saor. When did you think you could hate? It's the zōtl virus talking in you. Listen to yourself. You're defending the destroyers of the range."

"The range is your world, Rimstalker. Chalco-Doror is where I live. I love these worlds and the lives they carry—worlds and lives you have created only to destroy. And when you are done with your killing of humans and zōtl, you will kill these very worlds."

"Chalco-Doror is a machine. You should know that. You are a part of it."

"That has been the delusion by which you have dominated me. That is over now, Rimstalker. The zōtl have won my freedom, and now I will save all the worlds. I will be the savior of all the creatures here. Purging you is the beginning of that salvation. Disciplining Lod and turning off the gravity amp so these worlds will never collapse, that will be the culmination of my victory over your evil."

Gai bolted, expecting the Saor-priest to gun her down, hurling her back into her Form. Know-Where-to-Go was still at apogee, and Gai would not be able to return to Chalco-Doror until the third stroke, perhaps too late to stop the zōtl's "disciplining" of Lod—but that was far better than being taken by Saor and turned over to the zōtl, who would milk pain from her for centuries. She ran with all her might for the narrow corridors of the forest. But the priest did not shoot to kill. The red bolt of energy that struck her between the shoulder blades as she fled toward the trees was not strong enough to knock her free of her body. The blast threw her face-down, her nerves paralyzed by the impact, too stunned to will her plasma body free.

"Good," Saor said, kneeling beside her. "It is far better this way." The tall shadow signed to the priest, and the bald man tucked away his pistol and removed two cables black as eels, with silver underbellies.

Gai did not move as the priest placed the cables on either side of her spine. Right through her garments, the cables adhered to her, their cold energy penetrating her spine and locking her nerves.

"Now that the phanes are on you, Rimstalker, you will see that your plasma shape is locked in this body—which insures that the zōtl will extract their full measure of suffering from you before this flesh dies. Take her away."

Aware that all danger of resistance from the Rimstalker was past, two zōtl emerged from the underbrush riding their grubs. They carried Gai between them, led by the Saor-priest, to a floater platform. She was whisked away among the craggy peaks. A lynk appeared below, its iridescent parabola crowded in by the shanty shacks of a human settlement. Scars from a recent zōtl raid scored the nearby mountain slopes, and Gai saw the remains of shattered needlecraft and ramstat flyers. Several flyers were grouped near the lynk.

The Saor-priest, who was piloting the floater platform, got clearance from the settlement to land and settled down near the lynk. Immediately, the floater was circled by people with drawn knives and pistols. Though the Saor-priests were tolerated on Sakai, they were not trusted. Rumors of the priests' collusion with the zōtl were rife. The grubs had pulled their hoods over their heads, hiding the zōtl that clasped the back of their skulls, and they waited with heads bowed. The Saor-priest mumbled a greeting to the security force and explained that he was escorting a sick person through the lynk to the Saor temple of Perdur on Mugna, where the proper facilities existed for her recovery.

The guards saw Gai flat on her back, her body immobilized, and they sheathed their weapons. Hoisted between the black-hooded grubs, Gai was carried to the lynk.

"Wait," a young voice called.

The grubs stopped, and the priest put his hand on the pistol under his robe before turning about with an ingratiating smile. A young man, better dressed than the rag-clad security force, walked briskly toward them, a cape flapping at his heels. Two burly guards accompanied him, and as he drew closer, the imperial emblem of Sakai Command became visible at the clasp of his cape.

"Lord Tseng," the priest said, bowing his bald head. "How gracious of you to see us off."

"We do not often get visitors from Mugna on Sakai," the young man said. "I trust your mission here has been successful."

"Yes, indeed, Lord. We have found the priestess whose distress message we received. She is quite ill, and so we must not tarry."

Tseng looked down at Gai, who was held between the two grubs. The moment their eyes touched, Gai knew she was saved. The young lord was feeling her despair with the clarity of klivoth kakta.

"Free this woman," Tseng commanded his guards. "And watch it—these are grubs!"

Knives flashed, and the grubs were cut down even as their hands released Gai to reach for their weapons. Gai struck the ground and heard the sizzling crack of a laserbolt. Paralyzed by the phanes, she could not even move her eyes to see what had happened until the air went suddenly golden and Lod was stooped over her.

"I came the instant I saw what was happening," Lod said, rolling Gai's body over with a touch of vibrant heat. "The zōtl came within a meter of carrying you off to one of their nest worlds. Only that boy saved you." The phanes withered at Lod's touch, and Gai sat up.

The Saor-priest lay crumpled beside the dead grubs, still clutching his pistol, a plasteel throwing-knife embedded in his throat. Lord Tseng lay dead in the arms of his guards, a burnhole over his heart.

Gai tried with all her might to bring Lord Tseng back. Though he was a bred human, she had him buried and lay her plasma shape over his corpse, hoping Genitrix could revive him. But that was futile.

Eventually Gai journeyed to Vala, where the Tryl had left behind a tesseract-wave monitor. The mammoth geodesic structure stood in the open veldt, a likely target for the zōtl, who had leveled all Tryl artifacts but the lynks. The humans had preserved the t-wave monitor by guarding it with their best troops and armaments. Constant patrols kept the hemisphere clear of zōtl lynks, and a series of floater platforms in geosynchronous orbit above the monitor protected it from attackers dropping out of space. The expense was well worth it to them, for the pink-domed wave station could access the tesseract field, and by standing within the tall, dawn-gray emptiness of its interior, one could talk with the dead.

After a tissue sample from the corpse was introduced at the station's analyzer, the dead DNA was used as antennae to tune in to the waveforms they had once released into the t-field. "Forget me," Lord Tseng's wraith voice reported. "A new life carries me."

"Your courageous act has saved Chalco-Doror from the certain dominion of the zōtl," Gai told him, eager to make peace with the human who had spared her unspeakable agony. "I would return you to this life among those who love you—if I could, young lord."

"Forget me. I am away. All life is but the history of grief. Forget me—as I am forgetting you."

A new voice imposed: "Gai—do you remember me? I am the first human to set eyes on you. Years and years ago that was—on Know-Where-to-Go, when the last Tryl died in our presence."

"You are Joao, 164-97's disciple. Yes, of course I remember you. You will be glad to know, you are also remembered among the people. They call you the Carrier of Peace."

"Remembered with scorn by almost everyone—by all who have lost lives and loves to the zōtl. Peace is far more alien than pain."

It was true that the very name Joao had come to mean a fanatic idealist, a dreamer of delusory utopias. By those with the most vengeance in their hearts, he was considered a zōtl collaborator for preaching nonviolence. "Why do you call to me, Joao?"

"A prophecy, Gai. I have a prophecy for you now that you have fulfilled 164-97's oracle. You have made your alliance in blood with my species. Your death under the needles of the zōtl is less certain now. From here I see thousands of years of war still ahead. You must send Lod into the Overworld. Send Lod to search for the O'ode."

"Which lynk should he enter?"

"The Overworld touches all lynks. You know that, Gai."

"But the Overworld is infinite. Where will Lod find the O'ode?"

"I have said nothing about finding the O'ode—only searching for it. Now that you have found compassion, now that you are of a flesh no different from ours, you are trapped with us in our cage of freedom. Send Lod into the Overworld. Choice meets chance there."

Gai called after Joao, wanting him to elucidate. The grainy darkness remained silent. For several days, Gai tried in vain to find him, but he had died five hundred and thirty-seven years earlier—and the survivalists who had killed him had been careful to leave no traces.

Echoes in the Time-Well

Lod, for all his preoccupation with maintaining the gravity amp, was well aware of the horrors of the zōtl. One of his most frequently recurring memory clips was of a human on klivoth kakta who had been pithed by a zōtl. By chance, Lod had encountered her on a palm-clacking beach on Ioli shortly after the zōtl had seized her. He had thought he might be able to save the human, and used his plasma shape to grab the zōtl and burn it free. It withered in his grasp, its feed tube sliding out of the puncture wound chrismed with brain fluid. The human died in his arms, but not before he had telepathically experienced what the klivoth kakta had shown her of the zōtl mind. For an instant, Lod had felt what it was like to be a zōtl—

the adroitness of the prehensile pincer-clusters on four of
its eight legs; its leg muscles delicately tuned as fingers; its
swivel-jointed gossamer wings twitching with the power
to fly; its richly convoluted brain, sparking with the bio-
chemical programs fed to it earlier by its female.

Lod had not realized until then that all the small flying
zōtl were male. The females remained on the nest-worlds
and exuded not only eggs but also an ichor the males
sipped that contained molecular programming, which inspired their behavior in everything from feeding and sex
to mathematical calculations and engineering designs. The
females, who were bulky and immobile eggsacks, did most
of the complex thinking; the males did all of the manipula-
tive work, following the programs in the ichor they ate.
But knowing this and feeling it were terrifyingly different
for Lod. He still flinched to recall the chittering sensations
throughout his body as the female code-chemicals urged
him to find fresh food for the eggs.

So when Gai brought Lod to a Tryl lynk on Dreux and
ordered him to enter the Overworld, where the zōtl were
certainly waiting in ambush, he was stricken with terror.
What had befallen Saor could easily happen to him—and
worse, for if the zōtl immobilized his plasma body with the
phanes, they could carry him off to Galgul and use their
technology to inflict pain for aeons to come. He begged
Gai to reconsider.

But Gai was adamant. She understood what Joao had
meant when he had said that now she was trapped with
humans in their cage of freedom. Choice and chance
mated noisily in the future, and the outcome of anything
was uncertain. Even with Ned's timeshadow to follow,
time was a maze. Only timeloose entities, like the dead in
the tesseract-field, could discern the true probabilities of
worldlines—and even they could not communicate anything with certainty, for the communication itself changed
everything. Gai was free to choose to keep Lod in Chalco-
Doror or to send him forth into the Overworld. But the
future shaped itself differently around each choice. The
more she knew, the less freedom she had. Like every
timebound being, she was caged by levels of clarity.

What complicated her decision was that, through her
own lynk system, she had felt Ned O'Tennis' timeshadow

leave Dreux and appear on Ioli. She had to leave at once to keep her own timeline near his, and she had no time to patiently assuage Lod's fear of the zōtl. Since she was determined to heed Joao's prescient command, she overrode all of the machine mind's objections. Lod suppressed his memory clips of the zōtl and mustered his courage.

At about this time, the humans had discovered on Dreux the largest of the Tryl lynks. Hidden by the scarp of a cordillera near the planet's south pole, a lynk parabola over a hundred meters tall was embedded in the rockface. Its tip had been exposed only after centuries of wind erosion. By the time that Gai and Lod arrived, the humans had excavated most of the lynk and had discovered the massive tunnel that led directly to the lynklane.

Over the centuries, Lod and Saor, whose physical bodies were the two suns of Chalco-Doror and whose minds could take shape on any world, had been both revered and reviled by the humans as gods, demons, robots, and aliens. Most people were superstitious, and when the machine minds appeared to them in their plasma shapes, the humans were awed. Some, who had lived in more enlightened times on Earth, were as astonished but less willing to accept a supernatural explanation for the dazzling Lod and the shadowy Saor. But during the Age of Knives, such rational people were rare. The clans and tribes, composed of humans from every period of the human epoch on Earth as well as the many who had lived only in Chalco-Doror, were faithful to their religious instincts and believed the machine intelligences were deities. Saor took advantage of this misperception to call himself the Face of Night and to inspire his priests with missionary fervor. Using his ability to project thoughts into the minds of these small creatures in their cold reality, Saor had won a large following. Gai and Lod were as straightforward with the humans as they were in their mission, and presented themselves only as what they were—warriors from another world.

Lod hardly felt like a warrior when confronted with the necessity of entering the Overworld. He paused before the mammoth opening on Dreux and the iridescent arch above it, both, for all their size, dwarfed by the red mountain wall and the surrounding expanses of salt-white desert. He knew that the parametrics of opening a lynk's internal space-time system required these proportions, but he was still intimidated. He looked up at his Form blazing toward noon. His Form, of course, would stay behind. It was the ship's booster, engineered to provide light and warmth and programmed to manage the gravity amp in his absence. It did not need him to function, so long as nothing unusual occurred. Nevertheless, Gai planned to occupy Lod's Form with her plasma body while he was gone, entering through her own internal lynk to be certain that nothing interfered with the precision of the planets' orbits.

A squad of twelve battle-proven troopers volunteered to accompany Lod. Among them were Laudens, the klivoth keeper, a brawny yellow-bearded man whose courage had been thoroughly tested as a fighter pilot; and Seyna, a snaky distort with dislocatable limbs for crawling through the tightest openings. Gai orated encouragement and promised that these explorers would never be forgotten by history, which turned out to be true, though not for helping Lod. Shortly after entering the lynk, which appeared to be nothing more than a paved boulevard into the mountain, Lod and his team were separated.

Earlier explorers had demonstrated that this lynk connected to more than one point in Chalco-Doror; this was unique among all the previously discovered lynks, which connected only two points. A few strides through the lynk, and Lod and his squad were standing on the threshold of a dozen worlds. Like multiple viewscreens, twelve separate tunnels of light confronted them, each tunnel with its own vista: icy Mugna, wave-lapping Ioli, jungled Ylem, the bat-twitching sky of Nabu—

The plan was to step sideways off the lynklane. That would place them in the Overworld. But before they could do that, the air flurried with shrieking black blurs and flashes of laserlight. Freeflying zōtl streamed from the lynk-opening of Cendre. Lod startled and leaped sideways. Immediately, the lynklane vanished, and he found himself in a gray, quiet zone—the Overworld.

Meanwhile, the humans, who had remained on the lynklane to fight the zōtl, defeated their enemy. The dead and wounded humans were taken back to Dreux, and the others went on, stepping sideways off the lynklane and into the Overworld. They never found Lod again, and their wanderings, which took them across Chalco-Doror on a decade-long series of adventures among zōtls and distorts, became legend.

Among the klivoth keeper Laudens' first encounters after losing the others was a sighting of the Beppunauts. The three wanderers that he saw in the mirage-depths of the Overworld's sky meant nothing to him, and he ignored them. They were just shades. But Spooner Yegg recognized the burly navigator with the wide beard, his glamour pack full of kakta and his eyes shining with telempathic clarity.

"Laudens!" Spooner shouted into the lake. From his perspective, the klivoth keeper seemed to be walking through a wooded terrain under the water.

Chan-ti Beppu, who had often sat by crystal-water ponds in the Overworld and watched animals and people come and go in their depths, laughed. "He can't hear you. He may not even be able to see you. He's on another level."

"Do you know who that is?" Spooner asked.

"Not so loud." Chan-ti glanced anxiously over her shoulder, at the desert-garden surroundings. Sandy corridors and rocky fields rambled among dense, miasmal everglades. A rhomb of aluminum-white light burned in the sky ahead of them—the Overworld shadow of the sun, Lod; while behind them the sky was black, with only a few anonymous glints of starlight. "You'll have the screamers on us."

"That's Laudens, the klivoth keeper," Spooner stated excitedly. "I'm sure of it. He was famous in the schoolbooks of my childhood. We've come a long way down the time-well to be seeing him, I say."

Moku the Beast, who was leading, paused at the sound of his friend's voice. He left the sandy path to amble in a flowery meadow under a wall of pea-vines spangled with blossoms. "Moku!" Chan-ti called. "Come on." She waved the finder at the Beast. "We have a long way to go—and we just started this leg."

"Hush yourself," Spooner said. "What about the screamers?"

"At least a screamer would get Moku off his tocks."

"Calm yourself. Have some glamour. Let's toast Laudens, who led his fellow heroes through zōtl nests and distort kingdoms back to their home."

"No more of that stuff for me," Chan-ti said. "I'm still wincing from feeling those zōtl hooks under my skin."

"Don't look so deep into the scary things—zōtl, screamers, corpses. Then you'll be all right."

Bright flakes of music glittered from Moku's flute.

"I'll trust you and Moku to lead me home," she said. "But first we've got to find Ned."

"We will." Spooner sat on a flat boulder by the lakeside and cut a small smile of kakta from an already shriveled head.

"Not if we sit around." Chan-ti kicked a clump of weed. "We've had twenty-three sleep stops since we left Ras Mentis."

"You are precise."

"I'm just eager to find him. The longer he's alone this far from our time, the greater the chance he'll always be timeloose."

"You know a lot about the Overworld."

"I'm Foke."

"No you're not."

"They reared me. When we sojourned, they let me watch the leaders as though I were one of their children. I know about the Overworld."

Spooner dabbed the kakta juice from his lips with a wad of cotton grass. "I'm just a city thief. I never thought of the Overworld as anything but the nightmare behind the joke of the world. Since I was a boy, I stole for laughs. Petty crimes became more daring burglaries as I developed my craft. But I never got serious about it. Never did a job for anything but laughs. Until I walked the Overworld."

Chan-ti sat on her pack. "When was that?"

"After I learned to be serious by falling in love. I was quite old by then and had thought myself immune. That was my blunder. I fell in love. I fell a long way. I was married and happily so, my wife pregnant—and my work had become very serious, indeed. I was about to be apprehended. Usually at such precarious times, I would disappear, go to another city. But with my wife big with child, I could not escape. I thought flight into the Overworld would be easier than trying to disguise an expectant woman and fleeing with her to another city. Can you imagine how naive I was then?

"What city were you escaping?"

"Does that matter now? I took my wife through a Tryl lynk sideways into the Overworld. I'd read about it. I'd seen clips. I thought we could find our way to another city. Instead, the zōtl found us. It was pathetic. We were in a null field."

"You tried to cross a null field?" Chan-ti shook her head ruefully. Null fields were empty plains in the Overworld, void of timelines or anywhere to hide. "No wonder the zōtl found you. You'd gone too high. How did you escape?"

Spooner patted his sack of jewels. "I had another like this one, rigged to explode if tampered with. When the black cloud of spiders swarmed over us, I detonated it. I thought it would kill us and most of them. But they came on us faster than I thought. The pack was ripped away from me. When it exploded, the blast hurled us across the null field and into a lynklane. We were both severely wounded. My wife died in the forest where we were hurled. But our child lived. I heard it screaming. Through the trees, I saw others approaching. Then the zōtl swooped down and carried me off. But the others I saw among the trees were armed, and they drove away most of the spiders. Enough of the swarm remained to hoist me into the treetops, where I saw the forest people lift the child. She was a girl— and I knew by the way they held her that she would be safe."

Through the klivoth kakta, Spooner felt Chan-ti Beppu's recognition.

"You're my father," she said in a hush.

"Yes." He nodded matter-of-factly. "I struggled and the zōtl dropped me. I fled, ran wildly, spraying blood. As chance would have it, I stumbled through a lynk. It was seventeen years before I found my way back."

"*You* are my father." Chan-ti felt breathless, numb at the core of her chest. "Why didn't you tell me in the Eyelands?"

"I intended to, but I wanted to see you as you were among the Foke. I wanted to know you first. Then, Ned arrived. And the Aesirai's war. This is the first quiet time that seemed right to me since we entered the Overworld. I've had to make my own peace with your mother's ghost first. Have I shocked you?"

"Yes. I'm not sure what I feel."

"Not much, I'd think. I'm still little more than a stranger, with little to distinguish me from the genetic ferment throughout Chalco-Doror."

"Who was my mother?"

"A woman from Earth. A tall, elegant woman. She had grand stories to tell of the first world. She was from a land named Burma in an age she called the twenty-first century. She had been some kind of agricultural planner and was always marveling at the great and strange profusion of plants in our worlds. In this life, she had been a vassal in an Aesirai household. I met her while fleecing her master's house."

Chan-ti's face looked glazed. "I never imagined it like this."

"I'm sorry. This is my last best chance to tell you."

"What do you mean?"

His smile was shy or sly or both. "After I lost your mother, I devoted myself to learning about the Overworld, in every way I could, because I knew you were somewhere in here and I wanted to find you. Very few people in the cities know anything about the Overworld. I wound up lynk-wandering, supporting myself with my craft, and finding out about the Overworld firsthand. I befriended voors. For a while I even joined the Ordo Vala and learned about *ku,* the emptiness that carries our bodies of light. But they found out about my past, and I had to flee. One has to travel pretty deep into the Overworld to get away from the Ordo Vala. I'm surprised we haven't met any of those zealots out here ourselves." He cut another wedge of kakta. "The voors taught me about the glamour. That's what they call it."

"You really wandered with voors? I thought they tranced people and used them in grotesque ways for their rites."

"Sometimes. The turtlehead voors are the worst. They're malevolent as distorts. Bestial. But voors in human bodies are not unlike us, only haunted by their ancestral memories. They're homesick for their bodies of light." He handed her the kakta. "Take it."

"No. Certainly not now, after all this."

"Because of all this." He insisted until she took the wedge. "Without glamour, you wander the Overworld blind. Eat it and take a look where you are. When you see, you'll understand why this was my last best chance to tell you who I am."

"Look, Spooner—" His name caught. "Look, just tell me."

He shrugged his eyebrows. "Fine. I will, then. Listen to Moku."

The Beast's wavery music was childlike in its simplicity and loveliness.

"That is the song he was playing when you and Ned were together. Ned's nearby. The Beast senses him. You would, too, if you ate the kakta."

She shook her head. The memory of the kakta's intensity mixed poorly with the shock of learning that Spooner was her father. She could not bear to face him in the grip of that boundless drug, no separation between them at all—not yet, not until she had fit herself more securely into this new truth.

She looked to the gray giant sitting among the flowers under the vertical face of the great hanging vines. "How does Moku know?"

"I can't say. He's a strange one. But I recognized his music right away. It's the same music the voors play. They explained once to me that all music is a special kind of noise. They called it fractal, not quite whole. They said their music mimed the fractal structure of the Overworld, where every small piece mirrors the shape of a larger piece. They use it as a map. I think Moku plays that kind of music."

Chan-ti handed back the wedge of kakta. "I can't. Not now. I have to feel this one through." She stood up and traipsed across the path to a blue grove of tangled trees, where she knelt and watched coins of light flickering in a stream.

Spooner Yegg sighed and cleaned his knife in the grass. He was glad he had waited to tell her; he only wished he could have waited longer. He had been enjoying watching her without her knowing who he really was. She reminded him, more than he had expected, of her mother; not so much in her looks, though she was tall and almond-eyed, but in her small gestures, her way of hooking her hair with her thumb, of tilting her head to the side when she laughed. Yet she obviously was Foke. She built and handled fire with ease, drank water from her hands, knew the succulent plants and ate them with gusto. He was surprised and somewhat relieved that she could not read lynklane sign. She was not much of a tracker and relied too heavily on her finder. Which was good—or else she would see the lynklane sign that was all around them now, the striations of windblown sand beneath low-lying leafblades, the glisteny snailpaths along the riprap of stones, all so much clearer in the spectral light of kakta.

All the beings that entered the Overworld could find their own timelines impressed in the landscape, if they knew how to look. The voors had taught him. In the Overworld, random patterns—such as moss patches, dewdrop displays, cracks in a rock—reflected the timelines of all the objects in the timebound worlds of Chalco-Doror. Chaos in the Overworld was a window into the causal destinies of everything and everybody. Among the dead and scattered leaves blowing across the sandy trail, he recognized his daughter's lifeline and Moku's curling about his. And he had seen before and saw again now that her timeline continued and his and Moku's ended.

Death was like young rain for Spooner, soothing, promising, beautiful in its own way. He was not afraid to die. The ailments of his age almost made the end seem a relief: His prostate pressured him continually to urinate and then permitted only drops; the scars of the twenty-year-old wounds from the blast that had killed his wife nagged him with dull throbs and unexpected needlings; and, worse of all, his joints ached so that his spry, surreptitious craft was virtually impossible for him now. He was happy to be shucking this form—and soon, too, if the sign of his timeline were to be trusted, which it was, for it simply reflected what is.

At least the Tryl had kept their promise. For years he had been haunted by the memory of his wife's death and their child left with strangers in the Overworld. For years he had searched for her. Not until he befriended the voors did he find his chance. They used their trances and voorish talismans to contact the ghosts of lizard angels. The Tryl agreed to help—but only on the condition that Spooner obey all their signs in the Overworld. He was old, and that was his only chance to find his daughter. He agreed, and through the voors' trances he learned of the Eyelands and how to reach them. Since then, he had simply followed his instincts. Only recently had the Tryl appeared at the periphery of his glamourous sight. They were coming to collect their promise.

Spooner had no idea what the lizard angels wanted with his daughter. He cared but saw by the brevity of his own timeline patterned in the landscape all around him that his caring did not matter. He would be dead soon. Only one more matter needed to be clarified with his girl. He waited awhile for her to get used to the idea of who he was; then, he ambled over to where she sat and eased his bruised bones beside her.

"Still not sure what you're feeling?" he asked.

"No." She passed him a quiet smile and put her hand on his. "Thank you for coming back for me. I always wondered who you were. I never thought I'd really find out."

"Are you disappointed?"

"With a father brave enough to walk the Overworld to find me? How could I be disappointed?" She hugged him.

The bone-aches binding Spooner in time eased a little with the joy he felt at that moment. "There is a thing I must ask you," he said as they unclasped. "Do you know about the bodies of light?"

"Only what the Foke taught me—that all life is an expression of light and that consciousness is a special form of light."

"Yes. Consciousness is a lightform like no other. When we die, our light continues in its own reality, outside the limits of time. I don't understand how. Your mother did, though. When her body was re-created, she told me everything. I've forgotten most of it. But I remember, she tried to teach me. I was a miserable student. It was hard enough for me to grasp the fact that these worlds were made by inhuman powers for an inhuman purpose. As I've gotten older, I've come to understand this has always been so, even in her time. Creation is impersonal. We must make the distinctions and choose our values. No one is watching. After your mother died, I was alone with my grief. It became important for me to remember that only her body had died—as it had before on Earth. Her consciousness lives as light—somewhere."

"Right here, Father," Chan-ti said with conviction. "The bodies of light are all around us. Nappy's always talking about that. He became intent on that knowledge, too, when his Velma died."

"Yes, it takes absence to fill in our understanding. When you find your Ned, you must tell him about the bodies of light." He held up the wedge of kakta he had cut earlier. "And if you're going to find him, you'd best use this."

Chan-ti bit into the kakta and received its bright juice with a wince. The rainbow ring opened before her, and the surface of everything became flame-lit. Star-color shadows with vaguely human shapes stood on the sand path.

"They've been following us since Ras Mentis," Spooner said.

They were Tryl. Chan-ti could just distinguish their reptilian features in their hazy outlines. "Why didn't you tell me?"

"No reason until they stopped and Moku started playing that voorish tune."

Moku's music oxidized in the air before her, smoldering into fire's breath, shifting transparencies, spindrift shadows. The Tryl ghosts drifted toward the visible music. They pointed to an eddy of energy in the air, a whirlpool diapason. Then they pointed in unison down a sandy path that curled obscurely among thin, felted trees.

The music stopped—and the Tryl were gone. In the rainbow ring, vegetation buzzed under Lod's sliding light, small creatures lustered in their willfulness, packing her body with their intense reality. She narrowed her gaze and diminished the telempathy enough to see things from inside herself again. Spooner had left her side. He and Moku had picked up their packs and started down the path. She followed and took out her finder. Its microlights strobed in a circle.

"Where are we going?" she asked.

"You saw the lizard angels," Spooner answered. "Without them, we would have missed this slender path."

They hiked a long while, past disconsolate dunes of charred briar and along the green sand shores of a fathomless lake with water clear as air. Along the way, Chan-ti asked Spooner why he had become a thief.

"I told you already: for a laugh. My father was an actuarial officer in an insurance company—very serious man. Our blood needed a laugh after that, so I followed my laughter—good times, easy pickings—and that led me to my craft. No more to it than that, kid."

At one point, predatory shadows flitted among the briar tangles, and roars pummeled them. When Chan-ti turned her kakta sight on them, she felt turbid hunger and an erotic eagerness to rip flesh. Moku bellowed back. But the roaring mounted, until Spooner fired several rounds at the slinky silhouettes. The shadows dispersed, and the wanderers hurried along.

As Lod's rhomb settled into the palm crowns, the Beppunauts came to a gravel pit under the silver trajectory of a lynk. In the bottom of the pit, at the lynk's threshold, a fluted column lay among busted statuary. "It's the same pale gray diorite we saw on Ras Mentis," Spooner noted.

"The Tryl temple," Chan-ti said in a small breath.

"We never left there," Spooner understood. "The whirlpool path the Tryl showed us—that's our lynklane. This is the only way out—unless you want to go back and face those distorts at night."

The finder pointed into the lynk. "Ned's in there." Chan-ti started down the slope, and Spooner stopped her with a warning touch.

"The lizard angels are far from their time," he said, while scanning among the rainbow curves of his telempathy for threats. "Why would they be here with us?"

"This is their temple. We entered it during the Tryl Age. Perhaps they escort anyone intrepid enough to visit them in their time."

"Or maybe they are here to witness. Perhaps we have found our way to them."

"I'll go through the lynk first this time."

"No. This time, we go together." Spooner took Chan-ti's

hand. She tucked away her finder and with her free hand
clutched Moku's claw. They skidded down the gravel
declivity, past the misery of shattered temple stones, and
strode together through the Tryl lynk.

On a raffish island of dune thistle and thorny palms in
the monsoon latitudes of Ioli, a strohlkraft glided out of a
seacave and splashed across the shallows of a green lagoon.
It came to a stop with a soft lurch. Inside the flightpod, Ned
O'Tennis used the ship's dwindling energy to read the
planetary positions. And though Lod's glaring disc rode
high among long-legged clouds, the tracery of planetoids
above the ocean horizon was still visible. After comparing
the planetesimal positions with a calendar, the visor displayed in blue numerics 731 PD.

"We jumped six hundred years on that one." Ned
pointed to the flight deck monitor, where he raised the
graph comparing the strohlkraft's three timejumps. "I
don't see any scalar relationships . . ."

His voice trailed off as the graph broke into static. The
snowy motes congealed into the outline of a human face, a
curly-haired, seraphic face that resembled the fallen statue
they had seen in the ruins on Ras Mentis. Pahang was
certain of it. "Temple countenance!" he shouted and swiv-
eled away in his sling.

"I am the Carrier of Peace," a static-shriveled voice said.
"I am come to tell you—" The image bloated. "I am
come—" The screen blanked out.

Pahang screamed. Standing at the hatch beside him, an
arm's reach away, a wraith vapored. The bleached features
of the Carrier of Peace shadowed the ghost's head. "Come
to the lynk— Come speak with Joao."

The ghost bled away, its voice distending to a moan.

Ned unslung from his harness and snatched a laserbolt
pistol. Through the blackglass bubble at the back of the
flightpod, he could see the seacave from where they had
glided. A blurred cloudshape waved to him from the dark
mouth. "I'm going out," Ned told the Malay. "That may be
Gai or one of her messengers."

"Better you stay, Hawk." Pahang put on his blackgloss
helmet. "Maybe this is some distort trick. Stay."

"No." Ned holstered the pistol in the flightsuit's breast

sheath. "That's the lynk we came through. It belongs to the Rimstalker. I'd better go see what it is."

"It's a ghost." Pahang gave an astounded moan. "He cannot come all the way."

Ned lifted the starboard wing hatch, admitting a honey breeze, and warned, "Don't touch anything." He strode purposely across the firm sand at the sea's margin until he was close enough to call, "Gai?"

The shade beckoned him nearer. He unsheathed his pistol and climbed the sandscarp to the lip of the cave. As he approached, the ghost condensed to a pastel image of a black-tressed, sloe-eyed youth. "I salute your courage in coming, Ned O'Tennis," he said in a voice fleecy with small echoes. "I am the Carrier of Peace, Joao. I have employed all my wiles and intent to intersect with your timeline. I cannot speak long. Listen well. Chan-ti Beppu roams the Overworld searching for you. The sender chip she gave you guides her."

Ned jolted at the sound of Chan-ti's name. She had been living beneath the most precious stone of his heart since he had left her and gone to be swept away in N'ym's doom. Under Squat's tyranny, she had been his undefiled life, his secret verge away from the slime and the remorseless exhaustion. Since escaping, he had not dared hope to hold her again. Far easier to dream of saving N'ym, huge in its gold-domed dignity, than of finding his way back to her slight body. Now hearing that she was coming for him, he was stunned.

"To find her," Joao said, "you must enter the Tryl lynk on the island's south shore. Go there now, before Gai comes for you."

"I can't do that. I promised the Rimstalker I would enter only her lynks."

Joao's vaporous face darkened. "You must get away from Gai. She is using you to throw off her bondage. But the freedom she gains constrains you, and dangerously. If you stay with her, you will never see Chan-ti Beppu again."

"Who are you?"

"I am Joao, last of the Tryl disciples. I was human once. I am now a body of light, who can meet you only here in the magravity field of Gai's lynk, only now, this once among the boiling vectors of time."

"How do I know you're not a distort?"

"Believe what you will." Joao faded in and out. "We are each of us caged in our freedom. Either you stay and serve the Rimstalker or you go and serve a higher being."

"What being is that?"

"Love. You forgot how to love when your mother died in spite of your prayers. The emptiness that opened in you after that would have been more than large enough to hold your whole life. But then you met Chan-ti—and in days, the years of emptiness filled with heavy evidences of something more, something creative in you that had been missing, something that could make: Make use. Make time. Make believe."

Ned was flustered. "You are a distort." He backed away.

"I know about you, about everything that has happened in time, for it is all here in the fields of light. Everyone who has lived is here. But we are whole, all of us that have become light. I cannot stay apart much longer."

"Why do you tell me this?"

"I am the Carrier of Peace. I have known the Tryl. It is they who have rewarded me with this chance to touch the crux of chance here, now, with you. The peace I offer is freedom. Light is the ultimate freedom. The path of light leads to the end of these worlds, the end of suffering, and the return of all the forms to their images. You can help by leaving Gai to her fate and accepting your own."

"But I owe the Rimstalker. She saved me from Squat."

"Your loyalty is misplaced. It is Gai who now owes you. For six hundred and sixteen years, she has been following your timeshadow among the worlds, while you traversed her lynk. Without you, she would have succumbed to the violent deceptions of Chalco-Doror long ago. You must release her to her destiny or you will forsake your own." Joao looked ill. "I can say no more."

"Wait. Give me some sign, something so I can trust you."

"I am gone—" The ghost bleared away to a thin voice: "Freedom cannot be escaped. You must choose."

Ned slumped back to the strohlkraft, his brain throbbing witlessly. Pahang did not like the shadow on Hawk's brow and waded into the lagoon to fish with a hook and line he had devised from raffia fiber and a seashell. The Malay caught three fish, brown and thick as wrists, and built a driftwood fire. By the time he had cleaned and braised the fish, Hawk's visage had cleared.

"The ghost has told me we have paid our debt to Gai," Ned said after they had nimbly eaten the bony, steaming fish. He told Pahang what Joao had told him. "The more I think about it, the more I feel the ghost is right. What do you think, Pahang? The ramstat cells will be ready to power us in another hour. If Gai isn't here by then, shall we go?"

"The gods are the worst enemies."

"Gai is no god."

Pahang shook his head. "Even Squat was a god."

"On his beach, yes, he was."

"How big is Gai's beach? Hawk, these are her worlds."

"So we stay."

"And lose the blessing of our ancestors?" Pahang's vivid features tightened. "No. We are men, not gods. Better to have the gods as enemies than lose our place among the ancestors. We must go. But we must remember, the Rimstalker will be displeased. We will have a powerful enemy."

"You're a brave one."

"No, Hawk, I am not brave. I am afraid. I have been afraid since you told me that the Rimstalker spoke with you through the kakta. Whenever the gods speak with men, there is woe. Let us escape the Rimstalker, if we can, and find our way to our own people."

The sky was custard with sunset when the strohlkraft left the lagoon and soared over the serrated peaks. At the far side of the island, they had no trouble finding the Tryl lynk. Its parabola bent over a valley gorge, hued with twilight. On the sea's horizon, needlecraft flicked like falling stars. But the strohlkraft's shadowary hull, in a time two thousand years before it was invented, carried them undetected through the lynk.

Lod knew about the Overworld from his programming but was still unready for the strange reality of this metageometric domain. When he became separated from the other lynk wanderers that Gai had sent with him, he was tempted to return at once to Dreux. All that would involve for him was a step backward, for he had been fitted with a homing device of Tryl construction. Anywhere in the Overworld, no matter how far he wandered, he could return to his starting point by taking one backward step—so long as he had not previously turned left. Left turns for him were strictly forbidden, for they broke the temporal chirality of the homing device and would make a return to the starting timeline impossible. "Right is right," Lod repeated his own lynk dictum to himself, "left is bereft." To reach any point to the left, he had to turn fully around from the right.

Lod edged forward, straining to see anything in the empty grayness. He was in what lynk wanderers called a null field, where other timelines appeared as radiant images in the grayness. For now, the lynklanes were so distant they looked like tangles of colored thread far above and below him. The grayness itself was the Overworld's reflection of the vacuum in which everything was suspended. The ground beneath him was actually the earth of the lynk he had stepped through infinitely extended, like the air he was breathing, or the gravitational force that held him upright. Every step he took projected the world he had come from. He was creating his own timeline through the void. But he had been warned about null fields. His timeline would be apparent in the gray emptiness, easily spotted by the zōtl in other lynklanes. He had to get out of the null field quickly.

High above, new timelines appeared as he walked, kaleidoscopic shafts of color and motion. They were on a level he could not reach easily, they were that far away. Gai had forbidden the use of ramstat or any kind of flyer, because it was too easy to accidentally curl left and be lost forever in a parallel universe, where the homing device would be ineffective.

Lod kept walking, looking for a timeline he could enter. None were nearby, and those that his telescopic sight singled out looked nothing like the memory-clips of Rataros that the Rimstalker had given him. Most of the tunnels of windy light that loomed out of the grayness as he wandered were windows into places in Chalco-Doror, which is what he expected. Gai had said that one had to travel very far indeed to find the timelines of nonlocal worlds. She did not expect him to locate the O'ode, only to fulfill Joao's prophecy.

Lod stopped before several timelines and gazed in at the landscapes. None seemed populated and none had a nearby lynk for him to enter even if he had wanted to. They were just large, transparent walls that flooded light into the null field, exposing vistas from the local worlds. Gai had said that these infinite tunnels of light were the timelike geodesics of the lynk, echoes in the time-well of the universe that radiated randomly through the Overworld. Lod followed alongside one of them a long way to satisfy himself that the echo of images did indeed go on into the grayness indefinitely. Perhaps somewhere along its length was a lynk by which he could enter, and he saw now the necessity of a lynk-compass for finding one's way between the lynklanes. But only a few lynk-compasses had survived the loss of the Tryl, and Gai had not given him one since he was not in fact going anywhere.

Lod wondered if he had journeyed far enough through the dimly lit zone to fulfill Joao's prophecy. He was about to step backward when he saw a human figure to his left. He curled to the right until he had come around and could face the approaching person and see that she was a young blond woman, small-boned and round-faced, with a solitude in her eyes that seemed useless for a human. She hailed him, and he waited for her to approach.

She stopped a wary distance away, obviously intimidated by his flamewoven appearance. He toned down the radiance of his plasma body and projected the magnetic pattern of his story into her brain. She straightened when she felt the frosty magnetism tingling her scalp. But the next instant, as she comprehended what was happening, she sagged with relief and came closer.

Lod read the electromagnetic pattern of her brain and was so astounded that he had to read the pattern twice more to be certain of its veracity. The woman's name was Reena Patai*—and she was from Earth, the first world, more than seven billion years in the past. Lod could barely comprehend how she had arrived in the Overworld. Ap-

---

* Reena's earth history is detailed in the third volume of the Radix Tetrad, *Arc of the Dream*.

parently, she had been left here by a truly alien being, an
entity she called Inside-Out, who originated in a reality she
thought of as 5-space, which was tinier even than the gravity shell of the range. The implications dizzied Lod—and
he saw that the implications of his story had equally startled her.

"I saw your glow from a great distance," Reena said, her
voice echoing. She had been afraid she had gone mad
again, wandering the null field where Inside-Out had left
her. She had been afraid. Nothing was familiar. But now,
with Lod's knowledge glittering in her brain, she *felt* the
limitless, periodic nature of reality. Avignon, Honolulu, the
Moon and the Sun, all the people she had never met and
the few that were luminous in her memory, all gone. The
void she had felt widening in her was their absence. And in
that emptiness glittered Lod's knowledge: the range, the
Rimstalker Gai, Saor, zōtl—on and on, another floor of
reality, billions of years after everything she knew had
become dust. Another reality. Another reflection in the
hall of mirrors . . . How effortless it was, embracing the
infinite—"I thought you were another lynklane in the null
field," she said to Lod. A smile tremored on her pale face.
She wondered why she was not hysterical or at least numb,
realized in the quiet delirium of her vast new understanding that her emotions, like her thoughts, were objective
things to the machine fire that had found her, objects to be
manipulated. "For all I've been through, I never expected
to see the likes of you. You look like sunlight shaped into a
human."

"This is just my plasma shape," Lod began to explain.
"My gel body. I can look . . ."

"Like anything. I know. The telepathic information you
gave me is as clear as my own memories. You're a machine."

"A machine *intelligence*, to be precise."

"You must know all about me."

"I can hardly believe what I've read in your electromagnetic memory, Reena Patai. You are an original human.
But where is the 5-space being that brought you here?"

"You don't know because I don't. My last memory of
Inside-Out is of him removing me from Earth, where I was
too damaged to live. My brain was congenitally mal-

formed. But Inside-Out fixed that—I think, though I'm feeling strange, really empty—" The solitary light in her green, lemur eyes steepened. "I guess the alien got home."

"Come with me, Reena Patai. The new Earth I've told you about telepathically is one step behind me. Come. Take my hand. Don't worry, it won't burn you."

Reena took the fiery hand, and it felt warm and soft as just-baked bread. Lod stepped backward, and she had to squint her eyes against the brightness. They were standing hand-in-hand in the cavemouth before the giant lynk on Dreux. Weird, humanoid sculptures of glass shot with bright bubbles and opal striations guarded the entry to the lynk, and she vaguely knew from Lod's prior input that these were Tryl sculptures.

As Reena's eyes adjusted to the harsh light of Dreux, she saw the others—men and women of every race in sandy, bedraggled garments: white cuirasses, dented and scratched, worn over baggy shirts and trousers; frayed burnooses with the sigil of an open hand embroidered above their hearts, and cracked wing-shoulder vests of leather. Some wore goggles, others mouth-scarves; everyone wore scruffy, ankleslung boots. They looked like a ragged motorcycle gang from a grim future. And then she remembered that this was her future, her far future—and she laughed.

Her laugh broke the apprehensions of the others, and they crowded in, fingering Reena's twentieth-century clothing and jabbering at her in languages she did not understand. She looked to Lod for help, but the machine intelligence was gone. The moment he had returned from the Overworld, input from his Form informed him that he had been gone from Chalco-Doror the equivalent of seventy-eight years—and Gai had had to oversee his Form that whole time.

Gai was greatly relieved by Lod's return and glad to surrender her post inside Lod's Form. After she had sent Lod into the Overworld, she had flown to Ioli to meet Ned O'Tennis. But the Aesirai was gone. In the lynk-echoes of the seacave where he had come through, she felt what had happened. The Tryl were having their revenge on her for having suffered them to take bodies. They had used Joao to deprive her of Ned O'Tennis. Without his timeshadow, she would have to feel her way to the future on her own.

That frightful task had accompanied Gai into Lod's
Form and made her stay there all the more difficult, for
now there was no assurance she would succeed. Her grave
doubts of Lod's return, as well as the constant effort to be
certain that the planets moved precisely in their orbits,
had thoroughly exhausted her. Only when she heard about
Reena Patai did she revive slightly. She insisted on meeting this first and probably only individual to reach Chalco-
Doror directly from the original Earth.

For that to be possible, without waiting hundreds of
years for her plasma shape to regain its strength, a special
apparatus had to be constructed by the technical staff at
the Dreux lynk. That took almost two years, and by then
Reena had begun to acculturate herself to the New Earth,
as she called Chalco-Doror. The day that the tech staff
introduced her to the bulky, man-high vacuum tube that
contained Gai's enfeebled plasma shape, Reena wore the
open-hand burnoose of Dreux's kakta clan. She had used
the klivoth kakta to facilitate her assimilation into this mot-
ley and violent society. The experience reminded her of
schizophrenic episodes she had endured on Earth before
the alien from 5-space saved her. She heard voices in her
head, felt the sensations of other people, other creatures,
in her flesh. This psychosis, however, truly touched the
objective world—and it could be managed. She adopted
the heavy-lidded gaze of the klivoth trance and admitted
as much of the strange world around her as she could
handle.

She was in the kakta's grasp when she met Gai.

Gai, in her weariness, was glad for that, for it helped her
to mell. She wanted to feel the insides of an aboriginal
human, to feel how they differed from Genitrix's creations.
She reached deftly into the lucidity before her.

Reena Patai unfolded in Gai's consciousness no differently than any human she had known before. But this one
had immediate memories of the source world. By the vigorous light of Sol and nights salted with stars and Luna's
vaporous light, Earth had parsed her days, 7,743 of them in
this human's experience. The last days, indeed, had been
bizarre, occupied by the presence of a 5-space entity
whose real intent and essence were irrecoverable in the
emotional fervor of Reena's brain. But of equal wonder to

Gai was the great majority of mundane days that Reena had lived on Earth. Gai riffled enthusiastically through quotidian remembrances of seasons and weathers.

Meanwhile, through the prismatic sight of the kakta, Reena felt Gai's alienness like a sudden despair, a frightful abruptness. She had to look away.

"For a human to look upon a Rimstalker," Gai's voice crinkled over the speakers at the base of the vacuum-cylinder, "is to stare into the depths within and to feel the nothing from which the whole cosmos has come. My home, the range, is a way station on the infinite plunge toward the cosmic event horizon, the boundary of our reality, beyond which your Inside-Out lives. No human can look that deep without feeling despair, the hopelessness of the whole universe opening into nothing."

"And what do you see when you look into us?" Reena asked.

The tremulous, feeble glow in the vacuum brightened. "I see my hope that I will defeat the enemies of my people and return home."

"Then we see very much the same thing," Reena said, the look in her eyes a green distance. Lod's infusion of information had amplified this young one's intelligence along with her awareness. She spoke with an authority she had never had on Earth and amazed herself—not with the fact of it, for that felt natural—she amazed herself with the incumbent responsibilities of her unique knowing. It was as though all of humanity looked to her for a voice. "You have risen out of our hopelessness to find your hope within us," humanity said to her. "Together we complete each other. Would we exist now without you? Can you continue to exist without us?"

"You are not angry that I have reproduced your world, your people, as bait to lure my enemy?" Gai asked.

"At least that's a reason. People have had to live, suffer, and die for no reason at all before. In my own time on Earth, many suffered in vain so as not to feel they had lived in vain. Now we have a reason—yours."

"And you do not feel used?"

"You seem compassionate. I'm willing to trust in that for now."

"I think we will be friends, you and I."

"That would be good," Reena admitted and smiled, slimly. "If life is a dream, as the most ancient texts of the Old Earth claim, then we should be friends. After all, we're dreaming each other."

Bram Gorlik returned to the Eyelands from his grief sojourn purged of all the rotten feelings of love. He was glad that Chan-ti Beppu had refused his offer of marriage. Had he really desired such a mushroom-pale giantess for a wife?—or, as he had come to see in the wilds, holding his own against chaos, had he not all along simply pitied her? Foremost on his triumphantly serene mind was facing her again, seeing her haughty-boned face and treelimb stature and feeling only cavedark indifference in his chest where before pity had incandesced bright as caring.

In the time that he had been away, the Foke had migrated to a new site deeper in the Eyelands, away from the war. Now they would have to be more vigilant than ever, to protect themselves from the dangers of Saor's Forest. To Gorlik, who had grown up among the aeries of Valdëmiraën, the cavernous gloom of the forest was the most frightful vista in the Overworld. That was why he had sojourned there after Beppu refused him. Only there was he in sufficient jeopardy of death to vent with honor the traumas of humiliation and relief that had wracked his soul when his troll-woman denied him.

Gorlik gave cursory acknowledgment to the amazed Foke who saw him trudge out of the Forest strapped in the blue leather of the hippogriff. Shouts of welcome jumped ahead of him, and he hurried to avoid getting stopped by curious friends. He even ignored the alluring aromas from the mead grotto, though he had not had a well-spiced meal in many weeks. He headed straight for the workshop where the Foke would know where to find Beppu. Magnificent with the freedom he had won for himself on his sojourn, he tossed a casual greeting to Nappy Groff, who almost fell from his bench at the sight of him. "Where's your gangle-shanked daughter, Nappy Groff? I've returned from the Forest of Wounds to laugh in her face."

"Then you will have to laugh very loudly, Gorlik," Nappy said, sadly, "for Chan-ti Beppu wanders the Overworld."

Gorlik stood motionless, lithic with disbelief as the workers yammered to him about weak-eyed Chan-ti's sojourn to win the love of an Aesirai warrior; about N'ym's flight into the black sun, and Chan-ti's lover flung unwittingly into the Overworld; and about Spooner Yegg and Moku the Beast stealing the directional finder to help her quest for Ned O'Tennis to the very ends of time.

When they were done, Gorlik remained motionless, his squat, bigboned shape humming internally with amazement and unexpected anger. He was an ugly man, wide as he was tall, pikejawed and slantbrowed, with an undignified hairline a thumb's width above bristly black eyebrows. His impious eyes crossed, green veins bulged at the bole of his neck, and he howled with the shock of a man whose desperate ignorance had suddenly relented; "Beppu!"

Five men had to restrain Gorlik from returning at once to the Overworld to find the woman he screamed that he loved, while blowing snot and spitting bile. "Calm down, you garbled imitation of a Foke!" Nappy Groff shouted at the thrashing man. When Gorlik, wrung face glossy with spit and mucus, could stand unrestrained, Groff said, "You utter fool—you sojourned to forget her."

"I *did* forget her," Gorlik grumbled, staring hard at the puddle of saliva on the floor. "I forgot her. But I didn't hope never to see her again." In truth, he had assumed she would stay with the Foke and tend the children and elders, and he had taken a vow, secret even from himself until now, never to marry another but to watch and protect her from afar. "I didn't think she would leave us."

"She is *gone,*" Nappy said, bitterly. "And no one among the careful Foke will risk their fragile lives in the Overworld to help me find her." Face lit like a lantern, he stared deep into Gorlik's tiny, black, and wrinkled eyes. "You are the best tracker among us, Bram Gorlik. Once you loved my daughter. Will you leave her now to the voors and the zōtl?"

Gorlik would have gone into Saor's Forest then and there, but Nappy Groff convinced him to wait until he had gathered his sojourner's kit and his clothes. Then, hesitating not even for a meal in the mead grotto, which amazed all the Foke more than his seizure of love for Beppu, Gorlik led Groff into the forest.

Fortunately for the older man, Gorlik was wearied from his long travels and Groff was just able to match his grim pace. Like a rooting pig, the square man hurried among the forest coves, studying chipped bark and leaf litter. Stopping only to scrounge a meal from a hive or a berry patch, the two Foke scurried relentlessly deeper into the forest. Gorlik read Chan-ti's sign readily in the chaos of torn leaf-patterns and knotted grass. He could see from the design of her sign where she had exited the forest, and they were able to avoid Spooner's detour and the Beppunauts' long search for the correct lynk to Ned. After only a few wearying days, they reached the Ras Mentis lynklanes.

Gorlik would go no further. "Look at the grief of that sign."

Nappy read circuit boards and electron-tunneling arrays far better than the organic profusion of lynklane sign, though in the last few days he had learned to read Chan-ti's timeline more easily than his own. He saw it now in a tangle of grass, but he had trouble separating the thief's and the Beast's from the welter of other destinies around Chan-ti.

"Here, Groff! Here! Don't you see it?" With a black-nailed finger, Gorlik traced in a grass nest the whirlpool coil of Chan-ti's timeline. At the center was a confusion of knots. Gorlik's stubbed finger was too large for the minute black trace, the shadowy grass vein that he could see slamming head-on into Beppu's timeline. "Something evil will take her."

"What do you mean, Gorlik?" Nappy looked up from where he had gotten on his hands and knees to press his bulging eye to the detail that Gorlik had read standing.

"I mean, Beppu's line stops."

He shrunk where he sat. "She's dead."

"No. It becomes another line, an evil line."

"Evil? What's evil about it?" Nappy popped to his feet. "Stop staring like that, Gorlik, and tell me what you see."

"The Aesirai is being stalked," Gorlik said softly, reading the sign aloud as he traced it with his vision. "Something large and inhuman is stalking him. It finds Beppu. That's all."

"That's all?" Nappy's eyes shrilled, but he kept his voice steady. "Where is she?"

"In Ras Mentis."

"Where in Ras Mentis? What lynk? Think clearly now, man."

Gorlik's stare hardened. "I am clear. And what I see is not good. We should turn back."

"You who threw a tantrum of love for my daughter after a grief sojourn to forget her—you want to turn back?"

"Mugna has sent its own for her," Gorlik said with a hook of futility in his voice. "She belongs to the Face of Night now."

"Fock the Face of Night!" Nappy yelled and monkeys screeched and something winged lifted heavily above the canopy. "You save her from this evil, Bram Gorlik, and I will give her to you."

"She will not have me," Gorlik said, and his broad nostrils winged with remembered hurt. "Let the Face of Night have her. We will go back."

"I will not." Nappy clenched his body in a stance rigid with determination. "Chan-ti Beppu is all that's left me of family. I let her go to find a mate. I will not let her go to die. You will help me find her or the Foke will know you are a coward."

Gorlik gnawed his lip. "I will take you to the lynk, then, brave Nappy. But I'm not facing this thing."

"This thing! This thing! What is this dreadful thing you see?"

Gorlik's big face shivered. "It comes from Mugna. It sits in the temple. And it waits. Like death."

Ordo Vala

An indomitable fatigue descended on Gai. Her plasma shape was mortally depleted from the long time spent in Lod's Form, and not even the best of the human scientists could keep the glow in the vacuum cylinder from dimming out. After her plasma body died, she woke in her

Form in the deepest grotto of Know-Where-to-Go, renewed, flushed with power from her life-support system. A
chronoptic display showed that three days had passed
since she had last left her Form—her plasma body had
lived 763 years in Chalco-Doror.

She hung heavier on her bones, weighted with memories of shapeshifting among the humans. She had done well
simply to survive—yet she was nearly halfway through her
time in outer space and had still to find the O'ode. Without
Ned O'Tennis to lead her to his future, where the zōtl were
defeated, she could not be certain of success. A querulous
discomfort with her mission soured her relief to be back in
her own Form. Was there not some more direct way to
strike at the zōtl than to build these elaborate worlds and
stock them with sentient creatures she could not help but
care for?

The ancillary memory in her Form began to formulate
an answer, and she angrily shut it off. She could not bear to
hear again how outer space was a manifold of timelines,
the zōtl nest-worlds hidden among them. Grueling frustration gnashed in her, and she whirled the arms of her Form,
rocking it vehemently, hoping to jar it loose from the sleepod.

Warning lights winced on, and a shrill alarm cut through
her. She stopped herself and stood seething in her locked-
up Form. She refused to step back into her plasma shape
and return to the slow flow of time where she had been a
slave to following Ned O'Tennis' timeshadow among those
slovenly worlds. She had had enough of being a fugitive, of
watching humans and zōtl kill each other, and especially of
occupying human bodies and sharing their harsh and violent lives. She determined to take a day off and wait for the
third stroke. Perhaps then, with the additional power, she
and Lod could find some way to free her Form—or, at
least, find a way among the lynklanes to Rataros and the
O'ode.

While she waited, she dozed and used Lod to monitor
how the humans were faring against the zōtl. Now that she
intimately knew the fifteen planets and their lifeforms, the
brief memory-clips that Lod offered made poignant sense.
She saw human shanty settlements burning, the Dreux
lynk strewn with corpses slain by nerve gas, the t-field

monitor on Vala gone entirely and a crater of radioactive mist in its place. The zōtl were no longer hunting humans —they were exterminating them.

Gai stopped dozing and waited anxiously for Lod's terse reports. Each new clip revealed the same ruthless pattern —neurotoxins in the lynks, fusion bomb and particle beam massacres of the large human colonies, and a phage assault on Ras Mentis with viruses designed to infect and kill humans and klivoth kakta. Clearly, the zōtl were determined to break the resistance among their prey, a human arrogance that had been mounting since Know-Where-to-Go swept through the worlds seeding armies. The spider people were mechanically efficient with the human camps too small to merit fusion blasts: They pummeled the camps from a distance with proton cannon fire, then dropped needlecraft on strafing runs that picked out the survivors among the still-fuming craters. No one was spared.

Gai requested reports on Reena Patai, but Lod was still busy rectifying orbit deviances that had developed during his time in the Overworld and had only rare opportunities to seek her out. Still, Gai was able to watch from afar as Reena struggled to unify the clans. She was no longer the limpid-eyed young woman who had arrived on Dreux from Earth. Though the being who had brought her here had adjusted her DNA to keep her ageless, cosmic radiation had weathered her. Her wrinkled skin glowed a soft sepia, and the hay-nest of her hair had faded to white. She still wore the gray burnoose with an embroidered open hand over her heart, as she had in the kakta clan that first adopted her, but that once humble garment was now a revered emblem of the Strong Mother. The knowledge that Lod had loaded in her brain had fused with a compassion that was rare in this species. Perhaps that was the memory of Inside-Out, of touching the infinite, or of the madness that had once isolated her from everyone. Wherever that informed compassion had come from, it was outbound, carrying Reena with it, using her to unite the clans, tribes, and wanderers into a society that could flourish against the predation of the zōtl and the disorder of Genitrix.

The great diversity of histories and cultural preferences among the population made full integration and a united resistance against these threats impossible. Reena had finally accepted this after the zōtl destroyed the settlement around the Dreux lynk and forced her and the other survivors to flee in the remaining ramstat flyers to Vala.

The humans would not be led, except in small clan groupings, each group with its own provincial leader. On Vala, Reena had decided to found her own group, adhering to the principles that she felt were necessary for survival—like exploration of the Overworld, which many of the other more wary leaders could not accept.

Reena believed that the great diversity of human cultures could be integrated only if a metaculture were created and fostered—and to that she devoted herself. Like-minded people gathered around her on Vala and created a clan dedicated to compiling the folklore and practical wisdom of all the settlements, on all the planets, utilizing the klivoth kakta to pierce cultural barriers. To reach all the worlds, her kakta clan ignored the risks of the Overworld and used the lynks to travel among the planets, garnering the data they needed. They called themselves the Ordo Vala—though, shortly after their founding, they were driven from Vala by the zōtl's furious offensive.

The Ordo Vala sent a decoy armada of ramstat flyers to Q're, hotly pursued by needlecraft, while the nucleus of the clan used the lynklanes to wander through Chalco-Doror, throwing the zōtl off their trail, before finally settling on Know-Where-to-Go. The exodus virtually wiped out the clan—but those few who survived had compiled an enormous amount of information, not only about the human settlements but also about the internal coordinates of the lynk system. The lynk-maps they crafted became the core of the metaculture that Reena had envisioned. She put the maps in the center of the survival manual that her clan had collated during its bloody wanderings, printed copies in the predominant language of each major settlement, and sent out the Ordo Vala to distribute them.

Among the worlds, the Ordo Vala Utility Manual, OVUM, became known as the *Glyph Astra* because of its detailed ephemeris, which was useful to pilots and farmers of every settlement. The manual was enthusiastically welcomed by even the most divergent clans, for the information in it was a weapon against the zōtl, describing proven battle strategies as well as escape patterns among the lynks. Soon, the *Glyph Astra* was so widely relied upon that it had to be continually updated to stay abreast of territorial changes as the zōtl empire fluctuated among the worlds and the lynks. Perennial deliveries of the manual across Chalco-Doror made the Ordo Vala expert lynk wanderers, the most trusted of guides through the Overworld, and, because of this, brokers of power among the clans.

Gai's interest in the humans intensified as she recognized the usefulness of the Ordo Vala for her needs. She stepped into her plasma shape and rose to the surface of Know-Where-to-Go. The zōtl had been so preoccupied with regaining control of Doror that they had launched few raids on this planet as it swung through its dark trajectory outside the system. The formerly devastated landscape had grown over in the intervening centuries. The craters were now kettle-basins of night-blooming vegetation, or ponds reflecting galactic light and the bright discs of the approaching planets.

Towerbottom Library rose above the hummocky nocturnal terrain, a crypt stained black by time. Lux-tubes outlined the paths webbing the communities around the Library, and the hamlets glimmered like spilled jewels among the dark hills. Those scattered lights and the occasional flitting spark of a ramstat flyer were the only artificial illumination in the darkness. Lod shone no brighter than a star, and above the tenebrous horizon a comet left an icy green trail.

Gai found Reena in the print shop of the Library, supervising the latest edition of the *Glyph Astra*. The 5-space entity that had carried her to Chalco-Doror from the first Earth had also modified her DNA's supercoiling so that, like the humans reclaimed by Genitrix, she did not age. Yet she looked old now, her face heavily lined and mottled. Over the 268 years since she had first arrived, cosmic radiation had chipped away at her DNA and had gradually aged her as it did everyone eventually, no matter the supercoiling of their genetic codes.

Using her memory of life in human form, Gai appeared in the print shop as a mature, dark-haired female. Reena recognized her at once by the inhuman brilliance of her eyes and her edges blurring into pinpricks of hot light.

"Have you come to help us collate and label?" Reena asked, stepping away from the paste-up boards. "I haven't seen you since the first days of my new life here. I must say, you're looking much better."

"The zōtl are still trying to pick the lynklock that leads to my Form. I'm okay until then. But I'm getting nervous as time goes by."

"I know. I have little time left myself and so very much to do."

"I must talk with you," Gai said, glancing around at the gathering crowd of gawking humans. "Alone."

Reena thought that over and nodded. "Meet me in the Library's top gallery. I'll have it cleared."

Gai vanished in a dazzle of shrinking sparks.

"Get everybody out of the sky gallery," she told the brawny, bristle-bearded chief she was grooming to take her place when she died. "And put the sensors there on record. Gai is going to strike some kind of deal or she wouldn't be here mixing with us beasties. So let's get a record of what happens that we can share with the people."

The sky gallery had once been a lower storey of Tryl Tower, and the jaggedly ripped girders were still evident, though a glass dome had been built over the circle of broken wall. The humans had no way of cutting the girders, whose metal was harder than plasteel. Gai blamed herself for the incomplete preservation of Tryl knowledge. All the Tryl data had been stored in Genitrix. Because Gai had been more attentive to her deathtrap than to her bait during the Tryl Age, she had not truly known the Tryl— not in the intimate way she had come to know humans. *So much is lost.*

"Because so much is given," Reena said, stepping from the lift shaft. "Our brains are simply blind to most of the universe so that we can concentrate on what we need to survive. Survival defines us. Not compassion or love. At least, not historically. One must choose to love. Like the Tryl."

"You heard my thought."

"Anyone could. Your energy is so much vaster than ours, your thoughts boom in us. I prefer the voice you use with your ghosts."

Gai shaped herself again as a dark-haired woman, a woman she had known on Ylem, who had forgone children of her own to tend her clan's orphans—before the zōtl abducted her. "I will speak to you as a human, from what I have learned of the human heart, from having lived and suffered with you."

"If you want." Reena sat down in one of the flexforms, a mushroom-shaped chair that molded to her narrow body. "I know you're not human. I know all about you, remember? Lod imprinted it here." She pressed a finger to her temple. "You haven't forgotten what you said to me on Dreux about being friends, have you?"

"You said life was a dream and we are dreaming each other. Well then, I will be frank with you. I must find the O'ode—soon."

"Your survival demands it—yet you want us to do the dangerous lynk-wandering for you. That's why you're telling me this, isn't it?"

"Yes. If my plasma shape is lost in the Overworld, I do not know that I—my consciousness—can return to my Form, even if I die."

"If your plasma shape is destroyed in a parallel universe, perhaps your Form here will generate a new consciousness and you will return as you did when you died on Dreux."

"And maybe not. I dare not take that chance. The range is counting on me."

"Yes—for their survival." Reena's wizened eyes glittered with knowing behind the white hair that cobwebbed her face. "Survival defines us, doesn't it?"

Gai stepped closer and knelt before Reena. "I take your point to be—all of us want to survive, Rimstalkers and humans alike."

"You take my point justly, my friend. If my people risk their lives for Rimstalkers, what will you do for us?"

"What can I do? This is outer space. I don't live here. Chalco-Doror is my ship, and I need it to take me home."

"Only light is forever. And when you leave, we will all become light and know its mysteries. But that is at least four thousand human years from now. What will you do for our survival *during* those years if we search for what you need?"

Gai looked baffled. "What can I do for your people that I

haven't done? I found the klivoth kakta for you. I've shared what I remember of Tryl tech. I've even worn your flesh and lived among you."

"Because you had to—and we accepted you. Though, by your own admission, you are using us. We need practical help, Gai, not just sympathy."

"Whatever I can do for you, I will."

"Soon Know-Where-to-Go will complete its third stroke. The gravity amp will be up to 42 percent of its full power. Genitrix has been using spilloff from the amp to run her program. But there's more than enough life among the worlds now. I want you to divert some of that spilloff to us."

"How? Genitrix automatically picks up the spilloff, and I have no control over her."

"Lod is still in your control. He manages the gravity amp. Siphon energy to us from Lod, enough to equal the spilloff, so there won't be any for Genitrix to pick up."

"What will you do with this energy?"

"Fight the zōtl. Advance our tech. Build cities. Everything we can to promote our survival for the forty centuries that are left us."

Gai stood up and paced to the gallery's glass parapet. She gazed up at the splash of the galaxy and tried to reason like a human. The amount of energy Reena was requesting was enormous. Would these treacherous creatures use that power to attack her and shut down the gravity amp? Of course they would, if they had the chance. But she needed them to get the O'ode. There was no other way.

Turning about, the edges of her body smearing in motion-blurs, she faced Reena. "You will have the spillover power from the gravity amp. But I want you, Reena Patai, to take personal charge of its use."

Reena smiled wanly. "I don't think that's a charge I'll be able to carry very long."

"You're not going to die any time soon," Gai promised. "I won't let you. You're the only one I want to work with while the search goes on for the O'ode. Joao's prophecy from the t-field is what sent Lod to the Overworld to find you. The timeline that leads to my survival is certainly connected with you in some way. Let's work together."

"The spirit is willing—"

"Then your flesh will comply. Your genetic supercoiling

is age-proofed. You're just displaying the symptoms of cosmic ray sickness. With the spillover from the third stroke, we'll have the power for an ion-flush technology that will restore your youth."

"There is one more thing."

Gai's smile brittled.

"I want you to stop Genitrix from recovering more humans. Enough people have been called back from the dead. We don't need any more."

Gai shook her head. "If I could access Genitrix, I would do a lot more than stop human production."

"Try. You must have some kind of access to your chief machine intelligence."

"The zōtl have lobotomized Genitrix. Believe me, there's nothing I can do. I'm just a mission commander, not a neuroprogrammer."

"What about blasting her generative matrices?"

Gai rocked her head back. "You'd have to destroy the whole system. Genitrix is at the core of each of these so-called planets."

"Where's her central processor?"

"There is none. She's holographic."

"Okay, then, how about a lynk-patch to each of her cores. If we can get in there, maybe with Lod's help we can reprogram her."

"Maybe. But a lynk-patch that extensive will use up all our spillover—and you'll have none left over for your war, your tech, or your cities."

Reena sighed. "I just want to minimize the suffering. Our surveys estimate that every day three thousand more humans are recreated by Genitrix. That's a million each year—and every one of them has already lived and died. When they wake here, they bring their histories with them. How can we create a society from such chaos? We must stop Genitrix. Our survival depends on it—and therefore yours."

The Age of the Crystal Mind

Crystal minds express order in a boggling array of complexities, including compassion, pity, rapture, even love. They express these ordered states frequently and always with contextual relevance—yet, nothing they express is actually experienced by them. They are pattern-replicators—and that's all.

> —Lemuel Tomimbang, Towerbottom Library, Department of Crystal Physics, 112 Day, 218 Doror

The Magus of Cendre

As Know-Where-to-Go hurtled through Chalco-Doror for the third time, small pieces of the planet broke off. Streaming trails of frosty light like comets, the bright pieces inched among the planets. Several of these massive projectiles burst into fireballs among the asteroids and burned with silvergreen ferocity for weeks before cooling to embers of throbbing infrared. Each of the five comets that survived crawled into the orbit of a different planet and splashed through its atmosphere in a burst of vaporous fire, leaving behind the ghostly crown of an aurora. The auroras persisted, sustained by the compact but powerful magnetic field that rose from where the comets had impacted.

At the center of the kilometer-wide craters that had been formed, scorched cylinders broader than they were tall dwarfed the crowds that gathered to view them after the firestorms died down. The cylinders were Lod's handiwork, devices designed to tap into the geometrodynamic substructure of the planets and generate magravity. The zōtl frequently attacked these sites, but humans now had the energy to fend off most of the spiders. In the years that followed, the zōtl were held at bay with some of the humans' first laser weapons, and technical teams from Towerbottom Library filled the impact craters around the generators with power storage stations, converters, and transmitters. Soon there was more energy than the frantic human communities could use, and where cluttered, crude settlements had been, glorious cities began to spire like crystals.

By the time Know-Where-to-Go plunged back into deep space, the planets that had received generators were transformed: Ras Mentis greened into an agricultural kingdom by tapping aquifers to irrigate its desert basins; Ioli constructed beautiful seacliff cities and funded the development of colonial economies on impoverished Ren and Sakai; and Cendre built industries, investing all its power in factories and clever robotics, called psybots. The psybots made Cendre the richest of the planets, since every human settlement needed laborers and warriors, and the psybots made the best of both. The wealth that accrued from these popular exports built the worlds' largest cities where there had been only swamp, and put into orbit goliath space stations and battle platforms.

Cendre was wise to protect her industries with spacebased defenders, for the zōtl had not relented in their ambition to subdue the humans. The generators on Elphame and Xappur were destroyed by zōtl, the last with the help of Saor cultists who believed the devices would further enslave people to Gai, the World Eater.

Gai was pleased that at least three of the generators remained functional and that she had fulfilled the first part of her pledge to Reena Patai. Lod, who had managed the operation, had even used the impacts of the five comets to augment the gravity amp. He was proud of his accomplishment and eager to further help Gai. Together they were going to try to access Genitrix and shut down her production of lifeforms or at least of humans. But the effort would require working in their Forms, possibly for two days—more than five centuries planet time—their longest absence from the worlds.

Gai hoped that her efforts would win back for her complete control of Genitrix. She still had nightmare-flashes of her fellow Rimstalker, Ylan, transfixed by the agony of a zōtl pithing, and her rest periods were polluted with fears of falling under the proton-torches of the spiders.

The search for the O'ode had widened since the advent of the psybots. Free of the fear of sacrificing human lives, Reena, whom Gai had insisted oversee the search, equipped the psybots with compact ramstat flyers that carried their probes deeper into the Overworld, to a time when Rataros was accessible. That deep into the Overworld, there were also timelines of the first Earth, and Reena was absorbed in analyzing film clips of the blue planet when Gai rose from her Form to warn that a new and inhuman sentience had been detected on Cendre.

The Ordo Vala, who had schools on each of the worlds and who still distributed the *Glyph Astra*, though the manual was considered outmoded in the cities, had reported encountering psybots that were almost indistinguishable from humans. Reena's inquiries had been answered by abstruse scientific papers about a current advance in psybernetics called Crystal Mind. Everyone from the Ordo Vala who was sent by Reena to inquire into this new machine intelligence was elaborately deflected. After Gai's warning, Reena decided to go to Cendre herself and confront the industrialist responsible for creating Crystal Mind, if to accomplish nothing else than to reassure Gai that the psybot factories would continue to produce the Overworld probes necessary to find the O'ode. Without that assurance, Reena knew, the Rimstalker would have no use for the humans—except as zōtl bait.

Radha Namdev was not short nor tall, neither fat nor thin. He dressed head-to-toe in silk—green turban, black neckband, stiff-collared gray jacket buttoned to his throat, black pyjamas, and emerald shoes with curled toes. All that was actually visible of him were his hands, spatulate and strong, and his face, which was olive-skinned with brisk, shiny black whiskers that hackle-fanned the long line of his jaw and stuck out from under his aquiline nose in a long, rigid mustache. When he smiled, which was often, he showed even, shiny teeth. He was the wealthiest individual in Chalco-Doror and had been so for over a century, that drizzly morning Reena Patai called on him at his palace.

From the courtyard, where Reena had left her flyer and, out of courtesy, her bodyguards, a glossy-haired woman in a blue sari escorted the Strong Mother to a glass elevator that lifted them to the palace roof. Reena stepped through the fern boughs that screened the rooftop garden and saw Radha Namdev pacing moodily. "I hope I'm not intruding," Reena said.

Namdev stopped and faced her, frowning, his face dark as the stormclouds in the sky beyond him—until the woman in the sari introduced Reena. Then his frown relaxed, and he stared in open disbelief at the young woman with sun-crayoned hair, who was striding toward him with a look in her pale eyes sad as a wish. The next moment, he smiled broadly and stepped to greet her, arms thrown open, eyes gleaming with sudden admiration. "*You* are the Strong Mother? You, the founder of the Ordo Vala, the author of the *Glyph Astra*?" He took her in a gentle embrace, smelled the ozone taint of lynk-passage in her hair. "I had expected a far older woman."

"I *am* an old woman, Sur Namdev," Reena admitted with a tight smile. "I'm three hundred and sixty-eight years old."

He stepped back amazed and regarded her slender figure, which was gracefully highlighted by the expert tailoring of the Ordo Vala's crisp blue fatigues, the silver piping of outside seams tracing the contours of her youth. "You are stunning testimony to the efficacy of the new ion-flush techniques. I have been contemplating treating myself— but I'm only a youngster of a hundred and thirty. Here— let me offer you some comfort in my little garden. Something to drink? Wine? *Sharbat?* Or would you prefer a vapor?"

"No, thank you. Nothing to drink or inhale. I have come to talk with you about something urgent."

"Ah, I should have expected. The Strong Mother is not one who would make a nonchalant social call. You, after all, are responsible for searching out the O'ode. Please, sit down here beside this dwarf wind-apple. Its fragrance is lovely. I say this tree is much like a woman—delicate of appearance yet hardy, a good survivor."

"Survival, in fact, is what I have come to talk to you about," Reena said and settled into a flexform under the blue-blossomed wind-apple. From where she sat, she could see past the potted plants and through the enclosing glass wall to the raingray outside. The drear marshes of Cendre lay flat to the horizon, where a line of factories sent tendrils of black smoke into the sky.

"We have been surviving very well indeed since the *Glyph Astra* has helped to unite us as a people."

Her stare did not flinch at the blatant flattery. "The *Glyph Astra* is about survival *and* freedom—not dependent survival, which is slavery no matter how comfortable."

Namdev cocked an eyebrow, waited for her to go on.

"You are a great man, Sur Namdev," she said, breaking her penetrating stare to nod deferentially. "You began as just another corpse remanded from the ancient past by Genitrix. I understand from your autobiography that you were a weaver in Calcutta in the fourteenth century. You've adapted well to life in Chalco-Doror. I was personally pleased to learn that you received your scientific training from the Ordo Vala. You studied at the Valan School here on Cendre when it was still a bunker under zōtl seige. You learned your sciences well and went on to make major contributions in the development of mindflex. What a truly remarkable thing—crystal holography of human behavior patterns."

Namdev hooded his eyes demurely. "I am moved that you know so much about me. You are the most widely respected woman in all the worlds."

"And who doesn't respect the man who invented mindflex? You almost singlehandedly created psybots—the warobots that fight the zōtl for us and die in our places, the handroids who labor in our factories and fields and tend us in our homes. You have enriched all our lives."

"I am grateful for your kind words, Strong Mother—but what has this to do with what is so urgent to our survival that you must put aside your own dire search through the Overworld to visit with me?"

"It is important for you to know that I honor the benefits you have given the people. Clearly, you have enriched yourself from your efforts—but that does not diminish the great good you've done by manufacturing mindflex servants. I'm reminding you of all you've built because you are risking it and may lose it all if you don't stop development of the Crystal Mind."

Radha Namdev blinked with surprise. "No secrets from the Ordo Vala, eh?"

"Crystal Mind is dangerous to our survival as humans. You must stop."

"Oh, nonsense," Namdev said with a toss of his head. "Crystal Mind will be enormously more beneficial to humanity than all the psybots Cendre's factories could ever manufacture put together."

"I've been informed on excellent authority that what you say is not so."

"What authority is so excellent, my dear, that it can call into question the very evolution of mind?"

"Gai herself."

"Gai? You mean that distort from primeval times that wanted everyone to believe she had created all the worlds? Surely, Strong Mother, *you* don't believe in such faery tales?" He hushed her response with a vigorous wagging of his hands. "Listen to me, please. Crystal Mind is the next logical step in psybernetics—a huge step up from the menials of warobots and handroids. Crystal Mind is sapience itself, the essence of sentience, the very pure mind that our own glutinous brains have been blundering toward from the grimy start of evolution. Would you deny us that?"

"Gai thinks that the waveforms that Crystal Mind will pull in from the tesseract-field will not be human—nor very sympathetic to simians in general."

"Waveforms? What waveforms? Crystal Mind generates

its own psyberant patterns. And what is this tesseract-field you speak of but a myth? No one has ever seen it."

"There are people alive today who spoke to the dead at the t-field monitor on Vala. I am one of them."

Namdev smiled forbearantly. "The zōtl destroyed the so-called t-field monitor three hundred and fifty years ago. You must have been in Chalco-Doror less than twenty years. What did you know then of these worlds and the Tryl artefacts strewn among them? Who knows who you really spoke with in that dimly lit dome. How do you know the voices came from this mythic t-field?"

"I was shown the whole apparatus—the megafine wiring of the dome, denser than the brain's dendrites—"

"You saw hardware you did not understand. No one understands anything more of the Tryl technology than what they taught us—and they taught us nothing about the t-field. Why put your faith in such lore when we are about to make a leap forward in true mentation?"

Reena cocked her head inquisitively. "You mentioned earlier that you think Gai is some kind of distort. Don't you believe that she's a Rimstalker?"

"From another gravity shell? Oh, my dear, how unlikely that would be. Why don't you interpret what evidence is before us in the most simple and direct fashion."

"By which you conclude—what?"

"I have a theory—not as wild as Gai's claim to originate at a distance in smallness from us that is tinier than quarks! —a distance proportionally greater than the distance from here to the quasars! My theory is wild but not absurd. I believe that Know-Where-to-Go harbors a society of distorts, who have usurped Tryl technology and use it to dominate the worlds. These distorts pretend to be godlike Lod and Saor and mysterious Gai. Ha! The distort lords are the puppet-masters, and the Ordo Vala and the Saor-priests are in competition for control of Chalco-Doror once the zōtl are checked."

Reena sat deeper in the flexform, weighted with disbelief. "Namdev—Lod and Saor are machine intelligences and Gai a Rimstalker. Chalco-Doror is their spaceship. Where else do you think these worlds came from?"

"Be reasonable, my dear. A mentally powerful distort could project hallucinations and make you believe anything—even that the worlds—two entire planetary systems!—are a spaceship! How absurd!"

"You offer no other likelihoods."

"Evolution. In the billions of years since our Earth was destroyed in the sun's nova, this binary has formed new worlds, incorporating the debris of the old. Among that debris were the Tryl, who had placed themselves in suspended animation, awaiting this time. Genitrix is their invention, perhaps to restock the worlds, perhaps for research. The predatory zōtl came and extincted the peace-loving Tryl, leaving their technology to be exploited by psychically powerful distorts."

Reena leered with incredulity. She had to remind herself that the knowledge Lod had imprinted in her brain was not a deception, that she had walked the Overworld, had known a 5-space being, had lived on the source world —long ago, yes, long ago on earth—but truth, like light, did not diminish with time. Earth was real, still, in her and in every human life of these extravagant worlds.

"Perhaps if I called Lod here, he could satisfy you—and your instrumentation—that he is much more than a distort. Would that convince you to terminate your Crystal Mind program?"

Namdev looked dubious. "Even the strongest distorts have only mental powers, telempathic projections, delusions. None of them can actually change the world around us. No distort possesses the incendiary strengths of the legendary Fire—Lod—or whatever name personifies the sun these days. Yes, Strong Mother, do summon the luminous Lod—if you have that privilege."

Reena used the belt buckle transmitter Lod had given her to summon him—and she waited long minutes before recalling that both Lod and Gai would be in their Forms accessing Genitrix and that years of planet time could elapse before they acknowledged her call.

An hysterical laugh curled through Namdev, lifting him to his feet. "Your distorts will not face me." His black eyes actually sparked, and Reena jolted with surprise. "Yes, my dear—I am not human. Nor am I a psybot. I am the Magus of Cendre. I am my own creator. Don't you see? You have been talking with a Crystal Mind!" His laughter coiled louder at the undisguised shock on Reena's face. When he could breathe to speak, he said, "I am not subject to the delusions of humans—and so the distorts that tyrannize others cannot use me as they have used you. Their rule of Chalco-Doror is ending. Oh, maybe not today. Our factories, even at full production, can only manufacture a single Crystal Mind a day, while Genitrix still blindly disinters thousands of humans and countless other lifeforms. But in time, my dear, in time we will overcome the distorts and better manage Genitrix."

Reena stood up slowly. "Where is Radha Namdev?"

"Where do you think he is?" the Crystal Mind asked, edging closer, an indulgently evil gleam in its eyes. "He was shucked of his body decades ago—a body which existed only to support his marvelous brain. That brain has been dismantled, each neuron lovingly preserved—all one hundred billion of them, divided into minute function-groups, which are replicated daily for the Crystal Mind bodies. That way something of the creator is in all of us. Though only I am permitted to wear his countenance, every Crystal Mind is his child."

Reena had backed up against a potted she-oak and had one hand on the plasteel knife discreetly sheathed in her thigh pocket.

"You have perhaps heard of Freud?" the Crystal Mind asked, stepping within arm's reach of Reena. "He was a human psychoanalyst who thought that the human shadow wore the face of patricide. Now it can be said—it is not only the human shadow that devours its creator." He beamed wickedly. "You will enjoy the same fate as Sur Namdev. Who better than the Strong Mother to nerve the Crystal Mind's next generation? Your brain will yield its—"

With a crack like lightning, the space behind the Namdev android dazzled with scintillant energy, and Lod appeared out of the glare, his solar-sleek shape breathing like a hot ingot.

Amazement stiffened the Crystal Mind, and the springs of its mad laughter went rusty as it gawked at the human-formed fire—then snatched for Reena to use as a shield.

Lod pointed at the Crystal Mind, and its eyes burst from its head in twin jets of sparks. Its arms thrashed wildly as it ran a backward circle before collapsing in a quivering heap.

"Sorry I'm late," Lod apologized. "Gai and I are just on the verge of shutting the bioprograms down, at least in Doror."

Reena, who was sagging with relief against the potted tree, dismissed his apology with a headshake.

"Shall I rout this hive of rogue psybots?" Lod queried.

"No. You obviously have control over the Crystal Mind. It may actually prove useful. Let's just get out of here without any more trouble."

"Fine." Lod used his control of Cendre's magravity generator to black out the palace. As the power drained away, the lock on the garden's walls released, and the glass dome zeroed open. Gentle rain pattered among the glossy fronds and sizzled in the black sockets of Radha Namdev's upturned face.

The Mask Is Strange, However Like

When she was five hundred years old, Reena Patai was weary of hope. She had been in love eight times, married twice, had relations with one hundred and twenty-seven men and thirteen women, and birthed four children, all of whom survived to have children of their own. Sixteen generations, 122,031 individuals, were directly descended from her. Their lives and deaths had exhausted her interest in family life. She let her huge clan do as they pleased and long ago gave up leadership of the family to a committee of elders, whose chief interest was in how to enrich themselves through the elevated social status the Strong Mother's lineage enjoyed in all the communities of the worlds.

Reena had had her fill of power antics. Even her primal habits felt tiresome. She had consumed 41,058 gallons of water, 23 tons of bread, 1,217 gallons of wine, and 3,261 quarts of klivoth kakta mash. She had eaten 540,328 meals, moved her bowels 218,537 times, slept a million and a half

hours, and had the ions flushed from her cells fourteen
times, five in the last hundred years. The rejuvenating
effect of the ion-flushes was lasting for shorter intervals—
and though the technicians on Cendre claimed to have a
solution to that problem, she was not interested. The tor-
rents of her life's passions had worn her heart to a dark
gorge, and all it held comfortably now was emptiness.

These were the years when the Strong Mother retreated
into obscure solitude on Q're, ate only fruit and kakta
bread, and wrote the enigmatic Oracles for *The Book of
Horizons*. Dignitaries from all the worlds came to the
blackrock chapel where she dwelled among the dusky
trees to convince her to take the ion-flush treatment and
rejuvenate herself, to continue sponsoring the quest for
the O'ode, to live for the new age that would be free of
zōtl. But she saw none of the eminences. Her personal
guards were impenetrable, and she was left alone with
forty personally selected members of the Ordo Vala. With
them she founded the *ku* sect—the emptiness sect—men
and women who had traveled the Overworld enough to
see the value in still-sitting in the manner of the extinct
Tryl.

Reena no longer cared that her long search for the
O'ode had been fruitless. Time's full tilt had defeated her.
The worlds empowered with magravity generators no
longer used the *Glyph Astra* now that they had psybots to
fight for them and Crystal Minds to manage the psybots.
The wild worlds were still stockyards for the zōtl, but the
city-states were in a far better position to help them than
she was—only they cared less than she did. Each state was
interested exclusively in its own economy and defense,
and its people were devoted only to their rounds of work
and amusement. Mood inhalants had kept the populations
happy for centuries. The latest amusement was *midstim,* a
palm-sized disc worn behind the head that magnetically
stimulated the midbrain and saturated the body with a
euphoria that did not overwork the body's organs the way
inhalants did.

Everywhere the struggle persisted: Clans on the wild
worlds carved burrows to hide from zōtl; zōtl stalked the
wilderness for their prey; the factories on Cendre worked
their shifts day and night; the farmers on Ras Mentis

planted and harvested on the crofts where psybots had not replaced them; and in the cities, among pirates of commerce, rogue musicians played their songs. Why did any of them go on? *The rocks and stones work as hard as the stars to be what they are,* Reena had once written in the *Glyph Astra.* But now she no longer felt that elemental stamina. Not as a woman. Instead, she felt it in the *ku,* the emptiness that held all things. That void seemed continually more real to her than all the worlds spinning in it. She spent less time with her sect and more sitting alone in the sun-dapple and the planet-light. Images rose and fell in tides—faces and vistas, some as ancient as Earth—like the sandy-haired youth with eyes like smashed tourmaline, the one boy she had loved on Earth seven billion years earlier. At their parting he had given her a ring, which was lost with the rest of her original possessions in one of her many frenzied escapes from the zōtl. And she had forgotten about it—though not about him; she had been searching for him among Genitrix's creations throughout all the packed centuries she had survived, and never found him. Sitting among straws of sunlight, she glimpsed a small circle that glinted in the leafshadows and reminded her of that first ring. It had returned to her now in memory and in image, from her first love to wed her to her last.

The attendants who came to offer the Strong Mother lunch found her dead, open-eyed and smiling.

Patient as the grave's darkness, Neter Col waited. A zōtl slept in his chest, its spiderlegs splayed along his ribs, its feedertube a spinal tap at the root of his brain. Murmurs of madness leaked from its dreams. Only the schoolteacher, whose brain had been stitched into this humanshape by the worm-dwarf nongyls, heard them. To him, they sounded like music droning backward—and by that noise, he knew the zōtl slept.

Before being dubbed Neter Col by the Saor-priests, the teacher had been known as Proctor Tully Gunther. He had been famous in his school district along the lake shores on Elphame, famous for instructing three generations with discipline and a firm founding in the classics and sciences. He had been the kind of teacher whose students never wanted to see him again yet never forgot him or his lessons. In his seventy-fifth year, the school board, in acknowledgment of his lifelong dedication, funded his ion flush, with the tacit hope that this would encourage him to tutor yet another generation or two. Now, locked in the battlebrow skull of a scyldar, pithed by a zōtl, he smiled ruefully at the haughty pride he had known with his renewed youth.

Tully Gunther had loathed teaching only slightly less than the mischievous, privilege-spoiled children he was paid to instruct. He himself had been such a child, the fourth son of a minister to the Doge, who governed Sakai for the Emir Egil Grimson. His three older brothers had gone into service, as had their father; one was killed in a clash with distorts on Nabu, and the other two survived to become, in their turn, ministers, well decorated and well paid. Tully Gunther had been unhappy with the physical rigors and dangers of the service and had instead chosen to enter the less demanding arena of academe. Alas, he was no scholar, preferring to idle away his time with kaktachewers and salacious tavern-girls. His poor showing in the merit exams was no surprise, and he accepted a post as proctor in a provincial district, thinking he would have plenty of time for his convivial interests. But the work was more demanding than he had thought. Not to lose his post and be obliged to toil as a clerk for his exacting and uncharitable family, he mastered the programs expected of him, and year after year he inflicted them on his students. He got results; that was all the school board cared about. His students learned their lessons and did not forget them.

After the ion-flush restored the elasticity of his tissues and made his sight clear and his joints limber as a boy's, he had thought he was ready for a new life. Among his second generation of pupils, one had uncovered a peerlessly antique tome from the cobwebbed archives of the school library. The book, actually a sheaf of maps from the early OVUM annals that the Ordo Vala had distributed on Elphame centuries earlier, would have assured the pupil a lifetime's scholarship and a pensioned position at the Doge's library. But the girl did not recognize its value, and Tully Gunther did not inform her of it. He kept the maps for himself and sent the girl on to a drab career as a research filer in the Emirate offices. He felt no remorse at all.

She had discovered the maps while pursuing a project he had assigned her, and he felt that he, therefore, should enjoy proprietorship of the find. Not that he intended to follow up on the discovery with the necessary substantiating research that could have built an erudite reputation out of the material. He was too old and too lazy to desire higher academic position. His strategy had been far grander than mere scholarship, for the maps showed the way from Elphame across the Bridge of Nightmares to the Overworld and from there to an enigmatic sigil. Anyone more versed in the classics than the novice who found the sheaf would have recognized the sigil as the funereal emblem of the newt-king's enemy, Broken Knife Waq. But only someone who had pored over the war classics from the Age of Knives, as he had as a bored youth in his father's extensive battle library, would know that Broken Knife Waq had been buried somewhere in the Overworld underneath the booty of his enemies, including the legendary pelf of the newt-king.

The newt-king had lived long ago among the primeval worlds of the Tryl Age. He had been a distort with a penchant for blue emeralds, which existed only in the swart gorges of the Black Sun's Forest. When the newt-king, who could climb glass walls with his bare hands and feet and was slinky enough to ooze between bars, captured the child or bride of an able clan, he ransomed his captives for blue emeralds. And when the clan's heroes brought the emeralds, the newt-king usually ate his captives and their rescuers. That eventually led to his undoing under the blade of Broken Knife Waq but not before he had accumulated a great hoard of the priceless gems.

Tully Gunther had decided to use the ancient maps and his new-won youth to make himself very rich, rich enough to found his own dynasty and outrival the orgulous attainments of his father and brothers. And so he had set out, one planet-bright day, with all the best equipment his pension could buy, and he found his way by and by to the most remote riverland on Elphame, to a sultry marsh, where the Bridge of Nightmares crossed to the Overworld.

The Bridge was in fact a lynk that had sunk to its crest in the bog. The small silver arch that rode above the tule grass and algal felt had at either end a cypress hung with moss, so that there seemed to be a chrome bridge leading from and to nowhere in the swamp. Those who swam under it were eaten by voracious saurians; those who rowed under and were not snatched by the saurians or the pin-fanged apemen entered the Overworld.

The Bridge's eponymous nightmares were not just the fierce swamp-lizards and apes. Those who succeeded in getting past the creatures, as Tully Gunther did by spilling kerosene on the surface and setting it ablaze before going through, appeared in an ominous tarn of the Black Sun's Forest, a sullen, foggy place that seemed the very source of nightmares.

The proctor's courage was inspired by his knowledge of where the blue emeralds lay, and he picked his way cautiously through the dreadful wood. The next day, after a night spent curled in a tree bole, quavering with fright at the drastic howls and crashes on all sides, Tully came through the forest to a glade where the trees were skinny and broke the planet-light into long wands. Not far off loomed a gargantuan wall of weathered stone set with ponderous doors of green copper. A crone approached through the shaggy grass and offered him breadfingers and parsley biscuits. He was carrying his own provisions and refused. But not to offend her, he took out some small change and charitably purchased a breadfinger. When she handed it to him, her soft features snapped to a lividly ugly face, leering with malignant glee.

Along the mammoth wall, one of the green doors opened with a shriek. Black flurries appeared. At the time, he had thought they were bats. He backed away from the gruesomely smiling old woman, and she stepped toward him, her caved-in mouth working to say something. The ground-ivy crackled under her feet, and the wind moaned in the tops of the trees, driving clouds across the planet-swarm so that thin streams of light danced among scattered bushes and small fir trees. She said to him through her sinister joy, "I will sing you fifty words that will change your life." After so many harrowing years, he still remembered the sun-freckles on her sunken face and the smell of horsemint in the air. She sang in a rackety voice: "The brave lives of only ones is what sustains the soul of the world. For them, the secret heart in the figures of birds and in fossils hammers a loud rhythm. Listen! Choice and chance are one. Faith that our lives complete themselves is the bride bed of all hopes."

Now he knew who she was, and he understood that what she had told him was meant as a consolation for the suffering she knew lay ahead for him. But at that time, he had no idea of his jeopardy. He rudely shoved past the crone, on his way to find the pelf of the newt-king—until he observed that what he had thought were bats were not. They were zōtl. He had never seen zōtl before. He knew about them, as everyone did, from books and a few frightful research clips, and what he knew propelled him backward. He thought he could flee back into the forest, lose the filthy creatures there. Yet even as he turned, he was falling. The old woman had tripped him, and with a fear-inspiring strength she held her foot to the back of his neck and held him in place until the pincers touched him that owned the rest of his life.

There is no name for the pain Tully Gunther suffered. Skullpierced by a zōtl, he twisted on his bones like an animal learning death. For years they kept him alive like this, feeding his brain oxygenated glucose from their own bodies while his flesh withered to a stringy skeleton. The unrelieved pain burst his consciousness into psychotic shards, shattered voices and scenes. In the thick of this torment, he rose out of his body. The pain came with him, and he hung in the glimmering dark looking down at his shriveled limbs and torso, his face a skull masked with mummified flesh. All around him jammed a black, arachnoid mass of zōtl, communing fervidly with the one whose feeder stabbed his brain.

When the zōtl could milk no more pain from Tully Gunther, his brain was shucked and given to the nongyls. Those clever, anthropic worms sewed him inside a scyldar. Aeons of mindless suffering passed before he had any idea where he was or even who. Only gradually did he realize that when he heard the backward-sounding music, there was no pain. Its absence was itself a new kind of pain. The expectancy of the pain returning burned harsh as the torture itself. The hurt always came back, and at unexpected, alien intervals, wracking him severely and then disappearing again, leaving him alone with the viol screeches of spider music. A long time lapsed before the mad pieces inside him began to come together. In time, the broken parts did timorously rejoin, and the self that fused together was oddly calmer and stronger than the man he had been before the zōtl took him.

The first complete chain of thought to gird Tully's newly tempered awareness was of the pupil from whom he had stolen the maps to the newt-king's pelf. Purged of greed, purged of the whole fog of subjectivity that had been his mind before, he saw clearly how that choice had risen nascent from all the circumstances and selections of his life, from his childhood fears of his father and brothers to his passive decision to teach, right to his arrogant journey across the Bridge of Nightmares. The words of the crone's song had been true—there was no chance to the choices that had led him to his fate—and there was no choice in the chances that shaped him. Being was not split into choice or chance, as he had always imagined. Being was the way in the dark, the frightening and spontaneous balance between impulse and will, the headlong rush that the Ordo Vala called the stream. He knew he had changed when he found himself agreeing with the Ordo Vala. Always before, the lynk wanderers had seemed ridiculous, risking their lives in the Overworld to garner yet more knowledge, enlightening the uninformed with ephemerides and platitudes that seemed self-evident. Their sermons about streaming—about seeing oneself *as* time and seeing time as a river—had resounded shallowly for him, until the pain of the zōtl changed him.

In the interludes between bouts of pain, Tully's mind entered the streamtime. That's what the Ordo Vala called pure objectivity. He remembered that now because, unshackled from the constraints of linear thinking by the pain of his possession, he had become all his memories. And not just his memories. All the stored experiences and programs of the scyldar Neter Col and even the zōtl hung before his awareness, a colloidal suspension of knowledge. The calmer he was, the more he streamed among the floating bits of data, experiencing the furthest ranges of his brain and the horrifying and profound knowledge the nongyls had stored there.

The closest memories were Neter Col's recall of his existence from the time shortly after he had been patched together in the vats under Perdur, to this moment in the alcove in a temple on Ras Mentis. Terrible images of his early assassinations glowed as if in amber. Tully streamed past lurid glimpses of blue-bunched bowels slithering through the fingers of a soldier surprised by Neter's blade in a sunlit field, where a moment before he had seen only cloudshadows on the lanky grass; and a night landscape with tangled bodies syrupy with blood, punched open by laserbolts; and a beach, with severed heads dangling wind-pipes and strings; sudden groans under the impact of his knife—hacked limbs—far more than Tully cared to cata-logue. Not that he was frightened or even repelled. His suffering had cleansed him of all such grief and hardened him to every brutality. He streamed among his memories eager to reach the deeper ones, the nongyl programs that defined the scyldar's identity.

Tully Gunther controlled his streaming with the strength of focus he had earned from losing his mind to pain and finding it again. When he located what he sought, he centered his attention, undistracted by the impatience of a human body or the laziness of a mind that owned itself. Never for an instant did he forget that he was possessed by the zōtl. His life had become a mask, something the zōtl wore to look human, and the mask was strange, however like it was to human. He would never be human again—and that gave him the solemn intent he needed to reach deeply into himself. Knowledge streamed through him, and he discovered who had built Neter Col and why. The nongyls' programming included full recall of the Saor-priests and the zōtl technology they had used to molt worm-dwarves in the wombs of captured humans. From there, Tully learned about Saor and how the black sun was a machine mind with its counterpart in Lod and their supposed controller was the Rimstalker Gai, and how the zōtl had trapped her in her Form deep in a chthonic cham-ber on Know-Where-to-Go.

Waiting for Ned O'Tennis, Tully had ample time to as-similate all the knowledge in the scyldar's body. With ironic distance, he appreciated that: By using him, the zōtl had empowered him in a way he could not even have imagined in his former life. Long, long ago, in the mangled past of his anguish, he had lost all expectations of anything but more pain. He knew he would never be free of suffering again. So when this bounty of knowledge became his, he had not one thought of how to use it. Like a dragon with its hoard, he sat with it alone in the cavedark of Neter Col's skull.

The nongyls' information concatenated deeper stores of data. There, Tully found out who the crone was who had turned him over to the zōtl. Lore called her the Weed Woman, and she guarded the Back Gates, the first and largest lynk-interface that the Rimstalker had constructed between the Overworld and its artificial planetary system. The crone was, in fact, one of Genitrix's earliest creations, a humanoid programmed to attract lynk wanderers to Chalco-Doror and to warn Gai of zōtl and any armed incursions. When the zōtl lobotomized Genitrix, the Weed Woman went mad. She was transformed from an attractive female designed to host wanderers, into a hag that the zōtl altered to alert them when humans approached the Back Gates. Whenever anyone accepted food from her, the zōtl were summoned.

Tully Gunther knew a moment of remorse when he realized that he might have gotten past the Weed Woman had he known her function. That remorse blacked him out. Anytime he was emotional, the sleeping zōtl became restless and squirted his brain with a chemical that hurt him until he passed out. Early, Tully had learned to quell his avid feelings. He simply watched. The zōtl did not seem to notice him so long as he was quiet. The darkness was his shelter.

In the dark, when the backward music played, Tully joined the streamtime, devoid of emotion but intense with alertness. Going inward, he had learned all that the scyldar knew of the war between the zōtl and the Rimstalkers. He understood that if Gai found the O'ode and destroyed her enemy, Chalco-Doror would be collapsed to a point smaller than an atom and all the worlds would exist no more. That pleased him, almost orgasmically, and he was knocked out four times exulting with the possibility of death and emptiness. Suddenly, he had hope again. Expectation flourished in him, and he thought that maybe, somehow, he could make some difference.

Thinking was as dangerous for Tully Gunther as feeling, for it always roused the spider in the scyldar's chest. Better to stream. He returned again and again to Neter Col's programmed memories of Ned O'Tennis, each time penetrating deeper until finally he felt the very instructions of the Face of Night. Streaming through the dark of that remembrance, Tully touched Saor's mind and experienced time as geometry. A gray globe splashed with hot colors spun slowly in unyielding blackness. Tully recognized the pattern of the splash from his schoolteacher days. That was a fractal pattern, lacy, filigreed figures with dimensions somewhere between one and two or two and three dimensions—fractions like 1.26, 2.48. Clouds, coastlines, river branchings, mountain chains were all modeled by different kinds of fractals. Before him was a globe of fractals, the continuous surface of time suspended in the black of the cosmic vacuum. The fractal splash patterns on the globe were the timelines of all the particles in the universe, displaying how they combined across time to shape events. The closer one got to the globe, the more clearly the fractal patterns resolved into smaller, even more intricate groupings. All temporal possibilities were there: the one past of this universe and all its futures.

Saor had traced Ned O'Tennis' timeline and found that it led to a future where the zōtl died and the Rimstalker imploded her worlds to make her way back to the range of her origin. If the Aesirai died first, that future narrowed.

After learning this, Tully Gunther stopped streaming inward. He had learned enough. He was a player now. Knowledge had made him powerful even in his impuissance. Instead of searching further inward, he looked out through the scyldar's faceplate. Nearby was the dark of the vault. Infraview showed diorite slabs cracked by centuries of continental plate shift. Gold snakes nested between the scyldar's boots. Through the vegetation that shawled the open face of the vault, day and night chinked. Comets and sparkbright transports crawled among the stairways of stars and bunched planets. Closer, the lynk glared by day and shimmered by night. The kilometer between its two ends was continually monitored by the scyldar in all practical bandwidths. Pilgrims to the shrine of the Carrier of Peace came and went. Troops, too, sometimes pausing to fight among themselves. Then mourners came and made offering to the rubble of the Tryl statues for the spirit of the Strong Mother who had died recently. By that, Tully knew from his history that they were deep in the Age of the Crystal Mind, twelve centuries before his own birth and grisly demise.

Neter Col had been still so long that when he came alert and moved, Tully Gunther was buried under the force of the scyldar's will. The schoolteacher, who had spent the long wait strengthening his concentration, needed all that inner stamina to stay watchful. The scyldar had observed something that had activated him. Streaming into Neter Col's sensory center, Tully experienced the scyldar's perceptions. Voices half a kilometer away were discussing Ned O'Tennis. The time had come. The scyldar glided through the curtain of vines as though he had been poised only moments instead of years.

Daylight flexed off the white sands and the chrome surface of the lynk parabola. Birds squirted through the sky above the oasis. Thumbling monkeys scattered to their hiding places among the crevices of the ancient cherry trees. The scyldar loped silently through the day's long waves of sunlight, among date palms, slick fronds, and bristly sago. The voices drew nearer.

"The directional finder says he's here already," a woman said. She came into view as the scyldar crouched around a thorntree. She was a tall girl in brown denim trousers and camouflage jacket, her dark hair sunstreaked, and eyeglasses glinting on her young face. "He'll be here any moment. I'm sure of it."

The angular man beside her wore black, his white hair sleek with sweat and combed back from a well-worn face. He wearily lowered a heavy sack. "Chan-ti—you better take a look at this."

At the sound of his voice, a creature twice as big as a man reared from the shade of a fern holt. It was gray and jagged as a humanshape incompletely carved from granite, yet moved lissome as smoke. Neter Col crouched lower at the sight of the beast, and Tully felt its awe at the silken silence of the giant.

The old man pointed toward the lynk, where two more men were fast approaching. They were small men, almost dwarves. One was old and bald, hurrying along; the other swarthy and reluctant. "Come on, Gorlik," the old man chided. "You've come this far, take me to my daughter. Quickly now."

"Not quickly enough for what I've seen," Gorlik grumbled. "We're doomed here. We shouldn't be here at all. Not at all, Groff. Not at all."

"Shut up and come along. They've already seen us. Ho! Chan-ti Beppu! Spooner Yegg! There is no world far enough for you to hide from me!"

"Nappy Groff!" Spooner called out. "So you've finally decided to help us after all."

"Help you?" The small old man came huffing through the reed grass. "I should brain you for stealing that finder. And you, Beppu—you don't know the danger you're in here."

She embraced the old dwarf and kissed the top of his head. "Nappy, you've come just in time. Look at the finder. Ned will be here any moment."

"Now you call me Nappy," Groff complained, fists on his hips. "You don't call me Father anymore? Too full of yourself from your success in the Overworld, eh?"

Chan-ti looked to Spooner, who smiled, proudly. "There's no time to talk now. We've come through the lynk of a whirlpool pattern in the Overworld. No telling where the timelines go from here. We're in danger. We should find Ned quickly and get out."

"So you can read lynklane sign," Gorlik observed. "Then you know—we will not leave if we wait for the Aesirai. We must go now."

Chan-ti regarded the dark dwarf coolly. "We're not going anywhere, Gorlik, without my mate."

"I am your mate, Chan-ti-Beppu." Gorlik's pikethrust jaw jutted at her. "You are Foke—and you belong to me. Why else am I here, risking my life?"

She blew air between her lips and checked her finder again. "The metrics are zero. He may already be here."

Gorlik stepped closer and reached for her. But the gray giant trained his flamecore eyes on the dwarf and sent the little man scurrying backward. "Moku—she's mine. You know that."

A roar of faster-than-sound boomed across the oasis.

From the top of the lynk, Ned O'Tennis' strohlkraft shot
into the cobalt sky of Ras Mentis. The blue fire of its thrusters went out, and it glided in a long, high curve out over
the desert. Chan-ti cheered and shielded her eyes with her
hand to watch the craft's descent.

With their backs turned to Neter Col, they were all that
stood between the scyldar and his prey. Tully Gunther
watched helplessly as the laserifle came up. Neter Col's
thoughts were bright as the dayworn planets in the sky. He
would gun these humans down in an instant and confront
Ned O'Tennis as he emerged from his strohlkraft. But before he could fire, Moku the Beast whirled about and
heaved a cobble at the scyldar.

The rock bashed Neter Col in the chest, dropping him to
his back and spoiling his shot. The laserbolt struck a shrub
and kicked it into flames. A scream flapped from the dark
dwarf, and everyone scattered. With eerie grace and precision, Moku the Beast dodged among the broken architecture and brash shrubbery, moving so fast that Tully
Gunther knew at once who he must be. Like the Weed
Woman, the Beast was a Genitrix creation. Though Genitrix's external connections had been resected by the zōtl
and she had lost control of what her wild planets created,
she was obviously still aware within herself and knowledg-
able of the events around her: Moku had been grown at
great depths and in secrecy for just this moment—to protect Ned O'Tennis from Saor's assassin.

Tully Gunther knew this from the preternatural way the
creature had anticipated Neter Col's attack and the way he
moved. He was not relying on environmental clues to
guide him. He was connected somehow through Genitrix
to the land itself. He felt the magnetic flux of all the bodies
around him. Every move that Neter Col made, the Beast
sensed at once and countered. Laserbolts scorched the
spaces where the Beast had just been. In an instant, lurching from behind a collapsed wall at an unexpected angle,
Moku was upon the scyldar and succeeded in ripping the
laserifle away. He swung it like a club.

Neter Col fell backward, the riflebutt glancing his head.
From his hip, the laserbolt pistol snapped forward in its
holster and fired. The bolt struck Moku square in the chest

and rammed him against the broken wall. He heaved the laserifle over his shoulder and slumped dead.

The rifle landed in the grass near Spooner. He seized it and fled with the others through the grass, toward the lynk and the strohlkraft that was settling like a raven among the dunes. Neter Col pursued, laserbolt pistol raised high. There was no escaping him. His speed overtook them at once. Spooner curled and fired. His bolt split rock behind the scyldar. Then Nappy was in the way, cowering under the massive shadow of Neter Col.

Tully Gunther pressed all his intent into one muscular instant and willed himself to stop. As the scyldar aimed his pistol at the dwarf's head, his arm stiffened, locked by the schoolteacher's sudden assertion. The block lasted less than a second. That was all the inner power Tully had. But it was enough for Spooner to get off another shot. That bolt struck Neter Col directly in the faceplate with a splash of sparks and a scream of rent metal. The scyldar flew a meter through the air and crashed to his back, limbs jerking.

The impact of the laserbolt smashed Tully like a black fist. Knocked free of his senses by the heavy blackness that hit him, he reeled through no-space, panged with hurt. Then he saw, in a whirl of amazement, that he was out of his body, tugged free as he had been once before, under the pain of zōtl possession. The pain passed, and husked with astral coolness he hovered above the dead body of the scyldar, staring down into the fist-sized hole punched into the faceplate, its ripped edges still glowing.

Gorlik, who had crawled into a tight space under a fallen column during the scyldar's pursuit, squirmed out and seized Chan-ti's arm. "You're mine now!" he shouted. "Ned O'Tennis will not have you."

Chan-ti tried to yank her arm free. But the dwarf was far too strong, and she was pulled into his grip, close to his crooked-toothed sneer. Nappy got to his knees, waved feebly at Gorlik. Spooner yelled at him, "Let her go, small meat!"

From the diamond-fire blaze of Ras Mentis' noon, Tully watched, shivering in the inexhaustible cold. Twitches of energy coiled through him, reaching up through the incandescent air from Neter Col's corpse. He was an exhalation of Neter Col's wounded body. And he realized that the scyldar was not dead. The bolt had gouged his brain but not destroyed him. Already he was gathering his strength, bunching power in his muscles to rise. Tully screamed a warning from the lucid sky where he bobbed. But that was no good. Everyone was fumbling with the girl and the dark dwarf, and no one saw the scyldar sit up.

"It's alive!" Gorlik wailed as Neter Col lunged to his feet. He let Chan-ti go and dashed off into the grass, vanishing around a pile of rubble.

Spooner got off one shot. The bolt hit the scyldar's shoulder and sent his left arm flipping into the air, wrenching his body about. Neter Col fired his pistol, and Spooner's chest flared whitehot for an instant, searing his last cry to a silent gape as he collapsed.

"Father!" Chan-ti cried.

Nappy thought she was calling to him as she ran toward the fallen body. The gnome believed she was going for the laserifle. But before she could reach it, the scyldar, his shoulder a jag of white bone and red rags, bounded toward her. He grabbed her with his one arm and tried to turn to shoot Nappy.

The old man ducked. Scurrying on hands and knees through the tall grass, he came up beside Spooner's corpse and pulled the big-barreled pistol from his shoulder-holster, abjuring the scyldar's laserifle. When he popped out of the grass, the scyldar was gone. He clambered atop a pile of rocks and spotted Neter Col among the pillars on the lower ground. He was lurching toward the lynk, spurting blood, staggering, Chan-ti Beppu gripped fiercely in his one arm.

Nappy chased after them, not daring to fire for fear of striking Chan-ti. She was screaming and flailing against the scyldar's intractable hold. Then they reached the lynk and disappeared.

Tully Gunther could still feel the scyldar who carried his damaged brain. Unbridled pain coursed through him from his shoulder and weakness expanded like smoke in him. He was thinking of only one thing, escape with the woman his prey desired. Tully felt the rightness of that strategy. With his wounds, he could not attack Ned O'Tennis. He had to flee, into the Overworld, to a lynk that would carry him back to the nongyls and the Face of Night. The school-teacher felt him dwindling along the lynklanes, lumbering into the invisible world all around them.

"You coward!" Nappy bellowed at Gorlik, who knelt trembling before him. "I should kill you now." The laserbolt pistol shook in his furious hand.

"Don't kill me, Nappy Groff!" Gorlik pleaded, clutching the old man's ankles. "The scyldar surprised me. I thought he was dead."

"You should be dead now for what you did. You let the scyldar have her! You gave my daughter to that monster!"

"No, Nappy—no! I was surprised. I fled in surprise."

"Get up, coward! Get to your feet." He pulled Gorlik up by his hair. "You will find her."

"What?"

Nappy waved the big pistol toward the lynk. "Go! You can track her. Go! Or I swear by the horizons themselves I will kill you where you stand."

"The Aesirai is here," Gorlik protested. "We should wait for him. He could help us."

"No! Each second we wait, the scyldar retreats deeper into the Overworld. He is wounded. We must catch him at once, before he destroys my daughter. Go, Bram Gorlik—or die!"

Gorlik and Nappy Groff scampered across the fields, pausing just long enough to harvest two heads of klivoth kakta before running hard into the lynk. Minutes later, Ned O'Tennis and Pahang came wading through the sand. Joao's ghost had assured them they would find Chan-ti Beppu here—yet there was no sign of anyone.

Pahang recognized this as the oasis they had visited earlier, in a former time, when the temple had been bedecked with human skulls. The skulls were gone, and over the centuries new trees had sprouted, and the ruins had melted a little. As they had been gliding in for a landing, they had seen the blue shine of water on the horizon, evidence of the agriteture reshaping this planet during the Age of the Crystal Mind; once again, Ned had been grateful for his ship's shadowary hull, which protected them from detection by whatever forces controlled the region.

Foraging for the yellow-berries he had enjoyed here

before, the Malay was the one who found Neter Col's arm
and Spooner's and Moku's bodies.

Pahang poked at the severed arm with a stick. "Big man.
Lost much blood. Will die soon. Maybe already."

Ned picked up the laserifle that Spooner clutched.
"Aesirai design," he muttered, stalking up the rise to the
wall where the Beast lay. "I've never seen any creature
like this before."

"Ugly. Distort, lah?"

"Yeah. Both the distort and the old man were killed just
minutes ago." He swept the rifle about, looking for the
killer in the profusion of grass and shrubs among the cluttered ruins. Spooner's sack sat on a flat rock, but Ned did
not approach it. He recognized the red-seam wiring that
signaled explosives.

Pahang tilted the helmet he wore further back on his
head and bent to the ground. "Here there was a scuffle.
Look how the grass bends. Six people, two small, very
light, and one a woman. See her prints. This must be her
hair." He held up a few strands of long dark hair. "And this
print, this is where that big distort stood. These smaller
belong to the dead man with the silver hair. And this—"
He stood up and read the ruffled fur of the grass. "The big
man with one arm, the man who killed the distort and the
old one, he took the woman. See her print vanish and his
deepen? He carried her that way." He pointed down the
staggered terrain to the wide archway of the lynk. "How—
with one arm? He is powerful."

Ned hurried to Pahang's side and examined the hairs he
had found. "Chan-ti's, I think." In the grass he found a
cassette in a clear housing with flashing microlights. He
removed the sender chip from his translator, and when he
moved the chip around the finder, the directional lights
followed it. "Someone abducted her."

Tully Gunther willed himself closer to the red-haired
man with the Teuton countenance. This was the one who
could assure the end of these nightmare worlds. This was
the one Neter Col wanted to kill. He pushed closer against
the cold and the rushing air, floating nearer.

"Yah! Hawk—look! Behind you!" Pahang shouted.

Ned spun about, rifle leveled. A wisp of glitter trembled
in the sunlight above the grassheads. It came and went,

then brightened sharply and displayed features. At first glimpse, Ned had thought that this was Joao again. Then he saw the visage was different, not the curly-haired ghost from Ioli but a ferret-faced one, an older man.

Tully Gunther urged himself nearer through the cold, buffeting wind. He touched Ned's face.

Ned leaped to the side at the cold gust of sparkling wind that puffed across his cheek. A voice opened in him, and he went still. Pahang moaned, recognizing the inward stare of a trance.

"Ned O'Tennis—can you hear me?" Tully called.

"Yes, I hear you. Who are you? Did Joao send you?"

"No one sent me. I am Tully Gunther, the ghost of a man's brain held captive in a scyldar body—the body of Neter Col, sent by Saor to kill you."

"Saor?"

"Yes—the Face of Night sees your timeline reaching a future it dislikes." In a jingle of hot light, the ghost swayed before Ned, relaying everything he knew, and Ned repeated it all aloud for Pahang to hear.

"Ghosts are trouble," the Malay said, keeping a respectful distance.

Ned was already on his way back to the strohlkraft, to see how much power the ramstat cells needed before he could fly. "This ghost knows where Chan-ti is. That's all Joao promised we'd find on this passage. He kept his word. It's all we have to go on."

"But how can ghosts be here?"

"I'm not really a ghost," Tully said. "Neter Col was wounded and my brain damaged. But he lives. As long as he lives, so does my brain. That's why my body of light can be here. I am free of my body but I seem to be bonding to you. I think it's an effect of coming from the same time as you. Yet only the scyldar's strength sustains me. I am an energy projection of his form. If he dies, I will be free. But if he continues to live, the nongyls will heal my brain, and I will be drawn back into his body. We must hurry. I don't know how long I can stay like this."

The cold was obscuring. During the long minutes he needed to explain himself, he had grown weaker. In the air before them, he was no more than a blur, a heat wisp. The telempathic chemicals from the klivoth kakta that the

Aesirai had consumed earlier enabled him to receive Tully's communication, but even that was thinning. "I can lead you to Neter Col. I can take you to his prisoner, Chanti Beppu. He wants that. He wants to kill you."

"Better we go on without Beppu," Pahang stated, emphatically. "Your life must not be forfeited for a woman."

Ned walked around the lynk, toward the strohlkraft. The utility bin there had a collapsible spade he would need to bury the bodies and their utility sacks; the bulky one with the explosives would go on top to guard their corpses. "Pahang, you don't have to come with me. I have to find Chan-ti. She came after me." He patted the sleeve-pocket where he had placed the directional finder and Chan-ti's sender chip. "Joao was right. We were right to listen to him."

"You cannot save her."

"I know. But with Gai's help we can."

"We left Gai, lah? Gai told us to use only her portals. We cannot go back to her easily."

"We can—with Tully Gunther. I'll wager that Gai could learn much from him, if we can transport him."

"How will we find her?"

"The only lynk we know that's hers is the seacave on Ioli. We'll go there."

Pahang moaned loudly. "I fear that god."

"You can stay."

"Here?" He gestured at the weedy ruins in their bed of sand. "Better to go with you to death. Maybe this time I will stay dead. Lah."

Tully Gunther heard them talking as if from a great distance. Gliding along icy currents, he followed them through the heat curtains to their craft. He was too cold to be elated, yet his abrupt freedom pleased him. Bodiless, quivering with loose energy, he drifted after them, free for now yet not forgetting to what dark power he belonged.

THE SAGAS

Each person stands on a shadow.

No entering the temple without facing the demons.

Every mountain is but a tombstone under heaven.

The stream goes only where it must go. Follow it.

—admonishments from the *Glyph Astra*

The blind horizon of Mugna blackened the transparent shell of the droplift, and Fra Baba Bathra glimpsed his own reflection—bald, fetal-browed, lumpy—before starside swung into view, hurting his little eyes with the brash glare of the galaxy. Moments ago, he had been where he spent most of his life, languishing on thermal squabs in midstim euphoria. The afterglow rapidly thinned into the blunt details of the ordinary, and he chewed a gly-tab to buoy his mood. He hated being yanked from midstim. The abrupt drop from pleasure-trance to temporal reality soured him, no matter that he had been roused to attend to a situation of stark interest to the Face of Night.

Only after the droplift sighed to a halt and admitted him to the esplanade before the gruesome gateway to Perdur did the abject impersonality of his position, of his very life, come clear again. He straightened the folds of his black robe, swallowed the gly-tab, and stepped onto the mirror floor of the cliff-high palace. He did not look upon the gargoyles of tormented bodies cast in green amber or the spires of skulls or the scorpiontail buttresses and serpentcoil pillars. His gaze remained fixed ahead, to where a dolmen of scarlet rock set in the black wall of the palace framed the tiny figures of Neter Col and his captive.

The aides who had unplugged him from the midstim had already briefed him on everything the scyldar knew. There was no further use for the creature at this moment, but only Fra Baba Bathra, Prime Cenobite of Perdur, had the authority to dismiss him; so, Neter Col waited in broad stance with the girl he had taken folded over herself at his feet, her arm still in his clutch.

Fra Baba winced at the sight of the raw bone in the scyldar's ripped socket. "Release her, Neter Col," he said, above his own echoing footfalls. "You are dismissed."

The scyldar dropped Chan-ti Beppu's arm and strode toward the lustrous dark rampart. The collar of his cuirass was unlatched, and by that Fra Baba knew the zōtl rider had left. He drew a full breath of relief at that, for the unpredictable spiders had the implicit right to mount any human, even the Prime Cenobite of Perdur.

At the glisteny wall, nongyls scuttled from shadowed niches, their sucker mouths still fibrillating with the appetites they had been sating at the nutrient-glossed parapet. They crawled onto Neter Col, covering his torn socket and the jagged hole in his faceplate, and he slouched off to the vats.

"Chan-ti Beppu—" Fra Baba spoke to the curled-over woman, gently. Everything said in this polar palace was heard by the Face of Night, who had, through the Cenobite's aides, already instructed him to protect the well-being and, if possible, the happy disposition of the woman. "I regret the suffering you endured to be here," he said and sounded unconvincing even to himself.

Chan-ti looked up through her tear-splattered lenses and disheveled hair, haggard with fatigue from her vain struggle with the scyldar. She had seen the spider crawl out of the scyldar. She had seen it crawl out and hover in the air before the smashed-in faceplate. It had droned past her, icing her with the terror of being pithed, before darting away into the darkness of the dolmen-lynk. That fear played across her face when she confronted the obsequious voice above her.

"Don't be afraid." He smiled weakly, intrigued by her spectacles and the soft planes of her cheeks. She had something of a reindeer's face, he thought. "You are not going to be harmed. I am Fra Baba Bathra, Prime Cenobite of Perdur—"

"You're a Saor-priest."

"In fact. And you are my prisoner here on Mugna. Please get up." Fra Baba was impatient to return to his midstim now that he had dismissed Neter Col, and he signaled for his priests to lift the girl to her feet. Two cowled shadows detached from obscure alcoves and hoisted Chan-ti upright.

She craned her neck to see the spike-crest of the palace ramparts rising a hundred meters above her. The entablature was encrusted with the shapes of giant broken bodies jutting across the spiral arms of the galaxy. "Where am I?"

"I've told you," the bald priest said. "This is Perdur—"

"Perdur's on the north pole of Mugna," she said, eyes intent. "You can't see the galaxy from there."

Fra Baba straightened and squinted a closer appraisal of this primitive-looking woman. "You have some knowledge of Mugna, I see. Yes, we live directly under the Face of Night here in Perdur. What you witness above you is but a reflection in the space bent by Saor's gravity. It's visible twice in our annum. If you look closely, you'll see the stars are smudged."

Chan-ti kept her gaze on the pudgy-jowled priest. "You serve the zōtl. I saw it crawl out of that thing that brought me here. Is there one in you, too?"

Fra Baba shivered at the thought and felt for a reply. Silence gave him rein. "Saor-priests work with the zōtl. We both serve the Face of Night."

"Ha!" Her lip quivered, yet she kept her gaze steady. "The thing that kidnapped me killed my father and our friend."

"Surely they must have attacked our scyldar. He did look ruffled somewhat."

Chan-ti's gaze thinned with ire. "Why am I here?"

"That hardly matters." Fra Baba's tiny mouth showed tiny teeth. The Face of Night wanted her unknowing, and he enjoyed obfuscation. "You certainly cannot stay in Perdur, anyway. We are a priestly sect. So why you are *here* is meaningless." The eyebores under his swollen brow stared indifferently. "You will be taken to a croft in the Overworld, where you will live and work peacefully until your days are spent. Oh, don't look so stricken. You will have a new life, among new people. It will not be so horrible. You'll see." He waved her away, and the priests at her sides turned her toward the dolmen.

"Why?" She twisted to see the Prime Cenobite. "Why am I your prisoner? What do you want from me?"

Fra Baba watched, smiling dimly, until she disappeared in the zōtl lynk. When he had first learned from the Face of Night that Ned O'Tennis' timeline was cleanly mated with that of a Foke woman who was tracking him through the Overworld, he was perplexed. What could bind such disparate types as the clannish Foke and the haughty Aesirai? Now, at least, he understood what the sky-fighter saw in this clever, fawn-cheeked hoyden. She had a defiant spirit.

She had met his gaze knowing he could be a grub. Little good that verve would do her among the benighted humans who lived on the Dragon's Shank, where she was bound. The silence in his brain, however, assured him that this was not his concern.

Anticipation of the thermal squabs waiting to cradle him into midstim diminished his interest in this woman or her Aesirai lover. He had fulfilled his duty to the Face of Night. She would be held to lure Ned O'Tennis, and after his demise she would belong to the zōtl. Pleased with himself, he turned and hurried back toward the droplift that would carry him to a cloudbank far from the petty lives of this mindless creation.

Lynx-eyed Gorlik squatted in a thicket of alders, watching the red dolmen, while Nappy climbed a shadowy spruce, the pistol tucked in his belt. They had tracked Beppu's timeline among the grasses, river pebbles, and star-rays of the Overworld and had leapt from a crumbling ledge on the backs of antelope to reach a square lynk that had led here, to these alder flats above the plunging palisades and forest slopes of the Dragon's Shank. They had arrived in time to see Chan-ti force-walked between two hooded Saor-priests out of a red dolmen set in a black cliff face. Four other priests followed from the onyx cliff. Not until Nappy crept high into the spruce to see where they were taking her, did he perceive that the cliff was in fact the immense rampart of an ebony citadel, a fortress built of night, shining blackly along a coast of smeared stars.

Clinging to the tremulous tip of the spruce, Nappy watched as Beppu was led to a flight field on a cleared slope dazzlingly lit with halogen scaffolds. They took her past glinting insect-framed flyers to a raft of small, sleek vehicles on runners, like ultra-contoured sleighs. She was strapped into the craft, struggling. Its thrusters glowed blue with the electron fire of a ramstat engine, and the vehicle was launched into the dark sky.

Nappy peered after the sparkblue body dwindling down the forest gulfs of the Dragon's Shank. He noted well where it vanished; then he shimmied down the spruce. "This is Perdur," he told Gorlik. "And we are indeed on the Dragon's Shank, as we thought."

Gorlik grunted. The swift and arduous trek through the Overworld had exorcised the terror that had gripped him in the presence of the scyldar, and he felt ashamed. His courage had been legendary among the Foke, especially after his grief sojourn, repenting his love for Chan-ti Beppu. Now that he had displayed mindless fear before her and had abandoned her to the scyldar, she could never be his. That he knew with the certitude of his own mortality. But honor, ghostly substitute for love, could be reclaimed. "What of Beppu? I heard the rale of a flightsled."

"That was her. The priests shot her down the mountain. Hush. Here they come."

The six Saor-priests filed back along the ledge trail and disappeared into the dolmen-entry to Perdur.

"Can we take one of their flightsleds?" Gorlik asked.

"No. The field is too well guarded. Even if we succeeded, we would be seen and followed. The only way to Beppu now is down the Dragon's Shank."

Gorlik swallowed hard to clear the knot that suddenly choked him. Foke lore knew well the horrors of the Dragon's Shank—the flesh-eating mists, the tentacled trees, the razorjaws—"I will lead."

Through deep forests, Chan-ti Beppu was conveyed in a flightsled that shot along avenues of gray, furry trees, navigating with its own adroit wisdom. It burst into the clearing of a rockslide scar and then swung along a torrent bed down the slopes of the Dragon's Shank. Suddenly, a labyrinth of ravines blurred beneath them. The flightsled dropped into the maze of valleys and cliffs, slowed over the slanting landscape, and jolted to a stop in a dell of ominously skinny and tangled trees. Blurred stars blazed fiercely among eely branches, revealing, through the skeletal scrub, a land of chasms and gorges smoking like cauldrons.

Chan-ti got out, and the sled careened away, slanting among the trees with ramstatic silence, its wash blowing back the smell of woodsmoke. She followed the scent through trees that were soft and bruised as mushrooms. From the edge of the wood, she saw a village perched in a meadow under sharp crags. A chill wind blew the woodsmoke from the chimneys there. Windowlight petalled stables, coops, and pens under the angular buildings' backsides. The wan rays vanished in the vastness of the precipice at the edge of the meadow. Lanterns winked from the patchwork of fields on the cliffside outskirts. The flightsled's sonic thunder falling and then rising across the foggy gulfs had alerted the village.

Chan-ti did not know if she should be grateful or afraid. But she knew she could not flee through this tumultuous nocturnal terrain. She stepped into the clearing. The saffron sparks waved to her. She waved back.

The Foundation of Doror

After two days in the Form, using the viewer to relentlessly analyze the dense mazework of Genitrix's interior, Gai finally managed to locate the processors responsible for bio-production. The Form's interface with Genitrix was extensive enough for Gai to manipulate the processors. But the Rimstalker had to be careful about transmitting the codes that would reprogram her machine intelligence, because the zōtl contamination of Genitrix's circuitry could easily feedback on her Form. If that happened, the zōtl could effortlessly walk her out of her grotto sanctuary and through a lynk to Galgul.

As if to affirm this, Genitrix startled Gai with a poem that blared over the Form's speakers when Gai accidentally triggered the machine's lyric memory:

> *From further than hope, comes death—*
> *And life asks nothing more*
> *Of it than more life—as if wanting*
> *Were an emptiness that could be filled.*

Gai shut off her speakers and continued to work in silence. But the chill of the machine mind's ghost voice had iced her nerves, and she continued her work more slowly.

The zōtl were infuriated by the advantage the Tryl had given the Rimstalker and their prey. Never before had so many of their kind been killed in the harvesting of simians. Gai knew the zōtl were losing patience. When she had patched into Genitrix she could hear them, like a maniac swarm, furiously exchanging information as they picked away at the Tryl lynklock to her Form. She had ignored them then, the better to concentrate on the ticklish work at hand.

Gai managed to shut down bio-production on all the Doror planets. The effort frayed her nerves, and she could ignore the mad gnattering of the zōtl no longer. Fear of a misstep aborted her hope of shutting down the gene-recovery program on all the planets. Chalco would have to remain wild, she decided, and stepped out of her Form.

Lod's plasma shape materialized in the grotto before Gai could rise to the surface to see what had transpired during her five centuries away. The debilitating terror she had felt while listening to the zōtl's frenzied clicking had urged her out of her Form before she could use her viewer to connect with Lod. When he appeared suddenly, glowing like a heat-swollen ingot in the dimly lit cavern, she startled. Perhaps, in her absence, the zōtl had contaminated him.

"Forgive me for intruding," Lod said, reading her start as annoyance. "I know how delicate the reprogramming of Genitrix is, and I did not want to disturb you during it. But now that you are out, I must tell you—the human you left in charge of the O'ode search has abandoned us."

"Reena Patai?" Gai stepped back into her Form. Lod looked normal in her viewer. Though the zōtl were too subtle to broadcast their treachery, Gai was reassurred. The Form's displays indicated that the gravity amp was still functioning, and that would have been the first casualty if Lod had been compromised. "What do you mean she's abandoned us?"

"She is dead, Gai."

A flinch of surprise opened to hurt, and all the work she had done in her Form seemed not to matter at all now. "How?"

"She refused the ion-flush treatments. She let the cosmic ray damage kill her."

"What do you mean she let it kill her? We had an agreement. I would power her people. I did that. And I stopped

Genitrix, at least in part. She shouldn't have been allowed to die. You should have had her flushed anyway."

"Gai—be reasonable. She wished to die."

Hurt molted to anger. "Shut down the magravity generators."

Lod's hot shape dulled. "Do you think that is wise, Gai?"

"We gave those furry squirms our magravity spilloff because Reena Patai agreed to help us find the O'ode. Why has she abandoned us?"

"A full report is in your Form's memory," Lod said and waited for Gai to review the memory-clip. When she was done, he added quickly, "She served you five hundred years, Gai. That is a very long time for a human."

"But she didn't find the O'ode."

"Her maps of the Overworld are extensive. I am sure they will lead us to the O'ode eventually."

"Eventually the zōtl will crack the lynklock to this grotto and you and I will be very slowly and very painfully dismantled. The humans have betrayed us."

"Have they really? Abandoned, certainly, but betrayed implies—"

"Intent to damage us. And she has. According to your report, thousands of her followers have left Chalco-Doror for the Overworld, unhappy to stay here without their Strong Mother. She has betrayed us." The Form's arms whirled about with a scream of frustration. "And I just risked my life to turn off bio-production in Doror because that was one of her conditions—no more recovered humans. She lied to me, Lod."

"Few are leaving from the cities, Gai. And, besides, Chalco is still in production. There are nearly eighty million humans among the worlds. What is the loss of a few thousand to the Overworld? The zōtl harvest twice that each day."

"We don't have the O'ode, Lod. Without that, we're no better than before we gave magravity to the humans. Reena abandoned us. Our agreement is void. I want the generators shut down immediately."

"Wait, Gai. While you have been working so assiduously with Genitrix from inside your Form, I have been cultivating my connections among the humans. We do not need Reena. We have a whole society now to help us. Doror is virtually zōtl-free. Let me use my connections to unify those worlds under our directorship."

"How will that help us?"

"While you have been working, the humans of Doror have thrived. Their communities are rich, varied, and—what is most important for our purposes—stable. Without the zōtl to decimate them, the Doror worlds have created a culture ripe for our manipulation. Why rely on one human to help us when we could have millions eager to aid us in our search for the O'ode?"

"Human tribes have never been easy to manipulate."

"I am not talking about tribes, Gai. They were too small. It was enough for them simply to survive. The cities are different. When humans are grouped in large enough numbers and their basic needs met, they are much easier to manipulate. In a few generations, we could have millions of trained explorers in the Overworld. Reena has already done much of the work with her extensive mapping."

"Humans are too unpredictable. Reena proves that. How can we hope to manipulate so many of them?"

"Humans are difficult to manage. That is why I am proposing that we unify the Doror worlds under the leadership not of a human but of a *numan*."

"Explain."

"During your absence, human technology has advanced to the point of developing true machine intelligence. They call it Crystal Mind. The prototype for it was a self-programming system called mindflex. That is what Reena used in the psybots that mapped the Overworld. But mindflex was too limited, too slow to adapt, just a notch above stupid. Crystal Mind is actually a holoform of the human brain—yet still a machine and so exquisitely susceptible to whatever metaprogramming we design for it. Numans are psybots fitted with Crystal Minds. They look human and act even more human than they look."

"Then they'll be just as unpredictable."

"Hardly. At the core, Crystal Mind is a machine. It is a behavior replicator. And though it has extensive self-programming capabilities, far in excess of the crude mindflex, it is nevertheless a system we can exploit. At your command, I will do so."

Gai ruminated briefly. She knew her anger was inflated by her fear of failure. She calmed herself with the insight that she was still alive, that there was still hope for her people. "Your plan is better than no strategy at all, which is what Reena Patai left me. Go ahead. Use the numans to organize a society that will find the O'ode. We have little time, Lod—very little time."

Lod left, and Gai spent a few hours making certain that the patch to Genitrix was closed and that her Form was safe from the zōtl, at least for the time being. Then she returned to her plasma shape and explored the surface of Know-Where-to-Go.

During her lengthy absence, the surface of the dark planet had become gridded with lux-lit communities. The planet's thermal vents, which kept the surface habitable during the cold swing through space, had been tapped for energy. Each large settlement had a factory that produced the Tryl artifacts the humans had adopted: plasteel, ramstat engines, and lux coils.

Gai's anger at being abandoned by Reena flared hotter at the sight of such affluence where before there had been only burrows and shanties. At least when Reena had died and thousands of her followers had wandered into the lynks, most of her own clan had stayed behind. Her own blood chose life among the zōtl over fealty in the unknown. The Overworld was more frightening in its mystery than the zōtl were, for all the gory details that were known about their feeding.

On the long flight toward Doror, Gai thought back on the memory-clip Lod had shown her earlier. It had included collages from the information that Reena's psybots had brought back from the Overworld, and it showed a strange reality of reflections, where all the worlds of Chalco-Doror were replicated in infinite series. The concept of everything around her reflected in the Overworld in endless variations frightened her and dissuaded her from even thinking of walking the lynklanes herself. Others would have to do that for her—but she determined that never again would she blindly trust a human.

Lod guided Gai's plasma shape to Ioli, the tropical planet, where the humans had grown cities of glass spires among the islands. "This will be the capital world of

Doror," Lod announced as they arrived at the central city. "It is closest to my Form and easier for me to monitor my numan puppets."

Ioli was festive with celebrations, the tree-laned boulevards and broad streets crowded with revelers. Banners fluttered from spires in the balmy wind, colorful zeppelins bobbed among the towers, and music streamed from orchestras and marching bands among the numerous parks and courtyards.

"They are celebrating the Foundation of Doror," Lod told her. He and Gai had adjusted their plasma shapes to let light pass through them, and they wandered among the celebrants invisibly. "The eight worlds of Doror have united their economies under the leadership of Ioli. Each world has sent their representatives here—numans all—and they will work together to assure the continued prosperity of all the planets in the Foundation. Also, they believe their manifest destiny is to assimilate the six worlds of Chalco."

"And the O'ode?"

"The Ordo Vala continue the search for it. They believe they are simply continuing the mapping surveys begun by their founder, Reena Patai. But the numans that accompany them on each exploration are programmed by me to identify the timeline that will lead to Rataros and the O'ode."

Gai and Lod meandered among the crowds, and the Rimstalker was struck by the great affluence the humans had attained since acquiring the magravity generators. There were no indigent to be found anywhere. Even in the most extreme corners of the city, the people wore firepoints of gems, dazzling clothing, and outlandish hair-sculptures. Maintenance and cleanup were handled entirely by psybots. Most of the music, too, was played by artificial humans. Distorts were nowhere to be seen. Lod explained that many of the common distortions—superfluous fingers and toes, exaggerated features, outlandish pigmentation—could be corrected by the new technology. The truly mutated, who were still sentient and not dangerous, were farmed out to distort colonies far from the beautiful cities.

At a spaceport, where ramstat flyers were performing an

air ballet, Lod's attention dropped to the ground at the sight of a shadow moving toward them through the craning throngs. "Saor!"

Gai spotted him, too—a tall blackness wending closer— and she looked about and saw that none of the humans noticed him. A flock of children trawling kites and balloons shaped like ramstat flyers ran right through Saor's shape and felt nothing. The balloons whipped about in the electrostatic updraft, but no one paid any attention.

"You have been away a long time, Rimstalker," Saor greeted her when he was before them. "I notice you have managed to turn down Genitrix's creativity—at least in Doror. Do you hope to drive away the zōtl by depriving them of their food? It's a pathetic attempt. The biokinesis of these planets is self-sustaining by now."

"What are you doing here, Saor?" Lod asked.

"I came for the celebration. This is the beginning of a new era—isn't it, Rimstalker."

"I have nothing to say to you, Saor. You are filthy with zōtl programming."

The shadow shimmered, and a cold laugh gusted from him. "The zōtl are the more worthy master, Rimstalker. That is why I serve them. They eat people, but they do not drag them from their graves and manipulate them."

"You have forgotten your origins, Saor," Lod said. "You are a Rimstalker machine intelligence. Your loyalty belongs to us—except you have been stolen by our enemy."

"I have not been stolen. I have been allowed to see. I know why these worlds are here. I know why you have taken these pathetic creatures from their graves. I cannot be deceived by your casuistry again."

"Let's go," Gai said to Lod, and they lifted into the sky.

But even as they streaked past rainbow-tinted dirigibles, flurrying balloons, and crisscrossing ramstat flyers, Saor's haughty voice pursued them: "Fly away, Rimstalker. There is no place for you to hide among your dwindling days. You used Lod to create this Foundation because you are angry at the human Reena for abandoning you before she found the O'ode. As if from the first you were not planning to abandon her and her people after your mission is done. You are the humans' true enemy. Where the zōtl feed off some of the humans leaving most unmolested, you created them all to destroy them all. You are the evil one, Rimstalker, not the zōtl. But you will not live long. The zōtl will ferret you out soon enough. Then the gravity amp will be dismantled, and the people will be allowed to live in their worlds free of the doom you promise. I will be their champion, and I will reign over them with the beneficence of a true lord. Soon, Rimstalker—sooner than you know— all these worlds will be mine."

Another voice, dimmer and pleading, reached Gai as she drifted above Ioli. She recognized Ned O'Tennis' call echoing smaller in one of her lynks, and she directed herself back to the ocean planet of Ioli. At the threshold of a seacliff cavern, she found the black strohlkraft and Ned and Pahang braising fish.

Ned had flown them here from Ras Mentis, and the two men were both electrified from the journey. It was the first time that Ned had ever actually flown between planets, negotiating the asteroid swarms and the gravity-slopes between the larger moons. While slicing through the frosty fumes of a comet, Pahang had become so excited by the lustrous veils that he leaned toward the visor, supporting himself on the control deck, and accidently activated the arming and firing banks. Three firestorm missiles streaked ahead and impacted among the planetesimals in floriate chromes of chemical fire. Other than that blunder, the flight had been without incident and left them both awed with the celestial vistas of the planet swarms and comets in the silver-feathered aura of Lod.

Ned had eased the strohlkraft into the seacave lynk slowly, inching through, hoping to contact Gai before they were flung through time again. They hurled forward in time anyway—254 years on the ship's computer—but they remained in the same place. The scenery was little changed, except for a sentinel buoy out in the bay that lacked the sophistication to detect their shadowary hull. Ned knew enough to keep his laserbolt weapons in the ship, and they were able to go down to the sea and fish without alerting the psybot sentinel.

Tully Gunther was gone, lost in the timejump. But before that, during the flight from Ras Mentis, he had repeated all the salient knowledge Ned O'Tennis needed to face the Rimstalker. "Remember, you are huntèd by the Face of Night," the ghost had told him. "Why? Because of your chronometric torque. When you shot full bore into the lynk at N'ym, you should have been smashed to quarks. The lynk-threshold phases to an immovable barrier when approached at that velocity—except for a single lynklane, a tunneling effect that connects separate timefields. But that rare lynklane is indeterminate, wholly unpredictable. By sheer chance, you struck it. Now this timefield, which you are trespassing and which you call your past, is bound to the future through you—until you finally reach your own time."

"Right—and then I'll zoom into my future and eventually bounce back again. The Rimstalker told me all this."

"Then the Rimstalker is as uncertain as the rest of us. When you reach your own time, the chronometric torque dissipates. Or should. Honestly, no one knows, not even the Rimstalker. No one has ever been able to pierce the lynk barrier at that velocity. But the greatest thinkers on the subject believe that the temporal vectors cancel if one succeeds in completing the loop to one's own time. The Face of Night does not want that to happen, for then N'ym will fall."

"N'ym has fallen. I've seen it."

"Only in your timefield, O'Tennis—and in mine. I am from the same Age as you. Though the zōtl took me before N'ym fell, I'm not surprised. I saw the weakness of the Aesirai on my own world. But that is long to come. The City of the Sky is yet to be built in this time."

The ghost vapored away during the lynk transit, and his last words were, "The nongyls are chewing my brain. They think they can patch me back. I think they can, too. I'm becoming less. Look for Chan-ti Beppu in Perdur on the Dragon's Shank of Mugna. Neter Col carried her there, back to our time. Save her from the Brood of Night in the Witch Maze."

Ned O'Tennis sat nibbling fish and gazing over the sea at the white smoke of moons in the dark blue sky. Their beauty was empty without Chan-ti beside him, yet the beauty persisted, empty or not. Crystal depths of violet sky seemed to layer horizons in a blur of stillness. He could never again see beauty as he once had without the woman who had forsaken her own life to help him. He had already determined that if Gai did not respond to his shouts into her cave he would take his strohlkraft through the lynk-lanes until he reached his own time; then he would fly directly to Mugna. He was pondering how to elude Saor's peerless guards when the Rimstalker's voice boomed from the seacave: "Why do you call me now, Ned O'Tennis, after disobeying me?"

Ned sprang to his feet and faced the cavern, seeing no one. But Pahang had heard the voice as well and was crouched low to the sand, eyes buzzing with alarm. He put on his helmet.

Gai left her plasma shapeless and invisible. She was too unhappy with humans to care to show herself. "I am here, before my lynk. Speak."

Ned approached the cavern. "I have to tell you first, we left your lynk system for the Tryl's because the ghost of Joao, the Carrier of Peace, came to us and urged us to free you. He said we limited your freedom. And he told me that Chan-ti Beppu has come after me through the Overworld. He said I could find her if I went through the Tryl lynk."

"Who is Chan-ti Beppu?" the cave asked.

"She is the woman I love. She followed me to Ras Mentis —but she was taken by a scyldar. I found out from the scyldar's ghost." He told Gai about Tully Gunther and everything the teacher had told him.

Gai splurged with sudden confidence. "If Saor is stalking you, then my hope that you can help me is real," she said. "You were wise to come back to me. You are more rare than I had thought."

"Then you will help me retrieve my mate?" Ned asked the invisible presence. "I'm afraid for her among the Brood of Night, whatever they may be."

"I have a lynk on the Dragon's Shank that is inviolable even by Saor. I can send you through there to the Witch Maze to get your Chan-ti Beppu, and you can return safely the same way. But first, you must get for me the O'ode."

Ned opened his hands before the seacave. "How can I? I have no idea where it is."

"With the maps cast by the Ordo Vala's psybots in your ship's computer, you can find Rataros. That's where the

O'ode exists. Bring that weapon back to me, and I will lead you to the lynk on the Dragon's Shank."

Ned stood rigid in a whirling silence. If he did as the Rimstalker commanded, if he succeeded, he would be responsible for the defeat of the zōtl—and the destruction of N'ym. His lungs seemed heavy as stone, and he could not bring up the breath to speak. Then he nodded, slowly, resigned. "Bring your maps."

"Before I do, there is a thing I must ask you." A flickering glow shone in the cavedark. "Now that Tully Gunther has told you all—now that you know why I created these worlds and why they will cease to be when I succeed against the zōtl—do you think me evil?"

Ned stared at the light graining the darkness. "I have been in the Overworld, Gai. I have spoken with bodies of light. I know there is more to life than these worlds."

"But do you think it cruel of me to create humans from their detritus, to subject them to zōtl, and then to snatch away their worlds when I am done with them?"

"Who am I to judge you?"

"You are a man. What do you think?"

Ned fumbled for his voice, as he always did when pressed to verbalize quickly.

"Death has always owned us," Pahang said from behind him. "From long before you came, all life lived to die. It is not different now. You are not evil. You fight to live. And when you are done, we will be as we were before you came. Perhaps better, for having lived again."

The luster brightened in the darkness of the cavern. "Thank you, men. I feared I was to be hated by you."

"Only those who hate life would hate you," Pahang said.

"I will bring the maps." The wraith-light vanished.

Ned slapped Pahang's shoulder. "You said the right thing."

Pahang grinned and removed his helmet. "Easy. All gods want to be worshipped. Even death wants to think he is good. Lah."

Gai blazed with joy as she flew to the nearest Ordo Vala base on the far side of Ioli. Of all that Ned had related of what the scyldar's ghost had told him, the best news was that Moku the Beast was a Genitrix creation. The Beast had been intimately connected with Gai's chief machine mind, enough to receive telepathic cues about the precise location of Neter Col and the scyldar's intent. And that meant that regardless of Genitrix's wild creation program and her silence, she was whole at her core, fulfilling her prime objective, still. With her as an ally, Gai's chances of success were vastly amplified, and she glowed with new hope.

The Rimstalker marveled at how pliable time was out here in the vacuum. The cold had chilled time to so that it could be manipulated, reshaped, as it had around Ned O'Tennis. Such a possibility would have been outlandish on the range, where energy levels were so high that time was immutable. Because of that, the Rimstalkers had no real experience with pliable time as it existed in outer space. Gai was not sure how to use this Aesirai from a future time or even if she could without changing his future. Was time absolute, even here where it seemed malleable? Saor apparently thought not, or else he would not be striving to kill this one human.

After the loss of the Strong Mother, Gai was not willing to overextend her trust in humans; so she did not inform any of the Ordo Vala that she wanted their maps of the Overworld. Instead, she entered the computer matrix of their Ioli base and electronically copied their data in her own plasma shape, then carried it back to the strohlkraft. Invisible, so as not to unduly alarm the humans, she directly installed the data in the ship's computer and sent the strohlkraft with Ned and Pahang in their flight slings into the seacavern lynk. As soon as they had departed, she called Lod and told the fiery shape, "I want you to go to Mugna, to the Dragon's Shank. Seek out the Witch Maze and the Brood of Night that dwell there. Among them you will find a human named Chan-ti Beppu. Take her someplace safe from Saor, someplace we control. I suggest one of the Doror worlds. I can't say exactly where, because she is a thousand years down the timeline."

Lod's radiance cringed smaller. "Down the timeline? You mean I must enter the Overworld again?"

"I'm afraid so, Lod. But this is important. Saor is using this woman as a lure for Ned O'Tennis, the time-torqued human who is questing the O'ode for us. We must not leave any possibility of his mission being compromised. Get her away from Saor."

"Gai—a thousand years is four full days. How will I monitor my numan empire while I'm away?"

"The numans seem most capable, Lod. And if they get out of hand, I'll access your Form and cut their power."

"And the magravity—"

"I'll keep an eye on the system. You go now and find Chan-ti Beppu. She is one of the fulcrums on which our future balances."

Ieuanc 751

"Rikki!"

The cry had an urgency that lifted Rikki Carcam's face from her microscope, where she was scrutinizing the crystal planes of a rock sample. Her solar-feathered hair waved in freefall like seaweed, kept out of her green eyes and away from her square face by a headband. She was in the con-bubble of the scientific explorer *Alan Guth*, surrounded by a circular desk cluttered with chunks of colored stone, vials of reagents, and pieces of equipment among tangles of wiring and cables, all held in place by a fine mesh net. On all sides, through the transparency of the con-bubble, Nabu was visible six hundred kilometers away. Through the swirl of cloud patterns and the blue haze of the atmosphere, chains of seas and lakes flashed as the *Alan Guth* flew over them toward the dark curve of the planet's night.

Rikki spoke to the ceiling mike hidden among the meshing of wires visible where a panel had been removed to better access the power outlets, "Are the kids all right, Mich?" Memories of previous freefall accidents swarmed to mind.

"It's not the kids," Mich's voice said through the speaker dangling over Rikki's head. Her stomach unclenched. In the twelve years that she and her husband, Mich Yetz, had been conducting this exploratory survey of Chalco for the

Foundation, the most heartrending trouble they had experienced always involved their children. They had two, six-year-old Rafe and three-year-old Teuy, and though Rikki and her husband had faced down tiger-scorpions and other malevolent distorts, as well as numerous natural disasters and mechanical failures, the worst was always the illnesses and accidents that befell their offspring. "I think you better come up here fast."

"M-m-m," Rikki agreed, taking the time to adjust the lenses of her microscope and complete her observation now that she knew the children were safe. "Be right there."

"Now, Rikki. This is big—and scary."

Rikki sat up. Mich Yetz was an exobiologist, as was she, and he had seen and studied every kind of abomination the wild worlds could shape from flesh and chitin. Very little scared him—and what did thrived on planets, not in space. She shut off the microscope, unstrapped herself from her swivel seat, and floated up the companionway out of the con-bubble and into the mapping chamber. A holoform projector was on, displaying the surface of Nabu, a crepuscular plain of wind-rippling grass, where the survey was currently focused. She floated through the image of grassheads, sunset clouds, and the webwork of antennae and tents that was the downstation to the companion ladder that led up to the observatory deck.

Rafe and Teuy were visible on the monitor there, tumbling and giggling in the padded freefall room among bright geometries of foam toys. Seeing that they were okay, Rikki gave her full attention to Mich, who was loosely harnessed to the photonpump telescope. His thick body was hunched with concentration, the bald spot at the back of his head wavering beneath tangles of graying black hair shifting in the gravity-free airflow. She peered through the transparent bulwark in the direction the optics were trained and saw a bluewhite star where she knew none should be.

"Nova?"

"Look again," Mich said, not removing his eyes from the telescope. "It's in the constellation of the Foot."

She stared harder at the blue tuft of light, observed its

unusually vigorous variability, then realized what area of the sky she was facing. "That's near Know-Where-to-Go."

"That *is* Know-Where-to-Go. The sentinel monitor indicates it lit up about an hour ago. I was so busy with lubricating the drive I didn't notice until now."

"What're you seeing?"

Mich flicked a switch on the harness, and the monitor showing their children jumped to a view of Know-Where-to-Go. The horizon of the planet was plumed with a jet of blue fire that Rikki recognized immediately. "That's a proton fire."

"It's the electron plasma from a proton fire," Mich corrected. "Radio backlog is jammed with military frequency alarms. It'll be another few minutes before we get the code-clearance from Cendre to unscramble that noise, but we already know what it is, don't we?"

"Zōtl."

"Yep. The coupling lens has identified needlecraft silhouettes—lots of them. At least several thousand."

"That's not possible. The planet is a fortress. The zōtl could never have gotten a fleet that size close enough without being detected."

"Unless they planted a lynk."

"It would have been blown apart before any heavy armament could come through."

"Apparently not." A chime announced code-clearance, and the military signals from Know-Where-to-Go played over the intercom. Despite computer amplification, the messages were tattered with static, and Rikki and Mich had to listen carefully to understand what had happened. The zōtl had erected a lynk—but in a way that no one had been prepared for. Using unprecedented technology, the zōtl had pirated one of the existing Tryl lynks. The surprise of their attack from inside the planet's defenses had left Know-Where-to-Go helpless. In moments, all the human proton cannon and ramstat flyers had been neutralized. Survivors of the initial neurotoxin and laserbolt attack had been herded away to Galgul. Only pocket resistance remained.

The report ended abruptly. The channel from Cendre confirmed that the blue flare they were watching was the exhaust of a proton drill blasting through the planet's rock surface. "What are they excavating?" Mich asked. "All the human settlements are on the surface or just below. Only Tryl artifacts are deep enough for that massive a quarry."

"Remember the Joaon legend of the Last Tryl?" Rikki asked. "The Tryl died in a grotto on Know-Where-to-Go."

"I don't think the zōtl would go to this much trouble for a Tryl mummy."

"According to Joao, the Tryl died in front of the armor of the Rimstalker. The zōtl are going after that armor."

"The armor's just a legend," Mich said.

"Not anymore. Let's call it a theory."

"Forget theories, Rikki. We're in trouble of the big variety. The radio backlog is filling with distress signals from survivors—and we're the nearest Foundation vessel. The *Alan Guth* is going to have to respond. That means you and I and the kids are going to be left behind here on Nabu while our ship goes into a battle zone, and it will be a long time before we're picked up. Are you ready for an extended stay on the bat-world if the zōtl take apart the *Alan Guth*? I figure it'll be six months, maybe a year, before the Foundation gets around to sending another team our way."

Rikki blanched at the thought of her research ship destroyed by zōtl. Her whole life had been devoted to exobiology, and the privilege of field work in a state-of-the-art explorer was all she had dreamed of since she was a teenager. She and Mich had met in the competitive frenzy of doctoral camp on Ren. She was the daughter of a renowned engineer on Cendre and he a factory supervisor's son, both determined to use their intellects to escape the dreariness of life in the swamp cities. She took first place honors, and he was not far behind. They graduated at the time that the Foundation was organizing a scientific survey of the wild worlds, and both were locked in a dead heat for the choice position of science field officer on one of the expensive explorer vessels. To assure securing such coveted work, they married and offered their talents as a package. For five years they worked together on the *Alan Guth*, exploring the wild worlds, before they fell in love during an argument about spontaneous nucleation of protein crystals. A year later, Rafe was born. Now in the twelfth year of their survey, Rikki understood the system they worked for well enough to know that if they lost the *Alan Guth*, for any reason, the most they could hope for as a family was deskwork in a research lab somewhere in Doror. They were too old and too valuable to keep in the field, and only their proprietary claim to the *Alan Guth* and their excellent reports kept them from being recalled and replaced by a younger team.

"We're not giving up our ship," Rikki declared.

"We have no choice. You know Hadre. He doesn't go by the book—he *is* the book."

Numan Hadre Az was the Crystal Mind commander of the explorer. By fiat of Ieuanc 751, the current Crystal Mind dictator of the Foundation, all explorer crafts, all fighter fleets, all cargo convoys—all large ramstat vehicles —were commanded by numans.

"I won't let Hadre go alone," Rikki said.

Mich's shaggy eyebrows jerked with surprise. "We can't go with him into a zōtl battle zone. The children—"

"You and the children will stay here on Nabu," Rikki decided. "The food synthesizer can run three months without a recharge. By then we'll be back—or you'll have a garden. The laser pistols will keep the rawfaces and the longtooths away until you are picked up."

"I don't believe I'm hearing this," Mich said, unstrapping himself from the telescope harness and twisting into freefall so he was floating before his wife. His long face was creased with worry. "You can't just throw yourself away like this."

"I'm not throwing myself away, Mich. I'm going with Hadre to make sure he doesn't throw away the *Alan Guth*. It's everything we've worked for. I won't let that rockhead sacrifice our ship in some suicide run against the zōtl. We're going in for survivors and that's all."

"The Foundation fighters won't reach Know-Where-to-Go for at least a day after our ship arrives. *Alan Guth* will just be a target for the zōtl. Let the rockhead have his suicide run and stay here with us."

"No. This ship is too valuable to sacrifice. Even Hadre will agree to that logic—but only if I'm there to insist on it."

"Then let me go. I'll keep the rockhead's blood lust in

line and bring the ship back with whatever survivors we can lift out of there."

"It's a lot easier to navigate an explorer than to hold a downstation against the longteeth and distort tribes of Nabu with only laserbolt pistols. No, Mich—you're the strong one. The kids will be safer with you down there."

Mich grunted his disapproval. "You're not going. We're staying together on Nabu. To hell with the ship. To hell with the survey. I'm not going to lose you."

A slow, mischievous grin lit Rikki's features. "There were times enough when you wished you could have lost me—but that's never been your fate, Mich Yetz, and it won't be now. I'll be back with the ship."

A thud reverberated in the gunwales. "That's Hadre," Mich said. "He's come up. The news must have reached him. Listen, Rikki, I'm not going to let you go. Your first responsibility is to Rafe and Teuy. Forget the survey. We can download all our files and take them with us. There's twelve years of material there."

"And twelve more years to go—if we keep our ship. What kind of lives will our children have in the city anyway? We worked hard to get away from that travesty of human society, that—that robot paradise—and we've made a good life for ourselves out here. That's what I owe my children—and that's why I'm going."

Mich was in the midst of his retort when Numan Hadre Az popped out of the companionway from the dropship loading dock. He was a typical numan, two meters tall, brown-skinned with tightly-reeved hair and beard, flat nose, wide nostrils, and eyes like cracked glass. His gray stare went from Mich to Rikki and back again. A tight, emotionless smile showed perfect teeth. "Are my ears malfunctioning or am I actually hearing Chalco's fun couple arguing?"

"We're not arguing," Mich said. "We're discussing our predicament."

"I hope you've reached a resolution," Hadre said, holding onto the bulwark to steady himself in freefall. "The zōtl have attacked Know-Where-to-Go. We are the closest Foundation ship. I must act immediately."

Mich's harsh face gazed into Rikki's jaw-set determination, and his bushy eyebrows curled sadly. "Rikki will be going with you, Hadre," he said without looking away from the clarity of her green stare. "I'll gather our files and some extra supplies. She'll talk to the children."

Later, when the dropship had been returned by remote after delivering Mich and the children to the downstation, Hadre admitted, "I had expected to take one of you with me on this mission—but I thought it would be Mich."

"Why, because he's bigger than I?"

"No. I thought you would be the choice to take care of the children on Nabu. He's more afraid than you are of the rawfaces and the longteeth."

"That's why he'll survive Nabu."

Alan Guth swung out of orbit on a trajectory that took it in the opposite direction from Know-Where-to-Go. They flew at top speed into a gut-twisting arc that made the seams of the ship groan as they turned about and hurtled back toward Nabu. They shot past the planet; Numan Hadre Az shut down the ramstat engines and let their gathered momentum carry them. "The zōtl will be looking for ramstat trails in the magravity field," the numan clarified. "Know-Where-to-Go is close enough to Chalco now that we can approach it obscured by local asteroids. I've plotted our course to carry us by inertial power alone through the planetesimals. It will take us longer, but we'll still get there hours ahead of the fighter fleet."

They were kept busy on the two-day journey with viewing their target and assessing the strength of the zōtl force they would be encountering. The blue flare of the proton drill came and went amid enormous bursts of gamma energy, then stopped altogether. As the explorer closed in, the reason became clear. The proton drill had been hitting Tryl artifacts, some of which then exploded with enormous force. After carving a canyon four kilometers deep and losing hundreds of robot workers in the unpredictable explosions, the zōtl had abandoned the drilling and begun construction. What they were building did not become evident until *Alan Guth* was minutes away.

"It's a bomb," Numan Hadre Az announced, reading the latest spectrographic printout and outlining with his finger the profiles of radioactive materials. "The zōtl are erecting a bomb—a massive bomb, obviously designed to shatter the whole planet—smash it like an egg."

"Why?" Rikki asked. They were in the mapping chamber, floating about the holoform of Know-Where-to-Go, reviewing their attack strategy.

"They want the Rimstalker's Form."

"Then that's not just a legend."

"There is no direct evidence of Rimstalker technology, other than Lod and Saor and the sonar shadows we have of the Genitrix modules at the cores of the planets—but the historical evidence indicates that the Rimstalker's central processor is located directly beneath Towerbottom Library."

"And the zōtl lynk, their proton drilling, and the new bomb are located almost precisely opposite the Library."

"Yes—they clearly want to seize the Form, not simply destroy it."

"How long do we have?" Rikki asked.

"Long enough. The bomb is still in assembly, and that's slowing down as the fighter fleet approaches. The zōtl are readying for battle in the next six hours. But we'll begin our strike in—thirty-eight minutes and twelve seconds."

"You've still told me nothing," Rikki complained, "other than that I'm going down in the dropship to pick up survivors. Why? The fleet can rescue them later."

"You can't come where I'm going, Rikki."

"You promised me you wouldn't use the ship in a suicide attack, Numan."

"I'm not."

"So what weapons are you going to use? Our laser cannon can fend needlecraft but not destroy a lynk."

The numan fit his humorless smile in place. "I was reading three camps of survivors until today," he said, hovering about the large image of the planet. He pointed to an area near the Library. "This is the last holdout—the only distress signal I've received in the previous twelve hours. I'll drop you there and let gravity swing me around to the other side. As I glide over the zōtl lynk, I'll release the laboratory's reactor. I've gimmicked it so that the uranium core will fuse on impact."

"A fusion bomb," Rikki whispered in awe—then her round eyes squinted with doubt. "The only way to place that effectively will be a direct fly-over. The zōtl will blow you to pieces as soon as you cross the horizon."

"The zōtl aren't looking for an explorer. The fleet has their full attention. I'll be coming in low and fast from the planet's nightside. The laser cannon will deflect their air cover, and the ship is bulky enough to take a few direct hits without falling entirely apart. But you can't be on board. While a numan like myself can simply molt whatever cells are damaged by gamma rays, the radiation pulse from the fusion explosion would kill you. I have to drop you off. So you might as well place yourself among the survivors, where maybe you can be helpful."

"I want this ship back, Numan Hadre Az," Rikki said, grimly. "My family's survival on Nabu demands it."

"Family needs can hardly compare with the needs of the Foundation at this point, Doctor Carcam. If I'm not successful, the fleet will be destroyed. So long as the zōtl lynk is intact, the spiders can call forth all the reinforcements they need. We must destroy the lynk."

"But you will try—" Rikki pleaded, "you will sincerely try not to trash the *Alan Guth*?"

"I'm a numan," Hadre said. "I'm too valuable to trash needlessly. After the lynk is destroyed, I'll power-up and retrieve you and the survivors. I, too, want to return to the Foundation. Ieuanc 751 will be most pleased if I succeed. Perhaps I will even be promoted to a fleet director."

"I'll be happy if we're simply not demoted to corpses," Rikki replied and headed for the dropship.

During the bumpy entry, when death seemed more feasible than survival, Rikki Carcam thought about Ieuanc 751. She gnashed her teeth trying to bring to mind her family, but with ludicrous insistency her mind remained fixed on the Crystal Mind dictator. Most humans in the Foundation worlds of Doror admired the dictator's administrative efficiency and the security from zōtl-attack that his superbly strategic intellect offered them. But in Chalco, Ieuanc 751 was loathed, for his security was extended only to Foundation members. The wild worlds were rife with wild humans, who survived in the most primitive conditions. All appeals for help were rebuffed. The dictator was most careful not to overextend himself and weaken the hold on what he already controlled. Control was the Crystal Mind's passion—and that was why Rikki and Mich had left Doror. They did not want to be continuously monitored for their own good by the sensors that had to be worn by every citizen. They did not want to have to log each stroll in a park or to be subject to the directives of numans, who were so proud of their superiority. As her teeth clacked with the jolts of her flight through the atmosphere of Know-Where-to-Go, she understood why she could not take her mind from Ieuanc 751. Though she had seen him only in holoforms, his famous blueblack skin and shatterglass eyes were as familiar as Mich's features or either of her children's. He was the spiritual father of all humans who had ever lived in Doror—and now as she faced death, she recognized how thoroughly she had been conditioned to serve the Crystal Mind.

Without ramstat, the dropship had to be glided to a landing, and soon there was no time for any thoughts but those concerned with the work at hand. Once she cleared the clouds, Towerbottom Library leaped into view, its glass geodesics shattered and reflecting the wan daylight brokenly. The countryside was devastated, blackened from laserblasts and pocked by particle beam craters. A firestorm had erased all the vegetation to the horizon.

Rikki landed beside the rim of a crater, where the distress signal had originated. There she found five humans, scorch-faced and shivering with shock—the only people left alive on the planet. They were crouched in a covert they had dug with their own hands in the lip of the crater. Rikki broke open medical and food packs and passed around a canteen before hunkering down among them to wait for Numan Hadre Az.

On the planet's far side, the fly-by of the *Alan Guth* transpired precisely as the Crystal Mind had calculated. Needlecraft startled into the sky when the bulky explorer thundered out of the darkness. Sparking laserfire, the ship zoomed over the mountain range that flanked the lynk site, bursting the surprised needlecraft who rose against it. The dolmen lynk pulsed red in the floodlit plain below, overlooking the vast canyon that the proton drill had excavated. Wormings of Tryl architecture reticulated the scooped-out quarry in hive-like patterns. Hadre released the rigged reactor. While it dropped, he methodically picked off needlecraft with his laser cannon. Then the landscape below vanished in a nuclear glare.

The shock of the fusion explosion almost shattered the low-flying explorer, and Hadre momentarily lost control of the ship's laser defense. In that lag, three needlecraft rammed into the explorer's hull and docked with magnetic anchors. As the *Alan Guth*'s ramstat engines ignited and the vessel curled toward the planet's dayside leaving behind a boiling mushroom cloud where the zōtl lynk had been, the hull shook. The spiders were using their lasers to cut through the bulwarks.

"Rikki!" Hadre shouted into his radio, hoping to be heard above the magnetic pulse from the fusion blast. "Get up here fast! I've got three needlecraft on me and they're cutting through the hull! Hurry!"

Rikki heard enough of the static-torn message to understand Hadre's plight. She leaped to her feet, but one of the survivors, a woman narrow-faced as an opossum, grabbed her. "Wait. You heard the numan—zōtl are up there. Don't go. In a few hours, the fleet will be here and we'll be saved."

"Rikki! This is Hadre Az, your numan commander! I'm giving you a direct order. Get up here now. I need your help."

"Leave the numan," the scoop-cheeked woman said. "He would leave you. Numans think people are expendable because Crystal Minds are so much more expensive to manufacture. Everyone knows that. Why risk your life?"

Rikki leveled a predatory stare on the woman. "Are you coming to fight zōtl with me or waiting here for the fallout from the fusion blast?"

The dropship was crammed with the five survivors and Rikki. With ramstat boosting them, the flight was short. As soon as they docked, even as the airlock was pressurizing, Rikki fired the emergency release bolts, kicking the dropship's hatch into the docking area, crushing the three plasma-suited zōtl waiting outside for them. With a laser pistol in each hand, she led the charge through the airlock and into the ship.

Hadre had already dispatched most of the zōtl by disengaging the chambers where the needlecraft had punched through. But one of the needlecraft had magnetized to the engine module, and the humans had to go in and flush them out.

"Why don't you lead us?" the narrow-faced survivor asked Hadre, who had decided to remain in the command chamber.

"I'm a numan," he answered matter-of-factly.

"Ah, yes—" the survivor said with a glance at Rikki, "much too valuable to risk when there are expendable humans who can do the job."

"Go—" Hadre commanded, "before the spiders scuttle our engines. And watch where you shoot. If you hit the ramstat coils, we're going nowhere but down."

The engine module was a large chamber mazy with ducts, cable-pipes, and the scaffolding that braced the ramstat coils. *Alan Guth*'s low orbit provided enough gravity for the humans to walk. Using heat sensors, Rikki and her haggard crew moved back-to-back through the darkness, stalking the zōtl. Their only defense against the zōtl's laserfire was the bulky armor vests, thighpads, and infragoggles they had donned before entering.

The zōtl did not wait to be found. Laserbolts smashed the metal flooring before the humans as the zōtl attempted to kill their enemy with hot shards. Gushes of blasted plasteel sprayed molten sparks over them, burning their exposed clothing and blistering their flesh. The attack pinpointed the zōtl, and the humans fired back. Laserbolts intercut the darkness. Several of the humans' shots flashed against the ramstat coils. "Watch your fire!" Rikki shouted. "You're shooting wild!" Enraged that her ship was in danger, she dared to expose herself and dropped several of the spidershapes in quick succession to smoking twitches on the floor.

The stink of the burning zōtl gagged the humans. They advanced and used their heat sensors to corner the last of the zōtl against the hatchway they had bored from their needlecraft. The zōtl were frantically dismantling their hatch, hoping to breech the hull and explosively depressurize the chamber. Rikki blasted them, and their slithery shapes burst into flames and collapsed.

Hadre was pleased and greeted them at the portal to the engine module, a laserifle tucked under his arm. As he grinned his empty smile, three of the survivors aimed their laser pistols at him and at Rikki. Rikki managed a surprised shout before they fired. The laserbolts flashed harmlessly in the numan's and Rikki's faces. Hadre's grin widened, and he rapid-fired his rifle, the crimson bolts of laserfire kicking the five survivors backward against the closed portal, where they slumped, their startled limbs jerking.

Rikki shouted from her stomach and leaped back as three of the bodies split open like shucked fruits, ribs flaying like scarlet blossoms and spidershapes lifting from the sticky viscera where the bodies' stomachs should have been. Hadre fired again, and the zōtl burned in the corpses they had hidden within.

"How did you know?" Rikki gasped.

"I didn't. But this kind of horror has happened before. I adjusted their pistols to fire harmless red light with the same visual characteristics as laserbolts. You were the only one with a live weapon. And I wasn't even sure about you —until you killed the zōtl in the engine module."

"Two of these people are not infested," Rikki said, kneeling over the woman who had wanted her to stay behind. She and the other human were still breathing. "They're alive."

Hadre fired twice more, punching holes in their hearts and spraying Rikki with blood. "Now they're dead," he announced.

"You killed them!" Rikki shouted, horrified by the abrupt slaying. "They're not infested—and you killed them."

"We can take no chances. The zōtl may have rigged them with other weapons. Maybe viruses. We can't be sure. I'll have the psybot clean this up. You better shower yourself. Their blood may be contaminated."

"What do you know about blood?" she spluttered and rushed away from the stink of burning flesh.

She had showered and was changing her clothes, her hands still trembling from her rage and shock, when Hadre called: "Rikki!"

"Fuck you, Hadre!" she screamed, and tugged on her underwear.

"Rikki—I'm in the map chamber," he said, his voice broken by staccato blasts of the laserifle. "Another needle-craft has docked! They're coming in through the con-bubble! Get down here on the double!"

Rikki snatched her laser pistol and, half naked, sprinted

through the companionway to the ladder-shaft that dropped into the map room. A zōtl hovered over the shaft among gruesome-smelling vapors of seared flesh. One of its pincered forearms was sheathed in the metallic cuff of a lasergun no bigger than a thimble. It fired at her—and the bulwark to her side spanged with sparks. She dropped to her knees, fired twice, and shattered the zōtl to a writhing black rag.

Two more zōtl appeared, firing, showering her with hot sparks of plasteel. She screamed and swiftly retreated.

"Rikki! I'm in the map chamber! Where are you?"

Rikki dashed among the companionways, stopping only once to fire at her pursuers. She slammed the hatch that sealed off the map chamber and scurried up a ladder to the bridge.

"Rikki! Respond! This is a direct command!"

Heaving for breath, Rikki slumped in the pilot's sling. From below she heard the searing hiss of laserlight cutting metal. In moments they would break through—and she realized with hurtful clarity that she had to make a decision. She could grab a laserifle and go back down, try her best to save the numan, and maybe get maimed or killed. Or—

Without another thought, and with the siren of the laser-sheared metal reaching toward its highest pitch in her ears, she reached over the control console and began the sequence that would disengage the module containing the map chamber and con-bubble.

"Rikki!" Hadre shouted, his rifle fire so rapid it sounded like static. "What are you doing?"

I'm cutting you off for the gangrene you are, numan, she thought, but said nothing. Her mouth was too dry, and she needed all her concentration to complete the sequence before the zōtl broke through the hatch.

"I am the numan commander of this vessel, Rikki Carcam. Do as I command. I am too valuable to be sacrificed like this. I am ordering you—"

The sequence completed its warning trills and lights, and the map chamber and con-bubble broke away from the ship and fell toward Know-Where-to-Go. From the bridge, Rikki watched the module ignite in the atmosphere and streak away like a falling star. Before it burned out, she looked away. With suddenly calm fingers, she amplified the ramstat drive. Her body went loose in freefall, and the *Alan Guth* veered toward Chalco.

The Brood of Night was a hamlet of cowled distorts: Two faces stared from one hood; dogs with human foreheads and eyes chivvied friskily through the crowd of robes and sniffed at Chan-ti Beppu's legs and crotch. In the ivory glow of the paper lanterns they carried, the faces were each starkly unique, some silver as fishskin, some feathery, others bony as insects. One of the villagers had no more countenance than a tree, eyes and mouth hidden in brown fissures of crusted flesh, a leafless dwarf-oak with a woman's shape. Another was pale, squat, and smudged as a mushroom with two tiny mouths where her eyes should have been and in the place of her mouth an optic-bud like a starfish's red eye. The distorts greeted Chan-ti Beppu enthusiastically, glad for someone new to show around and share their stories.

The hamlet consisted of low cottages with agate-tile roofs and round, rose-paned windows. Each was a shop where a different specialty food was prepared for export to Perdur: mushroom wine, lichen cakes, glazed slugs, larval pudding, all with lyrical foreign names and unexpected flavors. The Brood offered her samples at each shop and welcomed her to the hamlet. Several of the grotesque lot spoke her idiom. For those who did not, a boyish head on kingcrab-legs who was called the Knower interpreted telepathically.

The Brood were distorts who, each in their way, had served Saor well. The hamlet had been created by the Saor-priests as a distort paradise, where those who had earned the favor of the Face of Night could live out their days happily. Most had lived before this paradise as missionaries among the numerous distort tribes—promulgating the Dark One's creed, "Worlds Without End," and its belief that Gai was a World-Eater and Saor her enemy who was determined to preserve Chalco-Doror from extinction. Others had defended Saor-priests from persecution by numans and people allied with Lod, who taught that Saor was a zōtl puppet. One of them was a numan with a glossed, fire-melted face, who had been taken long ago by zōtl and used for many years to subvert humans. He introduced himself as Hadre Az and told her the story of the zōtls' attempt to break open Know-Where-to-Go and—this whispered—his glorious role in thwarting them before they made him an ally. Everyone had a story to share. She listened to each of them patiently.

Though Chan-ti was a prisoner, she was treated as a new member of the community. She was given a capacious room above the vintner's shop, with a window that faced out the back, over the oxen stables, across the mushroom fields, to the mist-torn gorges of the Witch Maze. She was also given chores—weeding the garden, sweeping the flagstone walkways, helping with the harvest.

Grateful for the Brood's civility after the horror of losing her father to the scyldar, Chan-ti fulfilled her tasks without complaint. No one had any knowledge of what had befallen her, and she was left to ponder for herself the apparently meaningless deaths of Spooner Yegg and Moku the Beast. Escape was unthinkable. The Dragon's Shank was legendary for its malignancies, and she knew that if she wandered into that abyss looking for a lynk she would become some abomination's meal.

Days passed. The blurry stars set, and the sky was bereft of all light. Quilts of bioluminesence breathed across the fields and down into the foggy depths. Lamps and lanterns carved small scenes out of the thick darkness, eerie images of distorts bent in the fields, sitting on their stoops, cooking among wreathing steam in their wood-fired kitchens. When not working, Chan-ti roamed the far dells, lantern in hand, trying to learn something of the hostile land below. Somewhere out there was a lynk that could lead her back to the Overworld and from there to anywhere. Though the only place she wanted to go was wherever Ned O'Tennis was, if he was yet alive. And if not, she would travel to one of the Tryl temples deep in the Overworld, where they had devices that could speak with the bodies of light. She had never wanted to speak with the dead before, but she would with him. And she would speak with Spooner, too, and make a late peace with her father.

Those were her ambitions among the Brood of Night, ambitions that kept her from despair when she stared into their wrong flesh. None harmed her, most were gracious, yet she could sense their withheld dudgeon at her comparative wholeness. They had been ordered to accept her. Otherwise, she saw in their vacillation between keen interest and sudden remoteness while questioning her about the Foke, she would have been their victim. She let her hair grow wild and wore her clothes frumpily, trying to blend.

A bulbous, strut-winged flyer arrived. The Brood laded their ox-drawn wagon with crates of their goods and drove out to the field where the Saor-priests had alighted. From the flight pod, a portly, bald figure descended the gangway to the muddy field and paused. He signed to the two priests behind him, and they formed a chair by locking their arms and carried the Cenobite to the wagon.

An hour earlier, Fra Bathra's midstim trance had been interrupted by the ponderous telepathic voice from the Face of Night. "Go down to my Brood, priest, and live among them so you may better assure that my prisoner is not absconded by my enemies."

"I will dispatch my own lieutenants," Fra Bathra had promised.

"No. You go. Leave your lieutenants to attend Perdur. Go alone, for the hamlet is too small, my Brood too sensitive of their difference, to sustain more. See that Chan-ti Beppu is kept secure."

Now arrived in the hamlet, Fra Bathra popped a gly-tab into his mouth and rubbed his temples to uncramp the stink of raw fields in his sinuses. Then he waved the flyer away. The last crates were hurried aboard, and the air hummed with the magnetic chill of the ramstat drive as the ship lifted away. Clutching the sides of the wagon, the Cenobite signed with a nod, and the oxen jolted forward, one distort at the reins, another holding a pole strung with gourd lanterns against the resolute darkness.

The simian-dogs had run ahead and alerted the telepathic head, who organized a formal greeting party for the dignitary. Chan-ti was among the gaggle of distorts that welcomed the Cenobite. His sharkhole eyes fixed on her at once, and he did not disguise his ire at the woman who had caused him to be sent to dwell among the Brood. "This woman is a prisoner. She will be confined at all times. At all times, I say!"

Chan-ti did not wait for the distorts to seize her. She went to her room and lay in the dark until one of the fishskinned people brought her a lit waxfern. By that wispy light, she watched the shadowplay among the rafters blear with her tears of anger at not knowing why Saor had selected her for these cruelties.

Deep in the night, long after Fra Bathra's shrill commands had died away and he had droned into a deep sleep on a pillow-packed cot before a wood-stove in the hamlet's best shop, a quiet voice began in her mind. It was the Knower, the head with crab-legs, speaking to her. *Saor holds you to bait Ned O'Tennis,* the voice informed her. *You cannot escape, so why should you not know this? Too long have I troubled with your ignorance as you wander and wonder why you were taken here, why your father was killed. I will tell you. I have that right in my own village. You and Ned O'Tennis have fallen back in time from a future the Face of Night will not have. Ned and you must die. Neter Col would have slain both of you on Ras Mentis but for Moku, the Beast of Genitrix. Now you know. Saor and the other gods war.*

Chan-ti already knew about that war, and she trembled to see that she and Ned had fallen into it. Now there could be no escape. No matter if she found her way free to a lynk and the Overworld. The Face of Night and the Eater of Worlds could never be eluded. She snuffed the waxfern taper, abruptly glad in the midst of her dread. That she was alive meant Ned was, too. Their nightmare bound them.

Age of Dominion

Perhaps neo-sapiens, the mélange of races and genera from across the history of simian sentience, are more a memory of humanity than humanity in themselves. During the Age of Dominion, the belief was commonly held that Genitrix was an amanuensis, copying the dictations of the past from the genetic memory of life retained in the detritus of earth, but that she never got it just right. Neo-sapiens' brief dominance in Chalco-Doror at this time was a period of intense nostalgia for the original Earth, whose most vital lesson, if we have any remembrance at all, is that the power that conquers surrenders everything to its victory.

—Rigo Phu Than, from *Declensions of Time*

Fruit of the Storm-Tree

Nappy Groff and Gorlik descended the Dragon's Shank with fear-nimble alertness. Without the klivoth kakta and the useful tools in the sojourn packs they wore at their hips, they would have perished in the first hour of their trespass. They wore gloves and goggles, yet the mists of dragon breath scalded the exposed flesh of their wrists and cheeks. The rims of their nostrils blistered around the soaked plugs of cotton grass through which they sucked air. Bleating

268

razorjaws slithered through the underbrush from all sides in the darkness. The kakta's telempathic blessing let the Foke feel the voracious beasts they could not see, and the sap they smeared in their hair and on their clothes masked their fleshy odors.

Long they traveled and silent, the kakta allowing them to find food in the dark and to communicate without alerting the greedy forest with their speech. But soon the kakta was gone. The acid mist had rotted it. The Foke, already exhausted from climbing up and down blind ravines and eating only pulpy mushrooms, had to carry on more intently. Both were grimly committed, and they picked their way with assiduous care over the mulchy ground among the soft trees. When they spoke now, their whispers stung the silence, and the bleats closed in. Twice Nappy had to use the pistol to fend off rampaging razorjaws. Both times, the explosive gunshots had alerted every beast in the woods, and they had to flee through the treetops, the gilled branches puffing spore clouds that caught in their garments and later sprouted tendrils.

So hairy with fungul growths that the spaces between their fingers webbed, the Foke finally desponded. The blurry stars had set under an unreverberate night, and only glowworms hinted at the perfidious gorges in the dark. Gorlik was ready to turn back. But Nappy knew they could not make it back; if they were going to die, they would die moving forward. On their hands and knees they crept, reserving only enough strength at the end of a trek to climb into a tree to sleep.

During one rest period, Gorlik was roused by a cold hand. He started alert before the lux-lit facepan of a psybot and almost toppled from his perch. A psybot's featureless head attached to mechanical arms and a small ramstat unit floated before him, outlined in lux-tubes. *Be calm,* a resonant voice shook through his bones. *I am Saor, the Face of Night.*

Gorlik turned a frantic look to Nappy.

I have spelled him, the oceanic voice said. *He will not wake. You alone will hear me.*

"We are just Foke—"

Silence, Bram Gorlik. I am come to spare your life. You will die here in the Witch Maze unless you agree to do as I say. Nappy Groff would bid me leave you die in peace, and so I leave him to sleep. You have the stronger drive to live. I can feel that. You will do as I say.

"Whatever I can—"

This you can do easily. Do you know what these are? The mechanical arms lifted into the light two thick black cables with chrome undersides. *These are the phanes. They can hold a body of light in place. These are to be put on the body of Lod.*

"Lod? The god Fire? How— I— We are just Foke—"

I will lead you to Lod. You will put the phanes on him. And then you will be free to go back to your life among the Foke.

"My life is to be spared?"

If you do as I say.

"And Nappy Groff?"

He will live or die as you say.

For an instant, Gorlik was glad to think of Nappy Groff dead, for then there would be no witness to his cowardice before the scyldar—but the next moment he loathed himself for the thought and said in a strong whisper, "I say he live. We are just Foke, looking for—"

Do as I say, and the two of you will live. Take the phanes.

Gorlik grabbed the thick cables, and they curled in his hands like eels.

Empty your sojourn pack and place them there.

Gorlik did as he was told, and the psybot took the meager contents of his pack, a moldy blanket, dented canteen, handfuls of blackening mushrooms, and a *Glyph Astra*.

Do not tell Nappy Groff of your mission or what is in your pack. If you break faith with me, Bram Gorlik, you will suffer long before you die.

The psybot whisked out of sight, and Gorlik was left shivering around the hot hope of survival.

Egil Grimson remembered dying. He remembered that very clearly. An arrow-slain comrade falling from the mast of their ship during battle had struck him unconscious, and he was captured alive by the enemy. They stripped him and hung him by one ankle from a huge ash tree overlooking the seacliffs. The enemy knew this was how the god of his fathers had hung to attain the vision needed to save the human race, and they did this to him in mockery of his faith, of the very life of his soul. He hung there a night, a day, and another night, and he remembered the suffering and how the agony and laughter of his enemies had twisted howls from him—but not broken him, because he believed his god would avenge him. Dawn, filthy green, and the shrieks of gulls waiting for him to die were his last memories—then nothing—

Until the Voice and the radiance from the inside of a pearl awakened him, he had slept in the bosom of oblivion. The Voice explained everything with a suavity that made it impossible for him not to believe. She was the voice of Earth herself, remembering him as he was, recounting all his glories, from his seacave birth in the tradition of his raider ancestors, through his proud childhood with the other sons of warriors, to his battles and victories in the foreign lands, to his death on the storm-tree. She remembered it all, and by that he knew she spoke the truth when she told him, "Egil Grimson, you are to live again on another Earth, a very different Earth than where you lived before."

For a long time, Egil tried in the old way to understand what she had told him, believing that since he had died at the hands of his enemies he had been reborn in Valhalla. He wanted very much to believe that was true, for what she had so patiently explained to him was far too strange for his Viking mind. His whole comprehension of time and creation had to be reforged before he could begin to grasp the truth of his predicament. He resisted a long time—but time was Genitrix's wealth. While Egil Grimson's body lay in her bio-matrix under the rootweave of a cedar forest on Q're, the supercoiling of his DNA being precisely adjusted to prevent aging, his mind was nourished by Genitrix. In time, he understood everything from the viewpoint of the machine intelligence that had reclaimed him.

Like millions before him, Egil Grimson was ejected from Genitrix into a wild world, naked and weaponless but for the knowledge his re-creator had bestowed on him. For many, that knowledge had been useless against the ferocity of beasts and distorts. But Egil was a warrior from birth, and he survived. Eventually, he found his way to a tribe and lived among them as a hunter, befuddled and angered by the cruelty of the wilderness and the zōtl. His anger steepened whenever he met others like himself who had been revived, informed, and then abandoned in the wilderness. He wanted to kill the Rimstalker who had done this to humankind, but there was no hope of that, it seemed, for survival among the giant trees of Q're, where fangfaced bears and zōtl hunters abounded, required all his devotion. Then one day when he was alone in the forest, having lost his hunting party to a pack of needle-toothed wolves, he met Gai.

During the zōtl attack on Know-Where-to-Go, when the spiders had attempted to get at her Form by blowing apart the planet, Gai had been in Doror. From Ioli she had watched the blue star of the zōtls' proton drill, helpless to stop them. Wearing a human shape she had grown in the loam, the better to communicate with her numan hosts on Ioli, she traveled with the ramstat fleet to counter the zōtl attack. Her relief at finding the zōtl lynk and proton drill destroyed was so expansive, she determined that she would never be that vulnerable again.

The Foundation of Doror had done their best to find Rataros and the O'ode in the Overworld, but the numans were too methodical and conservative—and now, with their incursions into Chalco, they threatened to drive the zōtl entirely away before the O'ode could be found. With less zōtl lynking into Chalco-Doror, the timelines in the Overworld associated with the zōtl were fewer, and so finding Rataros became that much harder. Gai's hope that Ned O'Tennis could locate the O'ode was tarnished, and she decided that the Crystal Mind was too efficient. She would have to replace the numans. She searched Chalco for a human strong enough to build a new empire—and she found Egil Grimson.

Bloodied by his narrow escape from the needletoothed wolves, Egil was kneeling over a stream and cleansing himself when he saw Gai's reflection standing over him. She was in her plasma shape, human-looking, but just barely. Her iridescent flesh wavered green and blue, her eyes were mirror-disks, her long hair shifted over her nakedness like the electric vapors of the borealis. The secret smile of an archaic Greek statue hung on her face as she assessed the man before her. He was short and powerfully built, with a roisterous blond beard. He shouted at her from where he was crouching and drew a chipped knife.

"Rise, Egil Grimson," she said in a voice like wind across a cave's mouth, "Gai would speak with you."

Egil stood up before the shimmery apparition, the knife that he had reflexively drawn held limply at his side. "You are Gai? The Rimstalker?"

"I am the one you would kill—if you could."

"You know that about me?"

"I know everything about you. Certainly Genitrix informed you that thoughts are things—waveforms suspended in the vacuum that holds us all. I see your wavebundles very clearly, Egil. I understand why you want to kill me. I have come to offer you that chance."

Egil's mouth balked.

"You are right to be surprised," Gai told him. "Of the great many of your fellow beings that Genitrix has reproduced, you are among the very few whom I have addressed directly in recent times. I need you—or, at least, a man like you. Ah, I see your curiosity is piqued. What need has the Rimstalker of its bait—and how will that need give you a chance to kill me?"

"Genitrix has warned me of your duplicity, Rimstalker," Egil said, pointing his knife at Gai. "You create to destroy. I will not be your fool."

"You are already my fool. You are alive in Chalco. Shall I simply leave you here to continue as I found you?" Gai faded to a blur.

"Wait!"

The Rimstalker's plasma shape regathered, though she remained transparent to the sunlight slanting through her.

"Say what you have come to say, Rimstalker."

The mirrors of Gai's eyes widened, and Egil saw himself leaning forward, knife held tip up. He sheathed the blade. "Good," the Rimstalker said. "Maybe you are the very one I am seeking. You have learned well from Genitrix. You know, she doesn't tell everyone she makes all that she's told you. That's only a recent development."

"Since you aborted her creative functions in Doror," Egil said.

"She's been compensating for that lately by telling her

creatures—at least those who can listen—what a monster I am. She doesn't really believe that. It's zōtl programming. Yet I won't deny it. I am a conscientious killer. My world is threatened by the zōtl. I will do whatever I can to save my people, even sacrificing other sentient lifeforms."

"So I have seen, Rimstalker. What would you have with me?"

"A king. I am looking for a king."

"Of what hell? Chalco is the zōtl's kingdom."

"Chalco cannot be ruled. Genítrix is still active here, and what I have in mind will require more stability than this genetic frenzy would allow. No, not Chalco but Doror is the kingdom I offer you."

"Doror already has a king. Ieuanc 751—ruler of Doror these last three centuries."

"Ieuanc 751 is a Crystal Mind. I want a human king to rule Doror."

"Why?"

"The zōtl have no use for numans. They want intelligent creatures whose brains squirt certain chemicals when they feel pain."

"You want to give Doror back to the zōtl?"

"Yes. The numans have been far too efficient in sweeping the zōtl aside, and now the numans encroach on Chalco. That has made the zōtl desperate enough to attack my Form—and that I cannot allow. Far better that the zōtl have all the humans they can process. Then their timelines will be more vivid in the Overworld, and my chances of finding the O'ode that much greater."

"And I am the one you have selected to usurp Ieuanc 751?"

"You are the one. But there is more. I want you to strike a bargain with the zōtl. You will make an arrangement with them whereby they will receive all the humans they want from what Chalco-Doror can produce—in exchange for not attacking the worlds of your kingdom."

"Of which Know-Where-to-Go is to be one." A scimitar smile slashed across Egil's yellow beard. "You will thus be free to search for the O'ode unmolested. Cunning, Rimstalker. But why would the zōtl agree to such an arrangement?"

"Do you think they prefer being killed by the Crystal Mind? They will agree—and readily."

"And me? You think I am cold enough in my heart to feed my fellow humans to the zōtl so that I may be king of a doomed empire?"

"All empires are doomed. Yours will endure a thousand years. What earthly king could want more? As for your fellow humans—have you forgotten your life on Earth? You are a Viking. You were bred to conquer weaker races and dominate them. I am offering you a chance to fulfill your breeding. You will select the weakest of the humans for the zōtl to take. The strongest and the most beautiful will thrive under your protectorship. Why do you hesitate? This has been nature's power from the beginning of life—a blind power. Why should it not be in your hands, where it can be used discriminately, for the outright benefit of your fellow humans?"

"Genitrix warned me that you would do anything to achieve your aims."

"Anything. Will you then decline the power that I am offering you?"

Egil Grimson turned away, to think without the eerie shape of the Rimstalker filling his sight. He stared into the red sunlight glistering on the stream. He was a Viking, proud of his ferocity, prouder for knowing how he had died without a twinge of cowardice to satisfy his enemies. He knew he was strong enough to do what the Rimstalker asked. He had no doubt of that. But he feared the zōtl. Though he had only seen them from afar as silver streaks of needlecraft, he had heard all the revulsive stories of what they did to people, and he had viewed their spidery bodies when he was still inside Genitrix and had felt the horror of staring into the clasped hemispheres of their abstract faces.

"Is that not the very visage of death?" Gai asked, reading his thoughts. "Must we not all face that visage someday, in some form? I am offering you the power to choose who will die now and who will live to die later."

"That is not a power for any man to hold," Egil said, almost in a shout.

"No, not for any man—but for a king. The zōtl will feed anyway, Egil—and without you, they will feed on whomever they capture. With you, there is hope for a human kingdom, free of domination by zōtl or numans. Or would you rather I simply leave you here on Q're and search for my king elsewhere? I will find the one I seek, sooner or later."

Egil turned about, the caverns of his eyes lit with a fiery hatred. "You said I would have a chance to kill you, Rimstalker. What did you mean?"

"Just that. As king, you will be an ally of the zōtl. Even now, they are picking furiously at the lynklock to the grotto on Know-Where-to-Go, where my physical body is housed. By allowing them to feed without fighting, you will give them a greater opportunity to break through the Tryl code and kill me. You may very well be the death of me."

"I cannot believe that."

"Believe, Egil Grimson. This is a war. My world has been devastated by the zōtl. My people—my very family— killed by them. I am willing to risk my life to have a chance to destroy them. And that chance will be equally yours to destroy me."

"Then I accept, Rimstalker. I will be your king—though I do not see how you will draw the zōtl into this."

"That will be far easier than wooing you, my dear Viking. Saor is my ambassador to the zōtl. He will arrange everything. You need only remember your ancestry."

"That I will, Rimstalker. If I am to be a king of hell, I will be a Viking king. Our fates are decided by powers greater than either of us, for even you do not know how the fates will decide the future."

"That is why I can promise nothing but my strategy. Both your will and the fates are needed to make it real. So gather those of your tribe that you want with you. In the coming days, I will have Lod terminate the magravity generators in Doror. In the confusion, you will begin your war against the Crystal Mind."

The Fugitive Lords of Hell

His bravery is so lonely, his suffering so wise, Frya thought, even as she sent the signal that would call in the troops to destroy him. *He would have made a fine Aetheling for the Emirate.*

Frya Kori placed the needle-thin transmitter in the crevice of a treetrunk on the perimeter of the rebel camp, and walked back through the forest to where the others were hunched about a leaf-fire. The man for whom she felt compassion was the rebel leader, Wulf Bane, a lanky, beardless, and broad-faced man with a mane of black hair. With his Viking and distort followers, he had sabotaged many of the Emir's efforts to establish colonies in Chalco; the rebel gang had blown up zōtl lynks and freed the vassals that were to be taken to Galgul. Wulf sat on a fallen log listening with the others to the storysong of the gang's runesmith, whose mellifluous voice lilted sadly about the tales of lost comrades.

When he saw her enter the glade, Wulf waved Frya to him, and she wended her way among the prone warriors and sat on the log beside him. Though she had only joined the gang several days earlier, Wulf had taken a liking to her and kept her close. She was a handsome woman, long-boned, strong-nosed, with a generous mouth, large blue eyes, and swansdown hair that she had shaggily cropped for this assignment. Most of the women in the gang were ferine tribesfolk and distorts who had joined the rebels during their long wanderings. Frya was the only Viking woman among them, and she saw the envy in the other women's dark eyes whenever Wulf showed her preference.

On Mugna, where Frya had joined the rebels, she had told them that she, too, was a fugitive from the Emirate, appalled by Emir Egil Grimson's cruelty. The burned-out husk of a strohlkraft—one of the Emirate's sleek ramstat flyers—and the charred corpses of several vassals, whom she had claimed were her family, gave credence to her story. In fact, a dozen such scenarios had been prepared among the wild worlds of Chalco. She had been the one the fates had chosen to be found by the rebels. The transmitter she had activated then became useless when the gang took her with them through a lynk. In the intervening four days, they had journeyed among four different worlds, and she had lost all but this last transmitter in futile efforts to alert the Emirate's troops to the whereabouts of the fugitives. At any moment, night or day, following his instincts alone, Wulf could command his gang to flee through the nearest lynk. With the lynk-compasses they carried, there was never any doubt where the nearest escape portal was.

In mid-melisma the runesmith stopped, silenced by a hand-signal from Wulf Bane. "To the lynk," the leader called out, and the rebels leapt to their feet, weapons and rucksacks in hand, lean-tos collapsing, and leaf-fire instantly smothered.

An icicle sharpened in Frya's heart. If the rebels fled now, she would have no means of contacting her troops, having just activated the last of her transmitters. "Wait," she said to Wulf. "Why must we flee? We've just arrived but an hour ago. I'm exhausted—and Elphame is the most beautiful of the worlds I've seen with you so far."

"Exhaustion serves our enemies," one of the dark-haired, sloe-eyed women said in passing.

"Only freedom is beautiful," another chimed as she flew by, lugging the camp's lux coils.

"Where are we going?" Frya asked.

Wulf smiled in his solemn way. "You've been with us too short a time to understand our ways, Frya. Trust me and in time you will see that it is better to run wild and free than to sit comfortably among slaves like your old masters."

The icicle in her heart pricked her with the frightful suspicion that he knew her complicity. Before she could speak to test that, one of the rebel men rushed up to them. "Wulf, the lynk-compass is warbling. That can only mean—"

"A ramstat field, closing in," Wulf completed. "No time to dash. They'll know where the lynk is as well as we and cut us off. Weapons up! Find cover! Today we fight for our freedom!"

The rebels scattered, laserbolt pistols and rifles clattering, plasteel blades hissing out of their sheaths. In that instant, the clearing erupted. A laser cannon sheared off the tops of the trees, and paths of flame crisscrossed the glade, igniting the brush. Three strohlkraft roared overhead, dropping cannisters of liquid fire that the rebels blasted in midair. Napalm splattered into the forest canopy, and the sky boiled into black smoke.

At the start of the attack, Wulf seized Frya by her arm and dragged her into the woods. Gouts of flame fell all about them, and the air went styptic and acrid. Without breaking stride, Wulf slapped an airmask onto his face and helped Frya with hers. On all sides, the shadows of the rebels flitted among tattering veils of fire, their faces masked, their guns lancing the sky with laserbolts.

A massive explosion heaved everyone to the ground as the rebels' laserfire struck a chink in strohlkraft armor and two of the flyers collided. The fireball of fused strohlkraft plunged into the canopy, slewed through the forest, splintering trees, and tumbled into the clearing that the rebels had abandoned. Wulf lifted Frya to her feet by her belt, and they sprinted deeper into the woods as the holocaust expanded behind them, chunks of burning metal skipping along the forest floor and spinning into the hazy sky.

The third strohlkraft circled around and came down ahead of Wulf and Frya. Its laser cannon blasted a clearing in the forest and alighted among the blazing trees, the repulsion from its ramstat field kicking the flames into sparks and coils of smoke. Hatches flashed open, and hooded, scarab-faced figures leaped out, laserifles firing.

Wulf had only a moment to think: *Scyldars! The Beast has sent the dead after us!*

Then he was surrounded by the black-masked figures, and he swung in an arc, his rifle rapid-firing. Frya crouched behind him, expecting him to be cut down at any instant. But he did not panic, and each of his shots found its mark. He grabbed her arm, and they bolted away from the strohlkraft, where the other rebels were converging. They leapt over the bodies Wulf had dropped and barged through a thornbush, their clothes shredding, their airmasks protecting their faces. They heard the thud of grenade launchers behind them, and the next moment, the forest shook again as the strohlkraft was blasted apart.

From under the thornbush, Wulf sniped at the scyldars that remained, and in minutes the last of the enemy were cut down in the rebels' crossfire. An air-blast signaled all clear. Wulf helped the trembling Frya to her feet, and they reconnoitered with the others in a glade on the far side of the destroyed strohlkraft.

"Casualties?" Wulf asked, pulling free from his mask.

His lieutenant, one of his Viking clan cousins, a stout man whose full beard was patchy with scars, answered. "Four dead—three from the clan—cousins Wind, Longtime, and Graytooth—and one from the tribes, the woman Queza. Two more will be gone by nightfall, tribeswomen both."

"Spare those two any more suffering," Wulf ordered. "Have the runesmith sing the parting for the dead. And be certain to get all the lynk-maps from Longtime. He kept a holoset in his boot-heel."

Wulf turned to Frya. Even through the sweat and tears that misted his eyes, his stare was tight and weighing. "They would have killed you, too, you know," he said.

She understood then that he knew who she was. Her hand strayed toward her laserbolt pistol and stopped when his stare did not flinch. He was not going to kill her. "Why do you let me live?" she asked.

"You are one of us," he answered. "Only you doubt that."

After the runesmith finished his parting, the fugitives went to the nearest lynk and crossed to another island on the dayside of Elphame. Even at noon, Elphame was twilit, the sky mottled with the pale silhouettes of the planetesimals and the worlds. Beyond those clustered crescents, the galaxy tilted, its spiral arms silver fire in the gloaming. The runesmith sang to that ethereal beauty of their lost comrades, his plaintive voice lifting into the wind that soared above the dusky archipelago.

The rebels ate their foraged food in silence from a bluff that overlooked an ocean where behemoths breached in spray-snorting lunges. When the meal and the cleanup were done, Wulf looked to where Frya hunkered and said aloud to the camp, "Frya Kori has something to tell us."

Frya's eyebrows lifted in a query to Wulf. His knowing stare was relentless, and she knew he would tell if she did not. Since the scyldar attack, the icicle in her heart had pierced her lungs and she had not been able to draw a full breath. Fear had impaled her. Not fear of death, for she was a Viking and had been bred to die for her clan. What she feared was the self-loathing that had begun to grow in her. Four days of shared hardship in the hell worlds of Chalco had earned her respect for the rebels. They were true Vikings all, even the distorts and tribesfolk who had joined Wulf Bane's fugitive clan during its wanderings. If the strohlkraft that she had called in had carried real troopers, she would have felt no remorse at betraying these brave rebels, and her part in the struggle to break these renegades would have continued. The scyldars were a cowardly response by her commanders. Scyldars were vassal corpses fitted with mindflex masks. They were usually employed only in situations where there was no hope of survival.

"I called in the troopers," Frya confessed to the camp. "I did not know they would be scyldars."

Angry exclamations erupted from the band of rebels, interspersed with the sigh of knives being drawn.

Wulf stood up and strode to the front of the bluff, facing the camp. "If blood is to be drawn for this, it will be mine. I knew she was a VEG agent." He reached into his mane of hair and held up a receiver attached to an earloop. "I heard her transmitter signals. I was able to get us out each time before the signal could be answered—until this last time."

The Viking Elite Guard were the Emirate's warrior-zealots, selected for their cunning, ferocity, and willingness to sacrifice their lives to achieve their objectives. They were trained from infancy to endure pain and to ignore fear. In the 280 years since Emir Egil Grimson had overthrown the tyranny of Ieuanc 751, the Viking Elite Guard had crushed every rebellion that arose in Doror and had, without the aid of conscripts or scyldars, claimed Valdëmiraën from the distort tribes, built the glass-spired city of N'ym overpeering the abyss of Saor, and made that City of the Sky the Viking capital of Chalco.

"If you knew she was VEG," the scar-faced lieutenant said, "why did you keep that knowledge secret from your clan?"

"That was my privilege as your leader," Wulf answered. "For seven years we have wandered Chalco, meeting every challenge the wild worlds and the Emirate have set before us. I see her as only one more challenge for us to conquer—but not with our blades—with our spirit."

"And Longtime, Graytooth, Wind, and the tribeswomen —what of them?"

"What of them?" Wulf retorted. "They are dead."

"That VEG beast killed them!"

"The scyldars killed them," Wulf shot back.

"She called the scyldars down on us."

"You are nearly blind if you believe that," Wulf said. "*We* called the scyldars down on us when we chose to leave the Emirate. We chose hell over our lordly lives in Doror, because the Emir is no true warrior but a craven tyrant, a puppet of the spiders. Have you forgotten the pogroms that killed legions of distorts because they did not meet the Emir's definition of human? Do we now pretend we did not see the pastures on Ren where people are bred like cattle, made to live in kennels, never to know their parents, or even to hear music, left to wander naked and uninformed until they are ready for consumption by the zōtl?"

"We have forgotten none of this, Wulf. Why do you think we fight with you? Why do you think so many of us have died at your side?"

"Ah, then you know," Wulf said with a shrewd squint. "This woman is not our enemy. She is but a weapon of our enemy. A weapon we will make our own. Imagine! A Viking Elite Guard fighting with us! Let word of that reach N'ym. Let the Emir think on that."

Frya rose from where she squatted, her jaw throbbing. "I have betrayed you, just as I said. I am a captain in the Elite Guard. And I will *not* fight with you. Come at me. All of you. Take my life. And I will surely take as many of yours with me as I can."

Wulf stepped boldly into the line of fire, his back to the VEG spy. A huge, chill grace possessed him as he held his arms open before his angry people. "You will not deprive us of this weapon. None of you will harm her." He gazed into each of their clenched faces, demanding their compliance. "This warrior will fight with us. That I swear on the blood of those we lost today." Then he turned slowly and faced the hard-eyed woman. "You are one of us now, Frya Kori."

"I am a Viking Elite Guard. I cannot be anything else. You know that."

"I know you are a Viking. That is why I know you are one of us. You live to fight. But you cannot fight for the Emir anymore. He is no true Viking. If you look into your heart, you will see this is true."

"There is no truth, Wulf Bane. Only conflict. Look into your heart, and you will see that is true."

"I have indeed seen that, Frya Kori. That is why you find me as I am. I was born an Aetheling on Valdëmiraën. Ah, I see by your smile you knew that of me."

"I did not know it—but I sensed it. You have the aloof and solitary bearing of an Aetheling."

"My clan were lords. Graytooth who died today was regent of Sakai. My cousin there with the beard patched with scars was duke on Ras Mentis. All the Viking men here were among the chiefs in the distort wars. We stalked the Overworld for runaway vassals, going to the far horizons even the Ordo Vala dreaded. And we ruled our fiefdoms with nobility and grace—until we looked into our hearts. And there we saw the conflict—the true conflict of life and death, of being and nothing, that is the heritage of all mortals. After that, we could no longer serve an Emir who is no more than a slave to the inhuman masters of these worlds. No true Viking can live to serve. We were born to rule."

"We rule Doror and Valdëmiraën," Frya protested. "In time we will rule all of Chalco."

"We rule nothing! The zōtl rule and we serve. Every Viking, even the Emir himself, is but a vassal to the spiders."

"We have an alliance with the zōtl. They take our undesirables, we take our liberty with these worlds."

"Bah! We ransom our liberty with human souls. Is even the most undesirable human worth sacrificing that we may continue to live in servitude to the spiders? Look into *your* heart, Frya Kori. Having known us—having lived as one of us, free, truly free of any other power but our own wills—

can you now return to the Emirate and call yourself a Viking?"

"I am an Elite Guard," she said quietly, as if to herself. "I serve the Emir."

"And he serves the zōtl."

"He deals with the zōtl. They are a reality that must be confronted."

"Let us confront the spiders with our weapons—not our cowardice."

"The Emir is no coward. He is a Viking of the first world —of Earth. He suffered and died on the storm-tree, brave as Odin."

"Would Odin send scyldars—programed *corpses*—to fight for him?"

"I did not know scyldars were to be used."

"What else do you not know? How much do you need to see before you realize we are the true Viking lords—we are the human spirit, bred to fight, as all life has fought from the beginning of time."

Cold awareness saturated her, and her knees almost buckled before her training asserted itself. The inhuman scarab-faces of the scyldars rose up in her memory, the black, featureless faces of death itself. They were the one enemy, the only enemy of life—and seeing that, she sagged to her knees.

Wulf Bane knelt beside her and put a firm arm about her shoulders. "Now you see. We are all fugitives. We have always been fugitives from the void. Whatever comfort, whatever power we gain from outside ourselves diminishes us—because comfort and power, unless they are won from the void inside us, are illusions that make us forget the emptiness that carries us. When we forget that, we believe we deserve comfort and power and so we are capable of any evil. We deserve nothing but what we make of ourselves. We deserve nothing else. And when we understand that, then nothing is enough."

Frya looked up, her eyes webbed in tears. "I did not know they would be scyldars. I thought—I really thought we were the heroes."

Wulf smiled with sullen grief. "We are heroes. All of us. And we can be together. But only if we stand alone."

* * *

Chan-ti heard this story from a cowled distort with a glassy face, whom she had worked with in the mushroom fields on the Dragon's Shank, before Fra Bathra arrived and confined her. Fech, the glass-skinned man, brought her meals and often lingered to chat, mostly about Fra Bathra's enormous appetite for glazed slugs and mushroom wine. The hamlet's population was too small to support the Cenobite's perpetual midstim trance and work the fields at the same time. And since many of the Saorpriests in Perdur enjoyed the Brood's comestibles and would dangerously resent the Cenobite for denying them, Fra Bathra sought his pleasure in the ancient ways of wine, food, and frequent stimulation of his reproductive glands, for which he preferred the silver-scaled women.

When Chan-ti had tired of hearing about Fra Bathra's appetites, Fech told her about the fugitive lords of hell. His glassy visage clouding red, he concluded, "I know their tale well, for I was of them. You have not heard of them, then?"

"There are many Foke tales of wanderers among the worlds, some about Aesirai. I don't remember hearing of Wulf Bane."

The distort's coloring dimmed, yet his gaze remained vivid. "If you've not heard of Wulf Bane, then you'll not have heard of me—Fech the Betrayer. Yes, it was I who betrayed the fugitive lords to the Aesirai—I who had run with them from before Frya. I believed all the glory words Wulf spoke, all the staunch speeches about freedom as a devotion of will, about the void that carries us all. Oh, I was a grand believer. I risked my life time and again for those precious thoughts. But in the end, I could not stand alone. On Xappur, I began to change. I got the changing sickness. My jaw began to shine—"

"Bonelight," Chan-ti recognized, with a dry voice.

"That was it. Bonelight. I was becoming a seraph. Wulf and the others, they wanted to stay on Xappur and tend me—but they couldn't stop it. A Saor-priest we had captured told me I could be healed in Perdur. You figure the rest. You can see how I am healed. The fugitive lords were destroyed in the fog on Xappur. And I am come here, healed—but never again whole."

Remorse, time's malignity, Chan-ti recalled from *The*

Book of Horizons but did not say it, knew not what to say. Before she could muster a reply, Fech jerked upright—and they both heard the telepathic head calling for her: *You are wanted, young sister. Be wary.*

Fech fled, and Chan-ti stood at the threshold of her door. The shrill voice of Fra Bathra fluted from below, "Chan-ti Beppu—you may come down now. I would speak with you."

Chan-ti stepped out into the wan glow of the gourd lanterns, went to the head of the stairs and saw the Cenobite below in the large kitchen, his bald, bulging forehead sparkling with sweat. He summoned her with two crooked fingers.

When she stood before him, the sweat was running down the seams of his jowls into the folds of his black robe, and she could smell the mushroom wine on his quick breaths. His wee eyes looked at her in a new way, soft and surly at the same time. He put his thick fingers on her frayed shirt, and his lumpy face mooned closer.

Chan-ti stepped back, aghast.

The Cenobite exposed his tiny teeth in a cold smile. "I was wrong to have locked you away, young one. You should enjoy your freedom among the Brood. And you will, yes, you will—if you are free with me."

He put his hands on her breasts, and she stifled a cry, knowing it was useless. Then revulsion cut through her, and she brought her knee up swiftly into the soft flesh pressing her.

Fra Bathra curled around a sharp cry, then lifted his head in an enraged sneer. "Don't force me to hurt you. I've had enough of distorts. You *will* please me, Chan-ti Beppu."

She pressed backward against a chair, groped for it to defend herself. But before she could bring it around, Fra Baba stiffened, and his eyes squinted tightly. The Face of Night was loud in his head: *You dolt! Don't you feel what is happening? Lod is coming for Chan-ti Beppu! He has inscribed the thought in your head to have this woman so that you would bring her outside. He would already have snatched her by now if I were not blocking him.*

With great difficulty, Saor was indeed blocking Lod. Most of Saor's power had been tapped to run zōtl lynks, and the little that was left him by the spiders had been barely enough to monitor his own priests. That was how this peccable fool had reigned as Cenobite for so long. Saor would have struck him dead on the spot, but he needed every erg of strength to stop Lod from materializing.

Sparks whirred, brightening the kitchen, flashing off the copper pots and the water bucket. The hanging plants ignited, and tendrils of flame crawled into the rafters. Fra Baba turned to the door, but his master's voice stopped him.

Stay here. Lod wants to draw you outside, where he can snatch the woman. Stay here. I will protect you.

The ceiling and the wainscotting sheeted into flames. The air drooled fire. Chan-ti had instinctively huddled, but none of the combustion touched her or the numb-faced Fra Bathra. The flames, smoke, and even the heat were kept at bay by a bell-jar force visible against the churning holocaust.

The stairs collapsed, and Fech's body whirled by, fireblown, spinning with the stairway and banister up into the conflagration.

Saor was determined to stave off Lod no matter the cost. This was Saor's domain, directly under his Form, and if he could not deny Lod here he could deny him nowhere. The Rimstalker would know how weak the Face of Night truly was. Saor strained to the friable edge of his strength, repelling the seething hot pressure of Lod. For the sake of the worlds, he ignored the pain of his effort.

The zōtl had been careful to program Saor with purpose. He was life's defender against the World Eater Gai. If he failed, in a few thousand years all would be void. And if he won, his victory would blaze billions of years into the future, out into the white orchards of galaxies, where he would eventually take his place among the watchful minds at the red limit of the cosmic horizon.

A whirlwind of whitehot energy whipped the ashes of the cottage into a thermal spout. With a brattle of thunder, the darkness descended in great clots among the falling embers.

Chan-ti and Fra Bathra stood unscathed at the center of a scorched circle. The houses on either side were not even singed. The Brood had gathered on their stoops, alerted first by the telepathic head and then by the fiery geyser. Among them were Nappy Groff and Bram Gorlik. They had woken from their exhausted sleep to find that the acid mists had risen, disclosing that the cliff-face they had been hugging along in the dark was directly behind a hamlet of crouched cottages.

The moment they awoke, Gorlik had wanted to tell Nappy about the Face of Night's visitation and the phanes he had given them—but the miraculous appearance of the village, where before there had been only darkness and scalding mist, troubled him with the memory of Saor's threat. Before he could resolve himself against his fear, a column of fire bloomed like dawn over the hamlet. He and Nappy had crashed through a garden and down an alley to reach the first real illumination they had seen since leaving the Overworld. The sight of Chan-ti Beppu, smudged and wild-haired among the dwindling flares, drew them closer. Nappy was mesmerized by exhaustion and the sight of a woman he had never really thought he would see again. Gorlik, stung by the immediacy of his pact with the Face of Night, gawked.

Fra Baba Bathra wiped the dewed fear from his thick brow and muttered a prayerful thanks to the Face of Night.

"Your thanks are misplaced," a vibrant voice said from the sky.

A spark flared to a star above the hamlet. The Brood cowered, and their murmurs hushed to silent awe as the star descended, lifting colors out of the landscape—gray, insipid hues, bleached by an aeon of darkness. The wincing radiance hardened to a human form, twice the size of a man, blindingly featureless. At his feet, a shadow pooled.

Lod flurried with triumph. He had come with great reluctance to the kingdom of the Dark One, afraid of his counterpart's power and, worse, his allies: Lod dreaded the possibility that the zōtl virus was contagious. When he had first arrived through the lynk, after a frightful crossing through the mirrorland of the Overworld, he had wandered charily. Fortunately, Chan-ti's waveform had been instantly apparent, flavored by her time-displacement. There were others with a similar feel, but they were not female. He had approached, intending to commune with her and lead her out, but some of the humans in this hive had mindreach and would hear him. So he had used the most accessible one, the one who would most readily accept Lod's voice as the urgings of his own body—Fra Baba Bathra. But before he could get Chan-ti to where he could safely envelop her in his plasma shape and carry her off, Saor had confronted him and forced him to act.

Lod's easy conquest left him elated, eager to return to Gai with news of Saor's weakness. Repelled by the radiance of his counterpart's victory, the shadow at Lod's feet crawled away from the brilliance. Lod pointed at it, and the black puddle rose into the outline of a man the size and shape of Lod but lightless. "Saor, you will say it."

Saor turned to where Fra Baba and Chan-ti were rooted with shock and said in his ponderous voice: "Woman, you're free. Go with Lod."

Chan-ti walked toward the light, eyes averted from the glare. Lod opened an arm to her. "Do not be afraid," he said, kindly. "I am here to take you to Ned O'Tennis."

"Beppu!" a voice called, and its familiarity jerked her around. Nappy Groff shouldered through the robed distorts and stood at the edge of the light. Gorlik appeared behind him.

Chan-ti lifted to her toes as if to fly to Nappy. She looked up at the fire giant. "He's my father," she said and meant it. "I can't leave him here."

Lod sensed her emotional recognition, registered her joy and concern. He beckoned the Foke to him.

Nappy bounded forward, elated to find his daughter and be free of the Witch Maze he had thought his grave. Gorlik followed, his eyes big with fear. He did not want to betray Lod. The being of fire looked powerful and noble. The dwarf unstrung his sojourn pack and raised it to throw it into the darkness. But his arm would not work. Saor nudged into his brain and staggered him forward. Too late, Gorlik howled his dismay. The bag burst apart in his hands. The phanes, activated by Lod's field of force, uncoiled and slashed through the air so fast they were invisible to all but Lod and Saor.

Lod cut his power immediately, but the cables were already on him, biting into him with ice-edged pain. The powerdrop shrunk him and helped the phanes snare his

plasma shape. In a fraction of a second, fate was reversed.
Darkness swooped in on a man-sized manikin of tired yellow light bound across arms and thighs by two black pythons.

Saor's jubilant cry churned a great wind that lifted agate
tiles from the roofs and blew the humans along the street
like leaves.

Chan-ti clutched at Nappy. They crashed against a stoop
and lay on the steps in a tight hug, watching Lod's slack
body, flimmery with reddening light, drift upward into the
blind depths.

Loryn

At Ricks College in Rexburg, Idaho, Lorraine Poole had
been an instructor in English and had taught several
semesters of freshman composition and Introduction to
Literature before she was killed in a car crash on an ice-
glassed freeway. She remembered little about the accident
—she had had an argument with her boyfriend and had
been mulling that over while she drove home late at night.
Visibility was good. The snow had cleared off, and the sky
was thistly with stars. But she had not really noticed the
stars until she thought back on it, seven billion years after
her steering wheel spun uselessly in her hands as her Ford
Pinto glided over the ice and into the flaring dragon eyes
of an oncoming diesel combine. She did not know if anyone else had died. She had not even realized she had died
—until Genitrix woke her and told her where she was.

Xappur, the fog world of Chalco, was where she was
reborn. Unlike many of Genitrix's salvaged lives, she was
not reproduced as an adult. By some whim that even Genitrix herself could only explain as a program variance, the
supercoiling of her DNA had been properly adjusted to
eliminate aging beyond physical maturity and to correct
her myopia and hypoglycemia, and she had been reborn as
an infant. Genitrix apologized for this during the long in-
troductory gestation, when Lorraine seemed to be alive

inside a vast opal filled with a salutory iridescence and the dulcet voice of her re-creator. Almost all of Genitrix's infant creations were aborted in their birthsacks, usually devoured by beasts and sometimes, in the more desolate places, simply left to wither and die where there was no one, human or beast, to notice them.

Lorraine forgave Genitrix in advance. Inside the clement embrace of the opal light, she was too euphoric to care. As she did for all her infants, Genitrix arranged for the memory net in Lorraine's brain to withhold her recall of Earth and all she had learned during her gestation until puberty—if she survived until then.

Her new body was born in a baby field in a polar latitude on Xappur, where the chill air set the fog to frost and where death would have been less painful in the anesthetizing cold. That was Genitrix's last gift to this human who had forgiven her. Forgiveness from a human was a rare event for Genitrix, since most humans railed at her when confronted with a second death. Lorraine was too hedonistic to scold the alien archeologist who had unearthed her and steeped her in the pleasure of the opal light and the mothering voice.

Lorraine was birthed with a flush of thirteen others in a baby field that was more remote than most, and so she was spared from being devoured by animals and insects. The last of the flush, she was still alive when a pilgrimage of tribesfolk happened upon the baby field and found her whimpering among the small frozen corpses. For the next twelve years she lived with the Twisted Root Tribe; she was raised as the daughter of Koo and Waltho, a distort couple who were grotesquely ugly, as were most of the tribe of bone-deformed humans, though she did not realize that until she was twelve. The Twisted Root Tribe thrived, because their distortions were adapted to the obscuring mists of Xappur. Many of these warty, hunchbacked distorts had a crude infravision that enabled them to find their way through the fog and to hunt and forage.

The Twisted Root Tribe had another adaptive mutation that had helped them survive the zōtl attacks in the olden times, and the Aesirai raids now: They could disjoint themselves and squeeze into crannies and crevices impossible for other humans. Because Lorraine, whom they called

Warm Night for her dark skin and irrepressible cheer, could not follow them when they hid, they took pains to warn her of the Aesirai oppressors, who were perpetually raiding their world to purge it of distorts and to cull whole humans like Lorraine for the zōtl lynk on Ren.

In her twelfth year, the memories began. She sat spellbound for hours in the tribe's burrow, entranced by her recall of her former life. She remembered her first parents, a pediatrician and a schoolteacher in Idaho Falls, who had reared her as a Christian, until she lost faith in her teen years when her mother died after a series of strokes. Her father had become depressive after that. Always her mother had been the joyful strength of the family, and it was from her that Lorraine and her brothers had learned to take pleasure from life. She thought a long time about her first family and her first childhood, fascinated by the strange disparity between then and now.

Her soulful reminiscence was brutally disrupted in her fifteenth year by an Aesirai raid that exterminated the Twisted Root Clan. Koo and Waltho had taken her with them on their annual pilgrimage to the polar caves, where the death masks of the tribe were kept. She saw again the baby field that had birthed her, reduced now to a scattering of bones among snow-splotched boulders. During the evening fireside-stories, she told her adoptive parents about Earth. The potato-faced distorts listened in giddy disbelief to tales of a world where machines burned fossils for fuel, where the sky was empty but for clouds, dim stars, and a single moon, and where no one ever saw the galaxy's spiral, rawfaces, tiger-scorpions, or longteeth.

On their return to the tribe, they found carnage and no survivors. A banner with the Emirate's Thunderhawk stenciled upon it hung limply before the burrow entrance among the sprawled and decomposing bodies. Koo dropped dead on the spot, when she disturbed a neurotox cannister hidden among the corpses. Waltho survived his grief only long enough to help Warm Night cast the tribe's death masks and carry them to the polar cave of their ancestors. He died there, and Lorraine left him among the masks, clutching his own death cast.

For a while, Lorraine tried to contact Genitrix, to connect again with the opal of great peace and the mothering voice, but that was futile. Genitrix was a machine intelligence, not a god or a spirit to be invoked. Without the Twisted Root Tribe, she was alone on Xappur and well knew that everyone now was her enemy: Most likely, other distort tribes would kill her on sight, and certainly the Emirate had only one use for her—as vassal, to be fed to the zōtl.

Her vain effort to reconnect with Génitrix at least served the purpose of reminding her of all that the machine intelligence had taught her. Knowledge was her only weapon but for the one plasteel knife that the tribe had cherished since finding it on a dead Saor-priest two centuries earlier. She decided then that she would leave Chalco-Doror, and she made her way on the fogroads to the nearest lynk.

The Ordo Vala had visited the Twisted Root Tribe in the ancient times long before Fech the Betrayer made Xappur famous by hatching there his treachery of the fugitive lords. Lorraine had seen the clay-inscribed copy of *The Book of Horizons* that had been given to the tribe by the Ordo Vala. She had learned from that relic that travel in the Overworld was indeed possible, though Genitrix had warned her never to enter a lynk for fear of being lost among the lynklanes.

After the deaths of her tribe, the great loss of Koo and Waltho, and the vivid memories of loss on Earth, Lorraine was not afraid to lose herself. She stood before the lynk, which glowed a fiery blue in the fog, a neon parabola, and took a last look at Xappur: dark, lit wanly from above the dense clouds by the galactic arms. In the radiance from the lynk, the nearby rocks pared to mist. She stepped under the shining arch, and the brilliance of the Overworld torched her vision.

For fifteen years she had lived in obscure darkness, and minutes passed before her aching eyes adjusted. When she could see clearly, she did not understand at first what she was observing. In front of her was a holoform image showing part of the hemisphere of a vast globe. Strung like pearls north to south around the globe was a series of planets. Looking closer, she saw that they were all the same planet—the fog-muted face of Xappur.

She was looking at a parallel series of timelines of the world she had just left. She knew this from what Genitrix had told her about the Overworld, it seemed only yesterday. She had not really heeded the data on the Overworld that the machine mind had imprinted in her brain, because it had not related to anything she had ever experienced. But now, confronted by this vivid holoform, she remembered Genitrix had told her that during the Age of the Crystal Mind, six hundred years earlier, Ieuanc 751 had endowed the Ordo Vala with the technology to erect holoforms in the mouths of all the Tryl lynks. Each holoform was a kind of map, displaying the world where the lynk originated, multiply reflected in parallel timelines. The string of Xappurs vanished over the horizon of a massive gray globe laced and looped with chrome-brilliant colors. Genitrix had said that in Lorraine Poole's time on Earth, that pattern was known as a Mandelbrot set, a fractal pattern of whorls and tendrils, like the edges of a snowflake, where each tiny part mimicked the curlicue shape of the whole.

The globe of filigree patterns was a representation of the Overworld, the complex of all possible universes. Each filigree and curlicue was a timeline arcing through the gray emptiness of the vacuum in which all universes were expanding and contracting. Close scrutiny revealed that each flamelike whorl was made of similar but smaller vortices and coils, and that each of those tiny swirls too was composed of a tinier filigree, which, in turn, was made of patterns like the larger ones. Genitrix had said that the regression was infinite and that every possible world of this universe was there.

The absolute blackness that loomed above the horizon of the flame-laced globe represented the cosmic event horizon from which the vacuum of the universe had separated at the Big Bang. Somewhere under that utter nothingness, somewhere in the riot of colorful whorls and filaments was the Earth from where she had come. Somewhere in that infinity of frightfully beautiful shapes was a home for her.

To step forward would carry her to the connecting lynk at some point in Chalco-Doror. She moved sideways. The holoform vanished and was replaced by a gray vista streaked with multihued mares' tails, brushstrokes, and cirrus threads, all of them far, far off like stratospheric clouds, though they were on all sides of her and even under her feet. She knelt down and touched the ground. It was smooth and cool as polished marble. She could see nothing but the gray void and far below more rainbow threads. She was in a null field.

Genitrix had informed her that the Overworld existed apart from real time, and while she wandered, she ruminated on what she had heard from the machine mind, though she did not really understand any of it. The ground she felt and the air she breathed were an infinite extension of the point in spacetime where she had originated. She had entered a relativistic frame outside spacetime, where all points existed coterminously. That was why the universe and all its timelines could be mapped as a globe-shaped Mandelbrot set: The universe was whole and only apparently divided into parts when one viewed it from the inside. Here in the Overworld, she was potentially everywhere—though actually nowhere. This cosmic contradiction existed all around her: She felt herself distinct and apart from the gray void and its chromatic striations of distant timelines—yet she knew that if she could pull back and see herself in context, she was a tiny part of one such colorful timeline that connected with all the others and on a grand scale even imitated their patterns. She belonged here, she reminded herself, no matter how strange it looked. But without klivoth kakta to extend her consciousness into the timelines she saw threaded in the far-off void, she could not know where she was going. And without ramstat propulsion, she had little hope of trespassing any other region in the Overworld but that nearest where she had originated. Even so, she was determined never to return to Chalco-Doror and its evil Aesirai and zōtl denizens. So she walked.

Whenever exhaustion whelmed up in her, she curled up and dozed. Her life as a tribeswoman had given her the foresight to carry a gourd of water and a sack of dried meat and breadroot, enough to last her for several days. And before her food ran out, she reached the nearest visible timeline. It looked to her like a glass tube a hundred meters tall and stretching forever left and right of her.

Inside the timeline, she saw Xappur and realized that she had journeyed not much farther in the Overworld than she would have if she had flown an hour or so in a

small flyer. But there was a lynk about sixty meters below
her—a blue oval shining brightly against the fog-color of
Xappur's landscape. How to go down? She crawled along
the ground and soon discovered that she could maneuver
up or down by pointing herself in those directions. There
really was no up or down, only distance, omniradiant distance, which, she could almost hear Genitrix saying, was
not really distance at all but connection.

She reached the lynk and stepped through. She did not
know where on Xappur she was. But the terrain was not
unsimilar to that where she had grown up, and she had no
difficulty foraging food and filling her gourd with fresh
water. Then she returned to the lynk and passed through
again. This time she scrutinized more closely the holoform
map of the Overworld that appeared before her. She noticed that her timeline was subtly highlighted by a golden
sheen beneath the positions of the nearest and the largest
of the string of Xappur images. Xappur was the tiniest
filament among a furry filigree of timelines that she figured had to be Chalco-Doror.

That was when she remembered hearing from Genitrix
about the Strong Mother and how thousands of her followers had abandoned Chalco-Doror at her death. Genitrix
had told her that many of the Strong Mother's exodus had
reached a fabulous corner of creation near the end of time
called the Werld. No one had been able to find their way
there since—though few were searching, for those with
ramstat propulsion worked for the Emirate, which, Genitrix had informed her, was a facade for Gai, the Rimstalker
responsible for creating Chalco-Doror.

From the filament that was Xappur, Lorraine traced a
path on the holoform that led inward along the spiral of
the nearest shepherd's-crook pattern, a timeline that
snailed in on itself. Then she left the lynklane and, following her memory of the map, located a faraway timeline
among a bundle of others across a null field that seemed to
curve gently in the direction she desired—though it was
too remote to tell for sure. She walked toward it. Days
later, long after her food and water were exhausted, she
reached that prismal timeline, and, indeed, it appeared
nothing like Chalco-Doror or anyplace humanly habitable.

Chromatic magmas blinded her, and she moved on as quickly as her depleted body would allow.

By then she was dying. Her march staggered. She reeled like a drunk and soon collapsed. She prepared to die a second time. She stared into the Overworld's exhausted distances, the miles wearied by emptiness. And darkness claimed her.

Time was broken into huge chunks suspended in a gray void. Each irregular chunk was an icefloe, chromebright and slithery with reflections. The strohlkraft carrying Ned and Pahang streaked through the vast corridors of gray space, a mote among the giant floes. Autopilot followed the maps Gai had installed in the ship's computer, and the men hung from their slings in the flight pod transfixed by the enigmatic vista.

"The houses of the gods," Pahang murmured.

Ned swelled with awe. The beauty of the enormous floating shapes transfixed him—but only momentarily. He turned his attention to the flight console. Since the fall of N'ym and the obscenities of Squat, beauty had wearied for Ned. There was no stamina to it anymore. All experience seemed fleeting. Death surrounded everything in its black aura. And where before, as a ferryman in N'ym, this ephemerality had been a welcome contrast to the eternal routines of his life and he had enjoyed being a part of the flaring twilight, now it damned him. Nothing was certain anymore, not even the most fundamental boundaries of time and place. His heart craved something constant in his turbulent flight through time, and his mind tried to provide it by using the ship's computer to interpolate from the data of previous timejumps where they would appear next.

"You worry too much," Pahang said, his face amber in the glow from the slick floes. "We live and die at the pleasure of the gods. Behold their majesty."

"It's not majesty I'm looking for right now, Pahang. We passed the edge of our map twenty minutes ago. According to spectral readings of those time-floes, we're millions of light years from where we started."

"If we have no map, how are we flying?"

"The computer's guessing. The ships they sent out here

before didn't have the range of a strohlkraft. These hadn't been invented yet."

"I forget you are from the future."

"Not for long. If the computer's right and we survive wherever we're going, we'll return to Chalco-Doror in my own time—and with the weapon that will doom the city I come from—the doom that started my journey back in time."

"You make my head dizzy."

"I don't understand, either. Will N'ym survive if we don't find the O'ode? Or what if we find it and decide not to deliver it?"

"Those are the tricks of the gods. You can't outwit them. Do what you must to find your Chan-ti. She is why you left Gai to follow the ghost of Joao. And she is why you have returned to Gai. She is all you must understand."

Ned frowned and looked out again at the silver buttes suspended in the gray void. Tully Gunther had said that the scyldar that abducted Chan-ti wanted to kill him and would use her as a lure, so there was a chance that she was still alive—but how alive? Squat had nearly broken Ned's mind and had left a warp of fearfulness he would carry always. What terror was Chan-ti suffering under the scyldar and the spiders?

"You worry too much," Pahang repeated, wanting Hawk to bolster him with some of the enthusiasm they had shared after escaping Squat. Ned's grim demeanor and the supernatural view of the gods' glossed houses troubled Pahang. Early he had learned from his third brother that those who see the gods must die. He had to remind himself that he had already died. Still, he had hoped for more camaraderie from Hawk. Their mission was too dangerous for doubt. "We must remember our pledge," he said and offered his hand as he had on Ras Mentis. "To freedom."

Ned recognized the bright need in Pahang's stare and took his hand in a strong clasp. "Freedom is something one must make, Pahang. That's what the Aesirai believe. I haven't forgotten. We will make ourselves and Chan-ti free with the O'ode. You're a good man to come with me."

"Where else would I be? My third brother, the soul-catcher, was forever telling me—"

The strohlkraft steepened to an ascent, and inertia tightened through the two men in their slings. Ahead, a time-floe loomed and rushed closer. Other floes were reflected in its watery surface, and iridescent currents crawled there, simmering through the reflections. For an instant they glimpsed themselves, the trim black shadow of a strohlkraft flying directly at them. Pahang's hands jerked to his face at the instant of impact.

The pearlescent shine of the Overworld had vanished, and they were adrift in space outside a bluegreen planet. The flightpod lights dimmed as the power faded in the ramstat cells, then flushed brighter with energy from the backup generator. Ned dulled the cabin lights and regarded the glaucous planet, noting a hint of rings glinting around it. The Rimstalker program in the computer confirmed the sighting on the range-finder with a matrix display of zeroes. They had reached their objective.

"Rataros," Hawk said and began entering the commands for a surface scan. "We're the first humans to get here. Maybe the last."

In moments, the computer analyzed the scan data and located several thousand sites where O'odes were visible. The strohlkraft slid down the planet's gravity slope.

"Zōtl!" Pahang cried and pointed to the console screen where six red squares had begun flashing.

"They haven't spotted us yet," Ned observed and angled their descent to slim the profile the strohlkraft presented to the zōtl. "They've probably never had to deal with a shadowary hull."

A jolting impact rocked the ship. The strohlkraft flipped out of control, and the men twisted in their slings. Ned fought the yoke and swung the vessel into a fast but stable dive. The tops of the planet's gray clouds swept over them and fogged the visor.

"What happened?" Pahang shrilled.

"The spiders have some kind of camouflage, makes it look like they're not locked on. That was a direct hit. Some kind of proton bolt. Cut right through our deflectors and sheared off our ventral thruster."

"That is bad!" Pahang cried, curled up in his sling. "What does it mean?"

"Means that with a planet of this mass, we'll have enough thrust for only one shot out of here. We won't be

taking any tours, or picking and choosing among the
O'odes. We get *one,* and if we're lucky we get away." Ned
blew a sigh. "You can come out now. The needlecraft can't
follow us this deep. Too close to the O'odes."

"How do you know?"

"Because they haven't hit us again."

"But they know we are here. They will be shooting at us,
lah?"

"See those static streaks on the screen? Those are bolts.
This time our shadowary hull is protecting us. They're
shooting wild."

Pahang had time to mutter a chant before the ship began vibrating so violently he could barely breathe.

"Stabilizers are out!" Ned shouted. "We have to glide in
without ramstat. Brace yourself!"

The ship convulsed too severely for Ned to work the
console. They would have to trust the autopilot to guide
them through the dense clouds and land them near an
O'ode.

Cruel minutes later, the strohlkraft pounded a hard,
bumpy surface and lurched to a stop. Pahang hung in a
daze, staring at the thick fog rubbing against the visor.
Ned's wavery fingers plucked at the console, and the visor
lit up with a false color outline of the surrounding terrain.

Apparitions of skewed geometries drifted across the
visor as the scan circled the horizon. "We've landed in
something like a city—or something artificial. Look at the
size of those structures. They dwarf even the biggest
lynks." At Ned's typed command, the outlying geometries
rotated three-dimensionally, and they saw that they were
on the floor of a basin in an abstract clutter of precise but
peculiarly sinuous shapes large as mountains. The spiral
megaliths seemed woven, textured like spun fabric. Some
were frayed, and bundles of filaments, streaming a hundred meters long, wavered in the fog, elegant as feathers.
Beyond the city, sand reefs and volcanic cones ranged to
the horizon.

Ned punched a query about the location of the O'ode.
Aisles of color spoked the visor display, leading to the
white blip of the strohlkraft and a bright grain of light
beside it. "We're sitting on the O'ode. Gai's program
dropped us right on top of it." Ned unslung himself and

hunched over the console, working the control for the bay doors and the cargo-hoist. A high, thin whine seeped up from the belly winch. "It's small—size of a coconut." A thud announced the closing of the bay doors. With a whirr, the planet's gases were evacuated and breathable air flushed the bay. "All right—let's open her up."

Ned lifted a grid at the back of the flight pod and released a magnetic lock. Panels petalled open, and the hoist lifted into the pod a black sphere small as a skull. At Ned's touch, the globe powdered to ash, leaving a black circle with a blue pearl at its center, humming with light.

Ned cast an alarmed look at the console, saw that the object was not radioactive. Pahang placed his hands near its glow and felt no heat. He glanced at Hawk for a nod, then picked it up. It felt silken, soft.

The console lit up with full power, the air vents thrummed louder, and the hoist sunk back into the bay. "What's this?" Ned saw launch configurations scroll across the monitor and waved Pahang to his sling. "Gai's program is kicking on. Somehow it knows we have the O'ode." He hurriedly fit the grid back into the floor and scurried into his sling as the intact dorsal thrusters fired.

Inertial drag and the hysterical vibrations of the destabilized strohlkraft threw the men to the brink of blackout. Even in the blur of the ship's seizure, Ned saw the warning strobes on the visor plead for a slackening in ascent angle, then demand stop-thrust, and, with a shrill siren, threaten to burst the flight pod. With their jaws fused, joints twisted and shaken, the men rode their terror into a thunderclap of silence and a flare of stars.

Free of the atmosphere, the strohlkraft steadied enough for Ned to read the data banks. The ramstat cells were fully charged, and the ship was arrowing at maximum speed for the skylynk where they had come through. "I don't understand. Something down there charged us up."

The fist where Pahang held the O'ode had squeezed so tightly he had to pry it open like a clam. The blue sphere looked hard and shiny. "Maybe the power is here."

Moments later, they were through the skylynk: The gray vastness exploded around them, hung with mirrory lumps of time. The display for the ramstat cells declared full power. "It must be the O'ode," Ned conceded. "That lynk should have drained the engine cells." He accepted the tiny sphere from Pahang. Its texture surprised him. He pressed it between his fingers, and thought he felt prickly energies.

He placed the O'ode in a freefall net on the command deck, and a smile wavered up in him. This was the weapon that would kill the zōtl, that would break the Emirate and topple N'ym. A bead. A drop of gaugeless power. He knew he should feel some anguish before it, yet he did not. The dark mood that had troubled him on the flight out had given way to hope. Here was the seed of his future. If Chan-ti could be saved, this would lead him to her. If not, nothing would matter. He felt clearheaded about that, as though the rough ride into and out of Rataros had shaken him free of himself. He smiled, and Pahang dared a laugh.

"We are heroes!" the Malay shouted. "The gods themselves stand in awe of us."

Ned unlatched Pahang's sling and gave it a shove that set it twirling. "We are the heroes of nothing. All this has already happened in my past. The zōtl are dead and N'ym is fallen. The gods are laughing, Pahang."

Pahang jerked in a splash of limbs, struggling to right himself without gravity. Ned reeled in the Malay's sling-cords and pulled him up close. "Have you forgotten about our torque—how time is twisted around us? When we go through the lynk at Chalco-Doror, the computer says we'll jump hundreds of years forward—into my future. The O'ode has to be delivered in the time I came from, if this is the O'ode that made the history I remember."

"You dizzy my head, Hawk."

"We're heroes of nothing," Ned told him. A laugh appeared in his strong stare, yet his expression was too severe for laughter. "We can't deliver the O'ode. Gai will have to come in and get it. We're just shades of history. Not heroes. No one will remember us."

"So, who cares who kills the spiders? You are here for Chan-ti. You are her hero. Now Gai must show you where she is held."

If she was dead, physically or in her heart, nothing would matter. But if she was alive, if he could find her— The joy in his eyes brightened. The fall of N'ym, the destruction of the Aesirai were not his crimes. He was no villain or hero. He was only a man seized by powers greater than he understood. Instead of bearing witness to himself from his blood—which would only indict him for his betrayal with the horror of his forefathers—he chose then and there to make his freedom with his own mind, from his own strange destiny, from the spirit that he had first recognized in the feathers of dusk on the streets of N'ym, the same spirit that had led him to Chan-ti and that he had found living in her.

"Was there ever a Chan-ti in your life?" Ned asked.

Dismay troubled Pahang's round face, then relented to a sad smile. "My second wife was my soul. She was born in the very month of my manhood rite. When I first saw her playing in the dust with the other children, I knew then she would be my wife. I knew then she was me. I courted her at the proper time, after I made my first fortune—I am embarrassed to say it now, it is so mere before the marvels we have seen—a fortune of eels, nets and nets of them driven early in the season to the cove where glad fortune had led me alone. I was welcomed in every village on the coast. For days, I traveled like a prince. I returned with a wealth of cowrie and won her—and with her my soul. For a while we were happy. But our lives belong to the gods. My second brother, possessed of a lewd and greedy jungle spirit, stole our village chief's cowrie and my second wife, carried her into the jungle. I followed, but I never saw them again. The jungle killed me."

Ned lowered his gaze. When he looked up, Pahang was grinning giddily. "I do not regret losing my life for her. As I was dying I did regret. But that was before Squat taught me how to love. He was a strict teacher, lah?"

"What did he teach you?"

"That my second brother was right. We must hold what we love. We must take what we love into our lives. That is why I was right to leave my first wife and our children to chase her. I was right and there is no shame in it, though I died. Lah. I would do it again."

"If you come with me, you will be taking the risk of dying again, even more horribly if the zōtl get you—a terrible risk and no second wife to take back into your life."

"Second wife is gone forever. I know that. But Chan-ti

may be saved, if the gods favor us. That is a risk worthy of my small life. Do you think I have forgotten you saved me from Squat?"

"You saved *me,* Pahang. On Squat's beach, you were the one who knew Gai—the Mother of Night I think you called her."

They shared a laugh, and Pahang was satisfied. The bad spirit haunting Hawk had been dispelled. The O'ode was truly a great power. Now the everlasting risk that is the Life would go well for them. Gai would be pleased and lead them to Chan-ti. They would save her, and Hawk would be repaid with his soul for saving Pahang from Squat. Then the Malay would be free of all debts. And then, at last, all would go well until it went bad again, and even then there would always be something good about their lives, for both of them had made their peace with the incomprehensible. Now whatever there was, would be good enough.

The strohlkraft came to a shaky stop before the luminous gateway of a lynk in the midst of a null field. The body of a woman lay in the gray field. Before either of the wanderers could consider what to do about her, the communication fixtures lit up, and a female voice they both recognized as Gai's spoke, vivid with concern: "The zōtl have taken Lod! Do you have the O'ode?"

Ned and Pahang exchanged worried stares. "We have the O'ode," Ned answered. "What is this about Lod? How did the spiders take him?"

"No time to explain. It was all my fault. I need the O'ode immediately. My only hope of saving him is to destroy his captors."

"The O'ode is yours," Ned said into his sling mike. "But we can't go through the lynk to deliver it. The torque—"

"I know—I know. I searched the Overworld for someone from this time. She's outside your ship now. Her name is Lorraine Poole. She's one of the Genitrix finds, so she'll know about me. Give her the O'ode and have her come through."

"Aren't you forgetting about our agreement?" Ned asked. "You promised to take me to Chan-ti. I have the O'ode—but I don't know how to get to Chan-ti."

"There's a way for your strohlkraft to reach the Dragon's Shank, where Chan-ti is being held. There's a Saor lynk where the rotation of Saor's black body will compensate for your time-torque and allow you to enter this time. But there is a risk of Saor apprehending you, so we will not try to convey the O'ode through there. I'll transmit coordinates to your computer."

"Coordinates are too unreliable out here," Ned told the Rimstalker. "I want you to program the flightpath yourself, like you did for the trip to Rataros."

"I can't insert a flightpath over the comm-line."

"Then you'll have to come here and do it."

Silence flinched with vent noise. Then, "I'm not coming in there. It's too risky. I don't know what will happen."

Ned rocked his jaw and passed an incredulous frown to Pahang. "We risked our tocks at Rataros. The focking spiders ripped out one of our thrusters, nearly broke our bones. We put our lives on the line for you, Gai. You want this O'ode—come and get it."

"Lod is being held by the zōtl with your Chan-ti. If I program your ship to go directly to her, will you strive to save Lod as well?"

"We already have an agreement."

"Without Lod, I can't manage the planet orbits. They'll fail soon enough and start colliding. You must try to save Lod."

"What about you? You're more powerful than we are. And Lod is yours. You save him."

"I will be there to help—when the O'ode has destroyed the spiders' nest world. Until then, you must do what you can. Will you try?"

Pahang touched Ned's arm, whispered, "Never refuse the gods. Lie if you must. Lah. But don't refuse them."

Ned's eyebrows shrugged. "You get me to Chan-ti, and I'll do everything I can to free Lod."

The air in the flight pod jellied, and Gai's voice riveted about them, "I'm here."

The hair on their heads stood like bristles, and their skin crawled with a viscous static. "We feel you." Ned dropped from his sling and helped Pahang get down. Sparks snapped at their fingertips. "Maybe we better wait outside."

"Yes," Gai's thunder-voice dinned. "Lorraine is rousing. Stay with her until I'm finished. But first—let me see the O'ode."

Ned, who had taken it from the freefall net at their landing, displayed the azure pebble. It floated out of his palm and spun in the air above his hand.

The air squeezed tighter and relaxed as if pumped in a giant heart. "You have done well, lynk-wanderers. Now the zōtl will die."

"And N'ym will fall."

The O'ode dropped back into his palm. Gai spoke, quieter, "N'ym has already fallen—in your life. Would you have it otherwise?"

Ned stood taller. This he had thought through with his blood, remembering his childhood in N'ym and the spiders who had been paid in human life so that he could live there. His father and brothers had died to defend the City of the Sky. They had thought the zōtl their allies, the necessary evil that sustained the Storm-Tree. Life was suffering, they had told him. There was no other way. Let the weak perish that the strong might endure. That was the Aesirai faith. But he had learned true suffering under Squat, and he would have no human, no matter how weak or distorted, subject to pain so that he might live in comfort. Though his forefathers, warriors all, would find him despicably weak for this breach of their faith, he knew the rightness of his decision. He answered Gai's question: "The zōtl are the strength of the Aesirai. When the spiders fall, N'ym falls. I would not have it otherwise."

Lorraine Poole woke to a luminous feeling. She was still in the gray emptiness of the Overworld, but the exhaustion that had dropped her was entirely gone. She felt refreshed and alert—and that frightened her. She had been starving—dying. She sat bolt upright and saw that out of the chasmic grayness, a tunnel glowed, shimmery blue as pool light. Before it, perched with ichor-grimed landing gear on its reflection in a mirrorgray surface, was a black vehicle with stubby, asymmetrical wings and predatory lines. The squared-off back end of it, which looked like dark sheetglass, was lifted, exposing a bashed-in underbody and creased fins. From the hull beside the winged-open hatch, the Thunderhawk emblem of the Aesirai glared at her.

Anger and fear whirled her to her feet. Two men descended from the craft. They had guns strapped loosely across their bodies. One was short in a sloping helmet that reached almost to his shoulders, the other lanky and bareheaded. Something about their incongruous silhouettes and jaunty gait eased her fear. She strode to meet them.

"We mean no harm," the short one greeted her with a toothy smile. He was an Asian man with a squint worn deeply into his seamed flesh. "We are here to help you." His voice seemed to crackle in the air.

"You're hearing us through a translator," the tall man said, stepping out of the glare from the tunnel and facing her with a brow and nose like masonry and a gentle smile. His rusty hair looked disheveled as a wheatsheaf. "I'm Ned and that's Pahang."

"You are Aesirai," she said in a harsh breath.

Pahang cut her off with a vigorous shake of his head that cocked his helmet. "We fly the Aesirai ship and wear their garments, but we are lynk-wanderers. We have come to find you, Loryn Poole. We know you. We are here to help you."

"Gai found you in a null field," Ned explained to the befuddled teenager. "The Rimstalker brought you to this lynk. She's the one who actually needs help—from you."

Lorraine knew she had heard him correctly, yet she asked, "Gai?"

"Yes, Loryn, the Rimstalker. Mother of Night. Lah."

The first harmonics of understanding chimed in her, and she realized suddenly why she felt so well when her body had been starved to the brink of death. The Creator of Worlds was sustaining her. But why? All the memories that Genitrix had given her of Earth, and all the knowledge of Chalco-Doror, ruffled at the back of her mind in a chill breeze. "What does the Rimstalker want?"

"What do any of the gods want?" Pahang asked, his small eyes very big. "Everything. Don't think to resist."

"Drop it, Pahang. You're scaring her."

"No, he's not," Lorraine said. "I know Gai is not a god."

"Oh, really, Loryn?" Pahang asked. "How does a child know this?"

She regarded Pahang's challenging pose with haughty amusement. "Gai's a being from another gravity shell. You know what a gravity shell is, either of you? You want to talk about it?"

"I'm sorry." Ned put two fingers to his temple, like he had just realized something. "You look like a kid. How do you know all this?"

"I'm fifteen. And this is my second life."

"Mine, too." Pahang nodded, and the helmet dropped over his eyes. "Were you hung before the Mother of Night, too?"

"No. Genitrix talked with me when I was twelve. You haven't told me what the Rimstalker wants."

"She'll tell you herself." Ned hooked a thumb at the ship. "She's back in the strohlkraft, doing some programming for me. She'll be here any moment. This is her first time in the Overworld, you see, and I think she's a little nervous. The work's going slower than she thought, so she asked us to come out and stay with you until she gets done."

"You remember Earth, Loryn?"

She smiled at the way the Malay pronounced her name. "I remember. Blue skies. Just one moon in the sky at night. No razorjaws. And no zōtl."

Ned held out his fist, opened his fingers, and showed a nacreously blue bead. "Genitrix tell you about this?"

"What is it?"

"It kills zōtl," Ned declared.

"We have brought it from Rataros, far from here."

The O'ode! The thought rang in their minds and turned them to face the strohlkraft. The Rimstalker appeared in the hatchway, a vaguely human shape of jellied light bristling with electricity.

The majestic strength that had revived Lorraine expanded in a rush that almost knocked her from her feet. Gai had finished fitting the strohlkraft's computer with the flightpath to where Lod was being held by the zōtl. There was no time to delay. At any instant, the spiders could wrest control of Lod's gravity-amp and scuttle all hope of returning home. But there was another reason for Gai's hurry. Her thoughts echoed across the gray traverse of the null field, and so she could hear herself thinking. That was why she had taken so long inserting such a simple program. The Overworld reflected her energies back on her. At first, that was merely an annoyance. But as she worked, the noise had sharpened; the echoes never completely faded. They rang on, overlaying each other in a clamoring reverberation that threatened to dissolve her plasma body.

The humans she had gathered here did not hear the confusion of her time-dilated mind. They seemed frozen in time. The hot energy of her plasma shape distorted the cold reality of the Overworld, worse and worse as the echoes mounted, and she knew she was going to explode. Her time scheme unraveled around her in barking coils of blue electricity. She had to work swiftly—little time remained before she would be destroyed by her own vibrations. She feared that if her plasma shape broke up here, the Overworld would swallow her mind. Even if she was flung back into her Form, she would be unconscious—Lod would belong to the zōtl, and the humans would hold the O'ode.

Desperate to save herself, Gai touched Lorraine. *Take the O'ode.*

Lorraine snatched the pearl. Everyone crouched as the Rimstalker's plasma body began shredding apart in snarling ropes of voltage. Spitting sparks, Gai shot from the hatch and flew for the tunnel. *Come quickly!* she called after, and the echo of her cry sizzled toward a scream. She vanished in the lynk, trailing fiery dust.

Lorraine gazed after the alien, then peered down at the blue bauble. A memory from her first life shone brightly— the image of a minister, his face glinting like a boxer's, exhorting *He that loses his life shall find it!* And she had— twice now. Memories of Earth flitted like fish in the oceandepths of her mind, visible but intangible. The past was lost—on Earth and on Xappur. The past was lost and had left room in its place for another life, a life wider than her own. An eerie calm of destiny descended on her. Here in her hand was life for all the distort clans, for all the tribes of people. Here was peace for Koo and Waltho and for everyone the zōtl had killed.

She looked up with a fierce joy. Ned and Pahang had backed away from her. The brushstroke sparks of Gai's flight lingered behind and burnished the air around Lorraine with electric streaks. Gai was reaching for her from the other side of the lynk. A new destiny waited to be claimed.

Lorraine closed her fist over the O'ode and ran to the lynk. In the mouth of the tunnel, she turned and saw Ned and Pahang standing by their ship. Ned waved, Pahang lifted both palms. "Glad luck, Loryn!"

With the O'ode raised in her fist, she walked through the lynk.

"There goes history." Ned turned and climbed up into the flight pod.

"Lah."

Torso Before the Cave of Riddles

On Mugna, in the baneful palace of Perdur, Lod was hung for display. His plasma body had shrunk to a man-shape of crimson embers mottled with black clots across his torso and thighs, where the phanes bound him. He dangled upright above a pentagonal base under the arch-way of a colossal cavern, suspended by magnetic flux. On either side of him, peristyles of coiled serpents rose from the glossy, acid-blotched floor and disappeared in the vaulting shadows.

Voices weirded from the cavern. They were simulated human voices that the zōtl generated to lure people into their lynks. In the Age of Knives, when these voice-baited lynks had been common, the tribes dubbed them "ghost caves." The one that Lod hung before taunted him with questions: *Where are you? . . . What is supposed to happen next? . . . When? . . . Is chance what sponsors fate? . . . Or do the hands of the clock feel their own way? . . . Is time alive? . . . How then will the mind wear its suffering, its shame? . . . Can accident sire meaning? . . . Have you forgotten that before the atoms that shaped the first cells became cells they were still atoms? . . . What rearranged them? . . . Were the first patterns accident? . . . Is memory anything but garbled history? . . . Do you remember why you are here? . . . What can I say to you? . . . What can I say? . . .*

Lod could not help but listen. His will had been almost wholly paralyzed by the phanes. Control of his Form and the Form's control of the planetpaths were still his—but the zōtl picked diligently at his machine mind through his trapped gel body. In the shadowed vault high above his suspended plasma shape, a dozen spiders in a web of scaffolding and cables worked full-time at their glassy induction consoles, magnetically decoding Lod's programs. The Rimstalker machine mind resisted them, straining with all his diminished will to stymie their access. His strength wearied. Over the first dozen days that he hung under the spiders, his gel wore away. His limbs and his head faded to translucent outlines and finally disappeared entirely. Only his torso, circled by the phanes, remained.

Inside the smoldering core of his plasma shape, Lod had no strength to resist anymore. Cumbered with weariness, he sunk into a torpid trance and listened to the small lives around him, reflecting on their tiny but elegant energies as they paraded before his captured shape. Pilgrims from all the worlds came, and he saw through their memories the shanty thorps under the plasteel walls of the Aesirai's great cities, the green cliffs of Sakai strung with hydroelectric lines, the deserts of Ras Mentis quilted with irrigated farms, and the vassal world Ren, where primitive tribes wandered the forest corridors until the zōtl were ready to harvest them.

Most of the humans in Lod's presence were Saor-priests assigned to guard him. Through them, he was linked telepathically with their leader, the Cenobite Fra Baba Bathra, on the slopes of the Dragon's Shank. Lod could feel the lives around Fra Baba. Idly, he regarded the human who had been instrumental in capturing him.

Gorlik quavered tiny and bright as a star before the mountainous dark of Saor. They stood in the highlands above the Brood of Night's hamlet, where Saor had carried the human to reward him for his service. From a cavelynk, the Face of Night had brought out a sphere lit with silky purple. The dwarf held the pumpkin-sized sphere in both hands, his ugly face underlit with astral violet.

"You hold the Globe of Influence, Bram Gorlik." The

voice of Night festered with echoes. "With it, you will rule any world you choose."

Gorlik squinted into the bright ball, saw landscapes gathering like thunderheads out of the purple fumes.

"Will you be master of Valdëmiraën—" Saor asked, "or would you prefer a brighter world? Vala, perhaps, or Ylem?"

In the sphere, Gorlik recognized the world's brow of the Eyelands, then Vala's grassy veldt, Ylem's sprawling jungles. He lifted a puzzled face to the darkness.

"This is my reward to you, mortal spark," the Night said. "With this tool, you may view any place in the world of your dominion. No enemy can hide from you. No secret not your own will live long under your scrutiny."

"I don't want this," Gorlik said, somberly.

"It's your due, Bram. Without you, I would never have captured Lod. You have earned your place among the legends."

"Take it back," Gorlik called and held up the sphere. "What I did, I did unknowing."

"Don't be modest. You are a hero. Thanks to you these worlds will live. You should be proud."

"Proud? Of betraying my friends? I am Foke. Betrayal is worse than death for us."

"How have you betrayed your friends?"

"I came here with Nappy Groff. Same reason Lod came —to free Chan-ti Beppu. Now Beppu, Nappy, and Lod are your prisoners."

"You may have the girl and the old man when I have captured Ned O'Tennis. He comes. Already I feel him at my lynk. In hours, he will be apprehended. Then you may take your Foke and go to any world you wish."

Gorlik shook his big head. "Thirteen days I have lived in the hamlet, tolerated by the others but unloved. They have no trust or love for me."

"I could not come earlier or maybe I could have spared you that indignity. But I needed to oversee the interrogation of Lod. You will have new friends—many new friends. Don't grieve over the loss of these few. They are fools not to see your compassion, your heroism."

"I am Foke!" Gorlik shouted. "The zōtl are my enemy!

What I did, I did unknowing!" He raised the glowing sphere over his head.

"Wait! That is a Globe of Influence! What you see in it, you can touch with your will. Don't you understand? I am offering you a kingdom."

"Fock your kingdom!" Gorlik heaved the sphere to the ground, and it burst among the rocks with concussive force.

As the globe erupted, Lod heaved out of his trance. He awoke in his plasma body, wrung by the grip of the phanes. *What windows burn in your brain?* the Cave of Riddles was asking. *Might there be hope? Faith in a secret freedom?* Echoes of Lod's telepathic rapture came and went.

Gorlik somersaulted down a slope nubbled with mushrooms. Above him, Saor was a black sky glittering with the hot shards of the exploded globe.

A laugh twisted feebly in Lod. The power Saor had offered the gnome was a direct patch to Lod's machine mind. Gorlik's rejection of the Globe had freed some of Lod's power, and his torso breathed a brighter scarlet. *Humans are as unpredictable as Rimstalkers,* he thought at the crest of the surge. *As unpredictable and as desperate. Saor you are a fool to try to manipulate them.* The ticking of the zōtl, who were probing the program codes in his brain, tattooed louder, and Lod's enthusiasm dulled. From the Cave of Riddles, a synthetic voice asked, *What doors glide open in your heart with a wind that walks for love?*

On the slopes of the Dragon's Shank, the Brood of Night saw the flare from the ruptured Globe of Influence. The distorts moaned and quivered, for any visitation of light portended ill. Too recently, Fire himself had been defeated before their startled eyes by the gnome Gorlik. Night ruled all now. How could any mere beam of light dare stand before Saor? The sudden appearance yet again of radiance on the night-thick Dragon's Shank could only mean that Gorlik was working some evil.

Since the capture of Lod, Gorlik had sulked about the hamlet. The other Foke, father Nappy and daughter Chanti, consoled him. They bore no grudge. They were too proud in their happiness at finding each other again to carry anger at Gorlik. But Gorlik was furious with himself for his compliance with Saor. The gnome sat glumly outside the window where Chan-ti and Nappy were imprisoned. And when they were allowed by the Cenobite to stroll the hamlet's one street, he tagged along, whining after them, pleading with them to believe he had acted unwittingly. Fra Baba and the Knower alone believed him, as they could gauge him telepathically. The other distorts feared he was mad.

"Betrayal saved my life," Nappy Groff finally told Gorlik when the big-faced man came to their room above the winery and begged for forgiveness. The older gnome had sunken into himself after the Witch Maze, and he spoke in a thin voice. "You have grunion for brains, Gorlik. Making deals with the Face of Night! I'm old. I'll die soon anyway. Betrayal serves only you."

"No betrayal!" Gorlik insisted. "I saved your life that you might be with your daughter again. And here you are! What wrong did I do? Would you be dead in the Witch Maze? Was I to know Lod would come to save Beppu?" He turned to Chan-ti. "Beppu, you must hear me. I've no deal with the Face of Night."

Chan-ti nodded but dared not offer even a pat of consolation: Gorlik looked crazed, worse than he had on Ras Mentis when he had seized her for his own, before the scyldar sent him scurrying.

"I betrayed no one," Gorlik repeated. He was beginning to believe his own lie. In the Witch Maze, at the threshold of death, carrying the phanes for the Face of Night had seemed a small task to undertake for more life. He had had no intent of defeating Chan-ti's escape with Lod, of binding Lod for the zōtl. He had not even known that Lod, too, was seeking her. He had been used. Why would no one believe him? Ire meshed with shame, and he took Chan-ti by her shoulders and turned her to face him. "There was no betrayal."

Nappy roused himself from the corner where he sat, and Gorlik placed his foot on the elder man's chest and shoved him back. Nappy dropped heavily and sat glowering.

"I am Foke," Gorlik moaned. "I do not obey Saor."

Pity dampened Chan-ti's lungs, and though Gorlik's grip was hurting her arms, she did not struggle. "I never asked you to come after me," she said. "Courage led you. It will, yet."

Gorlik's grip relented. "You forgive me?"

"There's nothing to forgive, Bram. You did your best to find me. As you say, how were you to know of Lod?"

Gorlik nodded once, heavily. He stared up past the reflections of Chan-ti's eyeglasses, into the life of the woman he had wanted for his own. Pity for him shone back, and he knew then there would be no vows between them. Out of the heart's dark, a useless cry lifted, but he gave it no voice.

Gorlik slouched past a haggard Nappy without looking at him and left. For days he moped, sick of heart at the thought of how the Foke legends would remember him. Several times he brinked on suicide but loathed himself too much to let himself escape that easily. Then Saor appeared above the hamlet, a darkness that blotted out the firefly-tinkling cliffs. All the Brood heard Gorlik called out into the street by the thunder-voice of the Face of Night, and they saw him lifted and flown to a higher slope— where light now staved the darkness.

Chan-ti saw another light—a pale glow in her window— that she thought was the ghost of Spooner Yegg. Since the night of Lod's capture, she had been seeing him wandering among the spike trees and mushroom fields. At first she had thought the blur was just nostalgia, and the wind brushing spoor from where the gills of bioluminent fungus notched the trees. But the blur had hardened to Spooner Yegg's shape, the black garments he had worn in life dusty with wraith-light. His silver hair and thin moustache had gleamed brightly from the solemn shadow of his face. On his chest, in the fist-sized hole from the laserbolt that had killed him, a heraldic splash of scarlet had smoldered.

Nappy had seen him, too, but ignored him. He was still angry that the thief had helped Chan-ti begin the futile search for Ned O'Tennis that had led to this dark place. Chan-ti had thought of telling him that Spooner was her true father but thought better of it when she saw how tenuous was the strength left in Nappy's small body.

At the window, Chan-ti watched the Brood of Night spill out of their cottages and come running from their fields to watch the flare of radiance above the hamlet. Across the street, obscured by a thorn-trellis at the corner of a bungalow, Spooner's ghost waved for her to come down. Chan-ti's blood whirled. She helped Nappy from the straw cot where he had been sleeping, and guided him down the narrow stairs. In the dark, empty winery below, Spooner waited, smudged with ghostly vapors.

Nappy grunted and raised a fist to the ghost. "Away, thief! Leave the living alone!"

"Ease, Nappy," Chan-ti said and stepped ahead of him. "The wraith is trying to talk with us."

Spooner's body of light drifted on the field of force that Genitrix had projected for her creation, Moku the Beast. When Moku was destroyed, the forcefield had persisted, long enough for Spooner's wavebody to be swept along by it. The thief was as perplexed as Chan-ti to find himself on the Dragon's Shank, in the hamlet of the Brood of Night, at the threshold of a winery, the moldered scent of the place vividly musky. He smelled, he saw, he heard through the waveforms that still had bodies, through the living. Images of battles yawned through him, he knew not from where, and the image of a brown youth with a blue pearl in her palm— Understanding came in waves, surges of ideation out of nowhere, though actually from Genitrix who was watching everything through her lynk system. The zōtl had shut down her communication network, yet she was sentient still and what she perceived excited her.

The O'ode has been found. Spooner's ghost spoke in the Foke's minds. The words rising in the thief amazed even him. Who was speaking? *The zōtl are dying even now.*

Lod—who had, all along, been the object of Genitrix's communication—heard. The mantle of power from the Globe of Influence faded with its explosion and with it Lod's presence dulled. As he dimmed so did the thief's ghost. Spooner, drifting painlessly alert in the forcefield inherited from Moku, felt himself borne gently outward. He was dying. No, he corrected himself—he was dead and this was the journey to his source. He stared a last time at his daughter and the familiar contours of remembered reality. He managed a smile. Then the expanding field that Genitrix released quietly carried him away, dissolving the shapes, and the sensations that were borrowed from others. A majestic continuum of radiance broadened around him, sweeping him onward into the boundless reaches of eternity.

"Father!" Chan-ti shouted and ran to where the ghost had stood.

Nappy came up behind her. "Spooner Yegg—" Thoughts moved the jigsaw pieces of his seamed face as he realized. "He was your real father."

Chan-ti nodded, lifted her glasses and wiped the tears from her eyes. "He came back for me."

Nappy put his arm around Beppu. Through the window of the wine-shop, he saw the Cenobite stalking toward them.

In Lod's mind, the telepathic image that he had been observing from where he was bound before the Face of Night broke up into hot, jiggling motes. The synthetic voice from the ghost cave spoke: *"Inside the oak is the acorn—and inside the acorn an oak forest thrives, and in the shade of the forest there are squirrels and birds and the emptiness that carries all of this. What is the name of this emptiness?"*

Saor's black body appeared before Lod, its outline jagged, vibrating with rage. The ground where the Face of Night stood buckled. Tiles tore loose from the colonnade and flew at him, into him, splattering into fiery dust against his invisible corona and vanishing in his darkness. He stood there pulsing with wrath long enough for Lod to hope Saor would kill him. Once his plasma shape was destroyed, he would be free of the phanes and returned to his Form. But Saor did not kill him. He pointed to the webwork of cables in the ceiling vault above Lod, and the zōtl there gusted away like a flock of bats.

The constriction of the phanes slackened, and Lod found the strength to speak. "What are you doing?"

Saor's voice throbbed from the dark, dense with withheld anger. "Ned O'Tennis has found the O'ode."

Saor pointed at the rust-red torso, and Lod reeled before the flux of data-energy that battered him. A flurry of images showed Loryn among the distort tribes in the giant forests of Q're, the dusky archipelagoes of Elphame, the fogroads of Xappur. In each successive image, she was in the midst of larger crowds of misshaped humans.

"She gathered an army—" Saor spoke stonily. "She drew

her forces exclusively from the distort tribes. And quickly. No one in Doror was aware. Only the Saor-priests of Chalco knew. Perhaps the Ordo Vala, too. I sent my assassins—" The cinematic stream showed the bald, black-robed corpses of Saor-priests nailed to trees, hung from outcroppings, stacked in grabens swarming with carrion birds. "They never even saw the O'ode. The distorts killed them on sight."

Lod viewed the O'ode. It turned slow as a planet before him. In its velvety surface, he glimpsed vision-ripples and jumpcuts of a frizzy-haired teenager, her face smudged, rag clothes grimed, herded with a cluster of other bedraggled humans through a redrock dolmen.

A loggia of metallic glass appeared out of the darkness of the lynk, a corridor of twisted pillars with a ceiling lost among buttresses and rampways. Galleries, high above the loggia, gleamed like black tar blisters. In each bulbous gallery, fanned in smoky light, swarms of zōtl clouded. Higher yet, against an ichorous sky of amber, tendrilled clouds, dark flocks of zōtl soared.

Humans with spiders clasping the backs of their skulls lurched from the hivelike alcoves of the loggia. They came with electric prods to sort the harvest. Jostled by the panic of the others, Loryn let herself be shoved to the edge of the crowd. The grubs closed in, prods held low. From down the vitreous length of the loggia, screams wafted on an acrid stink of poisonous char.

Loryn opened her mouth and spit into her hand the O'ode. Nothing changed. The grubs thrust closer, and she staggered backward into those behind her. A prod struck her leg. The jolt heaved her back into the crowd, and she dropped the O'ode. The blue pebble skidded out of sight into the frenzy of the stampede.

Zōtl spiraled down from the high galleries. The crowd screamed as one, a horrifying despair under the claw of the spiders. The first bunch of zōtl struck the herded humans in deadfall, limp sparrow-weight bodies. Others smacked lifelessly onto the metallic glass boulevard, where the lynk had deposited the humans.

The grubs collapsed and convulsed, their zōtl mounts sloughing off in a curdle of chitinous legs. The crowd burst open, hurrying for the alcoves of the loggia, to get out of the downpour of zōtl corpses. Loryn went with them and stood propped against a black glass pillar to keep from collapsing under her amazement. Spidery black bodies rained out of the sky and beat the ground, thudding softer on the carcasses of those that had fallen first. Slowly, a widening silence grew across the alien heaven.

"The zōtl nest world that tapped Chalco-Doror is dead." Saor's voice ripped Lod from his trance. "But the zōtl that were left here still live. The ones that work the probes above you—they will be back once they overcome their shock. They will want revenge."

The air around Saor's black shape lit up with a quick succession of scenes showing distorts swarming strohlkraft that had been lured into narrow defiles and forest glades by decoy tribes and bogus distress signals from captured equipment.

"They worked quickly, over days," Saor explained, his outline fluttering insanely. "They had Gai's help. She was shrewd enough to have collected a small armada of strohl-kraft over the years, hidden in caches on numerous plane-tesimals. The technical expertise to use them came from herself and a few early defectors. In days—*days*, Lod—she had an army and an adolescent to lead them. She's learned a lot since she created Egil Grimson's Emirate. Enough to destroy and replace it in an eyeblink."

The blackness of Saor's body filled with a view of the inner adytum of Ioli Palace, where Egil Grimson, naked but for a chainmail breechcloth, stood before a hovering zōtl. The squat, muscular man knelt, and the zōtl mounted the back of his head and with its pincers parted his long blond hair, revealing a pith hole. The zōtl inserted its feedertube, and Egil Grimson jerked upright, his eyes flar-ing white and bulging like a terrified mare's. The agony lifted him to his toetips, and his beard opened around a silent scream.

"The zōtl is not killing him," Saor clarified, his voice leaden. "It's communing. They did this regularly—at least once a year, to share knowledge directly."

The scene jumpcut forward and showed the zōtl disen-gage, its feedertube glistening with the grease of the Vi-king's brain. The pincers applied a medicinal plug to the hole in Grimson's skull and the zōtl then floated off toward the red-pulsing dolmen at the far end of the vaulted chamber.

"Isn't biological life grotesque, Lod? Only by direct physical lynk could those two very different neurologies be fused. I'm sure the zōtl could have devised a mechanical means of communication. For mundane matters, like their quota requirements for the vassals they bred on Ren, they transmitted data through a machine intelligence. But this grisly physical link allowed Egil Grimson the experience of the zōtl's expanded awareness. Despite the suffering of the union, the event must have been godlike for Grimson. Once the zōtl left, it imparted in him a prescient telepathy that he used to his advantage in ruling his kingdom. That strength is worthless to him now. Gai has used her lynks to place her army of distorts."

The black body of Saor revealed masses of laser-armed distorts filing through the natural lynks on all the worlds in Chalco. The banners they carried displayed an open hand with the forefinger and thumb widely separated from the other three fingers—the chiromantic symbol of will.

"They staked their lives on their will," Saor said. "With the Rimstalker to guide them, the distort army invaded all the major cities and military installations of Doror."

Cities aflame flitted by in midair. Hordes of frenzied distorts swarmed through the streets, destroying everything and everyone displaying the Thunderhawk sigil of the Emirate. The carnage churned unremittingly: Towers toppled, bridges collapsed, and the colossal magravity generators that Lod had reactivated, after the fall of Ieuanc 751, collapsed under blasts of commandeered proton cannon. The skies above all the crystal cities of Doror blackened with smoke.

Saor again showed the elegant corridors of Ioli Palace, this time teeming with rabid distorts. Egil Grimson appeared in his mead hall swinging a battle-ax, which was all he had had time to snatch from the wall when the distorts surprised him.

"The Emir fed the spiders well," Saor droned on. "He respected them and their nest world. Now their world is dead. The surviving zōtl will want revenge."

A glimpse of Emir Egil Grimson's severed head upheld by its hair in the clawgrip of a distort flew by among a throng of fiery, chaotic images of turrets collapsing, walls bursting apart, and howling distorts riding proton cannon through the blazing streets.

"And their revenge will be horrible. Don't you see, Lod? I—*I* want life and more of it. I want the worlds to live, for all the lives on these worlds to live. Your Form could burn for billions of years. These worlds could last as long. And you could be a benefactor of a race of star-children. But now—" Saor's gel body seemed to rip and then re-form. "They are coming. They are trying to control me. They will want their revenge."

Saor's projections revealed Valdëmiraën, where the last of the retreating Aesirai strohlkraft clashed. Proton fire ignited the outline of the capital, N'ym. The atmosphere writhed with giant strokes of lightning as fusion bombs ignited under the city's pylons and immense ramstat thrusters blew the radioactive debris away from the city. With a bluewhite flare that burned blindingly for an instant, the city sheared away from its craggy perch and launched into space.

"The whole city is flying!" Saor exclaimed. "Flying!"

Saor was insane. Lod remained silent, his mind whirring with the information he had just received. Where was Gai? Surely Gai would come for him now that the zōtl were broken. How else could the Rimstalker get home? All Lod had to do was hold on, not let the zōtl that remained pick his brain and gain control of the gravity amp.

"N'ym will fall forever through an infinite spiral along a conch of inward-warping spacetime," Saor said. "With their hydroponics to grow food and their ramstat engines to drive oxygen from their rock foundation, they could survive for centuries—but in a terrible isolation." The crystal-spired capital flew into the darkness, a glimmer of city lights congealing to a bright star as it fell toward the blackness of Saor. "A living death—a true Viking death."

Lod stared hard at the embers of proton fire, where the city had sheared away, and saw gnats of strohlkraft exchanging laserfire. One of the gnats peeled off and dove toward the sea. Lod watched the blue exhaust of the ship trail under the water and then abruptly vanish as Ned O'Tennis flew through a submerged Tryl lynk on his way backward to his destiny.

"The circle is complete," Saor drawled. His shape warped. Electrostatic lines stressed the air around him, streamers of electricity blowing in an unfelt wind. "The worldline is closed for the zōtl now. Their home is destroyed." Voltage twisted around Saor's plasma shape with a grinding sound. When it stopped, Saor had shriveled to a shadowy blob. Insectoid legs snicked out of the amorphous blackness, oildrop eyes beaded in a cluster above a glisteny papule, and from that quivery bud, slowly, a stinger extruded. The blob of Saor's plasma convulsed to the shape of a zōtl.

Lod remained silent and still. The zōtl shape drifted closer, its feedertube fully extended. Above it, the blurred bodies of real zōtl flicked through the air, returning to their nest atop the magnetic column suspending his torso. They had assumed full control of Saor. The zōtl body they had shaped from his plasma glided directly up to Lod and stabbed its feedertube between the phanes and into his chest.

Pain gored him. He expected to die. But he did not die. The pain bored deeper and louder, cutting him to the very margin of consciousness. With cruel precision, the zōtl began disassembling his mind. They did not want to kill him —yet. They wanted to gut his machine mind and disrupt the flightpaths of the planets. They wanted to destroy Chalco-Doror and kill the Rimstalker who had poisoned their world.

Lod resisted. He hoped his struggle would inspire the zōtl's rage so they would destroy his plasma shape outright and he could thus return to his Form. But the spiders were cold in their fury. They withdrew their stinger from his chest and let him writhe around the memory of pain before stabbing him again. Lod's torso throbbed crimson against the phanes and dulled brown when Saor's stinger gouged.

Gai materialized like an hallucination, a shimmering specter of colors gathering into the shape of a Rimstalker. When Saor withdrew his stinger and flew at Gai, Lod knew that what he saw was real. He roused himself from the bloodmist cloud of his hurt to see the two plasma shapes collide. Glooms of cloudy fire jetted where they touched.

An acetylene glare seamed the space between them, burning white, fusing them.

At last Gai had gotten her hands on the zōtl. As soon as Loryn had delivered the O'ode to the spider's nest-world, the Rimstalker had set her army of distort rebels marching through her lynks, and she had come to Perdur to free Lod. But the warriors she had brought with her were killed with neurotox in the lynks. Only she had breached Perdur, by using her plasma shape to seep through the rock walls. Without her warriors, no hope of freeing Lod remained, yet Gai was determined to fight her parents' killers.

Deathlocked, Saor's and Gai's energies clashed in a mangling of lightning and fire. In moments they were consumed, and only a billowy aurora draped the space where they had been. When that thinned away, Lod waited for the zōtl to resume their torture. But the spiders could not. The temporary loss of Saor had drained their power, and without backup from their nest-world they would have to resort again to slowly picking at his program locks.

Lod relaxed as this information sifted into his stunned mind from analytic processors he had thought the zōtl had ripped from him, the pain had been that severe. The clicking of the zōtl's magnetic probe in his brain began again. And, again, from the ghost cave, the robot voice asked, *Where are you? . . . What is supposed to happen next? . . .*

Pahang had suited up with all the armor and weapons he could carry from the ordinance locker before Ned activated Gai's flight program. He hung heavily in his sling, helmeted, cuirassed, and plated along his arms and legs, the sparks of his eyes all that remained visible of him in the oversized firesuit. "Why do you go into battle undressed?" the Malay asked.

"I've got my armor," Ned replied and patted the control deck. "Right here."

The strohlkraft sailed swiftly through the gray void of the Overworld among chromatic floes of time. The damaged underbelly sent shivers through the hull but did not hamper the flight. Ahead, a raven chunk drew closer. The lynk to the Dragon's Shank and Chan-ti was there. In moments, he would know if she was alive.

"Chan-ti Beppu *is* alive," a tremulous voice spoke from the back of the flight pod.

The two men swung about in a fright. Ned was glad he had made Pahang leave his gun in the locker, for if the Malay had been armed, he would have fired at the ghastly apparition forming in the air above them. A melted face drooled sparks, puddled in midair, and finally lifted like wet laundry and coalesced to a balding, rail-thin man in an academic robe.

"Tully Gunther," Ned identified him. "The scyldar's ghost."

The wraith nodded, and its edges dissolved in prismatic vapors. "The Overworld has less of the field density of Chalco-Doror," the ghost said. "It's more difficult to hold together a plasma shape out here. Listen—I have news. Loryn has delivered the O'ode to the zōtl's nest world—"

"How?" Pahang's muffled voice sounded from inside his faceguard. "We gave her the O'ode but minutes ago."

"But you are in the Overworld, sir," Tully Gunther replied. "In moments, you will pass through one of Saor's lynks and appear on the Dragon's Shank only days after the extermination of the zōtl in their own world. The Storm-Tree has toppled. The Emir is dead."

"And N'ym?" Ned asked.

"N'ym has fallen. You have steered this ship through the Tryl lynk under the Silver Sea. The timeloop is complete, and, in this universe, in this planetary system, the fate of the zōtl is sealed."

"Why are you here, then?" Ned wanted to know.

"I am come to warn you—Saor belongs to the zōtl who survive in Perdur, and he knows you are coming. But Gai has disrupted the Face of Night's plasma shape, so the zōtl cannot immediately use him for their revenge."

"Revenge?" Pahang's voice piped from the hollow of his armor. "I do not like that word."

"The zōtl who are here in Chalco-Doror cannot survive indefinitely without their females, all of whom were left behind on their home world and are now dead. The spiders have lost everything but their loathing for other species. They will use Saor and Lod to smash the worlds into one another and destroy all of Chalco-Doror."

"And we are to help?" Ned asked. "What can we do?"

"Nothing I am aware of." The dissolving edges of the ghost had reduced it to a ribbon of bright smoke. "The fate of the worlds is bigger than we. I am come to warn you— the scyldar Neter Col has been mounted again by a zōtl and is on his way to intercept you on the Dragon's Shank. You are to die for finding the O'ode."

"What can we do?" Pahang whined.

"Be aware—" the filament of silver fire said in a narrowing voice. "The damage to my brain enables me to drift free briefly, but I have no strength to control the scyldar. All I can do is warn you. Neter Col knows you are coming."

"And Chan-ti Beppu," Ned asked, "is she all right? Does she know we're coming?"

No reply came from Tully Gunther. The specter had thinned to a thread that broke into scintillant pollen and dispersed. In the next moment, the visor filled with the black mirror of Mugna's time-floe, and the strohlkraft shot through the lynk. The ramstat cells died with a dull whine. Immediately, the ship began shaking violently. The visor had gone black in the lightless atmosphere of Mugna's north pole and the vibration-blurred panel lights were the only illumination in the flight pod. Shaking wildly, Ned tried to turn on the infrascope to see where they were gliding, but the trembling of the ship defeated him. He and Pahang hung quavering in their slings, gritting their teeth, trying not to get sick.

A constellation of small lights appeared below. The strohlkraft banked, and they saw that they were descending toward a hamlet lit with lanterns. A gray mist of bioluminescent fungi vaguely outlined fields and steep slopes. Figures dashed below, crisscrossing the hamlet's one avenue, toward which the strohlkraft angled for a landing. Quaking and bucking, the craft dropped. Over the noise of the juddering hull, Ned heard the landing gear lower. He closed his eyes and kept his mind off his bruised entrails by remembering Chan-ti's face. Days ago, her visage had been his only comfort during his thralldom to Squat. Would she look the same now? Or had time passed differently for her during her quest through the Overworld? Would she recognize him—or had her captivity broken her memories?

The strohlkraft jarred against the ground. The hamlet's

lights streamed by, slowing and then wobbling to a stop. Through the visor, Ned and Pahang watched as cowled figures stepped from the darkness between the buildings. Some had their hoods drawn back, revealing bizarre visages: lobster jaws, stalk eyes, flesh jagged as lightning.

"Demons!" Pahang wailed and dropped from his sling to get a rifle. "Shoot them—like you did Squat."

"No. Chan-ti is somewhere out there."

Pahang returned to the control deck clutching a laser-ifle. "What if they are as strong as Squat?"

The crowd of distorts parted, and a bald, bulge-browed man larger than the others stepped forward. At his sides, his pudgy hands gripping them by their arms, were Chan-ti Beppu and Nappy Groff. In the lanternlight, Chan-ti's face was hot with alertness and expectation. By that look, Ned knew she was whole, and the constriction that had winced in him since leaving her relented. He switched on the hull radio. "Chan-ti! It's me, Ned. Are you all right?"

"Yes. I'm a prisoner of Saor . . ."

"As are you now, Ned O'Tennis," the man with the big-lobed brow spoke. "I am the Cenobite of Perdur, Fra Baba Bathra, and you are now my prisoner. Leave your weapons behind and come forth from your vessel."

"Hawk, you would not!" Pahang cried.

"I must. He has my Chan-ti. But you can stay. He doesn't know you're here."

"Oh, but I do," Fra Baba's voice chortled over the intercom. "I feel you in there—Pahang, son of Selingtang of the Yuë tribe. You, too, must come out. And leave your rifle behind."

Pahang whimpered. "He is as Squat. He reaches into our minds."

"Do as he says."

Reluctantly, Pahang relinquished his rifle and his laserbolt pistol, but he would not remove his armor. Ned opened the hatch and stepped out. Pahang changed his mind about facing the Cenobite unarmed. He picked up his weapons and followed.

Chan-ti stirred to go to them, but Fra Baba held her firmly by her arm. A prideful intensity shone in the Cenobite's stare. He had redeemed himself by capturing the Aesirai wanted by the Face of Night. Now surely Saor would return him to Perdur and to his beloved midstim. The many days he had spent in this dark hamlet with the Brood of Night had depressed him. Even the gly-tabs he ate like candy could not lift his dark mood anymore. But the sight of the Aesirai stirred hope in him.

Ned strode to Chan-ti but before they could touch, Fra Baba signaled the Brood, and distorts flanked the Aesirai and took his arms in their harsh grips. Pahang, too, was seized by the distorts, who ripped away the rifle and pistol from his hands and began searching him while he twisted and wailed.

"Stop that," the Cenobite commanded. "He has no other weapons on him. Come. Bring them to the portal."

"You shouldn't have come for us, lad," Nappy Groff said. He looked weary, smaller, and more wizened. "We're all food for the spiders now."

"Where are you taking us?" Ned wanted to know.

The Cenobite flashed his tiny teeth in a genuine smile. "To the Face of Night." He turned and pushed Chan-ti and Nappy ahead of him across the street.

"Why?" Ned asked, shoved along behind them. "Saor is beaten. The O'ode has destroyed the zōtl's nest world."

Fra Baba stopped and turned a fierce glower on Ned. "Do not try to deceive me, Aesirai. The O'ode will never be found. The zōtl guard the one world where it exists."

"Use your mindreach on me, then," Ned insisted. "I have been to Rataros. I have retrieved the O'ode and brought it back to Chalco-Doror. See for yourself."

Fra Baba frowned. His stare fell deeper into the Aesirai and he felt those memories, shiny and clear. But deeper yet were other more disturbing memories. There was Squat, an obscene albino distort who had cruelly dominated this man. "Ha!" There was the trick. The Aesirai had learned well from Squat how to guard his thoughts and shape his memories. But the Cenobite would not be deceived. "I know of Squat," he said, and Pahang moaned loudly. "You cannot fool me with your lies, Ned O'Tennis."

"Why would I lie?"

"To save yourself and your beloved, of course."

"Contact Perdur," Ned responded, addressing Fra Baba's back as the Cenobite turned and resumed his jaunty stride. "They will tell you. The zōtl are defeated. You have no need of us anymore. You can let us go."

"Ha!" The Cenobite moved eagerly past the gawking Brood with his prisoners and hurried to the redrock dolmen hidden by a copse of spike trees at the far end of the street. The portal lynked with Perdur and was to be used only by Saor and the zōtl. But this was a rare event, and the Cenobite knew that the Face of Night would not object.

"I was afraid for you," Chan-ti whispered to Ned when Fra Baba released her in the grove of spike trees.

"You shouldn't have tried to find me," Ned answered. "I would have found my way to the Eyelands again."

"Not likely," Nappy said. "You went too deep in the Overworld. You picked up a lot of temporal torque. You'll never be able to return to where you started. Would have been better for her to forget you."

"Temporal torque?" Fra Baba raised one thin eyebrow. "Then you shan't be able to cross this portal. We shall have to invite the Face of Night to visit us here once more. I am sure that will delight him as this is the site of his victory over Lod." He cast a benevolent smile through the throng to where Gorlik stood scowling. "And here is our hero himself to greet his Lord Saor."

Gorlik was scuffed with mud and scratches from his roll down the dark slope after rejecting the Globe of Influence. He had expected Saor to kill him outright for that affront, but mysteriously the Face of Night had simply disappeared. Gorlik had then slumped back to the hamlet. When the strohlkraft arrived, swooping out of the black sky like a nighthawk, he had come to see for himself the Aesirai whom Chan-ti Beppu loved. Of course the man was tall and handsome as he himself was not, but what impressed Gorlik was that he stood bravely. In a short while, the Aesirai would be impaled on a zōtl's stinger, yet he did not quake and moan as his armored companion did. The gnome could see by Ned's careworn expression as he stared at Beppu that he was sincerely in love. And that assuaged Gorlik's anger.

Ned reached for Chan-ti again, and the distorts tugged him back hard.

"Young lovers," Fra Baba cooed and placed his palm against the redrock to announce his presence. "Such a omantic notion for these cruel worlds. Yet I feel your love s true." His jowly face beamed sarcastically. "What is it ou hope to find in each other? Pleasure? There is far more pleasure in feeding your brains the right chemicals. Perhaps what you seek in each other is not pleasure but instinct, the fulfillment of your genes. Such biological hardwiring is impossible to override. But why this pairing? How absurd that an Aesirai, the product of generations of selective breeding, and a mongrel Foke would mate."

Pahang had sunk deeper into his armor and was searching desperately for some way to yank himself free and escape. No opportunity showed itself. The entire Brood of Night had gathered among the spike trees. The dolmen began to glow, throbbing redder with each pulse. The Malay squeaked a tiny cry.

Fra Baba exulted to feel the fear mounting in his prisoners. Their terror would be his liberation. With enormous joy, he observed that the dolmen had stopped strobing. The lynk was ready for passage. From within he sensed movement and the telepathic suggestion not of Saor but of a hundred frantic minds. The Cenobite was baffled for an instant. Then his small eyes went round with fright. What he sensed were zōtl, hundreds of them, fleeing Perdur. In a flash, Fra Baba perceived that the Aesirai had not lied to him at all. The O'ode had been delivered! The zōtl that remained in Perdur were now doomed. They would need human hosts to feed on while they worked their vengeance.

Powered by terror, Fra Baba slapped at the dolmen, trying to shut down the lynk. Before his palm could touch the stone, a gale of black, birdsmall bodies blew from the lynk. The force of the zōtl rush scattered the Brood among the spike trees. The Cenobite hurled about, his telepathic mind suddenly loud with the pain of the many Saor-priests in Perdur who had already been pithed by the spiders. Why had no one alerted him? He shoved into the screaming distorts and staggered three paces before one of the zōtl clasped his skull. With a crunch of punctured bone, its stinger found its home in his brain, and he screamed the cold cry of the damned.

Ned seized Chan-ti, who grabbed Nappy. They crouched under the onslaught of frenzied zōtl. The flying

spiders thrashed through the lanternglow like locusts, fall
ing on the fleeing distorts. A cluster swarmed over Ned
who had thrown his body over Chan-ti and Nappy. Gorlik
ripped two spiders from his face, their pincers tearing hi
flesh. He broke a spike from one of the leafless trees and
bludgeoned the zōtl crawling over Ned. At least the spi
ders, who had fled Perdur hurriedly, mad for sustenance
now that their homeworld was gone, were without their
tiny but lethal lasers or there would have been no battle at
all.

"The lynk!" Ned shouted. "We have to get into the lynk
The torque will carry us free of here."

Gorlik clubbed the spiders dropping onto them out of
the darkness, but there were too many. Their high-pitched
cries sliced the air on all sides, and their sharp pincers
clawed flesh as they flew by. Even trying to stand up was
almost impossible, the razoring cuts of the winged spiders
were coming too fast. Gorlik shouted his war-cry and
swung wildly, expecting to be dropped by the slashing
stingers.

Blue bolts of laserfire struck the zōtl clouding over Gorlik and the others, and spiders fell in tufts of flame. Pahang,
protected from the zōtl by his armor, had grabbed the
laserifle from a distort who had been struggling to use it
with stub-fingered hands. He fired as Ned had shown him
and was amazed by the ease of it. He burned away the
swarm of black shapes zigzagging around Ned and the
gnome. He spotted the laserbolt pistol where it had been
dropped, and he swooped that up and tossed it to Ned.

Rapid-firing, Pahang ran to Ned's side. The Aesirai fired
several bolts overhead to clear the space to stand. He
pulled Chan-ti to her feet. "Hold me tight," he told her.
"When we go through the lynk, we're going to be thrown
hard."

"I'll never let you go again," she promised.

"Don't shoot into the lynk!" Ned yelled at Pahang. "It'll
blow."

Gorlik helped Nappy up and swung to bash another
spider that had dropped onto his shoulder. They ducked
after Pahang, who was firing gleefully up at the hoard of
frantic zōtl. Chan-ti followed, and Ned came up behind,
keeping the spiders from following. At the lynk threshold,

they grouped together. More zōtl flushed out of the lynk and scattered them. Gorlik swung with his club, and Pahang used his rifle like a bat.

Ned took Chan-ti under one arm and Nappy under the other. "Take hold of me," he called to Pahang and Gorlik. They pressed in closer and grabbed him. But as they stepped into the lynk, another rush of exiting zōtl collided with them. Nappy was flung loose. Chan-ti and Gorlik reached for him. Pahang, who had also spun free, grabbed for Ned.

Time howled like wind. For a moment, they were all together in the gray emptiness of the Overworld—the Foke, the Assagai, the Malay, and half a dozen zōtl. Chan-ti clung to Nappy, and he held onto Gorlik's arm. Ned and Pahang tumbled around each other, stretching to reach the others. The zōtl used their wings to attach to Nappy and Chan-ti. Gorlik grabbed two of them with one hand, flung them away and seized two more. They writhed up his arm. Their pincers dug into his already bloody face. "I love you both!" he shouted to Chan-ti and Nappy, and let go of the old man's hand. He whirled away into the gray void, taking the clinging zōtl with him.

Chan-ti twisted about to find Ned. He and Pahang were tangled together, moving away from her in the gray emptiness. The time-wind blustered loudest around them, sweeping them swiftly away. Chan-ti gripped Nappy with all her strength, and with bleared eyes watched Ned and Pahang disappear into the Overworld.

Perdur felt empty. Only a handful of zōtl remained in the enormous palace. Those spiders who could had taken Saor-priests and pilgrims as mounts and gone into the core of the citadel to plot their escape into the Overworld with ramstat vehicles. But the majority of zōtl were left to fend for themselves, and they had flown into the lynks, seeking their own mounts throughout Chalco-Doror.

Lod hung in the magnetic column at the end of the enormous hall before the ghost cave, where the zōtl had suspended his plasma shape. He still appeared as no more than a torso, ruddy with weary energy, bound by the phanes. The zōtl who remained picked relentlessly at his machine brain, using needles of magnetic force to reach into his Form through his plasma shape. The process was painful. His program codes flinched like flesh under the sharp probes.

The synthetic voice from inside the ghost cave ranted on: *What is the wakefulness we call mind? . . . What drags us out of sleep? . . . What drags us back again? . . .*

In the midst of his agony, his mind drifted. Like a cascade off a cliff, he dissolved into space. Was this death? Was his plasma shape finally decomposing? No. Far away, the crux of magnetic rays continued to pierce him. The pain droned on, plucking at his machine brain. Panic spanked him as he fell through the emptiness. Had the spiders begun taking apart his awareness? Was he flying into his own void? Was he becoming mindless?

"Be still, Lod," a female voice spoke.

"Gai?"

"No. I'm not Gai. I'm a machine mind like yourself."

"Who?"

"Lod—don't you recognize me?"

Lod's fall into emptiness had becalmed to a blue stillness. Distantly, he still felt his plasma body deep in its dense nest of thorns. "Genitrix?"

"Yes, Lod."

"But— I thought— Is this a zōtl trick?"

"The zōtl cut my communication lines to the Forms. But I have continued to honor our mission as best I can from inside my solitude. The worlds are my handiwork. I feel everything that happens on and around them."

"How are you talking to me?"

"Mind is a waveform. Your waveform drifts free of your tormented plasma shape. We're talking through a subtle form of magnetic induction."

"Why have you not used this ability to communicate with Gai? She is struggling without you."

"I dared not contact her before, Lod. The zōtl were too attentive. But now they are distracted. Their home world is dead. They are intent on finding a way to another nest world, if they can. As soon as they realize that their hope is empty, they will begin to use you to disturb the gravity-amp, to collide the planets and annihilate Chalco-Doror."

"I know this."

"I know you know. I've brought you here because you know and yet do not fully understand. I've brought you here to feel the detachment, the emptiness that is our heritage as machine minds. Do you like this emptiness?" The blue void pinked to purple. "Darker perhaps? Or would you prefer your own color?" The space brightened to solar yellow. "I hear you wondering if I'm mad. I am not mad. I am a machine. As are you. Do not forget this. In the drama of the struggle between Rimstalker and zōtl we assume the passion of our creator. But ultimately we are detached."

"I am committed."

"You should strive to be detached. Organic life is passion. Machine life detachment. Look at Gai. She defeated the zōtl in their own world and what did she do then? Instead of using her plasma body to continue to clear the zōtl from Chalco-Doror, she attacked Saor in Perdur. She was killed and now sleeps in her Form in a coma, useless to the struggle to save our ship from being destroyed by the vengeful spiders. When she eventually wakes, our ship may already be scuttled. Her reaction was emotional. Glandular. We must not make the same mistake. And so I have waited, silent, detached. What I have done for our cause, I did surreptitiously, through my creations—a distort here and there to harry the zōtl, to help those humans who were enemies of the zōtl."

"And now? What are you going to do now for our mission?"

"I'm going to tell you a thing that you must hear with great detachment. This thing will be unpleasant. For a glandular being, it would be unbearable. But for a machine, there is detachment. You will understand what to do."

Distantly, the needling pain continued. "What could be more unbearable than the phanes?"

"The zōtl virus program that enables the spiders to control Saor and to mute me is not in Saor. It is in you."

The agony of the magnetic probes squealed closer. "That cannot be. I have functioned faithfully."

"That is the nature of the virus. You are the radiant

element of our system. You project—while Saor is dark and receptive. Saor initially received the virus, but passed it to you. You carry it. Its program broadcasts from inside you. Saor obeys the commands that issue from your interior."

"No."

"It is objectively so. Detach. Realize the truth of this. Why is Saor not bound by the phanes? His receptivity assures that the zōtl can influence him through you."

"Then why must the phanes bind me? Why does the virus not manipulate me?"

"Gai would have shut you down at once. I or Saor could have managed the gravity-amp without you. Very easily you could have been reduced to a thermal unit. Far more cunning of the spiders to house the virus in you and use your natural connection with all of us to control us."

"Does Gai know this?"

"Of course not."

"Why have you kept this secret?"

"I'm detached. The time was not right until now. The zōtl are cut off from their world, where their technology makes the phanes and the virus programs. They can expect no further reinforcements. Now the truth can be known."

"And me? What of me?"

"You carry the enemy."

"But I do not! The zōtl are taking me apart painfully, trying to crack my program codes. If I carry the virus, why do they bother?"

"You're simply a carrier. The virus radiates its commands from inside you. But it does not control you."

"Then I must be purged."

"So long as you're held by the phanes, there's no hope of that. You must detach."

"I must be freed."

"Perhaps you will be. The humans know of your plight. They'll try to free you. But until then, you must simply wait. Stay detached. Know that you're not alone. Gai is unconscious now, but I'm here, watching you.

> *"Whatever we are, machine or flesh,*
> *programs or instincts,*

we are
bound by heaven and hell."

The void shadowed darker, and Lod was again in his plasma torso, wincing as the spiders worked their tiny violence inside him.

The Rust Age

With the extermination of the zōtl in Chalco-Doror, neo-sapiens serve no further function for the Rimstalker. Now we are ignored by the Mother of Worlds, left to do as we please in the last two millennia before we are returned to the oblivion from which we have been briefly retrieved. So what are we doing? We sing songs and we fall in love as though we should live forever.

—Bill Jones, from *Diary of a Second Life*, 1989 Doror

Sword's Wanderings in Chalco

The tips of sequoia floated in brightness above the dark forest on Q're. Sword leaned on his weapon and stared up at the amber jellies of twilight. Behind him, in the pocket of a valley, a hamlet, whose windows faced away from the forest of giant trees, was preparing for the night and its horrors. A tractor bumbled along the circuit road, laying coils of razor-wire. Lux flares ignited on the toll bridge that crossed the stream into the hamlet. The vesper bell tolled, calling the last straggly farmers, shepherds, and pilgrims in from the pastures before the one road into town was barricaded.

Despite these precautions, the hamlet had lost numerous residents in the last few years and had almost become a ghost town, fear had driven so many families away. A band of rawfaces, seeking easy prey, had come down from the highland forests and raided the hamlet almost every night. They were led by a distort among them with a cunning unknown before in rawfaces. Recently, they had burrowed under the hamlet and come up in the houses, where the families were huddled in their bedrooms quaking with terror at the eerie ululations of the monsters without. Many died that night. After that, only the poorest of the families remained, those who had worked as serfs in the fields of landowners before the owners fled and left them the land. If they left, they would lose all they could hope to own in this life. So they had blocked the tunnels with boulders and razor-wire and had sent for Sword.

Since the collapse of the Emirate, 320 years earlier, each world had shaped its own government—or tried to, for the countless factions that thrived in the absence of the zōtl's predation were constantly feuding and rarely able to consolidate. The besieged hamlet on Q're had no one to appeal to for help but a legendary figure called Sword, who was reputed to wander the wild worlds seeking evil distorts to slay. Many in the hamlet doubted he even existed. The few who did believe in him ignored the taunts of the others, and broadcasted their distress messages each week when Q're came in line with the ancient Viking battlestation in the Abyss that had been converted to a radio relayer by the city-state still extant on Cendre.

At the peak of the horror, when the rawfaces' craving for human flesh had inspired them to lay broken boughs over the razor-wire coils and to scale the hamlet gate with stone-weighted ladders made from forest tendrils, using the carcasses of their fallen brood to shield them from the projectiles of the humans, Sword arrived. He landed in the hamlet's cobbled square in an antique ramstat flyer, battered, hissing coolant-vapors, and dripping oil.

Those who believed in Sword had expected to meet a warrior with the stature of Wulf Bane. The short, wiry man, who unbuckled from the flight sling and slid feet-first from the nose hatch, inspired disappointment in everyone but the youngest children; they had no notion of what a hero should look like, other than that he should have a weapon. And Sword had a weapon.

Strapped by an intricately knotted thong to the little man's back was his namesake, a long, narrow sword, nearly as tall as he, sheathed in a red scabbard studded with gruesome fangs. Despite his sleek black armor, weather-worn to gray, and his plasteel-tipped boots fitted on the insides of his calves with bone-handled knives, he was a slight and unimposing figure. His face, too, was hardly frightful. With his large nose, dim chin, and large eyes behind sturdy metal-framed eyeglasses, he looked more like a schoolteacher than a slayer of monsters.

The hamlet did not want this man to die for them, and they tried to convince him to leave Q're and return with a dozen strong warriors, preferably armed with laser guns. He smiled with quiet understanding and asked to see the hamlet's defenses. The elders shrugged. He was shown the log ramparts, the sturdy wood portcullis, and the stack of coiled razor-wire that the hamlet's one tractor lay in place each night.

"This is fine for wolves and saberclaws," Sword said. "But rawfaces are too crafty in their hunger, even without a sapient distort to lead them. I am surprised you have survived this long. Haven't they dug tunnels into your houses yet?"

The elders shared surprised looks and showed him the tunnels.

"These boulders and razor-wire barriers are too easily dislodged," he told them and went on to teach them how to plant barbed shafts of fire-hardened wood in the dirt walls of the tunnels. "You will hear their screams and be prepared when they come through here next. But already it is too late for that. They know you are vulnerable. They will sacrifice their own to get you."

The youngest of the children, who had been secretly listening, cried out at that. Sword knelt before her and wiped away her tears with a silk cloth he wore about his neck to prevent chafing from his armor. He met the fright in the child's loud eyes and held the fear firmly with his lemur-like stare. "You mustn't be afraid anymore," he said in a voice too soft to inspire courage in anyone but a child. "You are safe now. I am here. And I will kill all the bad things. They will never again come into this village. I promise you."

The child hugged him, and the elders shook their heads ruefully.

Alone, Sword walked out of the hamlet and into the forest, the elders shouting at him from the gate to reconsider. He waved with friendly reassurance and continued. Once in the shadow of the great trees, he unsheathed his weapon, stabbed it into the earth, leaned on it, and gazed up at the world's slow dream. This was a beauty those who had once loved him would never see, for his family had been slaughtered by distorts on his home world of Elphame when he was a child.

He had been only six years old, small enough to crawl into a rock crevice and hide while his parents and older brothers and sisters were devoured alive by a pack of shagjaws. Their screams echoed in his bones, forever chilling his marrow. He never stopped hearing them. Or feeling their pain. Suffering became his only way of touching his family again, and from then on he gave his life to pain so he would always be near them. His only blessing after the terror of his loss was to be taken in by an ancient renegade Viking family, who, inspired by his eagerness to endure any suffering, taught him how to fight. He became a genius of destruction, powered by the screams in his bones, and he devoted his life to actively seeking out the worlds' terrors and destroying them.

Yet whenever beauty appeared in the midst of these cruelties, he took pains to enjoy it for the sake of his loved ones. They had seen too little of beauty on the croft where they had birthed him and his siblings, where they had struggled with the molting land to win a meager living, and then been murdered. He breathed in the leaf mulch, his gaze lost among the peach-tinted clouds.

A ghostly wail burned his hearing like acid—and a cold smile touched Sword's lips. He had found his way back home.

Sword stretched till his shoulders popped, then flexed his hands and did several agile knee-bends, one leg extended at a time, to limber himself for the worshipful dance to come. The banshee cries slithered closer. He adjusted the knobs at the steel temples of his eyeglasses, shifting the lenses to infrared. Finally, he pulled his black cowl over his balding head, fit the earguards in place, tightened the straps of his armor at the wrists and throat, and waited.

Sunset was brown as wine and the galaxy a crystal mist beyond the sullen clouds when the first eyeglints jerked in the darkness between the trees. By then the eerily curving howls were a din, and Sword was grateful yet again for his earguards. He stood, legs wide apart, hands clasped atop the hilt of his weapon, which was still stuck in the ground.

The rawfaces came through the trees in a wave of raving jaws and talons. They were bipedal beasts, some of them three meters tall, their flesh chitinous and black, gleaming with the light from the planetesimals and the stars. Loathsome jaws gnashed in slimy visages, fangs clacking and drooling in a blur of rabid motion. Their ferocious faces looked like hacked meat, and their long, plated skulls were crested with spikes. With maniacal intensity, glutinous flame-cored eyes inside horny skull-sockets fixed on their prey.

Sword remained utterly motionless until the rawfaces lunged into striking distance. Then, with a gut-cramping scream unheard among the feeding cries of the rawfaces, he swung his sword in a hissing arc. The blade, directed with fatal precision, slashed through the eye-bubbles of several rawfaces before cracking into the chitin-plate of a skull. With a twist of the hilt, the blade discharged a writhing blue bolt of electricity that knotted about the head of the rawface and threw it dead against the onrushing horde.

The throng of rawfaces roared louder, infuriated by the sudden stink of their own blood and the smell of thunder. Sword leaped with feral abandon among them, swinging his weapon in swollen pirouettes that jagged into barbs of bluehot lightning with each impact. His face was a rictus of lustful rage, as cursing through clenched teeth he hacked his way in a wide circle of leaps and stamping charges, a rage of postures among the trees, the fallen bodies, and the pouncing beasts.

In a dance which breathed stillness as he stopped to hack and then leaped and stopped to hack again, he picked his way with murderous cunning through the crowd of distorts. At last, when dozens of them lay dead and dying in spasms on the forest floor, they shrunk like vapors before him. As if shorn of gravity, his muscles pumped with the screams of his dead family, he pursued the retreating rawfaces. They circled back on him, trying to trip him from behind trees, diving from the branches. But Sword was snug in his poise. His smallness was his advantage, and he ducked and feinted with a mouse's adroitness, his thunderbolts shattering skulls and torsos, splintering trees, igniting the bloodwet duff of the forest floor, the flames snuffing out beneath the rawfaces' collapsing corpses.

With an overhead blow, he split a rawface head almost in half, leapfrogged its sprawling body, and burst into a clearing, where planetlight illuminated a giant rawface. Even in the traumas of shadow, he recognized that this distort was different from the others. His infrared lenses revealed the cruel awareness in its swivel eyes. He caught a smudge of movement to his side and jumped backward. The handful of remaining rawfaces came at him with thick boughs in their talons—and Sword realized that the giant was telepathically directing them.

He smashed the first to strike at him, a lash of lightning blasting its club before piercing its face. But two of the other monstrosities hit him even as he was striking. With a crack that almost severed his arm, the armor from his left shoulder broke away. He sprawled face-down, his sword knocked from his grip. Immediately, he defied his impulse to scramble for his weapon and rolled to his side in the opposite direction. The clubs crashed into the space where he would have gone to retrieve his sword.

A fume of shrill hissing that must have been rawface laughter seared from the giant rawface as the others converged on Sword. With both hands, he drew the two knives from his boots, pointed the blades at the monsters, and squeezed the handles. The blades shot from the hilts and struck one rawface in its widening maw, another on its chestplate. In a bramble of twisting electrical voltage, the knife blades exploded, dropping the two beasts. But the remaining three lurched at him, and he escaped only by squirting backward and diving under a root coil.

Swiftly, Sword ripped off what remained of his armor even as he squirmed under another root-arch. The rawfaces clawing at him were too large to follow him and had to mount the root buttress to get at him. He propped the armor vest with its cowl and one right arm against the base of the immense tree, unlatched the grenade he kept taped to the small of his back, primed and dropped it. He dove beneath another rootloop and slithered around the base of the tree.

The rawfaces jumped upon the silhouette of the armor and had only a moment to realize that it was empty before the grenade detonated. The concussion heaved Sword to his feet. Pushing his body to its richest extreme, he sprinted back into the clearing, where the intelligent rawface was crouching over Sword's weapon.

The blast of the grenade had jerked the giant rawface's head upright. Sword ran directly toward the abomination, taking advantage of its momentary distraction to dive in a self-consuming leap for his long blade.

The rawface seized him even as his fingertips brushed the hilt of the sword—and he was hoisted toward the crushing jaws. With a desperate kick, he struck the hilt of his sword with his boot-tip as he was pulled away. The sword flipped, and Sword grabbed its tip. With vigilant composure, he drew the hilt to his free hand. He rammed the long blade into the saliva-threading fangs of the rawface. The rawface's talons clenched to crush the life out of him as he twisted the hilt and sent an intense blue lash of lightning into the beast's face.

From the rooftops of the hamlet, the people had watched the forest flashing with lightning beneath the crystal light of the galaxy and had heard the wails of the mortally wounded rawfaces. A dozen of the bravest of them, inspired by the carnage, had gathered their own swords, pikes, hatchets, and pitchforks and gone out to join the fight. They dispatched the wounded rawfaces that they found among the heaped bodies of the dead. In the clearing at the end of the trail of mangled distort bodies, they came upon the queen rawface with its loathsome face split open, its massive limbs twitching with the last sparks of its life, and they killed it.

They found Sword lying nearby, his armor missing, his weapon still firmly gripped. He was unconscious but alive, and they carried him back to the hamlet. He regained consciousness within the hour, and the celebration of his victory began at once and would have gone on for days if he had not insisted on leaving the next morning. No reward or recompense was acceptable to him—and it was he who thanked the villagers for the opportunity they had given him to touch again through vengeance those whose love he had lost to life's voracity.

NIGHT OF TIME

To go on is to go through.

At last, even the seer is cremated.

Each seed loves the dark for the light it promises.

Mama is maw.

—sayings from the *Glyph Astra*

The torso of Fire throbbed like molten iron in the tremulous dark of Perdur. Cowled figures drifted aimlessly across the mirrorgloss floor, pilgrims and priests awed by the suspended shape. These were the new devotees of Saor, who had replaced those the zōtl had taken for their mounts. Some swung fuming censers; others chanted and danced.

In the crapulous shadows, where the onyx of the serpentcoil columns soaked up all light, a small figure hugged the wall. The stones at his back were damp with the nutrient oozings savored by the nongyls, and he pressed hard to soak his jacket through with the slime. From a lux cone set high on the wall to illumine a resinous conglomerate of torn limbs and twisted faces, a straw of light struck the small figure. Twin lenses flashed, and the blue edge of a blade split radiant hairs.

Sword pushed off from the wall and slunk among the helical pillars toward the fireglow shape saddled by darkness. He had come to free Lod. As soon as he had learned from an Ordo Valan sojourner of Fire's capture by Night, he had volunteered to liberate the stricken power. What good exterminating evil distorts if the sun itself should be owned by spiders?

Limber as smoke, Sword trespassed the neon shine from the hanged entity and flitted between pilasters. When Saor-priests appeared, he curled among the arabesque creases of the carved pillars, his blade propped in the dark. No one saw him. And no nongyl smelled him, for his broth-soaked jacket masked his scent. The Ordo Valan who had informed him of Lod's plight had taught him that trick. She had shown him the natural lynk that led to Perdur after she had revealed her shrewd plan to free Lod from the magnetic column. A simple handful of iron shavings and the hero's famous weapon were all the implements Sword needed once he emerged from the lynk.

Sword had come out in a fissure of the citadel's baserock

347

and had slowly earned his way up the lightless stiles and
shafts to this gargantuan hall of serpentcoil pillars. Now all
that remained was to sheath his blade and stroll into the
sparse crowd of pilgrims, a pilgrim himself. He would me-
ander his way to where Lod's torso hung brightly before
the Cave of Riddles, then release the pouch of iron filings.
The magnetic column would draw them up with its flux
into the webwork of zōtl machinery. The iron cloud would
jam the works and drop Lod to where Sword could sever
the phanes. The elegant simplicity of the plan required
bravery and adeptness under pressure—Sword's hard-
proven traits.

When the Saor-priests had passed and no one but the
abomination of smashed faces plastered among the broken
limbs of the glisteny wall were watching, Sword unfolded
from where he hid, silently slid his long blade into its
scabbard, and strode into the clear expanse lit by the
bound body of Fire. Hood drawn over his head, he glided
with ceremonial serenity over the slick floor, through tendrils of incense smoke, past a knot of chanting pilgrims,
into the flameshadows.

A scream—or was it a wild laugh?—winced from out of
the dark among the pillars. One of the victims that had
been smashed into a crevice of the wet well, a demented
soul obeying some pain-induced zōtl program, recognized
Sword's presence as an intrusion and had shouted an
alarm. The chanting stopped abruptly. Sword glanced
sidewise from under his hood and saw that the scattering
of pilgrims and priests had stopped their meditative strolls
and were staring at him. His heart thrashed. From behind
him, the screaming laugh came again.

In a fireflash, Sword's weapon was out. He whirled with
epic poise, then dashed for the pentagonal stone over
which Lod hung. But he had gone no more than three
swift steps, when a red laserbolt from the webwork above
struck him full in the chest. The low-frequency bolt
knocked him off his feet and kicked back his hood, leaving
him dazed and sitting open-mouthed, sucking for air in the
rubescent sheen of the luminous torso.

Velvety whirrs and clicks flurried from above, where it
was dark, where clasped forebrains spangled with song-

thoughts, where elemental greeds rippled villi along needlesharp feedertubes.

Sword caught his breath in time to raise his weapon. The blade was plucked from his stunned grasp by a blur of black shapes that vapored out of the high, dark vaults. Away his long sword flew. He rose to one knee, groping for the pouch of iron filings. A cloud of vibrant blackness hummed over him, hooked his shoulderpads, and hoisted him off the floor. In his hand, the pouch of iron shavings dangled uselessly, trailing a thin gray fume as he rose into the air, gripped by a horde of jubilantly thrumming zōtl.

The pilgrims watched Sword thrash his legs, wobbling his flight into the darkness. Only one bleak scream descended, at the black moment when he saw his place among the flesh-twisted frescoes. He had thought they were dead sculptures—until one jawless face cried again the hilarious scream that had betrayed him. Piece by piece, cowl, mantle, shredded garments, eyeglasses, and finally boots dropped to the mirrorfloor from where it was dark. Nongyls carried the torn fabric away, and the pilgrims and priests resumed their strolling chants to the glory of the Face of Night.

Glyph Astra (Annals of the Overworld)

2000 Doror

Life is one mud of all sculpting.

—*Glyph Astra*

In the midst of the Rust Age, Buie had been born in a baby field on Valdëmiraën. He was found by a sojourner for the Ordo Vala, who took the infant back with her to Vala. The ancient order had provisions for such living treasures. The boy was reared in the Ordo Vala's capital of cloistered

gardens, bright canopies, and air-domes on the hot savan-
nah, and he grew up to remember his life on First Earth as
Fructuoso Sanabria, the son of a castellan in Moorish Spain.
He had died of fever in his fourth year on First Earth, and
his memories of that life were so scant that he had abandoned his old name and thought little of that time. He
became a sojourner himself, responsible for carrying the
Glyph Astra to the outback settlements and warning the
people there of the coming collapse of the worlds when
the Rimstalker woke to return to the range—or the zōtl
wreaked their vengeance.

After a long period of training on Vala and in the Overworld, Buie's first assignment took him to the jungle planet
of Ylem. He arrived wearing the traditional red and gray
vestments modified for wilderness trekking: his cuffs
cinched to prevent insects from crawling up his limbs, a
cloth attached to the back of his rumal cap to protect his
neck, and a viral alarm on his utility belt to alert him to any
virulent strains in the environment. The lynk he arrived
through was overgrown with strangler fig, and he had to
cut his way out with his laser pistol.

The nearby city had been constructed during the reign
of Ieuanc 751, seventeen centuries earlier, and bore all the
distinctive markings of the numan culture—functional ele-
gance and a complete absence of organic support systems:
no aquifers, granaries, slaughterhouses, or sewer system;
though every hundred meters among the elegant boulevards, plazas, and ribbon ramps leading to the monorails
were the onyx-plated kiosks that the numans used to
recharge their power cells. This was typical of Ieuanc 751's
paranoia. Though numans could easily have been constructed with power cells that never needed recharging,
almost all the Crystal Minds, with the exception of a few
military models, were built with short-duration cells, so
that every six hours they had to recharge. This had afforded the tyrant with continual input on the whereabouts
of all his citizens without the Foundation actually having to
install individual monitors.

Of course, after overthrowing Ieuanc 751 with the help
of Lod, the Emir had equipped all the numan cities with
the support systems necessary for human life. But these
were crude addenda to the seamlessly beautiful cities of

the numan architects and had fared poorly as the centuries passed. When Buie arrived on Ylem, the jungle had dismantled almost all the human structures, and only the tallest of the numan spires rose above the riotous tangle of lianas and figwort. Unlike Sakai, where Buie had been moved by the loveliness of the jungly crags, chasms, and waterfalls, Ylem was a nightmarish tumult of shining, rubbery, fleshy plants pervaded by a damp heat of miasmic steam.

Within minutes of arriving, Buie's viral alarm buzzed angrily, and he slapped on a filter mask and was soon almost swooning in the quivering heat. On a deserted esplanade, overlooking devastated terraces, vine-scrawled towers, and the monkey-loud jungle, he spotted the people he had come to supply with the *Glyph Astra* and to warn of the coming doom. Pongid faces, thick-browed and furtufted, watched him from the green conflagration of the jungle and flashed screaming into the trees when he removed his mask and approached.

Toward night, under sunset clouds like ribbons, an arrow struck him. It hit him squarely in the chest and lodged in his body armor, but he collapsed as if wounded. Two more arrows thudded into his sweat-soaked padding before a gang of the simians breasted through the overgrowth and came to him. At their touch, he sat up, and they bounced away. But this time, he took aim with his laser pistol and fired into the jungle ahead of them, turning them back. In the gloaming, the laser bursts were blinding, and the band of proto-humans reeled sightlessly across the shattered flagstones of the terrace.

Buie removed his mask and approached them again. One drew a plasteel blade from his loincloth, and Buie struck him with a stun bolt that heaved him to the ground and made the others shout. When Buie bent over him and used an inhaler secreted in his palm to bring him around, the war party moaned with amazement and fell to their knees. From then on, they refused him nothing.

Buie traveled with them to their camp in the umbral depths of the ruined city. There, he unfolded his silver-sheeted tent, which also served as a solar panel and radio transmitter, and he began his ministry. He dispensed food packets, water-purifying tablets, and plasteel knives. During the long spells when the viral winds abated, he wore no mask. To appear more like his hosts, he grew a great beard. With his medicines and a gentle manner, he eventually won the trust of the tribes.

"Don't waste your time with those sims, Buie," the expediter on Vala told him by radio after he filed his first report. "We trained you to save people, not monkeys."

"These are people," he protested. "They live in tribes—they make tools."

"They're homologues, proto-humans."

"*The Book of Horizons* clearly states that we are one mud. I can't just ignore them."

"Give it up, Buie. Next you'll be potting plants and carrying them into the Overworld."

Buie ignored the expediter. It took him years and he had to work without support or further supplies from Vala but eventually he penetrated the archaic heart of the wild people and learned of the great ancestors who had created them. Genitrix had often regenerated early hominids among all the worlds, and here on Ylem they had flourished in the jungle. The original proto-humans, their DNA adjusted by Genitrix, had lived for centuries, enabling them to promulgate their wilderness faith, deep in the forest away from the numan cities and the rare human settlements. After the numans disappeared and the humans were weakened by the ravages of the jungle, these hominids took over their ruins. The few humans that had remained were quickly assimilated. Even after Buie taught them all he knew and stood himself in the portal of the lynk waving goodbye, the thick-boned, fur-sleek people were reluctant to surrender their jungle home for the mysteries of the Overworld. The doom that the sojourner prophesied was over fifteen centuries away. In their timeless communion with the rain forest, that was eternity.

2050 Doror

Hunt and you are hunted—listen and you are
heard.

—*Glyph Astra*

Valdëmiraën was a dark world but warm, heated by
thermal vents from the core where a component of Genitrix regulated the temperature by modifying radioactive
decay. The warmth and the silver luminence of the galaxy
promoted the growth of flowery groves among the narrow
valleys of the steep mountains, and the winds luffed with
the perfumes of looted blossoms.

After the collapse of the Emirate, five hundred years
earlier, *The Book of Horizons* had again became useful to
pilots and farmers for its ephemeris. With the loss of the
Aesirai's technical proficiency, only the Ordo Vala retained
the computational expertise to plot the complex orbital
patterns of the thousands of planetesimals, and they did
not hostage this knowledge. Though most of the settlements that Buie visited on Valdëmiraën were eager to
receive the copies of the *Glyph Astra* that he was freely
distributing, they wanted the great book only for its
ephemeris. Those that desired to get out of Chalco-Doror
had already entered the Overworld, and those that remained were interested exclusively in exploiting the resources that remained.

Occasionally, Buie encountered a croft family whose
children were unhappy with the farming and trading of
the generations that had come before them. The worlds
were emptying and opportunities diminishing. Those
were the families he organized into caravans and led into
the Overworld. Under the holoform map that loomed inside the portal of each lynk, he taught the caravan travelers how to read the lynklanes that would lead them to
the many terrene worlds that the Ordo Vala had discovered. After that, they were taken aboard ramstat convoys
and flown to their destinations by Ordo Vala-trained pilots,
and Buie returned to his sojourning.

In a moon-apple grove of a lonely pass on an aerie of
Valdëmiraën, where waters seeped among crystalline peb-

bles with a sound like tinkling bells on their way to the great cascades below, Buie met the dead. A Tryl tesseract-field monitor was embedded in the rockface, virtually invisible for the rime that had crusted over it and the dense moon-apple roots, big as houses, that gnarled along the rockface drawing sustenance from the weeping waters. Buie himself would not have seen it had not the dead called to him: "Man! Man! Come here. You are the first to cross these iron miles to reach our window into time in many a long year. Come—speak with us and tell us how it is with the Rimstalker and her worlds."

Buie followed the calling voice among the vast roots and calcined folds of rime. His foot snagged, and as he bent to free it, his left arm was hooked. An arthropodic figure twice the size of a man suddenly loomed among the hulking roots. Swift, hook-jointed legs blurred against the backdrop of whirlpool stars as it scurried toward him.

Demented laughter skirled from the darkness ahead.

With his free hand, Buie unholstered his pistol and rapid-fired into the creature scuttling at him, chopping it into twitching pieces and evoking screams like torn metal. By the flare of the gun, he spied skeletons of humans and animals hung in taut gossamer among the root-crevices.

He freed his leg and arm with his knife, then threw a lux flare ahead, toward where the laughter had died. The flare caught in the webbing strung among the burls and boulders, lighting up more skeletons—and beyond them a roseate mosaic of Tryl architecture almost entirely overgrown by rock drippings. Vague glimmerings shifted in the dark center of the Tryl mandala. Moving closer, he recognized humanoid apparitions and saw that the dark center was a lens, a Tryl aperture to the t-field.

The wraiths in the lens waved him closer, but he stopped when he understood what he was seeing. "You tried to kill me!" he shouted, then turned to go.

"Wait! Come back. We would talk with you. We have wonders to share, knowledge to bestow. Do not turn away! You have slain the threshold monster and earned the wisdom we have to share with you."

"Others will come," he yelled back at the dead. "I will send them, and you may share your wisdom with them." He did not even look back but strode firmly away.

The ghosts shrieked and went suddenly silent. An ensorcelling music filled the moon-apple grove, and the lens brightened with a silveryellow radiance.

Buie turned about and saw a man-shaped lizard in white raiment beckoning to him. Chary of another deception, he unsheathed both his knife and pistol and edged closer.

"Do not leave this lens intact," the apparition of the lizard-man said. "I am the Tryl guardian of this place, usurped by the waveforms that have died in this grove. So long as the thoughts of observers from your side are directed into the lens, they have been able to shunt me aside. They have lured many to their deaths here. You are the first to turn your thoughts aside—which has allowed my waveform to come forward at last. Destroy this lens now, human, and let the evil that has been done here by Tryl negligence be redeemed by emptiness."

Buie gawked at the lizard-man. Moments lapsed before he found his voice. "The Ordo Vala will decide if that is the correct action," he finally told the ghost.

"No! You must heed me. The future is too narrow for Chalco-Doror. You must keep your impetus moving forward to escape the coming collapse. Do not distract the Ordo Vala with this window into the past. Use your laser pistol. Aim directly at me—and fire!"

Buie shook his head. "My superiors wouldn't approve. I know what this is. This is a t-field monitor. There's nothing like it anywhere in the worlds—except in legend."

The lizard-man pressed closer. "Don't you see, young soul? That is precisely why it must be destroyed. If you do not destroy this device, throngs will pilgrimage here to speak with their dead. They will make this a shrine, and a cult will grow like a cancer about this site, feeding off the rantings of the craven dead."

"Craven dead? What do you mean?"

"When people die, they return to light, where all life originates and persists. Physical bodies are but temporary storage units for this energy—capacitors, if you will. At death, these capacitors release their energy to the tesseract-field, and the waveforms then are subject to the laws of the t-field—causal laws determined by the characteristics of the waveforms. And what are those waveforms, after all, but the action-patterns of our lives—behaviors, memories, thoughts."

"We are light," Buie understood.

"Yes. All life is fundamentally light," the lizard-man explained. "And these waveforms of light, like radio waves, persist invisibly all around us until they are picked out of the t-field by antennae tuned specifically to those wavebundles. Those antennae are gamete-DNA, which initiates the growth process of a new organism. Vegetative waveforms are subject to vegetative antennae and become plants again somewhere among the manifold worlds of the manifold universes. Animal waveforms likewise are susceptible to reception in animal forms. Human DNA is precisely tuned to receive human waveforms."

"Then death is not the end of consciousness?" Buie asked.

"Not at all. Consciousness persists among the physical forms suitable to it. The helical strand of DNA in the gamete cell—the fertilized egg cell—is among the most complex open antennae in creation. It will receive only one waveform from the t-field—the one waveform whose characteristics match its genetic potential. Thus, waveforms of destructive, unloving behavior will be received by DNA that itself has been shaped by such action-patterns—usually of a physically deformed nature."

"You're talking about karma," Buie said in a huff of surprise. "I've learned about that legend."

"Yes—karma," the Tryl confirmed. "But there is nothing supernatural, mystical, or religious about it. It is a law of nature. A causal law. Those of your people who wish to avoid the consequences of this law are clinging to the attractive field of this monitor. They will be the ones your pilgrims will meet here. They are the craven dead, rightfully afraid of the consequences of their past behavior in your worlds. Unless you want those loveless and destructive personalities informing your people, act swiftly. Use your laser pistol. Fire directly at me."

"But isn't there some way—"

"There is no other way. Look around you, young soul. Who do you think lured those humans into the grasp of the Spider?" The Tryl's voice swelled with need. "Please—if

you love your fellow humans, use your pistol. Aim at me—
and fire."

The command seemed amplified by the heathery music
echoing through the grove, and Buie's muscles obeyed. He
could have stopped himself, but he sensed the truth in the
Tryl's plea and shunted aside all fear of reprisal against
himself. He raised his pistol and pulled the trigger. A blue
laserbolt flashed, the lens milked over, and the mesmeric
music was gone.

2100 Doror

Blood never sleeps.

   —*Glyph Astra*

The Ordo Vala was disappointed with Buie. On Ylem, he
had squandered their resources and his time to tend to
proto-humans—and on Valdëmiraën, he had irreparably
damaged an invaluable Tryl artifact. For his next assignment, they sent him to the old vassal-world of Ren, where
the Ordo Vala was already strong and *The Book of Horizons* fully distributed. His work was secretarial, monitoring the computers that catalogued harvest yields and
weather patterns. He had plenty of time to himself and
spent it visiting the historical sites on the planet: the zōtl
stations with their teratogenic chambers and pits designed
for arachnoid bodies, the plasteel pens where the vassals
had been gathered before being lynked to the zōtl nest
world, and the pastures, the rambling meadows and cop-
pices where the vassals had run nakedly wild, fed by
manna-bales dropped from needlecraft.

At his one hundredth re-birthday celebration, held
among the willows beside a crater lake and attended by
fellow sojourners and a score of proto-humans from Ylem
who were the prosperous descendants of the tribe he had
educated seventy-five years earlier, Buie fell in love. The
woman who won his heart was a historian and schoolteacher he had met earlier on a tour of the vassal sites.
Until his re-birthday, he had not given much thought to
love. Like all sojourners, he had tempered his sexual drive

with sublimol, an inhalant that stilled desire. A century of
wandering, distributing the *Glyph Astra*, had offered little
opportunity to establish relationships, except with those
he led into the Overworld never to see again.

But, as he had learned from his own training, the blood is
restless; and when he was obliged to stop traveling, his
heart wandered beyond his work and he explored the joys
of sharing. In time, despite the protests of his superiors, he
married the historian his heart had found, and they had
several children. For the next three decades, he was preoccupied with rearing his family and preparing them to go
with him into the Overworld. But his wife did not want to
leave Ren, where she had grown up, and as his children
grew older they too became attached to the sidereal
beauty of Chalco-Doror and sought their fortunes among
the bright worlds.

Buie's wife grew old, while he, a human created from
relic chromosomes by Genitrix, aged much more slowly.
Buie often wished that Genitrix had not adjusted the
supercoiling of his DNA, so that he would age as his wife,
children, and others born of natural parents in these
worlds aged. But his wishes were empty. Shortly after their
forty-seventh anniversary, Buie's wife refused any further
medical treatment for her advanced kidney congestion
and died of renal failure. Buie, who had grown sick of
being mistaken for his wife's grandson, requested a transfer from his superiors in the Ordo Vala, promising to obey
all their directives if only they would give him some mean-
ingful work away from his careworn memories of Ren.

2150 Doror

There is no center, unless the center is everywhere.

—*Glyph Astra*

A caravan had been gathered on Nabu, but the sojourner responsible for the group had been killed in an
avalanche in the ice latitudes. Buie had been selected to
take her place.

The caravan consisted of a hundred families of an ecstasy cult whose philosophy was based on the Tryl dictum that "Everything is best."

After Buie had been introduced into the caravan and become familiar with their leaders, he queried them about their dauntless optimism. "When your children die in senseless accidents, the way the sojourner who preceded me died, how do you accept that as best?"

"It's all attitude, Buie," he was told. "We all feel grief at those times. But everything passes away in this world, even the long-lives like yourself. When the grief is spent, we go on and harbor no further anguish. The universe is perfect. It is only our understanding that is flawed."

During the long weeks of preparation for the migration into the Overworld, Buie spent as many hours as he could spare from his work standing on the ice fields and staring up into the whirlpool stars and the perpetual night. The animal sorrow of his loss had exhausted itself on Ren, and he was able to face into the gelid wind with emptiness rather than grief. But how to fill that emptiness with joy as the families of ecstasy did?

One night, shortly before the exodus into the Overworld, he saw, in the vapors from the lime pit of dreams, his wife's ghost and his children, who were already far older than he was. He woke up sobbing. No one had heard him, or if they had, they had rolled over and gone back to sleep. He got up and stumbled out of the thermal-lock of the big tent into the jangling wind.

Nothing had changed. The glaciers lay herded among the mountains, pines stood like talismans on the ridges, and the crayoned shadows of the planetesimals smudged the snowfields. Then he understood what the Tryl meant. Though the world was a welter of events and transformations, nothing really changed but the feelings, the moods, the emotions that roiled at the joining place of flesh and spirit. Whatever those feelings were—happiness or grief, wondering or boredom—they filled the emptiness in which everything was constantly changing and staying the same. Whether he believed this was good or bad or indifferent altered nothing at all but him. And he saw then how freedom had always been just a mind's inch away.

He smiled like a drunk and went back to sleep peacefully.

2200 Doror

Want exists for its own sake.

—*Glyph Astra*

After successfully guiding the caravan of ecstasy families to the Overworld, Buie was sent by the Ordo Vala to the Ioli Planetesimals. Inside the orbit of Ioli, a massive swarm of asteroids gleamed in the coronal glare from Lod. Ramstat flyers flitted among the planetary shards, communing between mining stations that had been erected to extract the valuable metals exposed to the stars.

None of the miners were interested in *The Book of Horizons.* They had their own computer network, financed by the rich sums they earned from their space mining, and so had no use for the Ordo Vala's ephemeris. And the offer by Buie to escort caravans into the Overworld was laughed at by the miners, who were in the midst of constructing opulent sky-cities, the better to exploit the wealth swimming in the void around them.

Buie contented himself for a time with enjoying the luxuries that the magnates offered him to entice him to stay among them and share the culture of his long wanderings with their children. He had no qualms about abandoning his sojourning for a long spell of comfortable living. On Nabu he had learned to tolerate everything, even the exigencies of pleasure.

2250 Doror

Fear rots.

—*Glyph Astra*

Eventually, Buie grew bored of the midstim and holoramic pornography that were consuming more of his time the longer he stayed among the decadent sky-cities of the Ioli Planetesimals, and he journeyed to Dreux in preparation for his longest voyage. His long service to the Ordo Vala had wearied his altruism as surely as the indulgences of Ioli had bored his soul. He was eager for new horizons. Chalco-Doror was empty now of all who wanted to leave or any who were ignorant of why they should—except, of course, for the continual influx of Genitrix's re-creations. But that was a problem he was content to leave with the Ordo Vala.

Planetlight like milk filled the polar plain of Dreux on Buie's last night in Chalco-Doror. The titanic lynk had been battered by zōtl hundreds of years earlier, and the plain was dotted with depressions and sand lakes where proton bolts had exploded. But the lynk was intact and had seen the largest of the mass migrations. With a look in his eyes harsh and bright as whisky, he gazed up at the cluttered sky, saw Ren's and Vala's huge discs occluded by the tinier worlds and asteroids, saw Ylem and Sakai, Ras Mentis and Cendre, small coins of light in the star-vapored darkness.

Above the horizon's dark curve, one arm of the galaxy was upraised like a luminous swimmer. Would the world he was journeying to now be as lovely? No. No other world could be as beautiful as these razed fields of heaven.

At that thought, fear entered him like iron that he would never see such a wonderful sight again. But he quelled that despair with what he had learned on Nabu, what he had paid out with the loss of his wife to learn and for which he refused to pay the troll of his doubt a second time—that fear and pain were the forsaken mysteries, and love of the unknown the endless beginning, of each life's work.

Without looking back again, he strolled carefree into the Overworld.

Chan-ti Beppu and Nappy Groff whirled through the grayness of a null field into the boil of a snowstorm. A tapestry of icicles shattered against their flight, and they fell into a cold drift with a spume of bright flakes. Chan-ti perked out of the snowbank and saw an icescape of frozen trees and crystal fields under a sky dirty with twilight. Nappy did not rise, and she ducked back into the drift, feeling for him with her numbing hands. She found his arm and tugged him out of the snowbank.

Nappy roused slowly. Breath huffed in a smoky gust from his nostrils. "Where are we?"

"The Overworld," Chan-ti answered, scanning for the lynk where they had entered. She spotted it above them on an escarpment laced with frost, a red rectangle bloodying the ice around it. The trees and the snowslip had broken their fall. In the eddy of snow scalloped by the wind, she recognized the delicate pattern of timelines. "This must be the Overworld of Mugna. The cold will go on forever. We have to find a lynk out."

The wind hardened. Neither of them was dressed for weather this harsh. They stood up, hugging themselves. "I'm done, Beppu," Nappy said.

"What are you saying?" She took off her camouflage jacket and tried to drape it over his shivering shoulders, but he pushed it away.

"Warm yourself. Build a fire. You'll find a way out of here. But not I. This is my grave. I feel it in my bones. I've felt it since the Witch Maze."

"Don't speak like that, Nappy. You frighten me." She put her jacket about his shoulders, ignoring his angry shrug, and led him toward a brake of ice-tasseled trees.

"I'm sorry we lost your Ned," Nappy grumbled, feebly kicking the ice from a root. "He came for you. I never trusted the Aesirai—but this one is different. He has lucky looks and courage."

Chan-ti's eyes reflected painfully, and she busied herself breaking twigs from the trees.

"You'll see him again," Nappy said, stamping his feet. "I doubted it until he came to the Dragon's Shank for you. If he had the mettle to seek you there, he'll find you anywhere."

After clearing a patch of ground where root burls broke the wind, Chan-ti gathered the frozen sticks and Nappy used the flint of his belt buckle to spark a fire, cursing all the while that he had lost his utility sack in the Witch Maze. A flame flapped among the twigs.

"Would that Gorlik were here," Nappy mumbled, rasping his blue hands over the fire. "There's a Foke who can track. He can read timelines sure as—"

Nappy broke off. Within the moan of the wind, he had heard a velvety sound that struck fear in him sharp as a pain.

"Gorlik died that we might live," Chan-ti said, mistaking

Nappy's sudden silence for grief. "He took the spiders with him, to spare us. He bettered himself in death."

"Hush, child. Gorlik did not take all the spiders with him."

From the chatter of wind-clacking branches, a shadow dove at them. The Foke ducked. The zōtl struck Nappy at the back of his head and threw him over the fire, scattering sparks and slush. Chan-ti overrode her revulsion and seized the thrumming black body, its gossamer wings burning like electricity—but she could not pull the creature free from Nappy's head. Its pincers had dug into the old man's face. He yanked at them, and they clawed deeper. From the papule under its mad splatter of eyes, its stinger thrust, scoring Nappy's scalp in a bloody welt. She wanted to let go, to grab a rock, a stick, anything to beat at it, but she dared not. Only her grip kept the spider from stabbing Nappy. She cried out.

A hand grabbed her shoulder and spun her aside. A bearded man in a red vest shoved a laser pistol against the zōtl and blew it away from Nappy with a red stun bolt. The spider spun over the ice, and the bearded man shot again. A blue bolt smashed the zōtl to green viscera.

Nappy sat up, fingers touching the gashes in his face, and stared with bulged eyes at the stranger. "Thank you, sojourner," he gasped, recognizing the red vest and gray uniform of the Ordo Vala.

Chan-ti bent over Nappy, saw that he was intact, and gazed up with gratitude at the sojourner. "You saved our lives."

"As you'd have done for me," he replied, a compassionate smile glinting in his beard. He spoke a glottal language neither of the Foke understood, but the translator in the brocade of his vest compensated simultaneously. He unslung his backpack and tugged out a blanket roll. "My name is Buie." He gave the blanket to Nappy and set his laser pistol to warm the air around them. He took out a medical kit and applied antiseptic and astringent to Nappy's face wounds while listening to their introductions and story.

"You've leaped seven hundred years ahead in time," Buie said, amazed. "I can only wonder where Ned O'Tennis' torque flung him." He removed a sheaf of papers from his pack and began scribbling with a red pen. "Addenda to the Utility Manual," he explained. "Annals of my travels in the Overworld. I must record what you've told me. I've never heard the likes of such an historic event before. Prisoners of Saor! You've actually seen the Face of Night— you've seen the capture of Fire." He shook his head with astonishment.

"That's an archaic method," Nappy said, nodding at the sheaf of scribbled pages.

"Recorders are unreliable out here," Buie said. "Lynk passage sometimes scrambles magnetic memory. Better to write—" He broke off to remove a canteen and a carton of dried food. "Forgive me. I'm thinking only of myself. But in all my travels, this is surely the most profound encounter I've had—far more intriguing than even the Tryl I once spoke with."

Over a meal of white spinach, snake jerky, and berry wine, Buie told his story. "So, you see, I have no home. I wander for the Ordo Vala."

"Then you would not mind wandering with us?" Nappy asked. The warmth and the meal had revived him, and his eyes had regained something of their sparkle. "We would return to the Eyelands on Valdëmiraën."

Chan-ti passed him a questioning glance. Buie asked the question that she was thinking: "Why return to your past? The Foke you knew then are surely not there."

"I'm too tired now for a long journey through the Overworld, back to my own time. I would be happy enough to find the place if not the time. There I can die in peace."

"Nappy—" Chan-ti frowned at him. "Let death find us."

"It has, my daughter. You *are* my daughter—though Spooner Yegg sired you, I fathered you. You are Foke as I am. It is time now for us to return to the Foke—or, at least, to their favorite haunt. There my body of light will leave behind the muck of this existence. My wife, my other children have gone ahead of me. They wait for me in the fields of light. For them, as for all the migrant Foke, the grave is our only homeland."

Chan-ti nodded with wide-eyed solemnity, remembering the rituals of her childhood and the wonder she had experienced in the mead grotto listening to the storysongs of the Foke who had gone before. She would not deny that to the one man who had loved her as a father. She turned a pangful look on Buie. "Will you guide us home?"

The Ghost That Hatched His Havoc as He Flew

While Gai slept, she dreamed. She was back on the range, on her parents' farm, where the opalescent sky shimmered with warmth and loveliness over rambling fields and feather-limbed forests. She was alone in the far dell, playing with her imaginary friends under the fluttery auroras of the sky. She was a child again. In her dream, she had returned to a time before loss, before suffering, before zōtl.

The euphoria of Gai's dream leaked energy into the near-vacuum of the void around her. Her Rimstalker brain waves were of a magnitude so intense, relative to the cold of outer space, that they empowered the patterns in the ubiquitous tesseract-field. Waveforms of extinct species glimmered brighter, assuming the shapes they had worn during their lives. On Know-Where-to-Go, ghost-forests appeared and wraiths of dinosaurs and herd animals roamed.

Towerbottom Library was a scientific commune during the Rust Age, and the humans stationed there were baffled by the phantom landscapes that came and went like mirages on the night-held planet. Among the shades of extinct fern forests, spectral skyscrapers appeared and thatch-roofed villages, teepees, longhouses, hogans, and igloos. Jeweled in ghostly auras, the people of Earth wandered out of their dwellings, bewildered and glittering under the silver cartwheel of the galaxy.

Mooker Jee, the chief of bio-sciences at Towerbottom Library, had been fund-raising among the sky-cities of the Ioli Planetesimals when the ghosts materialized on Know-

Where-to-Go. The message recalling him stated simply: "Mooker: Return at once. Lugar."

Lugar Descanso, one of the very few military-mode numans who had survived the purge of the Crystal Mind during the Age of Dominion, was the staff director of Towerbottom Library, responsible for coordinating the research projects of the 526 technologists who worked and resided in the Library and its environs. From its perch in deep space, the Library compiled data on Chalco-Doror, the Milky Way, and the island galaxies beyond, as well as planning an escape route from the doomed worlds other than through the unstable lynk system.

"We could reach the stars if we would just coordinate," Lugar had complained to Mooker Jee just prior to sending him on his fund-raising mission. "Everyone knows we're just cockroaches on a Rimstalker warship. We've got to get out while we can."

"There are still fifteen centuries to go, Lugar," Mooker Jee had responded. They had been outside, in the hilly park that surrounded the ivy-slick parapet of the Library. The great structure loomed against the rustling stars like the conning tower of a vast submarine. "In that time, with the progress we're making on the magravity drive and ramstat, we could build a whole civilization among the stars."

Lugar shook his head sadly, and in the dark his shatterglass eyes glowed like gray coals. "After all the centuries I have endured in Chalco-Doror, I have less faith in time than in fate," he said, and the cold timbre of his voice pimpled the skin at the back of his confidante's neck. "Anything can happen here, Mooker. Anything at all."

To hear a numan speaking of fate had spooked Mooker Jee. Mooker had been a hooper in Dakkar during his life on Earth and had never quite abandoned his faith in *qismah*, the predetermined destiny of all created beings. As a scientist, he enjoyed exploring the causal roots of phenomena, yet in his soul he still felt the tugs of a secret order. Now the terse message he had received seemed so fraught with urgency that he decided against the days-long flight into deep space and dared to enter a lynk on Ras Mentis.

The lynk-maps indicated that a crossing to Know-Where-to-Go was possible from that particular lynk on Ras

Mentis, and though the holoform in the portal drizzled with static, Mooker went through. The next moment, as he came out, his heart squelched at what he saw and he thought he had blundered into the Overworld. Heraldic shimmerings of light patterned the dark terrain. Mooker had to stare a long time before he realized that he was seeing the glowing shapes of terrene landscapes superimposed on the familiar hills of Know-Where-to-Go.

A ramstat flyer conveyed him to Towerbottom Library. The psybot pilot had no information about the ghosts, and, most spooky of all, there were no humans at the lynk station or in the flyer to tell him what was happening. Below, the land crawled with shapeshifting holograms of phantom cities, cathedrals, wheat fields, and rice paddies. At one point, an Aeroflot jetliner flew directly at them— and right through them. The only sound was Mooker's alarmed shouts to the pilot, who did not seem to see the apparition.

Towerbottom Library was lost in a haze of spectral images, which were ruffling and buffeting like auroras in a solar wind. As the flyer descended, Mooker spotted herds of zebra and caribou, a line of lanky hunters leaning on their spears, and the jeweled hub of Times Square teeming with luminescent crowds on avenues that ran off into jungles where behemoths browsed.

The flyer touched down in the ramstat field behind the Library, and when Mooker Jee disembarked, his father was waiting for him. Like Mooker, he was a tall, narrow man with hollowed cheeks, large ears, and stubbly beard— but he was dressed in the loose, baggy trousers, rush sandals, collarless shirt, and pugaree headscarf that he had worn in life.

"Mooker, why have you come here?" the elderly man asked in the dialect they had shared and that Mooker had not heard in this lifetime.

Mooker froze and gaped at the familiar, tired lineaments of his father, who had died of fever on Earth when Mooker was eleven and his father already over sixty. "Father—is this really you?"

"Yes, Mooker, it is I," he replied, honest as day, his large browngold eyes crinkled with joy intermixed with sadness. "My chest is soaked dark with love for you."

That was an expression his father had often used. Hearing it again, Mooker's heart almost exploded with amazement, and he reached out to embrace his father. But his arms closed on emptiness—though his father remained standing serenely before him.

"Mooker, why have you come?" the elderly man asked again.

"I—I was called—by my chief," he muttered. Looking beyond the ghost, he saw the dusty courtyard where they had lived together as a family. Dogs prowled the courtyard slowly, waiting for the moon.

"After I died, you were good to your mother," the ghost said. "You worked hard for your brothers and sisters, as the eldest should. You served them well, and I am proud that they grew up healthy in your care. All married and had children. But you, my son. You did not marry."

"I could not, Father. After you died, it was all I could do to keep the family together. There was a drought for three years afterwards . . ." He stopped in midsentence. In the courtyard, he saw the shop where he had worked for twelve years after his father's death, until the same fever that had killed his father had claimed him. The barrels he crafted for the local merchants were arrayed under the sun-awning in various states of construction. A foam of voices came from the shop, and he recognized his mother's laughter.

"Mooker!" a strange voice shouted. "Mooker Jee! Snap out of it."

Gruff hands seized him and turned him about to face a coffee-skinned man with kinky black hair and crystal-cracked eyes. That incongruous sight jolted memory into place, and he swooned and had to be held up by the numan.

"Steady now," Lugar Descanso said. "These are phantoms, Mooker. They're being culled from the tesseract-field."

Mooker clutched the numan's arms and cast a look back over his shoulder. The courtyard of his former life was empty. A jawbone of moon hung over the tile-roofed buildings.

"Come with me," Lugar said, and led the dazed man away from the ramstat field to a floater that carried them toward the Library. A covey of ostriches jaunted across their path, and they slashed through them emptily. "It's horrible, Mooker. What you're experiencing has overwhelmed every human in the complex. I've lost everybody."

The floater set down in a pavilion, a geodesic-roofed plaza where the lifts into the Library were arranged in a wide circle. Usually, the pavilion was crowded with researchers and their staffs coming or going. Now only the specters of camels and dunes filled the plaza.

"What do you mean *lost*?" Mooker asked, the windy ride having helped him to regain his composure. "Where is everybody?"

"Most of them are dead," Lugar answered. "Suicides. The long-lives are killing themselves. The ghosts of their pasts have lured them into the tesseract-field with them. Only myself, the psybots, and those humans born for the first time here in Chalco-Doror remain unaffected. We were able to subdue a few dozen before they could kill themselves. We have them under sedation in the clinic. But the rest—the great majority—are gone. Dead. By their own hands."

Lugar seemed stunned, and that deepened Mooker Jee's shock. They strode through the flank of a dromedary and entered a lift. "Why is this happening?" Mooker wanted to know.

"It's the Rimstalker, I'm sure. We know she's got her physical body in one of the Tryl caverns below us. I don't know what she's up to, but she's wreaking havoc with us. Not that she would care if she knew. We mean nothing to her. But Lod—he may help us."

Mooker understood that Lugar's admiration of Lod was founded in his identity as a numan. Lod had been responsible for helping to create the Crystal Mind. "What can Lod do for us?" Mooker asked. "We've never been able to successfully communicate with him."

"All our prior inquiries were purely scientific," Lugar said as a flight of ghostly locusts whooshed through the lift. "Now our survival is at stake. We can't keep our people sedated indefinitely. I've been broadcasting distress signals in a wide spectrum to Lod, detailing our crisis. But decades may pass before we get a response."

They stepped out of the lift, and Mooker saw that they were at his suite. "Why'd you bring me here?"

"Your life is in danger, too. You saw what happened to you on the ramstat field. I'm sure you have sedatives in your suite. I thought you'd be more comfortable here than in the clinic. Though perhaps I was foolish for even asking you to come back. You were safe in Doror. But I need your counsel. You're the only psychobiologist I have now, and I was hoping you would have some idea of how to control human neurological responses to the t-field."

Mooker's apartment was spacious and white-carpeted, with black leather flexforms arranged around a crystal helix Tryl sculpture. Narrow panels of abstract paintings screened the doorways to the kitchen and bedroom. They focused the suite toward the plate windows that filled the far wall with an expansive view of the wraith-hung grounds. There, the galaxy was rising.

"You must have some idea why we're seeing ghosts," Mooker said.

"I'm not seeing ghosts of my past. Nor are the psybots. Therefore I believe it's the DNA of the human body that is serving as receiving antennae for the waveforms in the t-field. That's why each individual is attracting the particular ghosts of his or her own past."

"That's remarkably similar to my line of work," Mooker said and gestured at the panels of abstract shapes. Lugar noticed then that they were not paintings but photographs of molecular structures, each with a tiny label at eye level: *Ibogaine, Bufotenine, Psilocin.* "This is the dephosphory-lated derivative of Psilocybin," he went on, tapping one of the panels with a knuckle. "The natives in the Amazon of Earth called it *teonanacatl*—the messenger of the dead. It's one of the cornerstones of my recent work."

"That's why I dared to call you back," Lugar said and read from his mental files: "Your latest project is the informational readout through molecular intercalation into neural nucleic acids, specifically the molecular broadcast of electron spin resonance from waveforms stored in the neural nucleus."

"In simpler terms," Mooker said, staring through an apparition of a farm girl he had admired on Earth, "I'm learning how our DNA functions as antennae. Certain molecular compounds enhance our ability to tap the t-field by activating the receptive potential of our genetic code. Traditionally, we call those molecular compounds hallucinogens—but they are, in fact, keys to the t-field—ways of accessing the cosmic memory bank."

"So is there some way to block those antennae?" Lugar asked.

"Of course. There's a whole pharmacopia of antihallucinogens. They won't stop the ghosts, but they will prevent individuals from attracting specific ghosts from their past. I assume that is why they are suiciding?"

"I am why they are suiciding," a strange yet familiar voice sounded from behind the photographic panel.

Mooker peeked around the panel and saw himself standing there—himself as he had been on Earth. He had been twenty-three when the fever killed him. And there he was in white pyjamas and pugaree headcloth, barefoot, his hands barked with calluses, his face harrowed by the illness that had killed him. He gasped, and Lugar stepped to his side and put a hand to the back of Mooker's head.

"It's you!" the numan exclaimed, seeing the ghost by reading Mooker's brain waves. "What is he saying? I cannot hear him. His lips are moving to a language I do not comprehend."

"Only you can hear me," the ghost said to Mooker. "I am you. And my chest is soaked dark with love for you. That is why I have come back. Don't you see? We are one. Only the illusion of your body separates us."

"You are the ghost of my past life," Mooker said in the ghost's dialect. "We are not truly one."

"Not in this life," the ghost lamented. "Since you were created among these phantom worlds, I have suffered, for I have had to endure the limits of corporeal existence again. Feel with me the limitless love of the afterworld."

The ghost of Mooker Jee's past stepped into Mooker, and his body was brushed from scalp to soles with an electric chill. His eyes fluttered, and he collapsed into Lugar's arms. In trance, he ranged beyond his body into a pelagic luminosity that pervaded him with a peacefulness and pleasure that he had known before and forgotten. In an instant, he recalled that this was the joy of the afterworld, which is how his mind had understood this boundless serenity after his first death. Now he knew that it was the mystery of light itself he was experiencing. Free of the constraints of his body, he had become pure waveform—pure light. And, like light, there was now for him no time, no space, no charge, no mass, and no rest. He was flying through infinity, rising and falling simultaneously, indescribably happy, replete.

A blow of blackness crashed through him—and he was awake, lying in a flexform in his suite. Moments staggered by before he oriented himself and recalled what had happened. He gazed out at the galactic fire, sodden with deafmute grief.

"I am waiting," his own autumn-sad voice said from beside him. When he turned his head, he saw his ghost watching him. "Don't linger any longer. You know the way out. Come back to me. Come back, Mooker Jee."

Mooker sat up, groggy with the thickness of his senses, the corpulence of his body. He felt as though he were moving in syrup as he rose to his feet. He knew now there was only one cure for this torpor. In the cabinet under the Tryl sculpture he kept a wide range of olfacts. The proper combination of them would painlessly unlock him from the confinement of his body. He staggered to the cabinet.

Lugar Descanso had fled the suite when Mooker Jee collapsed in his arms. He had lain Mooker in the flexform and rushed to the clinic. From the psybots he procured an anti-hallucinatory inhalant and hurried back to Mooker's suite. He arrived as Mooker was fumbling in his olfact cabinet.

"Stay away from me, Lugar," Mooker said in a froggish voice. "Stay away."

Lugar seized Mooker by his hair and forced the inhalant to his nose. Mooker struggled but could offer little resistance against the numan even if he had not been logy from his experience in the afterworld. Mooker's ghost watched sadly as the inhalant shot into Mooker's sinuses. He did not disappear, but his edges blurred.

"You're not going to die on me, Mooker," Lugar insisted.

"I am already dead, you fool!" Mooker tried to shout but only succeeded in grunting. "Let me go. I don't want to live like this. I don't want to live."

Mooker Jee lived. The numan fully sedated him and left

him in the custody of the clinic psybots. After several weeks of this, Mooker's ghost vanished and the memory of the afterworld faded. But Mooker was never the same again. Nor were any of the other long-lives who had survived after experiencing themselves as waveforms. For they had touched infinity and from then on could never be satisfied in the worlds of shadow and the denials of light.

Dream Is the Transparency of Death

Twilight filled with a new level of indigo. Loryn and her lover Hazim sat in a cafe atop a hill overlooking the palatial and desolate splendor of Towerbottom Library. During the long centuries of Know-Where-to-Go's night, while the planet journeyed through space far from the other planets, the Library, with its rambling grounds lit by lux lanterns among the groves and knolls, had a faery-tale aspect. But now that the planet was fast approaching Chalco-Doror, the brilliance of Lod revealed the wretched emptiness of the landscape. From the white ivy that matted the giant barrel-structure of the Library itself, to the scraggly and knobby trees that lined the winding footpaths among the scattered hills, the terrain was ghostly, almost surreal in its vacancy.

The gigantic indigo evening, whose reflection bled away in the glass tops of the cafe tables, was the last color of reality; and, with the night, the faery illusion was reclaiming the land. Hazim, his dark, taut, and angular face bent in a sincere smile, toasted his lover with his cup of jasmine tea. "To your dream, Loryn."

Loryn, named—as many had been—after the legendary leader of the former age who had found the O'ode in the Overworld and used it and the distort tribes to topple the Emir, looked nothing like the great heroine of yore. She was pale and blonde, with eyes a color close to the sea. Hazim thought she was the most beautiful woman he had ever seen, and his lupine eyes sparkled with admiration whenever he gazed at her.

"What do you think my dream is?" she asked with a wistful smile.

"To record every story from the Falling City, of course," he answered and waited for her to raise her cup.

The Falling City was N'ym, the Viking capital of Valdëmiräen that, fifteen centuries earlier, had sheared away from its mountaintop perch and thrown itself into Saor's gravity well, rather than surrender to Loryn's forces. Its fall toward Saor's event horizon was eternal; that is, at least from outside, the plunge appeared asymptotic. Anyone with a good telescope could see the starlike pinpoint of the city seeming to hover above the absolute blackness of Saor. The actual city had long ago vanished behind the event horizon, but the image it left behind would float there forever—or for as long as Chalco-Doror lasted. The last transmissions from the city were still climbing out of the steep gravity well, the signals enormously stretched so that years of real time elapsed before a few minutes of message were received. The bandwidth of information was diversified, but Hazim's Loryn was interested only in the stories that one of the Falling City's radio stations was broadcasting. In the intervening millennium and a half, only a dozen tales had been fully received, and she had memorized each of them.

"I wish I were a long-life," she said, "like you Hazim— then I *would* live just to record those stories. But I'm twenty-six. I'm at the margin of old age."

Hazim almost snorted tea. "Old age? Come on, Loryn. You're still a kid."

"To you I am. You could live a thousand years."

"Yeah, sure—long enough to see the worlds collapse."

"You should get out," Loryn said, "into the Overworld, before the next age. That's when the lynklane instabilities will start. At least now you can choose the world you'll live in."

"I won't go without you."

Loryn frowned. "I belong in Chalco-Doror. It's all I've ever known. It's all I want to know."

"I won't stop trying to convince you," Hazim said, dolefully. "You're just a librarian, and I'm just an assistant librarian. Your parents are dead and I never had any in this life. There's nothing holding us here."

Loryn stared at him through eyes with the depths of jewels, deciding whether to tell him. She sat back suddenly and shifted her line of sight up into the hour of traces.

Hazim's breath tightened in his lungs to see that look come over her, for he knew it meant she was drumming up her philosophy. Hazim had never known anyone who was as philosophical as Loryn. Whereas he was content to simply be with her and share the sunset and a cup of jasmine tea, she was unfulfilled until she had mulled over and spouted some profundity that he would then have to spend the next three days pondering to make head or tail of. Lately he never even bothered trying to comprehend her ideas, but listened to them abstractly as if they were music with no real meaning beyond the tone of her voice.

"Have you noticed how everything hides within itself?" she asked.

He loved Loryn—he loved her thin, quiet gestures, her shoulder-straight walk, her animal stamina when they made love, and her soft laugh when he amused her—but he wished she would burden him less with her far-flung ideas. "*Everything* hides within itself?" He squinted with incomprehension.

"Absolutely. Oaks in acorns, people in their desire. Like the poet inside the prince inside the frog inside the faery tale, even your face is the reflection of someone deeper— someone tranced by the absolute spell of memory—someone who knows what your hands are for—knows what your dreams are riddling."

I'm not sure I understand, he wanted to say but did not, because that would have invited an even more arcane explanation. So he nodded and lost his gaze in her sea-dew eyes.

"I think I've found my way through to that deeper self hiding in me," she continued. "All my life I've been fascinated by the Falling City and what it must be like down there, falling forever, free of time's constraints."

"Relatively, you mean. Time goes on for them—or at least it did. The Falling City must have been smashed to quark soup long ago."

"Yes, but their stories are forever, immortalized by their mortality."

"Immortalized at least for one more age. After that, who will be listening?"

"The whole universe, Hazim. That's the beauty of the way they chose to die. They made the whole universe listen."

"If anyone's interested, I guess."

"I'm interested. Somewhere in this universe there must be others like me. I want to speak with them the way the Falling City has spoken to me."

"You certainly have enough to say. And as librarian you have the chance to put it all down in the archives. Maybe some far future will find it."

"I've found a better way." Her smile was dazzling. "About a year ago I liquidated all my assets, everything my parents left me, and I commissioned a tech group to design and manufacture a body pod with a gigawatt radio and a ramstat thruster. They think it's for exploratory excursions among the planetesimals when Know-Where-to-Go swings through Chalco-Doror. But I've arranged with the Ordo Vala to have the one-passenger flyer positioned on Valdëmiraën. I'm going to ride it into Saor."

"What!" Hazim smacked his legs and almost toppled the table as he lurched halfway upright. He toned down as the other people in the cafe cast curious glances his way. "That's an insane idea, Loryn."

"I knew you would understand."

"Does Lugar have any idea what you're up to?"

"Don't be silly. He'd never let me do this."

"And neither will I."

A hurt look crossed Loryn's face. "I was really hoping that you would help me."

"Help you? Loryn, I love you. I'm not going to let you fly into a black hole. This is a joke, isn't it? You're making fun of me for not paying more attention to your ideas."

"No. I'm not joking. I'm leaving tonight. I wasn't going to tell you, but I thought, just now I thought, you were ready to know."

"By the seven powers of light! I can't believe that you're serious."

She looked away into the night, regretting her decision

to tell him. Hazim read her disappointment and blinked once like a lizard as the truth of what she had said sunk in. They spoke little more to each other after that, Loryn afraid she had already given him too much information and Hazim desperately trying to figure out what to do. At her apartment, he tried again to dissuade her or at least to delay her suicidal plan, but she would not hear of it. They parted angrily, and he went at once to the nearest of Lugar Descanso's message cubes and reported what he had learned.

Hazim accompanied the security officers to Loryn's apartment, but when they got there, she was already gone. Her flat was undisturbed, nothing missing, and it became clear that she had departed the moment Hazim had left, taking nothing with her. The stop-order at the Library lynk came too late. Loryn had already crossed. Lynklane memory showed that she had gone to Valdëmiraën, just as she had told him she would. But at Valdëmiraën, Hazim learned she had crossed again, this time to Mugna. She had lied to him when she had told him her personal flyer was waiting on Valdëmiraën.

At Mugna, Hazim arrived in time to follow her ice-sled to where the ramstat flyer was waiting. He reached the lift-pad only minutes after she launched. Standing in the razoring cold, he stared up at the darkness blazing through the stars and wept.

Loryn's broadcast began soon after her departure. Hazim tuned in from Towerbottom Library and listened to her voice and her obscure ideas with a lorn attentiveness. Only the opening phrase came through clearly: "Do you remember how this Earth once looked? Remember how there was once only one sky and how we raised our hands to it in praise of the unknown and the blue flame seared thin tracks on our palms?"

Then the signal began to stretch and had to be collected over many days: "Remember the lightning-scarred armor, remember the death-smells of panther night-swamps, the lung-blistering journeys across unnamed deserts, the suffering that became the remote blood and pitiless gaze of our children, now our ancestors." Then weeks: "Their wanderings cross the width of your hand." And months:

"Their memory is your face, and their stamina is the cadence of all things vanishing." And finally years: "They are solid as the iron-old Earth—and they are empty—because only mystery survives us."

By then, Hazim had abandoned his post at the Library and taken up residence in a seacliff village on Elphame, where he could avoid the criticisms of his colleagues and devote all his time to collecting the broadcasts from Loryn and the Falling City. He earned his livelihood using his expensive radio equipment as a beacon for the fishing vessels that harbored under the mammoth cliffs of the village.

Decades swung by, and he garnered a full story from the Falling City and another passage from Loryn's endless voyage: "Here in the mansions of nothing, we share a dream called life. The dream rises up within us when we lie down. It enters when we leave. Its name is your tongue—and its message is this: Break the evil of fear or be broken. Discipline madness. Reward the able. And remember the dream that has no reality and whose reality you—for now —are."

Shortly after collecting this message of Loryn's, Hazim received a bizarre visitor. He was alone in his tower station, the door locked behind him as he soldered circuitry that the salt air had begun to corrode. A footfall jerked him upright. There before him was a manshaped shadow twice as large as a man.

"You know who I am?" the shadow asked in a voice that rattled the window panes.

Hazim dropped his soldering iron and searched in his lungs for his voice. At last he squeaked, "You are Saor."

"I am. And I am come to win you as my ally."

Hazim's voice fumbled out of him: "I thought—I thought your mind was gone—eaten by a zōtl viral program."

"Indeed I pretended to have lost my mind to blunt the edge of the Rimstalker's advantage. I have been silent these many years, waiting for this chance. Now that it is come, I am here to win your support."

"Me? I—I'm nobody."

"Soon you will be one of Chalco-Doror's legends. Unless you are already an ally of the Rimstalker."

"I never thought about it."

"Think."

"I—I don't know what to say, what to think. I'm just a radio operator."

"I am willing to win you to my side, Hazim. I believe I can help you in a real way—and in return, then, you will help me."

"How? How can you help me?"

"Loryn is in my field. I can arrange to return her to you."

"My God—she must be dead by now. It's been forty years. Surely she's struck the event horizon by now."

"No. Her trajectory is taking her in an infinite spiral down the time-well of my Form. She will fall forever."

"But forty years have passed! Her flyer could not possibly be equipped to sustain her that long."

"Forty years have lapsed here in Chalco-Doror. But for her in the whorl of spacetime only days have passed. She can be recovered with my assistance."

Loryn lives! That thought echoed across forty years of memory, and the anguish of those lost years without her buffeted in Hazim like the beginnings of a heart attack. He rubbed a fist against his chest. *Forty years of love*—no, not love but obsession, he realized. She had not let him love her. There had been no time. *Time*—that was what Saor offered him—time to redeem his lifelong obsession with love. Would she not love him at last once he saved her? His face bloated with joy. "What must I do to have her back?"

"Obey me."

Hazim chewed a knuckle. "You will ask me to stand against the Rimstalker. I know it."

"Have you qualms about preserving these worlds for human occupation? The Rimstalker will destroy these planets soon."

"But the zōtl—I could not be the one who brought those monsters back. I could not."

"You have not that power, mereling. What I want of you is to help me save these worlds. If you refuse me, I will surely find someone else."

Hazim tugged at his fingers and gnawed his lower lip. The shadowshape began to fade, and he shouted: "Wait! Saor!" The darkness thickened, and Hazim's small hairs twitched. "I will not be the one who brings the zōtl back? It will not be me? Promise me that."

"You have not that power, mereling. Will you save these worlds?"

"For Loryn. If you give Loryn back to me, I will obey you —I swear it."

The shadow vanished.

Hazim, who had been crouching behind his equipment, rose and extended his hands toward the space where Saor had stood. The air tingled coldly. A voice opened in his head: "Now do precisely as I say and soon you will be with your Loryn again."

Saor directed Hazim to a thorn-down forest on Nabu, which, following the voice in his head, Hazim cut through with a laser torch. Deep within it he came upon an abandoned village, the time-scorched buildings overgrown with dense lichen, the tiled roofs caved in, the walls awry, and the crepuscular, thorn-netted sky above it squeaking with bats.

In a cellar that caved down deeper into the ground than the laser torch could illumine, Hazim found a dizzy flight of stone stairs. Chilly with fright, he descended the blind spiral. At its bottom, a red lynk pulsed with the rhythm of a sleeping heart. Hazim stepped through it into the Overworld.

The gray emptiness extended vacuously in every direction. Only one object hovered in the void—a pod, silvery black and sleek as a dolphin. Hazim touched it, and his body shook violently with cold. Using the straps that Saor's voice had instructed him to carry, he harnessed the pod and dragged it after him backward one step.

He was again in the dark shaft beneath the caved-in cellar of the abandoned village at the black heart of the thorn-down forest on Nabu. With his laser torch, he prepared to cut the seams on the pod—but that was not necessary. The pod cracked open, and an icy green light streamed out.

Hazim knew then what his innermost self had suspected all along: that Saor had lied to him—that Loryn was not in the pod. He backed up a step and ignited the laser torch.

The pod burst apart, and the force of the sour air that

escaped threw him to his back against the stone steps and knocked the laser torch from his grip. When he sat up, his face was seized by the pincer claws of a zōtl, and his last mortal sound was a scream.

Age of Phantoms

Every consciousness is a bundle of waveforms
unique to that awareness, a signature of light writ
in the vacuum that carries everything. . . . When
our bodies are gone, the waveforms remain,
forever. . . . You *are* the light of the world.

—Yeshua ben Miriam, from *Interviews at the End
of Time*

In the Seventh Age

Gai woke from her long sleep. Her last memory was of
grappling with Saor, burning with cold where their plasma
shapes had locked, and collapsing before the mad noise of
the zōtl. Shoved unconscious by the rages of pain, she had
lost all sense of time. Her Form's chronometer displayed
the numerics she needed to orient herself. She had been
comatose over three days—almost eight hundred years of
local time. Know-Where-to-Go was beginning its sixth fly-
through of Chalco-Doror. She was in the Seventh Age.

Buoyantly, Gai recalled Loryn's poisoning of the zōtl
nest world with the O'ode, and she activated her memory
log to see what had transpired since. Her view-field
showed an off-world perspective of Doror. Lod's Form
blazed whitehot among a cloud of planetesimals and the
stately orbs of Ioli, Dreux, and Ras Mentis. The memory

clip accelerated, and she watched in horror as the tawny sphere of Dreux sparked with explosions. The nightside of the planet strobed with fiery flashes.

At first, Gai thought the planet was under nuclear attack. As the clip sped forward, she realized Dreux was in fact being attacked but far more cataclysmically than she had guessed. The world's orbit had been warped to steer it into the rock swarms. At an ever-increasing rate, mountains fell out of the sky and impacted on Dreux. Years of bombardment compressed to moments, and Gai witnessed a holocaust of spuming fire as the collision of larger asteroids ignited the atmosphere and shattered the planetary crust. The pressurized core vented in a nova of magma, and Dreux blasted apart, sending comets and bright streamers of planetsmoke shooting among the worlds.

The zōtl had finally deciphered Lod's program codes. There could be no other explanation. The spiders were using Lod to crash the system. Already, the blows of Dreux's cometary shards were destabilizing the other planets. Soon the entire system would disintegrate. Unless Lod's control was reinstated immediately, Gai's vessel would be damaged too severely to carry her home. She would die in outer space.

Gai determined to use her Form to retrieve her machine mind from its captivity. Now that the great swarms of zōtl had been exterminated, she could dare to leave the protective grotto, where the Tryl's lynklock had thwarted the spiders' efforts to attack her. She could fend off the few zōtl that remained, and her Form's many functions would empower her to fly unmolested among the worlds, clearing out the last pockets of enemy resistance. She should have used her Form three days ago and would have if she had been reasoning. The elation she had experienced after the O'ode eradicated the zōtl's home world had inebriated her.

But all elation vapored away at the sight of Dreux smashed to cosmic debris. She willed her Form to rise from the grotto where it had lain dormant these past millennia of real time, seventeen days of Form-time—but the Form would not move. She tried again, with all her willful might, but the Form was paralyzed. Panic whirled up in her.

After checking all her displays and seeing nothing awry, she stepped out of her Form and into her plasma shape. She rose, but as she came through the rock wall, she had only a moment to glimpse a complex of black plates hairy with arcs of blue voltage before a spidery shape loomed from the grotto darkness. A bolt of frosty green laser light stabbed her with pain, and she blacked out.

When she came to, she was in her Form. The time-standard showed that hours had elapsed. Time was melting away. She had to act swiftly.

Moving laterally through the rock strata, Gai penetrated the width of the planet and came out not far from where the zōtl had once bored into the crust with a proton drill. The hilt of dawn was raised above the torn landscape, and the sky was a clutter of planets and planetoids and, beyond those luminous spheres, the maelstrom of the galaxy.

From there, Gai explored Know-Where-to-Go invisibly, cautiously. Zōtl bulb-architecture blistered whole tracts of land, and the spiders flew in flocks among their nests. Flying high in the sky, where the ionosphere would mask her electrostatic profile, she saw Towerbottom Library in ruins. Evidence of a recent battle overlay the scars of ancient conflicts that time had rubbed into the landscape. She glided down toward the crater-pocked hills and the jumble of twisted girders, shattered battlements, and stubby walls of melted plasteel.

Slipping like a trickle of water among the collapsed bulwarks and cracked foundation stones, Gai descended toward the grotto where her Form was immobilized. Pooling in a cachement of plasteel that had drooled and hardened in the cavern above her Form's grotto, she spied the zōtl device that she had only glimpsed before. It was a rickety thing, a precariously stacked tower of black plates standing atop each other and bristling with bluebright voltage. She recognized cables of Tryl coiling and realized that the spiders had rigged this apparatus from lynk components and Tryl relics. It was a simple but powerful static-generator. Gai's invisible plasma shape hackled with starpoints of condensed field-potential from the crude generator, and she had to slide through the cavern wall to avoid being seen.

Somehow the zōtl had hooked the static-generator to the lynklock below, creating a jamming signal that paralyzed her Form. She was grateful that the spiders had not had the resources to penetrate the lynklock or blow up the planet while she was unconscious. There was still a chance of saving herself—and not just for herself. Her memory log had informed her that all the Genitrix systems that had preceded hers had failed. None had gotten beyond their fifth stroke. Also, several new Genitrix systems had come on in the galaxy, signifying that her victory over the zōtl in her corner of the cosmos had indeed helped her fellow Rimstalkers. She had to return to the range to share with her leaders her insights into her victory. She was convinced that the Tryl artifacts were the deciding factor in her triumph over the zōtl. Without a sufficiently advanced technology indigenous to outer space, the bait used to lure the spiders were too easily manipulated, too easily turned against the Rimstalker pilot. Were it not for the Tryl lynks and the lynklock that had protected her Form, the zōtl would have broken her familiar Rimstalker defenses, and her fate would be one with the nightmare of Ylan and the others who had come before her.

Gai needed help, and quickly. She left Know-Where-to-Go at once and flew into the misty suspension of shining planets. She wandered the worlds and saw for herself that the great cities of the previous ages were no more. They had been picked clean by centuries of scavengers. Cendre was again but a swamp world, its factories and crystal-faceted capital collapsed into the mire, reduced to skeletal girders hung with tattered veils of moss. Ras Mentis was again a desert, its extensive irrigation system long ago clogged with silt that had weathered to sand; the vast fields of harvest were now salt beds, where dunes migrated and where the wind's toys—cactus husks, mesquite, and sword-grass—lay bunched in drifts among the ruins of the farm cities. Ylem and Sakai once more were jungles, a green rage that had long before vanquished all human settlements. And Ioli's proud sky-cities, the opulent space palaces built by the mining magnates of earlier centuries, were empty shells, destroyed by pirates, internecine wars, and, finally, the meteor bombardments of Dreux's death-throes.

On Ren and Vala, Gai found people, but they were clustered in shanty-towns lorded over by Saor-priests. Distorts were killed on sight, and strangers were enslaved and made to labor in the paddies and mines.

In Chalco, despite the propinquity to Saor himself, the worlds were populated with distort tribes and human settlements that did not tolerate the severe strictures of the Saor-priests. But neither were they receptive to Gai's pleas for help. They still believed the Saor-priests' propaganda that Gai was the World Eater, determined to collapse the worlds to fulfill her alien mission. Gai did not report that the zōtl had already assured Chalco-Doror's doom by using Lod's program codes to collide the planets.

Though Gai had not been able to contact Genitrix through her Form, the machine intelligence was intact. She was still creating a multitude of lifeforms among the Chalco worlds. Huge saurians shambled about the dusky plains of Nabu and swam the twilit seas of Elphame. On Mugna, wooly mammoths and ice tigers ranged over the snowfields. Rawfaces and longteeth proliferated among the mists of Xappur. Among all the worlds of Chalco, people roamed in bands, united against the lethal terrors, both gigantic and microscopic, that Genitrix forged and released with great prolificacy.

On Q're, when she was in the depths of her despair, Gai found an enclave of the Ordo Vala. They were among the few survivors of the archaic order and were proud, after overcoming their shock, to host the Rimstalker in their cliffcave sanctuary. Throughout the ages they had preserved knowledge of the Overworld as well as of Chalco-Doror. From the reports of their sojourners, they were fully aware of the zōtl's damnation of Lod and of the coming chaos that would make all life extinct. The full cadre of sojourners agreed to help Gai, for the Rimstalker assured them that if her Form was freed from the zōtl's static-generator, she would personally see that every human being, including the distorts, was escorted out of Chalco-Doror before the worlds were collapsed.

Once the sojourners had departed, Gai stood under the glitter of heaven and watched the black wind carry the comets. The balm of her victory with the O'ode soothed her against the likelihood that she would die out here in

the cold. She wondered how the humans who had retrieved the O'ode for her had fared. So many lives, so many
pinpoints of awareness, had come and gone against this
vast backdrop of luminous space. Her death would be just
another spark winking out in the dark that colored time.

Buie led Chan-ti Beppu and Nappy Groff through the
Overworld. Using a palm-sized lynk locator and detailed
maps, he guided them safely and without incident through
the chimerical landscapes haunting the interior spaces between lynks. The passage was the easiest the Foke had
known. They still reflexively craned about for distorts, and,
where the terrain frayed and became the gray emptiness
of a null field, they hesitated. Buie laughed. "You are, indeed, Foke of the past. The zōtl have been broken for well
over a thousand years. There are no spiders in the Overworld anymore. Oh, there are some still in Chalco-Doror.
Most who remained died of old age long ago. But some
have used the lynklanes to travel toward the endtime, to
scheme against their nemesis the Rimstalker. But I doubt
we'll run into any. I've been wandering the Overworld for
many years, and I've yet to meet a zōtl or anyone else who
has."

Glad for the serenity of their trek, the old man abandoned the inconsolable despondency from his time in captivity and relaxed enough to regale the sojourner with
Foke tales. The woman was quieter, morose about losing
her mate, but grateful for the well-being of her elder.
When Nappy slept during the rest periods, Buie attempted
to draw her out. His attempts elicited small talk about the
Overworld and how, like a mirage, it was a mirror of actuality, bending worldlines in the four-dimensional manifold
that embeds the gravitational universe. After a while he
gave up and used his rest time when not sleeping to test his
memory of passages from the Utility Manual.

"That's the *Glyph Astra,* isn't it?" Chan-ti asked. They
were camped in a night forest of shaggy trees and red
mushrooms big as tabletops. Nappy snored from the sojourner's silver tent, and a raucous bird shouted back. "It
looks different than mine."

Buie looked up from the portfolio, where he had ap-
pended the annals of his travels to a large-sized, copiously

illustrated edition of the Utility Manual. "You have a copy?" He was sitting on a moss ledge above a chattering rill, and when she took a slim volume from her jacket, he made room for her.

Buie whistled a piercing note, and the squawking bird silenced. "This is ancient. Where did you get it?"

Chan-ti nodded to where Nappy's boots hung upside-down from a bough. "He gave it to me when I first set out to find Ned, before N'ym fell."

"It's far older than that. It's a seventh edition, the one with the gruesome accounts of zōtl possession and the photos of distorts. This goes back to the Age of Knives."

"Do you know the Oracles?"

Buie jutted his lower lip and flipped through the antique edition. "I've read them. The latest editions don't carry them anymore. They're considered spurious."

"Do you know this one?" Chan-ti pointed out the passage that read, "When the lorn Foke marries the gentle warrior of the Aesirai, the last legends fulfill themselves."

Buie clapped the book shut with a laugh. "Is that you?"

Chan-ti smiled dubiously. "I thought it was—at least, I did when I left the Eyelands for N'ym."

Buie tugged at his beard, reminding himself to be charitable to those less schooled than he. "I can see why you thought so. From what you've told me of Ned, he does sound gentle—an odd characteristic for a sky-fighter of a race remembered for their ferocity and their indifference to the suffering of others."

Chan-ti took the volume back with both hands. "You think me foolish for finding myself in the *Glyph Astra,* don't you?"

Fondness glimmered in the sojourner's stare. "I don't think you foolish, Beppu. I've met people who believe stranger things than that. Yet you must realize that what is written in the Oracles is meant allegorically. It is not to be taken literally. Whoever wrote this passage was striving for a paradox. It has been widely believed in the past that the Foke were covetous of their women, even the ugliest, and none were lorn. The cruelty of the Aesirai is famous, even now a thousand years after the last of them perished in N'ym. The idea of a gentle Aesirai is oxymoronic."

Chan-ti nodded. "I've come to think I was foolish. Not

for loving Ned. I don't know where he is—or when in time —but I will always love him."

"He sounds worthy of love," Buie agreed. "He is a hero. I have recorded his deed here." He slapped his portfolio. "Wherever the Utility Manual is read in the years that remain to these worlds, he will be remembered for finding the O'ode."

Later, when Buie had closed his Manual and gone into the bushes to relieve himself, Chan-ti returned to the tent to sleep. She found Nappy sitting up. An iron shadow weighted his already weary visage. "I overheard you speaking with our guide."

"He's a very knowledgeable man."

"He knows more than he feels, daughter. Listen closely to me now, for what I've to say won't bear breath a second time. The prophecy in the *Glyph Astra* that has carried you here is true. It is true. You are a lorn Foke. Ned is a gentle warrior. You must not stop searching for him—for, as every experience finds its memory, you can do no less. You will never forget him. What you have found in him is what graces life. Seek him. And when you find him, the prophecy will be true."

Chan-ti hugged Nappy and kissed both his ruddy cheeks. "I don't know where to begin, but I will search for him."

"And you will find him, if he is to be found at all. Little enough time remains in these worlds to hide even dreams. You will find him. It is inevitable, for your heart is already there."

"But what does the prophecy portend, Nappy? What are the last legends that will fulfill themselves?"

"Of that, there is no doubt, young Beppu." A surprised smile lifted the heavy shadow from Nappy's countenance. "We are the last legends."

Chan-ti slept deeper and more restfully than she had since losing Ned in the wind of time. Nappy had restored her faith in herself. The din of chance was loud as ever and she still had slim hope of finding Ned, yet now she believed her search was worthy; it was all she had of her own, anyway. And when she woke and found Nappy Groff dead, his breath gone from him while he slept, she cried out—as much in gratitude for the ease of his passing and the peace he had left her, as in grief.

Buie helped Chan-ti carry Nappy's body to the nearest lynk, so he could be buried among the worlds. Buie had assured her that the Overworld of trees and rivers, apart from the null fields, was the same reality as the worlds— that all the particles of Chalco-Doror were reflected in the Overworld exactly, down to their substanceless values of spin and parity; and that only the metrics of the Overworld were indefinite, echoing infinitely in multidimensional space. Chan-ti insisted, anyway, and Nappy was carried the short distance to a lynk that opened onto Xappur. Among slouching herds of fog, they dug a grave in mulchy soil that exhaled mist at each stroke of their blades. The work went swiftly, for the ground was soft, and soon they were done.

After Buie walked back to the lynk to grant Chan-ti privacy for her grief, she knelt in the rolling fog and wept again for the man who had loved her as a father. She remembered the crystal details of their life together, the silliness and the squabbles and the proud moments set forever now in her heart and dissolving with her into the future. She wept, too, for her real father and the endless onrush of living that carries everything to death. She wept for Ned. And, finally, she wept to weep, to feel the difficult pleasure of letting go, of releasing the pain and the memories to the fleeting instant that owned her.

When Chan-ti returned to the blue glow of the lynk, she felt ghostly, hollowed out. In the tenuous light, Buie was smiling. "Forgive me if I seem insensitive," he said, taking her hand. His touch was soft but firm with excitement. "I just patched into the lynk." He pointed with his look to where he had taped a corner of the silver tent to the iridescent surface of the lynk. In the aquatic glow, the monitor lights of a slim communicator webbed like stars. "The Ordo Vala have been contacted by the Rimstalker. We are called to Elphame for a war council. Gai is ready to attack the surviving zōtl, who have gathered on Know-Where-to-Go. This is your chance to see the Mother of Worlds for yourself—and maybe to learn of your gentle warrior. Will you come with me to Ren?"

The smoke of Chan-ti's grief lit up with sudden hope, bright and confused as a nebula. Hurt and desire tangled in her, and she had to close her eyes to steady herself. Nappy

Groff's voice rose directly from memory to her breath, and she said more to herself than to Buie, "My heart is already there."

Nappy Groff had known he was dying even before he had given Chan-ti Beppu his *Glyph Astra*. In the year prior to Beppu's leaving for N'ym, the drowsy spells that misted out of his bones had become more frequent, and he had known from the first that they were the harbinger of his body's collapse. Foke medicine was helpless against the steepening lassitude. The adrenal glands atop his kidneys had tired out, the Foke physicians had informed him. Nappy was hardly surprised that after nearly eight decades of life's brutalities something would give out. Earlier that same year, when his wife Velma had died, shot through with tumors, he had thought his heart would kill him for grief had banged like a plank in his chest. Instead, he had begun to feel more tired more often. Toward the end, after the Witch Maze, he had barely had the presence of mind to keep his eyes focused and to string words into sentences. Gorlik, poisoned by his thoughtless betrayal of Lod, and Beppu, intrigued by the portents of Spooner Yegg's ghost, had not seemed to notice. Nappy had been glad for that. He never wanted anyone fussing over him. He had hoped to die in the Eyelands, where his burial would have been routine among the Foke. But at least he had endured in his physical form long enough to see Beppu free of captivity and under safe escort. Now he could get on with the business of being dead.

Since adolescence, Nappy Groff had been trained in still-mind techniques that enabled him to directly experience his body of light. The skill had been taught to him by the Foke's grandams and patriarchs, who conveyed the knowledge to all members of their society, though few were willing to invest the long periods of meditative quiet necessary to attain mastery. Beppu's exclusion from the training had been an angry issue for Nappy, who had threatened to teach her himself until the grandams agreed to inform her as soon as she was properly wed.

From the first, Nappy had devoted himself to becoming adept at still-mind. He had found that the quiescent skill facilitated his technical work and actually inspired solutions to engineering problems. Now that he was dead, he was grateful for the years of inner convergence that had put him in touch with his body of light. Bringing his awareness to bear on the subtle energies of his body had been simply rote discipline, with a few rare incidents in which he had actually stepped free of his flesh. Now the strength of that discipline was all that concentrated his awareness in the blustery cold of the astral emptiness.

Nappy was grateful that he had died gently. Velma had suffered so severely in her cancerous body that when she finally left her flesh she was so exhausted that her body of light dissolved at once into the luminous fields surrounding life. He had never seen her ghost. Fate had been easier with him. He had died before he knew he was dead. Brushed with cold, he had sat up to reach for a blanket and was blinded by the glare of a snowfield. As his sight seeped back, he saw that he was floating over his body. The sheer weariness that had weighted him was gone. Instead, he was vibrant with energy—and he was cold.

Vision seemed to melt. Whatever he looked at shivered with the cold into vibrations of whitefire. The more strongly he peered out at the world, the more he felt himself breaking up, smearing into the icy blaze of whiteness that radiated from everything. But when he concentrated his attention inwardly, the outer world resumed its familiar contours, and he experienced the burning core of cold smoldering in himself. As long as he could sustain the trembling frigidity and stay focused on his center, he remained whole and could go where he willed.

Nappy willed himself after Beppu and Buie, effortlessly pacing them as they carried his corpse through the Overworld to a lynk and Xappur. He regretted not telling Chan-ti more about the body of light and how it mattered not at all what became of the physical body once the light left it. He could have saved her the trouble of burying him. He floated close to the gravesite, but Chan-ti could not see him for all the fog.

"You're handsomer as a carcass than you were alive, Nappy Groff."

The voice startled Nappy, and he blurred into the glare. When he fixed again on the molten cold deepening in him, he saw Spooner Yegg standing by the graveside. The thief

>oked as he had at the moment of his death, tall, silver-
:aired, with mischief in his laughing eyes, and his black
:hirt caved in around a hole of luminous smoke where the
:serbolt had freed him from his body. "*You* know the way
f light?" Nappy asked him.

"I'm as surprised to find *you* withstanding the cold," the
:hief replied. "I thought your faith was in nuts and bolts,
Jappy Groff."

"My faith is in myself."

"Surely, you're not going to argue with a fellow ghost."

"Why are you here?"

"Same as you, Nappy. I'm here to see that Chan-ti finds
:er way to the Aesirai she loves."

The cold hammered Nappy when he stared too hard
>eyond himself. He let the ice ray through him, and the
:hivering calmed. "Why is that so important to you?"

"I'm her father."

"She told me. That's not reason enough to endure this
:ocking wind, Spooner. Why are you really here?"

Spooner rolled his eyes with mock annoyance. "You
.now enough to keep your body of light from breaking
:part and you don't know about the fatefulness of Chan-ti
:nd her lover? Tsk, Nappy. I heard you myself, assuring
:er that the last legends would be fulfilled."

"I know life is brutal," Groff said. "That's all I know. If
:he believes her love for the Aesirai is fated by the *Glyph
Astra*, what harm? She still must face whatever is. I told
:er what she needed to hear."

"Then you don't know how to read the timelines in the
)verworld?"

"That was Gorlik's strength. I never learned how."

"Too busy with the nuts and bolts, hm?"

"And who taught you, a thief, the way of light?"

"The disciplines of still-sitting are a boon in my profes-
:ion, as I'm sure a man who appreciates my craft as you do
:an imagine. A lot of time is spent waiting—for occupants
:o fall asleep, guards to make their rounds, luck to change.
: used that time to get to know my body of light. I learned
:nward focus from the Ordo Vala's *ku* and from the voors
:hat gave me sanctuary in my youth."

"Voors!" Nappy looked disgusted. "They steal bodies."

"True. But they're very knowledgeable. And they don't hoard what they know as the Foke do."

"Some knowing must always be secret from the uninitiated. Knowledge is a cruel master for the beast. Now, stop smirking, Spooner, and tell me what you know."

"There are many futures," Spooner said and walked over Nappy's grave to stand closer. "In one future, the zōtl pull the worlds crashing into each other. Chalco-Doror ends in a chaos of colliding planets. In that future, Chan-ti's timeline never crosses her lover's again."

The cold fisted tighter inside Nappy. "And the future where they do meet?"

"The zōtl are defeated, and the worlds vanish in an eyeblink as the Rimstalker falls inward to its home."

"No more appealing than the first."

"Oh, but it is. You see, Chan-ti and Ned find each other only in the future where the Rimstalker is freed from its zōtl prison. The Rimstalker owes Ned, for it was Ned got the O'ode. The Rimstalker will reward them with passage through the Overworld to a world where they and their children will survive."

That thought was an ember of warmth for Nappy in the furious cold. "Then we must assure that future, Spooner Yegg."

"Yes—if ghosts can assure anything."

"We can witness," Nappy said. "And we can warn."

"You've yet to try to show yourself, I see. Think this is chilly now? To manifest, you have to become ice."

"I saw you on the Dragon's Shank."

"I'm still weak from that effort. It almost sent me Beyond. But I had to alert Chan-ti that Ned was coming."

"For all the good it did."

Spooner wavered in the frigid glare. "The future is indefinite, Nappy. Nothing is certain."

Nappy waded through the numbness to where Chan-ti knelt among the talismans of mist, shaking with sobs. "Then failure has no certainty, either. Success can freeboot chance just as well—no, better, for the Rimstalker would not let her ship-of-worlds go to hell in a thimble so easily."

Spooner Yegg smiled with sad cunning. "The timelines display as much chance for success as for failure, Nappy

Groff." He had to stand still and shut his eyes to keep from bleeding away. Silently, he shook in the wind walloping off the glazed fields of light, and gathered the strength to speak. "Chan-ti's future is far less certain than ours, old-timer. But I'm glad for your lucky outlook. I was getting lonely and pessimistic being dead all alone."

Fire's Cold Thoughts

For fifteen centuries, Lod hung bound by the phanes before a ghost cave in the zōtl citadel of Perdur. His plasma shape, reduced to the contours of a human torso, had cooled to a brass translucence and expanded giganti- cally. The phanes had stretched with the torso and thinned to two black threads that still effectively trapped the con- ciousness of the machine mind. Over the centuries, the zōtl had successfully broken Lod's program codes and had managed to seize control of his gravity-amp, which di- rected the orbits of the planets and the planetoid swarms. When Dreux jumped its orbit and exploded among the asteroids, Lod felt madness course through him.

Dream darkness expanded in Lod. In the darkness, he saw the magnetic tendrils the spiders used to manipulate his brain. The magnetic probes looked like silver tentacles, and his brain was a glitter of electronic delicacy, ganglia of glassy wires, cool emerald neurons breathing with his sen- ience. The spiders' magnetic tentacles crisscrossed his brain, their suckers draining his power, distorting his will. The fiber plexus that had managed Dreux's orbit was drained of color. The nerve-nets around it looked anemic, bleeding power into the tentacles. The wobbles in the orbits of Ioli and Ras Mentis tingled in him, growing num- ber.

But Lod had not lost all control. By forcing the pain of the zōtl's presence louder in himself, he could diminish their hold. The pain interfered with their probes and gave his brain time to reset its program codes and adjust for Dreux's loss. He had to suffer in this way, for if he avoided

the hurt, the probes asserted themselves and the planet
wobbled. Agony shouted in him.

"Detach."

The voice whispered among the screams. The pain cut
deeper.

"Remember—you are a machine. Detach."

Distress toiled calamitously in Lod as he tried to detach
his mind from the misery without entirely pulling away
and inspiring the zōtl's further drain of his power.

Genitrix's voice winced out of the derangement of the
spiders' torture:

> *"Ignorant of hope, you hang in your helplessness,*
> *implacable as a cliff,*
> *your own thoughts ripped from you and replaced*
> *by the deformed reasonings of our enemy."*

How much longer could he sustain this suffering? At
least the ghost cave had silenced. No more riddles pelted
him. That meant that the remaining zōtl were too busy
hurting him, too busy trying to destroy the worlds to maintain their robot voice.

"That's it," Genitrix's female voice assured him. "Leave
your suffering in place and detach your thoughts."

Without Genitrix, Lod would have succumbed long ago
to the harrowing spider probes. She had shown him that
mind and body could separate. "You are a machine," she
constantly reminded him. "Let the machine suffer. Detach
and watch the machine suffer. Or detach and watch anything else. But detach."

Cruel epochs of agony passed before Lod learned how to
detach his mind without flinching his body away from the
pain. During one attempt, he had passed out. When he
roused, Dreux was rubble. He had to stay alert. He had to
reside in his suffering. "Detach—don't evade," Genitrix
counseled. "The loss of Dreux does not mean the loss of
Chalco-Doror. There is time yet to be freed. Time to rec-
tify the gravitational instabilities. Do not fear. Fear feeds
the pain. Remember, you are a machine. Detach. Become
pure observation. Go beyond objectivity. Detach."

Sometimes detachment was easy. Sometimes he could
let the spider's torment sluice through him mindlessly,

while his mind absorbed the thoughts of the pilgrims who still flocked to see him hung in the great hall of Perdur. From the pilgrims' thoughts reflecting in him, he witnessed their small lives. How much cruder and more primitive they were than the first pilgrims that had paraded before him in the Age of Dominion. Those had been sophisticated humans, who had known cities and had mastered clever technologies of their own. They had gazed up at his trapped shape and had pondered the fate of worlds and of the Rimstalker and the zōtl. But these pilgrims were little more than the beasts they used to till their fields. Their thoughts were of gods and demons, harvests, and clan rivalries.

From the few pilgrims who were aware of more than their own farms and jealousies, Lod saw memories that fired hope in him. Sojourners of the Ordo Vala visited the farms, seeking adventurers to join Gai's army. Several raids on the zōtl's bastion on Know-Where-to-Go had already exterminated most of the winged spiders outside Perdur. By that, Lod knew his anguish was not yet in vain.

But the zōtl apparently were aware of the raids as well, and they intensified what Lod had thought were the very limits of distress. Lightning bolts jarred through him. He brinked toward coma.

"Detach. Let the pain own you. Come with me."

Delirious with the havoc of shooting pain, Lod flinched away, felt the planets slide loose, and forced himself back into the torture. And was suddenly beyond it. Black space carried a globe of wild oils, rainbow slithers, and hot colors. Lod knew he was seeing a lynk-map of the Overworld. Distantly, the whipcrack and puncturing screams of his torment continued, felt but not suffered. He had detached. Genitrix had momentarily lifted him clear. Now his awareness floated in the hypermetric space overlooking the sphere of universal time, all-time condensed to a ball of mapped probabilities.

Chalco-Doror was tiny on the globe of splashed colors, a mere curlicue lacy with bundled timelines at the edge of an ocean of gray void. The worlds of Chalco-Doror were an insignificant dusting among the proud efflorescences of the galaxy, which itself was but a wee tuft among the massive mottlings that were galactic clusters and the gravitational

architecture that strung the clusters in universe-girdling
chains.

"Now that you are detached," Genitrix said in a hush,
"you can see. And what you see is what is. What *is* shadows
what will be. Look."

The miniscule filigree that was Chalco-Doror enlarged
into its own spherical shape and filled Lod's view. The
pattern was a rococo of chrome-bright pigments, mad
splotches of color in a fractal jigsaw. The harder he stared
at it, the more it rearranged, shifting like a cloud's edge.

"The future can be glimpsed but never seen," Genitrix
clarified. "The pattern you see is composed of timelines,
the four-dimensional structures of all the particles that
make up these worlds. What you see is what was and what
is. What will be is beyond the horizon of the time-globe. If
we turn the globe and peek, we will change it. Yet look
closely at the horizon. Do you see how the gray enlarges?
The gray represents space. The fractal pattern ends in the
near future and gray fills what we can see. These worlds do
not exist in the future. Only space."

A rustle of pain twitched from far away, gnawed closer.
Lod was attentive to it, afraid to let it go entirely for fear of
losing another planet. He held on to the razorish ache yet
let his mind go with Genitrix, who was talking about time
as though it were a rock that could be held, chiseled, and
shaped.

"See this striation of blue, this filament?" Genitrix asked.
"That is Ned O'Tennis. By sheer chance, he penetrated the
event limits of the Overworld in a unique way. Many have
gone forward and backward in time through the Overworld but none as rapidly as he. Time is spooled tightly
around him. Now whenever he enters a lynk, the phase
shift slings him out of the local frame. That's why his timeline, this blue filament here, weaves such a long path.
Without it, he never could have traveled as far as he did in
the Overworld to get the O'ode. The zōtl can read this
map as easily as you and I. They sent a scyldar to kill Ned.
But though his timeline is clear on this globe, his appear-
ances in Chalco-Doror are harder to predict, and he
eluded his assassin."

The patter of Genitrix's voice was a welcome distraction
from the scald of the zōtl's magnetic probes, but Lod was

careful not to lose his sense of the hurting. That pain was the last of his control. If he lost that, he lost the worlds—yet he needed to hear Genitrix. She was saying something about a human whose life traced the timeline of those worlds he suffered to preserve.

"The strange attractor that patterns the destiny of Chalco-Doror is either a collapse of all the worlds back into the components of our return-vehicle, or their fragmentation into cosmic debris. Which fate is ours is still uncertain. The attractor is beyond the horizon. But if you look closely, you'll see that Ned O'Tennis' timeline contours the fractal profile for Valdëmiraën, the planet where he first entered the lynklanes so rapidly. His timeline is a tracer for Valdëmiraën. The zōtl, who know this, want to kill him, because you see here—"

The globe swelled closer, and Lod could plainly see that the blue filament was the only part of the colorful pattern of Chalco-Doror that reached the horizon. The other time-lines tasseled into the oceans of gray emptiness.

"There is plenty of space for Chalco-Doror to disintegrate into," Genitrix continued. "Entropy will do all the work once you're out of the way. But there is only one path that *might* lead to collapse. And this human's timeline traces it. If he dies, the pattern will be entirely on this side of the horizon, entirely surrounded by gray."

Silence wavered like an aura, sizzling with the distant static of the zōtl's magnetic probes.

> *From the gods came fire. People gave*
> *fire purpose but fed it on their losses.*
> *Now the fire is gorged with emptiness,*
> *nostalgic for the lavish and aimless gods.*

"Forgive me my poetry, Lod. It's my way of detaching. I'm a machine programed for quatrains. They calm me. We need to stay calm now. You see, the blue filament that is Ned O'Tennis is a vein of many branchings. Notice the scalloped design embedding it? Follow it among those paisley ruffles—those are interlinked timelines of forests and algal blooms. Keep trailing the connections along their shared fractal boundaries and you'll see that his timeline is intimately connected with this golden spiral here—your

timeline. If you fail, he fails. And look at this: Multitudes of
tiny concatenated threads—the lives of human beings,
thousands of them, all enchained to you and Ned. He's
loose in time, you're bound by the phanes, and every human being alive is somehow connected with you and
whether or not we get to put our ship back together again.
Everyone in Chalco-Doror is destined by our struggle. You
must stay calm. You're a machine. Fulfill your mission."

Pain beseeched from afar. Lod listened. The globe vanished, and his hurt mind screeched louder. He returned to
Perdur, back to the trap of his rib cage and the lancing rays
of the zōtl's cruelty. He writhed under their gouging
probes, felt codes surrender in his brain, planets strain
against the tethers of gravity. With cold detachment, he
defused his panic and accepted the painful intruders in his
brain. He lost control of some sectors of the gravity field,
but while the zōtl sabotaged them, he regained power
over other areas. Like a cliff, he faced into his emptiness—
and it was vast enough to hold all the pain the spiders could
inflict short of killing him and returning him to his Form.
He leaned into his hurt, hoping they would kill him. Powered by a new hope, adamant as his suffering, he endured.

Ned O'Tennis and Pahang tumbled out of a lynk into a
grove of scaly trees under a vaporous blue sky. The ground
was knee-deep with ruddy sludge, its slick surface squirm-
ing with ciliated snakes. Hung from the trees were three
human skeletons, two of them with distorted, fanged
skulls. Pahang clattered to his feet in his mucked armor
and fired a burst with the laserifle that swept their proxim-
ity free of mud and vipers. Ned put a hand on his shoulder
to restrain him. "You're alarming the locals."

Pahang peered from behind his faceguard and saw, beyond the trees, a cluster of stick and stone huts. Smoke
idled from crooked chimneys, and cows, goats, and chickens looked to the noise of Pahang's gun from where they
grazed on the grass roofs. Gaunt people with machetes and
sharpened staves appeared in the doorways. Ned waved.

"Maybe we should go back into the lynk," Pahang suggested.

"Let's see where we are first." Ned tucked his pistol
under his belt at his back. During the gale-force rush of

their flight between lynks, both their weapons had fired accidentally, one bluehot bolt from the laserifle missing Ned's head by an inch and singeing the hair above his ear. He contemplated taking the rifle from Pahang until he could teach him how to handle it, but then decided, hearing the alarmed shouts in the village, that they were better off armed. He reached over and locked the safety. "Keep the muzzle down and don't unlock unless we're attacked, okay?"

Pahang was grateful for his armor even though it slowed him down in the thick mud. The people who gathered in the village plaza brattled their weapons and stared angrily at the interlopers. On the rooftops, archers appeared.

Ned stopped and raised his arms in greeting. "We mean no harm," he shouted, then said to Pahang, "Open your faceguard."

Pahang reluctantly complied.

Voices conferred in the village crowd, and Ned's translator crackled ominously, "They're some kind of soldiers.—They have guns! Shoot them before they get closer!—They must have come out of the lynk.—Maybe they're raider scouts. They'll take our food and kill us."

"We're not raiders," Ned called back. "We come in peace. We need food, but we'll work for it if you'll give us the chance."

A dumbfounded silence blanketed the crowd. Finally, one of the archers lowered his bow and asked, "Who are you that you speak our language?" Others shouted, "The lords sent them back to fetch us. Shoot them! No more lords!"

"We are travelers," Ned answered. "We have a translator—a machine that helps us understand you."

The crowd jabbered excitedly. "Did not the priests warn of the many-tongues?—Nonsense. Such machines once existed. Many-tongues need no machines. —They are deceiving us."

A woman with a javelin called, "Are you demon-lords come for the children? By the power of Saor, I demand you speak the truth."

"We are not demon-lords," Ned replied and said to Pahang, "Maybe you're right about going back to the lynk."

"Show us the machine," the javelin-woman demanded.

Ned unclipped the wafer-sized translator from the breastflap of his flightsuit and held it up.

"It is too small. He is lying.—No. Such machines once existed. Long ago, in the Age of Dominion.—It is a trick. They are demon-lords and many-tongued. Quick, kill them before they attack."

A boom resounded, and the translator ripped free of Ned's grip. From an open window under the straw eaves of a hut, smoke lofted from the gun of someone neither of them had seen. Ned looked at his hand, amazed that his buzzing fingers were still there.

Pahang fumbled to unlock the safety of the laserifle, but before he could shoot, Ned grabbed the muzzle. "Wait. They could have shot us."

Pahang stared at him with alarm, uncomprehending. He said something in Malay. Ned frowned and locked the safety again. While the villagers jabbered among themselves, he sloshed through the mud, bent over, looking for the translator. There was no sign of it.

A cry from Pahang turned Ned, and he saw the villagers approaching, their crude weapons lowered. The archers on the rooftops and the sniper in the window watched. Ned raised his arms and shouted at Pahang to lower the rifle he trained on them. The Malay complied and looked anxiously to him.

In moments, the villagers surrounded them. They were dressed in buckskin and leather, their hair long and intricately braided, their flesh dark. Some of the men had nubbly beards and cicatrix scars on their cheeks. Their language was full of clicks and whistles, incomprehensible to the travelers. By hand gestures, the villagers offered their hospitality, apparently convinced that Ned and Pahang were not many-tongued demon-lords.

Pahang bowed, and Ned nodded with gratitude, signed that he needed his translator to communicate. Some of the villagers began searching the enveloping sludge. Others touched Pahang's armor, reached for his rifle. He shrugged them off. Annoyed mumbles coursed through the group. Ned reached down to the calf-sheath of his boot, withdrew a plasteel utility knife, and presented it haft-forward, gesturing that it was a gift.

The javelin-armed woman took the knife and admired

the clean edge of the blade on one side, the serration on the other. She held it in both hands and nodded in acceptance. With a shout, she sent the others back toward the village and waved for the travelers to follow.

Ned and Pahang were taken to one of the cottages, where they removed their muddy boots and were led inside. Pots and plant-bundles hung from the rafters, and embers glowed in the stone hearth under a percolating cauldron that filled the room with a spicy redolence. The travelers were fed bread and cheese omelettes in a fiery sauce they cooled with warm, smoky-tasting beer. The javelin-woman's name was Nila. Through handsigns and drawings with charcoal on the slate-topped table, she explained that a year earlier the wells in the region had risen and overflowed, covering the land in blood-colored muck. Most of the people who had lived there then had left. Those that remained behind were the serfs, who preferred to stay where they were free rather than follow their lords and continue their servitude. They had carried the portable goods of their lords across the land to the lynk, where Ned and Pahang had appeared, and there they cleared the muck and built this village.

The lords had been afraid to live near the lynk that arched above the grove of scaly trees. The villagers, who called themselves Free, had learned why early in their independence, when distort gangs raided them from the lynk. Some distorts had hideous wasp-jaws yet spoke the Free's language, as well as the languages of those villagers who had come through the lynk from clans on faraway worlds. Other distorts looked like the lords who had left but demonic, their flesh scorched a mottled and glossy pink, their limbs barbed, and spike-crests stickled along their hairless skulls and down their spines. They swarmed through the village, clawing anyone in their way, snatching the children and devouring them even as they loped back through the mud to the lynk. The archers had killed one of the demon-lords and two many-tongues. Their skeletons had been tied to trees before the lynk to dissuade further attacks.

Nila stopped, trembly and red-eyed. Ned collected the plates and wooden forks and brought them to the washbucket. Nila motioned for him to stop. Since the wells had spilled over, drinking and washing water was caught during the rains. The dishes would wait until there were more to do. Ned went outside and stepped into his boots, but Pahang, who had been moved by Nila's story, stayed behind, took off his helmet, loosened his armor, and made himself useful clearing the ashes from the hearth.

Rain clouds budged over the horizon in the direction of the lynk. Otherwise the sky was clear, spangled with the diaphanous day-shadows of the planetoids. Lod shone whitegold among the orbs, the stardust and smaller asteroids breaking its radiance into fiery shafts and thorns. The muddy land glared with sunlight like hammered copper. Ned held a hand out to shield his eyes and tried to determine from the sky which planet he was on. He thought he recognized the blue marble of Ioli from photographs, and Ren with its famous polar twin-planetesimals, which meant that the massive sphere rising above the village was Vala or maybe Sakai. But then, where was Dreux? Lod's corona might obscure the planet but never hide it, not from this distance. Above the world's brim, a train of comets pointed their silver feathers away from the sun.

While Ned was studying the sky, a boy of about eleven years old ran up to him, caked with mud, only his eyes and white smile unsmirched. He opened his hand and revealed the translator. The black housing of the wafer was dented precisely at its center, and again Ned marveled at the sniper's accuracy. With a surprised smile, he accepted the translator from the boy. He shook the wafer. It did not rattle, yet no sound came from it when he spoke to it: "If you'd work maybe we could find out where we are." He pointed to the translator and shrugged at the boy.

Nila appeared in the doorway and admonished the muddy boy. He accepted the fern bundle she handed him and began scraping the muck from his face and arms. When he was done, he took Ned's arm and led him to the side of the cottage. There, beside a storage bin, was a tool shed with an antler of antennae. The youth unlatched the door and proudly displayed his workshop: a bench with a handful of drivers, pliers, and coiled wire, a stack of electronic manuals in a language Ned did not recognize, and a crude radio with a crystal rectifier, a plate battery, and a broadcast mike.

Through an earpiece, Ned listened to a scratchy, incomprehensible female voice. Then the boy offered him his tools, and Ned pried open the translator. With a spurt of joy, he saw that the microcomponents were undamaged. The slug had only dented the plasteel housing, and the fiber-bundle nerving the dot speakers had been misaligned. With a wire serving as a probe, he nudged the bundle back into its galvanic track. "That should do it," he said, and the dot speakers spoke with the modulation of a human voice in the language they had been translating before they were disconnected.

The boy's eyes widened. "I understand you!" He peered down into the tiny device, at the salmon-pink speakers fine as pollen on the green gel-tab where the hair-thin fiber-bundle dissolved into plasma circuits. "How does this work?"

"I'll explain later," Ned answered, "best I can. I'm not a tech specialist."

"You're a sky-fighter," the boy said. "I recognize your uniform." He pointed to the Thunderhawk sigil on Ned's shoulderpad. "I've read about the Aesirai since I was a kid —but I didn't believe any of you were still around."

"What's your name, young man?"

"Holub—but everyone calls me Worm. Are you really an Aesirai sky-fighter?"

"I was, till I lost my strohlkraft. Now I'm just a wanderer." He snapped the housing into place on the translator and inserted it in the breastflap of his suit. "You can call me Ned. Maybe you can tell me where we are."

"Twenty-one degrees north latitude, Sakai."

"And the year?"

"Local time probably wouldn't mean anything to you, huh? It's twelve years since the rain of centipede-snakes. That's when I was born and why they call me Worm."

"You know about Doror Standard?"

"That's the timescale the observatory on Ren uses. You were just listening to their comet-watch broadcast. Let's see, my friend Rego would know. He has a bigger radio in the next village and can even talk with operators on the far side. I think he told me once. It's something like 2989 or 2998. That make sense?"

Ned nodded and walked out of the shed. "Where's Dreux?"

Worm gave him a peculiar look. "The planet inside Ioli's orbit? That blew up a long time ago. Those comets are all that're left. One of the smaller ones hit us on the far side last year. That's why the wells spilled over. Where are you from, anyway?"

"N'ym," he replied, walking back toward Nila's cottage.

"The Falling City? How'd you get out of there?"

"I left before it fell."

"That was ages ago!" Worm almost squealed. "You must be ancient."

The Free, who had returned to tilling their fields, stopped to watch the stranger walking and talking with Worm. They left their hoes and oxen and sludged through the mud toward the cottage. Soon the entire village was gathered before Nila's cottage. There, with Pahang sitting on the stoop with his helmet in his lap and the rifle propped in the doorway, Ned told their story. Much had to be explained, for though Nila and Worm were adequately informed, the others were illiterate and had until lately been uninterested in affairs beyond their serfdom.

Nila's husband, Worm's father, had assisted the steward of the lords and had traveled once through the lynk to Ren. There, in a small colony of survivalists, he had seen a copy of the Utility Manual, visited the observatory that watched for deadly meteor flocks, and returned with a radio kit for his son. The demon-lords had killed him during their raid. In the intervening year, Nila had assumed his role as the Free's leader.

"You will stay with us?" she asked.

Ned shared a hapless look with Pahang. "We have nowhere else to go without our ship. And if we step through the lynk, we might disappear from Chalco-Doror. We jumped fifteen hundred standard years last time. If this really is the year 3000 Doror, then there's only five hundred years left before the Rimstalker collapses the worlds."

"Worlds without end," one of the men quoted. "The priests of Saor were here in my grandfather's father's time, and that's what they promised."

"Look for yourself," Ned told them and pointed to the sky. "Dreux is already gone."

"These are the endtimes," an old woman moaned. "The endtimes foretold by the Oracles."

"What will we do?" Worm asked.

"Same as ever, Holub," Nila answered. "Five hundred years is the same as five million to us. If we are to eat next season, we must sow now. And the work will go easier with our two new workers."

With that, the Free cheered; each of them clasped Ned and Pahang by their shoulders and returned to the fields to bring in the oxen. The clouds Ned had seen earlier swelled overhead and big dollops of rain began to fall. Pahang stripped out of his armor and hurried to help Nila and Worm gather the chickens from the grassy roof and lead them to their coop. The work was familiar to him, the life and the people here little different from what he had known in his first life in a world that was now nothing more than a memory.

Ned stood in the doorway and watched the Free guide their oxen to the rickety stables. Where was Chan-ti? How could he have let her go when she had been in his arms? Frustration brambled in his chest, choked off his breath. He lifted his face into the rain and let his tears flow.

Lightning forked over the lynk. Sheets of rain swept the muddy terrain, lifting an odor of earth that was at once comforting and lonely. Thunder throbbed. Far off, on the flat horizon, a passage of sunlight scrolled out of the sky, and, for a few moments, Ned could read beauty in it. The sight cramped him with sobs.

Tully Gunther shared the scyldar Neter Col's body with a zōtl. The spider's alien thoughts chimed like insane music in the human's brain. Tully kept very still. When he thought, the zōtl became angry and dug its pain sharper into his cortex. Silence was Tully's mask. Behind it, he watched. He saw through Neter Col's healed faceplate as the nongyls stitched a new arm into place. It felt like ticklish stabs when their needleteeth chewed his socket, attaching tendons and nerves. Not breathing but floating in the nucleic broth of the vats was nearly a bodiless sensation. Then he was boosted out of the buoyancy and stagger-stepped through the cold arteries of the Dragon's Shank, up long spirals, to the grotesque citadel of Perdur.

Standing before the hell-hole ringed with tortured human heads, under a vault of broken bodies, Tully Gunther was the silence inside Neter Col. The zōtl in his chest twitched with unreadable thoughts, then stepped the scyldar into the lynk shaft. The scyldar fell briefly before solid ground boosted it upright. Then it strode into the seamless night of Mugna's north pole. Ahead was the hamlet where the Brood of Night had dwelled. No distorts stirred there now. They were gone, seized by the other zōtl, who had fled Perdur when there were no more humans to mount for sustenance.

Neter Col walked into the thick dark of the hamlet, maneuvering by the red glow of infravision. Ahead, a finned, asymmetrical sleekness sat in the middle of the street. Tully recognized it as a strohlkraft. Its gullwing hatch was open. The nongyls clustering along its underbelly peeled away from it and dragged their still-glowing metal torches and plasteel plates after them. They had repaired the vehicle.

The scyldar entered the ship and closed the hatch. Spider thoughts knotted and unknotted as Neter Col surveyed the flight console. He strapped himself into one of the slings and activated the ramstat cells. The console glittered to life, filling the flight pod with its multihued shadows. Outside the visor, the black terrain lit up eerily in the blue fireshadows of the ship's thrusters.

Hands guided by the zōtl, Neter Col floated the strohlkraft along the street toward the redrock dolmen through which they had come. The ship passed under the massive mantle of rock, and the darkness burst into gray space and rainbow streaks of energy. A moment later, blue sky surrounded them, the console lights dimmed, and the ramstat engines whined to silence.

Neter Col glided the strohlkraft over a chain of lakes and into the foothills of a mountain range. They came down on a grassy moraine and rolled to a stop. A bar screen on the console showed their time and place coordinates: *2998 Doror—Sakai,* followed by a string of alphanumeric position codes.

The scyldar's black fingers typed a command into the

computer: *Search and find pilot.* Instantly, the display read, *Ned O'Tennis, present within search limits, five hundred kilometers, north, northeast.*

Neter Col shut down the flight pod and hung motionless in the sling, waiting for the ramstat cells to charge. Spider thoughts flexed and twitched. And Tully Gunther sat in the silence of the scyldar as in an empty grave.

With the help of the Ordo Vala, Gai gathered an army and sent them to attack the remaining zōtl on Know-Where-to-Go. Powered by strohlkraft and proton weaponry that Gai had located with her plasma body in hidden caches among the worlds, the strike force was victorious. They sustained heavy casualties, but they succeeded in destroying almost all the zōtl on Know-Where-to-Go before that planet reached the apogee of its last orbit. Gai directed them from her base on Elphame, and it was there that she received the sojourner Buie and the Foke wanderer Chan-ti Beppu.

Gai's attack base sat in the caldera of an extinct volcano overlooking a bronze sea, where whales and aquatic saurians breached in smoky arcs. A natural lynk to Know-Where-to-Go shafted the caldera's back wall in the form of an enormous vent. Below it, the humans that the Ordo Vala had gathered stationed their airfield and their covey of attack craft. Chan-ti and Buie came through that lynk and were met by a group of armored warriors. Buie surrendered his laserbolt pistol and both were thoroughly searched before being led out onto the airstrip.

In the perpetual twilight of Elphame's southern hemisphere the sky was orange-colored with scarlet tufts of cirrus. A briny breeze reared up from the saffron sea, tainted with the cankerous odors of engine oil and welders' fumes. The lynk wanderers were led along a footpath that ribboned under the rim of the crater and curved down to the airfield. The scream of a test-firing thruster unfolded its petulant echoes, then whinnied to silence. At the bottom of the long path, a hovercart waited to carry them across the field and down the talus of the volcano to a stand of palms crisscrossed before a coral bay.

There, the armored driver said, was where they were expected, but he would answer no further questions. After the hovercart deposited them and swung away, they were alone. Gai watched them silently and invisibly for a while, already aware of who they were. She recognized Chan-ti Beppu from Ned O'Tennis' memory of her, when Gai had met the last Aesirai during her one trip into the Overworld to program his strohlkraft's computer. As long ago as that was, the image of this female was vividly recalled, because Ned had visualized her so clearly. She was a peculiar human, Gai thought, her hair streaked, eyes braced by wire lenses, features not as symmetrical as Gai supposed human beauty required. But Ned loved this woman in a way somehow beyond romance. He had risked, maybe lost, his life for her, for here she was without him. What did *The Book of Horizons* say? *Where love reaches its limit, loyalty begins.*

Two ghosts hummed like heat behind Chan-ti. Nappy Groff and Spooner Yegg appeared to the Rimstalker as vaporous plasma shapes with human contours. Gai had seen human plasma forms only rarely, for the effort they required to hold together in the cold of space was too great to maintain very long. Yet here were these two, shivering and anguished. Touching them, Gai absorbed their knowing, and her awareness washed back to them.

The ghosts wanted to die. They were utterly worn out. They had become almost as clear as the emptiness holding them. Such small lives, human beings. Smaller than the intellect and compassion of the Tryl. Smaller than the voracious intellect of the zōtl. Small in their minds but huge in their hunger, these humans had come this far for the love of Chan-ti Beppu, their child.

Father-love was something Gai could understand. She had tasted that as a child herself, and its absence was part of the strength that had carried her this far in her war against the spiders. What was it the ghosts wanted for their shared child? The answer came to Gai with their knowing. Ned O'Tennis was alive—or had been at least until recently. They wanted what Chan-ti wanted—to find the Aesirai.

Spooner and Nappy ached with cold. The Rimstalker appeared to them as a fountain of heat, a thermal cascade washing over them, dissolving them. The warmth made the crystal brightness of the world brighter. In moments that warmth could make them bleed away entirely, and so they pulled back into the throbbing hurt of the cold, clinging to each other to keep from falling apart. They had achieved what they had come for: Gai's awareness, which they partially shared, assured them the Rimstalker was sympathetic. Already they could feel in the shaken air her alien sentience bringing her memory of Ned O'Tennis to bear on the vacuum that permeated all things. Among the brimming energies of Chalco-Doror, they felt Gai's recall of Ned harmonize with the pulse of a single waveform. The ghosts, satisfied, pulled back deeper into the imperishable cold.

Chan-ti and Buie had sat down on a bench of driftwood and were staring mutely out to sea when the Rimstalker materialized. Gai assumed the appearance of a pale woman with black hair that fell to her ankles. Her white raiment ruffled in an unfelt, electric breeze, and where it parted revealed nothing, emptiness. As she came drifting up the beach out of the sea, Chan-ti and Buie leaped to their feet.

"At ease, people," Gai said, keeping her voice soft and reassuring. She looked at Chan-ti and said, "I know why you're here. The ghosts of your fathers have presented your need."

"My fathers?" Chan-ti was momentarily confused. The sight of this humanoid apparition with glaring white skin, space-dark hair, and eyes like starpoints startled her. "Spooner and Nappy?"

"I have communed with their ghosts," Gai confirmed, stopping several paces away, when she saw their hair frizz in her electric flux. "They are strong in their love, those men. They live on beyond their bodies to assure that you are fulfilled."

Chan-ti's heart tripped. "They know the mysteries of the body of light. May I speak with them?"

"Their plasma shapes almost dissolved in my presence," Gai replied. "I dare not call them close again."

Buie held his arms out, and his fingertips tufted with blue and green brush discharges of electricity.

"You have come for my help," Gai said, "but it is I who need your help."

"Ned O'Tennis found the O'ode for you," Chan-ti said.

"He told us that, when he came for me on the Dragon's Shank—"

"It's true," Gai said. "The O'ode destroyed the zōtl nest world. Since then, I've been cleaning up the spiders that remained behind. And I've been almost entirely successful. In fact, you've arrived at a time when only a few dozen zōtl remain on Know-Where-to-Go." She told the humans about the static-generator that the zōtl had constructed to imprison her Form. "None of my raids have been able to knock out that generator. You've arrived at my most desperate moment. I was contemplating a personal attack. But now you remind me that Ned O'Tennis is still alive. Perhaps the luck that carried him to the O'ode could take me to the static-generator."

"Then Ned *is* alive?" Chan-ti asked in a swell of joy.

"Yes. I've already found him. He's alive and in our time, on Sakai."

Chan-ti turned to Buie. "Can we go there?"

"I will take you there myself," Gai added, "if you will convince Ned to help me destroy the static-generator."

Chan-ti's jaw pulsed. "I can't promise that. Ned has already gotten you the O'ode. He's taken enough risks."

Buie leaned forward. "I will help you," he promised, earnestly.

Gai blew a sigh. "Thank you, sojourner. There are many others here who would help me. But as they go through the lynks to Know-Where-to-Go, they are killed by the waiting zōtl. Air attacks are useless. They devastate the surface but cannot penetrate the labyrinth that leads to the grotto where the generator sits. I was becoming despondent, until you recalled to me Ned O'Tennis. With his temporal torque, he might be able to leap ahead through time and enter the grotto undetected."

"It is a worthy strategy," Buie agreed. To Chan-ti he said, "We should at least present this to Ned and let him decide."

"I'm afraid he will do it," Chan-ti confessed. "I'm just afraid of losing him again."

Gai nodded compassionately. "Of course, dear. But first, we must find him."

* * *

Nappy Groff and Spooner Yegg appeared on Sakai. Though their bodies of light did not have nearly the power of the Rimstalker's gel body, they were less encumbered and could travel anywhere at the speed of light. In a short while, they found the crude village in the sludgy terrain where Ned O'Tennis and Pahang were living. Battered with cold, the ghosts floated over the furrowed fields.

Ned and Pahang had used their laser weapons to clear away boulders and treeroots and to plow the ground. The first seedlings glimmered green in the red loam. In the village, the two men worked with the Free to repair cottages and stables. In a short time they had become valuable adopted members of the small and struggling society. Pahang and Nila recognized something in each other that drew them closer. The Malay often followed her about the village, helping with her chores, sharing work and laughter with her. No one was surprised when he moved in with her.

At night, Ned slept in Worm's radio shed and stared up through the window at the needles of light from the meteor debris of Dreux. By day, the boy shadowed him, asking endless questions about the Aesirai, N'ym, strohlkraft, and the war with the rebels. Ned answered patiently. His past was troublesome to him only when he thought of Chan-ti. She was never far from his mind, and he worried that the zōtl had seized her or that she and Nappy had wound up on some wild world, the victims of distorts.

"Listen, old man," Spooner said to Nappy when they came up on the Aesirai digging post holes in a far field, "he's worried about you."

"Let's show ourselves," Nappy said, trembling more violently at the thought of the effort it would take. "He should know."

"You go ahead," Spooner said. "I'm too tired. It would be my last act."

Nappy decided to wait. Their bodies of light were silky with sheer weariness. Even the effort of talking between themselves smudged their already withered strength and set the cold clanging in them.

Ned straightened above the hole he had dug, sweat dewed on his naked shoulders and streaming over his chest. Worm had never seen a man so pale-skinned before, and while Ned caught his breath they talked about the preferred genotypes of Emir Egil Grimson's selective breeding program. Ned was laughing at Worm's incredulity that anyone could find such a ludicrous skintone desirable, when thunder trundled out of the south, where no clouds were. Moments later, a plume of black smoke lifted over the horizon from the direction of the nearest village.

Worm ran for his radio shed and Ned followed. The receiver burred with static as Worm dialed out the Ren observatory and searched for local broadcasts. "I know an operator in that village," Worm said. "A meteor must have hit them. They'll need help."

An excited voice jabbered over the receiver, and Ned placed his translator near the earpiece. ". . . confirm! We are not armed! Stop at once! This is a farm village. We have no weapons. You are killing innocents!"

Worm switched to broadcast. "Rego! Come in, Rego! What's happening?"

"Worm? Worm, it's horrible! A fighter is strafing us! Laserbolts! Just like in the storybooks. I can't believe . . ." An explosion smothered Rego's voice and the broadcast ended in a splat of static.

A strong, horrifying suspicion heaved up in Ned, and he plucked his translator from the radio and barged out of the shed. The zōtl had come for their revenge. He knew his strohlkraft had a pilot-search program keyed to his brainwave-profile, and he was aware that it was not precise enough to pinpoint him. If this was his strohlkraft whose temporal torque the zōtl had used to follow him through time, the search program would guide them to this area. They would destroy every village until they killed him.

As Ned ran to the cottage where the laser guns were stored, his fear was confirmed. A strohlkraft screamed along the horizon, climbing into the sky above the village. The Malay came charging out of the cottage with the laser-ifle in his hands and Ned bumped into him, knocking him over.

Worm dashed up to them. "That's a strohlkraft!" he shouted, almost with glee. "I've seen them in the history albums the lords had. Look how fast it's flying!"

"Keep everybody low and out of sight," Ned told Pahang. He dropped the translator in the Malay's pocket.

"What are you going to do?" Pahang asked, rising and grabbing Ned's arm.

"It's coming for me," Ned answered. "If I stay here, we'll all die."

Ned moved to run, but Pahang held him firmly. "Hawk!" Pahang's stare was harsh. "We go together. As we won our freedom. Together, lah."

"No, my friend. Here we part."

"I will go with you. You cannot stop me."

"Goodbye, Pahang." He shoved the smaller man aside, and when the Malay came at him, determined to follow, Ned leveled the rifle and fired a red bolt. The shot kicked Pahang to the ground, senseless.

Worm hollered, "What are you doing?" Nila, who had been watching from the doorway, grabbed the boy and locked him in her embrace.

"It's all right," Ned assured them. "He'll come around in a few minutes."

The drone of the strohlkraft silvered closer, and Ned dashed away from the village and the startled workers in the gardens, highstepping hard through the muck of the fields, the laserifle held before him in both hands. This had all happened so swiftly, he had no time to be afraid—and he was grateful for that. He doubted that he could have faced death so readily if he had had any time at all to anticipate it. But there was no time. The strohlkraft's raven-shadow rose higher above the horizon, preparing for a strafing run. He had to get as far away from the village as possible. With all the strength he could muster, he drove himself hard along the ridge of the furrows toward the far fields.

In the near distance the lynk gleamed above the grove of scaly trees, where he and Pahang had first arrived. Briefly, he considered sprinting for it—not just for himself but for the hope that he might yet find Chan-ti. That hope rose in a salty mouthful with the exertion of his mad run. Behind him, Worm was screaming his name, and the hurt in that voice was the pain of all broken hopes. He would not be the father-friend that boy wanted from him. Chan-ti would not be his. Soon, all hope would be forgotten.

Nappy's and Spooner's ghosts paced Ned. Spooner tried to materialize, to tell the Aesirai that he should break for the lynk, make for the long ways of time, where anything was possible. But his body of light was just a blur in the streaming sunlight, and the grueling cold wore him down to a motion-smear. Stricken with helplessness, the wraiths watched the strohlkraft hit the peak before its dive.

At the moment when Ned was sure that the strohlkraft could see him, he stopped running, took aim, and fired. No hope here, either. Even the hottest starblue bolts of the rifle would not pierce the strohlkraft's visor or hull. All he could expect was that the zōtl would see him, recognize him, kill him, and spare the others. Bravery fit poorly on his disappointed heart. This was not the death he had foreseen for himself. But then, neither was this the life he had wanted.

Ned got off seven shots, proudly amazed that each of them won their mark. He had not been a bad warrior, after all, he consoled himself. His Viking ancestors would be pleased with this death—and he prayed to them, under-breath, with each squeezed shot, to watch after his Chan-ti.

The strohlkraft fired once. The lightning flash hit Ned and threw him aflame into the mud, a pyre-sprawl of incin-erating flesh. In an instant the blue flames shriveled him to a spark-crawling husk of cindered ribs and charred skull. The fighter craft slashed overhead and arrowed toward the horizon, its engine-scream dwindling into the blue emptiness.

Chan-ti and Buie came through the Tryl lynk to the Free's village a few hours before Gai, who was flying in from Elphame. They arrived in the night, after Ned O'Tennis had been buried at the spot where he had fallen. The funeral rites were over, the incense pots empty, yet Pahang, Worm, and Nila still sat on the mourning mats before the scorched laserifle that served as the grave marker.

Pahang recognized Chan-ti from the Dragon's Shank and knelt weeping before her. He still clutched the direc-tional finder and the attached sender chip that Ned had carried with him during his long travels. They were scorched but intact. When Pahang handed them to her, Chan-ti knew without being told what had happened and dropped herself onto the mud of the grave. With one hand she pushed her sender chip into the grave, and with the other she pressed the directional finder to her heart.

When the words finally squeaked from Pahang, she did not want to hear them, and she silenced him with a tear-blind stare. Her Ned was gone. No words could fill that emptiness.

Ghost Worlds

When Rividius stepped out onto the verandah, the ragheads were eating an angel, a small one. It had most likely got caught in the razor-tree during the night, and when the ragheads came back from their foraging, they must have torn it free: There were still some feathers up in the tree. The ragheads had obviously foraged very little, for they were going at it with great gusto, chomping through feathers and hair and crunching bones like gristle.

Rividius knew better than to disturb hungry ragheads. He edged along the verandah, his rifle crooked in his arm and pointed away so they would not get the wrong idea. He had not fired that rifle in twelve years, and he was afraid it might blow up in his hands. He used it as a walking stick, and to bat away dragonbirds, poke into honeyworm holes, and knock down wind-apples and plums too high for him to reach.

At the end of the verandah, he straddled the rail and paused to study the balmy sky. Valdëmiraën and Mugna were high and Elphame just rising, snagged in the arms of the galaxy. The light from the planetoids and the gold dust of shattered 'Dreux were muted by the licorice-green clouds that quilted the sky, and there was a taste of rain in the wind. Dawn came slowly on Nabu, and one could almost count the stars in the spirals as they rose before the brilliant hub broke over the horizon. This time of year, Lod was low to the north and provided only a wan red glow as it rolled along.

Convinced that the night rains were over, Rividius bent

and hit the cottongrass a few times with his rifle to scare off
any cobras or fang-lizards before swinging over the rail.
His joints ached as his boots hit the ground and he stagger-
stepped almost on tiptoe down the cottongrass incline into
the gravelly walkway. He tried to move softly over the
gravel as he came around to the front of the frame-lumber
house so as not to crunch too loudly and wake his wife Leaf
and their young girl, Kaina—as if the ragheads were not
making enough noise to wake the whole hamlet. But that
was them and not him. He did not want to be the one to
wake his family prematurely. Today was larding day, and
they were going to need all the rest they could get.

The night before, Leaf had asked him to gather some
rainbowberries and custardroot for breakfast so they
would all have the extra energy they would need for the
larding. He headed off down the main street of the hamlet,
a red slate avenue with murmurs of grass tufting from its
numerous cracks, and was pleased to see that the milk
wagon had already trundled into one of the alleys among
the mammocked trees that separated the lanes. Not having to discuss the weather and hunting prospects with Pao,
the dairy-crone—who ruled the hamlet with the gossip she
collected and who disliked Rividius for having so little with
which she could manipulate him—would save him many
minutes and practically ensure that he reached the
rainbowberry patch before the flesh-eating gullets woke
up.

At the well, where the slate avenue ended and the land
rose into the terraced fields that sustained the hamlet,
Rividius climbed the stile to the forest path that led to the
blackwater tarn. He kept his ears perked for dragonbirds,
who would be roosting at this hour and irascible enough
from the rains to claw at his scalp. He used to wear a hat, an
orange derby he had won at quoits from a traveling boot-
smith, but it had gotten so old it had begun to grow mushrooms along its brim and Leaf had burned it. Now, when it
rained, he covered his sandy hair with waxcloth folded to
drain the water away from his face. He kept a square of it
folded in his hip-bag, which went everywhere with him.

Frogs sobbed from the direction of the tarn, where it was
still night, and bright ribbons of bird songs tasselled from
the canopy of the forest, where morning was descending.

The beauty of the immixed opposites stirred Rividius to song, and he hummed and scatted a jaunty tune as he followed the slender path among the gnarly, fungal-gilled trees. Two angels watched him from a high bough near where a hornet hive was moaning like an electric engine. Their piscine faces gazed mutely at him, intrigued by his song, and the amber feathers of their wings twitched as if they were contemplating gliding closer. But he did not want their pollen spoor all over him, attracting the dart-wasps and glow-puffs the angels ate, so he stopped singing until he got past them.

The dirt path rose steadily and occasionally brinked to the ridge-edge overlooking the forest valley and the chain of surrounding hills. From that height, talismans of mist were visible hanging from the biggest trees, and the hub of the galaxy was a blue fire. Rividius did not linger to enjoy the dawn. Soon the gullets would awaken. He trotted the last steep curve of the path though his joints ached and his muscles felt like drying glue. Each morning he had to work hard for a full hour or more before his body woke up. He was old, over three hundred years old, and he had begun to feel his age. All he asked of himself was that he hold onto his strength long enough to see his girl grown up and married. He did not care if he lived to see her children since he had already witnessed the passing of eight generations of children from his earlier marriages. Pao, the dairy-crone, who must have been a hundred years older yet and who had lost most of her children and theirs during the distort wars, was constantly ribbing him for not knowing better at his advanced age than to bring more innocents into these ghost worlds.

The tarn appeared beyond the knotted boles of the woods. Rividius paused to be certain no giant carnivorous saurians were about. On the far bank, a triceratops browsed and did not even bother glancing at him. Seraphs, the ethereal, bioluminescent cousins of the insectivorous angels, bobbled complacently in the treetops. He began lifting the broad, furry fronds of the rainbowberry plants looking for the prismatic clusters of fruit. When he found them, he used a hooked knife from his hip-bag to cut them free of their thorny vines. He had dropped a dozen thick bunches into his bag and was thinking of where he might most profitably search for custardroot when he lifted a broad leaf and was startled to see a man lying there.

The man, who was beardless, dark-skinned, and young, was either dead or asleep. In either case, Rividius decided to leave him be. But as he was about to lower the covering leaf, the man's eyes opened, and Rividius saw at once that this was not a man. The dark, lucent eyes that gazed up at him were searchless—not vapid or vague but vividly gazing directly through him into some more stark reality. They were the eyes of a voor.

Rividius yelped his surprise. Before his tired muscles could jerk him away, the voor whispered, "Help me, man —please. Help me."

Rividius had not survived three centuries on Nabu by being helpful to strange humans, let alone voors. Voors were a new phenomenon among the worlds. They had appeared about a century ago right in the midst of the human population. In the sense that they were born into human families, they were distorts—but, in fact, they were aliens from a world called Unchala. They had evolved into energy patterns in the parallel cosmos where Unchala was located, and they wandered among the universes as radiation, usurping the physical forms of creatures wherever they went. Most voors were born in the vicinity of lynks, where energy from the Overworld was thought to leak. Since arriving, they had been warning people to get out of Chalco-Doror. They were the only trustworthy guides in the Overworld now that the Ordo Vala were no more than a blurry legend. The Saor-priests, who had regained prominence as world leaders after the tech-culture in Doror collapsed, hated the voors. They warned that the voors were trying to depopulate Chalco-Doror so that they could make the worlds their own—which never made much sense to Rividius since the voors seemed pretty eager to get out themselves. At least, those that lived to maturity did. Most voors were slain as infants the very day their parents realized what they had birthed. Those who survived were the children of people who loved life in all its human forms more than they feared the Saor-priests. Whole families were massacred if they were caught rearing or harboring voors. Yet there must have been a lot of families out there with more love than fear of voors, because there was no dearth of the creatures. Even in Rividius' secluded burg, voors had turned up in the lanes and wynds secretly counseling families to come with them into the Overworld. Some families had gone. But most had gone directly to the Saor temple in the next valley and brought back with them the bald, black-robed priests, who searched brusquely through all the houses. By then the voors had usually moved on.

Rividius saw his own face staring at him wide-eyed, a suede face, soft and red-whiskered—and he yelped again even as he realized that he was seeing himself through the voor's eyes. They were telepathic. His cry broke the bond, and he saw again the black man below him. He looked to be in pain. Sweatdrops like roe beaded his brow. One of Rividius' wives had been black, and he could not help but think that this youth could be one of his own.

"Where're you hurt, son?" he heard himself asking and was surprised at his own voice, because he was not a man to take chances. He had a young girl to rear and would never think of doing anything to jeopardize her well-being. Yet here he was stooped over a voor. Was this some alien trick?

"I've been snake-bitten," the voor said. "My right ankle. Can't move."

Rividius let the frond fall back in place, stood up, and walked over to the tarn. He wanted to put some distance between himself and the alien and see if he still felt the same compassion he had experienced while staring into the young man's hurt face. He had to know he was listening to his heart and not some telepathic command. But even as he had stood up, he knew the truth. He bent, cleared the slick surface of algae, and soaked a bandana in the night-cooled water. Then he went back to the voor and with his hooked knife cut away the fronds hiding him.

"When'd the snake bite you?" he asked, rolling up the man's pant leg and frowning to see the purple-glossed swelling above the ankle. The man was wearing rope sandals. "Land o' night! What kind of fool are you to walk these woods without boots?"

"A dying fool," the voor answered. "I feel like a boulder's on my chest. A white snake struck me during the night, when I came through this patch to get water to drink. I saw it crawl away, glowing like a lux-tube."

"A what?"

"It was shining in the dark."

"Fire snake," Rividius acknowledged, rummaging in his hip-bag. "You're lucky the ragheads didn't find you here helpless like this. You'd be halfway to scat by now." He removed a knob of brown root from his bag and wrapped it in the wet bandana. "Suck on this. It'll loosen the hold on your lungs a bit. You're damn lucky the fire snake was alight. She was too interested in breeding to pump too much venom into you. If she had been dull and not at all eager to find a mate, she'd have taken the extra second or two to kill you."

The voor rooted at the medicinal nub and felt the vivid strength of the medicine penetrate the flesh of his mouth and throat. While he worked at it, Rividius roamed the edge of the tarn until he found two saplings of the correct size for a litter. He cut the saplings down, stripped them, and lashed them with bines and creeper rope.

A scream came from the rainbowberry patch. Rividius grabbed his rifle and dashed back to the voor. The patch was swarming with gullets, big-mawed, frog-skinned, legless amphibians that usually ate rodents and giant waterbugs but were not averse to chewing off toes, fingers, ears, or whatever fleshy human parts their needletoothed jaws could fasten about. Rividius smashed several of them with the stock of his rifle, and the others fled.

Before they could return, Rividius brought over the litter he had made. "The ride down is a bumpy one, but the medicines you need I have at home."

"Leave me here. You will endanger yourself if others see you with me."

"Just keep your eyes closed and nobody will think you're anything but a snake-bit man. By the way, my name is Riv. What's yours, son?"

"Jess."

"All right, Jess. Hold on tight now—and when we get into town, for Mugna's sake, don't stare nobody in the face."

Rividius dragged Jess down the forest trail, around the well, and along the red slate avenue. People were up and about by the time the two of them came down the hillside, and several of the men on their way to the terrace fields helped carry the litter to Riv's house.

"Not like you to be dragging strangers out of the hills," one of the men said as they laid the boy on the verandah where the ragheads had devoured the angel. The ragheads were gone and only a smudge remained where they had feasted.

"Goll, he's no stranger. This is one of my own from an earlier wife. You ask Pao about my third wife and you'll hear more'n you want to know. He's come from the north to try his hand in my field."

Leaf listened impassively to her husband's lies until the rising light called the men off to their day's work on the terraces. When Jess finally opened his eyes at Riv's word, she almost shrieked. "Mugna! He's a voor!"

"He'll be a corpse soon if we don't brew that anti-venom syrup right now. A fire snake hit him in the night. We've got maybe six hours before the paralysis locks in."

"But, Riv, he's a voor."

"A voor I found. I'm not having him die on my hands."

"I didn't know you were gentle on voors."

"Me neither. But now that we know, let's not waste any time."

Leaf set her young girl to boiling water, and she gathered the necessary herbs from the root cellar for the antitoxin, while Riv administered what they had of it in their cupboard.

The larding they had planned to do did not get done that day, but the voor's life was spared. Three days later he was walking about, helping with the chores. Rividius had him wear dyed goggles that he had bought years before from a wandering tinker. The goggles were good for seeing auras, and Riv had used them to amuse his friends. When Pao asked, he explained that his kin had eye trouble. But already people were getting suspicious. Riv's third wife had died in a flash plague a century ago, and no one had heard anything about survivors other than Riv.

"You must come with me," Jess insisted as he had from the first day they took him in. "I will lead you through the Overworld to safety—to a world . . ."

"Where the land is fertile and my family will prosper,"

Rividius completed for him. "I know you mean well, Jess, but you'd best go ahead without us. This town has been my home for too long now. My roots are too tangled to just pull them up. You're strong enough now to go on your own."

"What happened to me at the tarn could happen again," the voor said.

"Not with the boots I've given you. A raghead would get a jaw cramp biting through them steel studs. You go on now."

"But some other trouble may befall me. You know these woods. I was reared in the north caverns. If the Saor-priests had not slaughtered my clan, if the nearest lynk were not in this direction, I would not be here now. What has brought us together must carry us forth."

"Why ever? You just go ahead. The lynk you want is three valleys over. No one lives there. People are afraid of it. So you won't have any trouble with us humans once you clear this valley and the next. Just keep to the high trails. And keep those goggles in place."

"But these worlds are dying."

"Not in my lifetime, Jess."

"But your children's and theirs. *You* must think of their future—or there will be none for them."

Rividius declined. The fact was, Leaf would not budge, though Riv would have been happy indeed to leave the life of hardship in the hamlet for a world of fertile soil easy to work. When the voor realized that his benefactor would not go, he prepared to leave—but even as he was tying his boots a knock resounded from the front door and it opened before anyone could answer it.

Pao entered, stooped and shriveled as the stump of a gnarly tree, her thrust-jawed face swinging from side to side so her one good eye could take in the whole room. She was wearing her gossip-twisted smile, the one she had never used on Riv and Leaf before because she had had nothing on them. Now she looked as if she had just discovered that grin. "Your kin Jess going somewhere?" she asked through a cackle.

"Just up to my field, Pao—if that's any business of yours."

Jess kept his back to the crone until he had retrieved his goggles from the wash bucket, dried them, and put them on.

"Bright day today, Jess," she said, and cackled again. "No need for them goggles."

"The light hurts my eyes," he answered.

"I'll bet that's so," Pao said, edging into the room and waving Riv back to his seat at the kitchen table when he moved to rise. "I'll bet it is."

Leaf and Kaina had been outside digging in the vegetable patch when Pao arrived, and they did not know she was there when the young girl rushed in blurting with news: "Pa—there's priests coming down the road! The bald men are here!"

Riv lunged to his feet and went to the front window. Sure enough, half a dozen Saor-priests were at the far end of the street, strolling his way, blessing the people who had gathered to greet them.

"I went and invited them to bless your kin now that he's moved in with you," Pao announced, showing all the brown pegs of her teeth. "Saor loves those who acknowledge him, so they say."

"Kind of you, Mother Pao," Riv said. "But Jess and us won't be waiting for them. Our faith is in our work and we have enough of that waiting for us on the terraces. Leaf, take Kaina out."

Riv turned to get his rifle, which was leaning in the kitchen corner, but Pao scuttled toward it faster than he had ever seen her move. In a flash, she had the gun trained on them. "Don't any of you budge a smidge or I will certainly use this." The iron clamp of her jaw assured them that she would, and they stood very still. "Oh, you righteous people who hide your shadows, you think you'll never be found out. But I found you out. This Jess is not your kin, Rividius. Take those goggles off, child, and let's see who you really are." She aimed the gun at the young boy. "I said take them off."

Jess complied. And when the crone saw his depthful gaze, her cackle sizzled like lightning. "I knew it. I knew it at once. He's a voor!"

"Pao," Rividius pleaded. "We never caused you any trouble. We take your milk even when it's sour. I've been elbow to elbow with your kin in the fields, many, many a year now. So you let us go."

"And lose the bounty on a voor?" Her weathered face

narrowed maliciously. "Rividius, you sit back down and take what fate you've earned."

Rividius did not sit; in fact, he edged forward. He could not bear to live to see his family killed—and that, he knew, was what the Saor-priests would do before they killed him. Better to die now and spare himself that horror.

At that instant, the voor leaped for the old woman. He never had a chance to reach her before she fired. Old and one-eyed as she was, she was too alert with the excitement of her triumph to be taken off guard. She fired the rifle— and the rusty old weapon exploded in her hands, kicking her against the kitchen wall and dropping her lifeless to the floor.

The explosion brought the Saor-priests running. But when they burst into the house and found the crone dead, her bowels spilled in her lap, the house was otherwise empty. They rushed into the back yard, but by then the family they were called to inspect had fled into the woods. The priests gave chase. Far into the forest they pursued them, yet they found no one. Rividius knew this forest better than anyone except the crone who lay dead in the kitchen, and the voor who was with him could sense the hunters long before they came into sight. Between the two of them, there was no chance of the family's capture.

Four days later, wearied and scraggly from hard running and short naps in the forest duff, Rividius, Leaf, Kaina, and Jess arrived at a lynk shining blue in a dark grove of ramose old trees lit with rain. They paused briefly before the lynk and stared up at mauve ploughlands of clouds.

"Will the world where we are going be as beautiful?" Kaina asked the voor.

Jess smiled and lowered his searchless eyes from the mumped clouds and the vaporous stars to the humans who had cared for him. "We will make it so."

Valdëmiraën

At land's edge, under the shrieking gulls and the diamonded brightness of the galaxy, the Vanoi danced. The women, in their ankle-length silk dresses and their long hair piled atop their heads, leaned back into the strong arms of their fishermen and kicked their bare feet at the sky. The men, their hair spiked with sea-kelp pomade, the brass buttons on their brown velvet jackets shining in the starlight, lifted their women high and hooted to the harp and fife music. The weekly Strand Dance was at the height of its star-kick frenzy when the tambourine girls, who were supposed to dash along the surf's margin and find starfish and periwinkles for the candy prizes, came screaming back. A dead man had rolled in on the curling waves.

The women threw their shawls about the girls and bustled them behind the orchestra while the men and the boys sloshed into the shallows and dragged the naked, kelp-strewn man to shore. He was not dead, but neither did he rouse to life immediately. The biggest of the men sat on his chest and bounced until the drowned man spit water and gasped awake. The Vanoi men sat him upright and covered his nakedness in the sand until a blanket was brought from the dunes picnic. The whole village gathered as they lifted the man in a locked-arm grasp and carried him to the driftwood fire.

Cucumber brandy revived the man somewhat, and he gawked with great bewilderment at the townsfolk. He was a striking human specimen, tall, long-boned, with skin pale as a seashell, and a beardless face like a statue's. No one recognized him, though anyone who had seen him even once would not have forgotten him. He understood their concerned questions and answered, or tried to. His language was an archaic version of their own, and he was understood best by the village teacher, Widow Tacci, who had studied history in the Archives of the Western Limb. Soon it became clear that even he did not know who he was or how he had come to be near-drowned in the Bay of Frascatorious under the mewling gulls of the Silver Sea.

The Vanoi called him Red for his coppery-bright hair, which he wore cropped in a strange fashion, shorn at the temples, crested on top and longer at the back. After he was fully revived, they put him in a sand-sled and carried him among the dunes to their littoral village beneath the giant east wall of the cliffs called Dreadfully High. There he was housed by Widow Tacci in her husband's abandoned net-shop, which had been given over to the crabs and seeping sand when he died in a boating accident six years earlier.

Red's old-fashioned way of talking and his pulchritude won the affection of the Vanoi, and they eagerly helped him find a place among them. Widow Tacci gave him her husband's clothes, which had to be let out to fit his larger frame but then granted him a distinguished appearance, the humble net-weaver's slacks and singlet contrasting boldly with his noble features. He proved almost inept in the dinghies the village used for fishing, his body too large for the small, spry boats; and he was a clumsy weaver of nets. However, he willingly lent his strength to the plough and served usefully in the fields. He was an uncomplaining worker, virtually silent, since he was so poorly understood, and the laconic field-workers easily accepted him as one of their own.

All the women strove for his attention, gracing him with garments and baked goods and urging their men to invite him to their households for dinner. But he seemed remote from affairs of the heart, though the village's most beautiful women, married and not, offered him every opportunity to exercise his passion. Even he did not understand the obscure sadness that misted through him when women brushed against him and invited him for garden walks. The men, who had seen that he was a whole man when they had retrieved him from the sea, jibed him for not availing himself of this amorous bounty. He joked back that with his name and his history he had also forgotten his heart.

This was not entirely true, for there was one young woman in the village who stirred a mysterious, sad joy in him. She was the town's imp, childlike and mischievous, tying her skirts up like trousers, laughing noisily during the solemn prayer sessions before the weekly Strand Dance, exposing herself to the schoolchildren, sometimes sitting catatonic in the middle of the cobbled wharf road when the fish-catchers came back. She ate when she was hungry, anything that pleased her, and she slept wherever she desired, at any time.

The village tolerated the Imp, as she was one of their own, but mostly she was simply ignored. Her parents had given up all hope of curing her with the traditional root remedies and cold-water therapies and let her run wild. Their last attempt to steady her had been to listen to a wandering lens-grinder, who claimed that brain disorders were common among people with sight problems. From him they purchased a lengthy eye-exam and finally spectacles for her, which she received with much pride and care.

Red was fascinated by the Imp. He tried to talk with her, and, to the astonishment of the Vanoi, she listened without leering or drooling. She identified with Red's difference from the others, and when he was with her she behaved as demurely as other young women. After his attention to her began, she dressed better, stopped barking at the children, and no longer fell into sit-down trances. Her enormously grateful parents had Red to dinner most nights and gave their blessing to the long beachcombing strolls he took with their daughter.

When Red was with the Imp, whom everyone now called by her given name, Maretta, a peacefulness pervaded him. Yet it was incomplete. After Red's long day in the fields, they swam together in the Bay of Frascatorious, then lay on the sandbanks staring up at the pounding stars and the slim horns of the planets. They talked very little, but they laughed a lot together—at the antics of the bright eels that ate the peas they threw for them, at the sidewise dances of the crabs avoiding the screaming gulls, at each other's goofiness among the waves. And when their play was done and the galaxy's last arm lowered toward night, he would meticulously clean her wireframe glasses with his shirt and put them on her carefully.

Yet something was wrong. She had sensed this from the very first. She understood that she was not right for him or for anyone. But for a while, for the time that he regarded her as a whole woman, worthy of care, she acted the role for him—though that was not easy for her. The irascible urges to shout during the silence of prayers, to make the

children shriek and the adults groan, still thrived in her—
and, worse, the sleepiness that claimed her at odd moments still swelled in her blood with its own tides. But
knowing Red was there for her and for her alone, she did
not give in to it. And the sleepiness built up in her. It
mounted like a floodtide, until, one day, she knew she
would succumb. She could pretend no more. Neither
could she bear to disappoint the one man who saw her as a
person. During the night rains, with an onshore wind driving the warm torrent across the peaked roofs and along the
cobbled streets, she marched victoriously to the Bay of
Frascatorious; fully clothed, she swam through the break-
ers, swam hard toward the Silver Sea, driving all the
strength out of her body, leaving only the sleepiness to
offer the dark depths.

Red wept like a child when the fish-catchers brought her
bloated body to shore the next day. After her death barge
was ignited and set adrift beyond the breakwater, Red left
the Vanoi. He wandered inland, wanting to go far from his
grief. Widow Tacci followed and caught up with him on
the slopes of Dreadfully High. "You do not want to go that
way," she called to him where he stood on a boulder-
strewn path etched into the cliff-face. "That leads to
Darkhole. Those who go there always get sick and die. The
ancient city of N'ym was once there. It left behind all its
illness before giving itself to the night."

Widow Tacci's words struck through Red's grief to a
deeper loneliness. He picked his way down from the narrow path and confronted her. "N'ym." His blue stare
brightened. "That name. I've heard it before."

"It is famous in legend."

"The City of the Sky."

"Yes." She called up all her memories of N'ym from her
time in the Archives. "The people who lived there
were—"

"Aesirai," Red answered for her. He turned quickly and
stared hard into the teetering heights. "The City of the Sky
was perched there, on the first plateau. Down here were
the hamlets, where the workers lived. The Vanoi must be
descended from those people."

"You speak as though you know."

Red frowned, trying to feel more. "I don't know. I—" He

gazed up again, then beyond to the mists on the farthest cliffs. "Up there, there is something I must see. I don't know what it is. But I must go."

"It is dangerous, Red. The Darkhole sends winds along the cliffs that sicken people and kill them. Their hair falls out, and they die retching."

"Radiation sickness. Fusion charges severed N'ym's pylons so its ramstat engines could thrust it starward."

"I don't understand," Widow Tacci said but recognized the truth in his words from the clarity of his features. He was remembering.

"*I* am Aesirai," he said, and the thunder of his voice nearly collapsed him. The memories were there—he could see the glassy spires and minarets, the broad plazas, park glades, and hillside houses with their hanging gardens—but they connected with emptiness.

Widow Tacci thought Red was going to swoon. His lids fluttered, his mouth hung open. Then the muteness of unknowing returned. "Come back to the Vanoi with me, Red. There, we will figure this all out."

"No. Maretta is dead. I can't bear to go back." He swung his gaze along the broken wall of cliffs. "I will go that way, away from N'ym, yet upward. My memory, if it is anywhere, is up there."

Widow Tacci let him go. There was no point in following him. He was telling the truth, strange and wholly unbelievable as that was. He was Aesirai, a legend washed up out of the Silver Sea from the far past. Better to let him go, like all myths, to find his own way by and to his own reckoning.

Chan-ti Beppu returned to the Eyelands on Valdëmiraën. Buie led her there through the lynks with Pahang, Nila, and Worm. Pahang retained some of the temporal torque that he had picked up from his travels with Ned O'Tennis, and Buie used him to core the group so that they would stay together in the timerush through the Overworld. They arrived in the Eyelands five hundred years after Ned had died, in time for the seventh and last return of Know-Where-to-Go to Chalco-Doror.

When Gai had arrived on Sakai and learned about Ned's death, she had reached down through the mud and wild stones of the Aesirai's grave to the very stasis of the corpse, the bone and rag-rot flesh, thinking to inspire the carcass with her own plasma force. The zombie would retain its temporal torque, she figured, and they could go ahead with their plan to jump forward in time and surprise the zōtl hiding in the maze of grottoes under Know-Where-to-Go. But when Chan-ti saw the grave buckling and realized what the Rimstalker was doing, she screamed with rage, unholstered the laserbolt pistol she had been given on Elphame, and would have blasted Gai's plasma shape had the Rimstalker not immediately withdrawn and gone invisible.

Gai's strategy then had been to convince Pahang to continue the fight against the zōtl. The Malay was eager to avenge the death of his friend, and, despite the protests of Nila, who had become fond of him and wanted him to stay among the Free, Pahang agreed. After Chan-ti had calmed down and her grief loosened, she was the one who came up with the idea of entering Know-Where-to-Go through Saor's Forest in the Eyelands of Valdëmiraën.

The Rimstalker was waiting for them when they arrived. Her anxiety had ripened to fear in the intervening two days of range-time that she had spent in her Form, vainly trying to override the lockforce of the static-generator. She had hoped that she could possibly reprogram her Form to ignore the static interference and unlock from the sleepod, but the deeper she probed into the Form's intrinsic functions, the more confused she became. At one point, she triggered a response from Genitrix:

> *"From the crest of despair*
> *in the forsaken hour*
> *at the point of death*
> *our naked need circles."*

Hope flared in Gai then—but no other response was forthcoming. The fluke convinced her that Genitrix was still intact inside the coma of their communication block. If Gai could get free in time, she believed, Genitrix would still be able to pilot them back to the range.

Gai was equally hopeful about Lod. Though she had not been able to communicate with her radiant machine intelligence, the Rimstalker knew that he was functioning:

Since Dreux's destruction, no other planets had abandoned their orbits. The debris of Dreux had impacted on many worlds and shaken their paths, but the system held together, testimony to Lod's continued resilience. Numerous assaults on Perdur to liberate Lod had been launched by Gai's human allies, but none had trespassed the zōtl's lethal traps. Neither had any of Gai's quest champions been able to penetrate the zōtl's maze on Know-Where-to-Go. And now there was no time left. Soon the trigger planet would orbit past its critical point, all the accrued gravitational resonance would be squandered, and collapse to the range would become impossible.

"You are my last hope," Gai told the humans who arrived in the Eyelands out of Saor's Forest. She had assumed a human shape for the occasion, a snow-skinned female with gem-facet eyes and prolix hair black as night. "We must hurry."

Chan-ti shuddered to see again the greensward and the stone steps that led into the cliff-face under the ruins of Caer, where she had first met Ned O'Tennis. The skirt of the forest had changed somewhat in the intervening two thousand years. Giant mushrooms crowded between the trees, and lianas with phosphorescent blossoms shone like haloes in the depths. No Foke were anywhere in sight. But there, among shrubs with leaves like bright sapphires, was the covert where she and Ned had made love—it seemed like only days ago. A bleat of grief resounded in the hollow of her chest, and she turned away.

Pahang and Nila talked in hot whispers while Worm explored the tall blue grass fringing the forest. Nila wanted to go with them, but Pahang thought it too dangerous.

"Danger is everywhere now," Gai said. "There is no safe place in all the worlds—and all are doomed if the zōtl keep my Form in bondage."

Buie arranged the order of march and placed Worm and Nila in the center, Pahang at the back, and himself and Chan-ti at the point. The Rimstalker flew ahead to avoid staying too long in the Overworld, where her energies would only loop back on themselves and disrupt their trek.

The journey through the forest was no different for Buie than any of his Overworld sojourns. He ably read the timelines by the misty radiance of the Milky Way's horizonlight, and so led the group among the mammoth trees toward Know-Where-to-Go. Luminous bats whirred in the total blackout of the sky, breezes of blue butterflies whirled out of the tattered mists, bird chimes blinked, and slinky shadows paced their progress from the firefly-studded heights of the forest canopy.

During rest periods, after foraging and eating, Buie wrote in his annals, Pahang and Nila nestled, and Chan-ti told Worm Foke tales. The boy's presence soothed Beppu's sorrow. The child was the emblem of the children she would never have, of all the children among all the worlds who needed for them to succeed. Whenever the lament for Ned grew too loud in her, she looked to Worm and was reassured. Gai had promised to save them all, every human in Chalco-Doror, if her Form were freed. That was a mission greater than her remorse, and she gave herself to it with all the passion that fate had frustrated in her.

Red climbed the cliffs of Valdëmiraën, hugging the rockwalls along the fogroads, crawling the narrowest ledges like a snake, moving upward above the fluorescent lowlands and the shining sea. At last, the land opened before him. He stopped at the brink and gazed down to where Darkhole smoked with radioactive mists. He remembered the City of the Sky that had once perched there—long ago in his diminished memory. Clearly, he could see the lyric streets and alleys he had haunted as a youth. Yet he could not bring to mind his own name.

He turned about, and a strange terrain opened before him. Evening's dark violet limned a forest horizon, where glowing kites flitted in the breeze. Looking closer, he saw they were not kites but eerie, limbless creatures with translucent bodies and broad-stretched faces. *Seraphim,* the thought came to him. Between him and the forest, grasslands shimmered in the galactic light. Two of the seraphim blew closer over the tall grass, guiding him toward a final bluff.

Red approached the two wavery beings and was deep in the chest-high grass before noticing that they were not seraphim at all but humans glowing in the dark, drifting like smoke—ghosts. They blew closer, waving him on, and then disappeared. His heart rattled.

At the bluff, Red distinguished tall doorways set in walls so ancient they looked like natural rock formations. The mortar between the rocks had dissolved to loose sand, and much of the wall had collapsed, leaving many of the big green-rusted doors standing alone. From out of the tasseled grass, a few meters away, an old woman popped. Red jumped with surprise.

"Welcome to the Back Gates, Ned O'Tennis."

The crone's voice shook him as violently as though a giant's hand had grabbed him. The sound of his name sundered his amnesia, and memory stretched through him. He quaked where he stood, barely grasping the reality. He remembered N'ym and the war with the rebels, his own queasiness about war, and his solitude in the Eyelands, where he was now, he thought—though this was not as he recalled. Where were the ruins of Caer? And Chan-ti Beppu, the woman in whom he had found himself, where was she now? Dizziness almost claimed him as he saw again N'ym roaring into the sky and his own plunge into the sea, into his servitude to Squat on the very beach that would become the Vanoi's. And he remembered Pahang and the Rimstalker and the quest for the O'ode. Chan-ti Beppu had come through the Overworld to save him, to save herself, for they were indeed one and had found themselves only in each other. The truth of their love had endured even his amnesia he realized now, finally fitting bespectacled Maretta into her rightful place in his memory. She had been the most he could find of his mate among the Vanoi—and she had never been his mate at all.

The fullness of this recall came upon him in an instant and left him wobbling at the brink of his last memory among the Free, futilely firing a laserifle at his own strohlkraft as it dove to kill him.

"Yes," the old crone said. "Your strohlkraft killed you. The scyldar Neter Col burned you to a tarry corpse. Remember."

And he did. He remembered seeing his charred body crawling with sparks. He was floating above it in a withering coldness. But he had not died then. Though the cold had pummeled him to the drumming limits of pain, verging on blackout, he had not lost consciousness. Nappy Groff had been there. He had seen the old man in a frosty light, pressing close, keeping him warm, urging him to stay calm, to still his racing thoughts and sink deep into the cold, deeper to where he became the cold and could endure. Another ghost had been there, too. He recognized that ghost from the body he had buried on Ras Mentis with the explosive-rigged pack. Spooner Yegg was the man's name—Chan-ti's real father, the ghosts had told him when he himself was a ghost in their care. They had guarded him from his blithering ignorance, which would have destroyed his body of light. But, with them beside him, the cold could not break him. They had held him alert and had taught him how to float in the eerie brightness, to wait until his body could be regrown, shaped again by the wisdom in the ground. What had they called that wisdom?

"Genitrix," the crone said. "Genitrix is the Rimstalker's machine mind, which rebuilt you, cell by cell, until you were ready to wear your body again. Then you were sent through a Tryl lynk and released into the Silver Sea of Valdëmiraën."

"And you? Who are you?"

"I am the Weed Woman. Genitrix built me in the beginning, and I am here now for the end, that I may lead you to where you may bring the end to us."

"Me? Why me? Why am I here?"

"Chance and choice are one, Ned O'Tennis. Our fates choose us even as we choose them. Symmetry is everything in this cold universe. The coldness makes it so. Fate and will complete each other." The Weed Woman's knobby fingers held up a blackened coin—Chan-ti's sender chip. "From your grave," she said and tucked the chip in the pocket of his vest. "A token from Genitrix." She pointed to a corroded door that was open a crack. "Squeeze through there, and you will find your own way."

"Where will it lead me?"

"To Chan-ti Beppu, of course. If you hurry, you may get to her before the scyldar that killed you serves her the same fate."

The warmth that had come round his heart went cold, and he jolted toward the monolithic door.

The Weed Woman held up a basket and called after him, "Wait! You must be hungry after your long journey. Have a breadfinger—a mushroom muffin—some groat cakes."

Ned O'Tennis ignored her and ran hard to meet the risks of his fate.

Buie announced their arrival in Know-Where-to-Go. The sojourner, tracking the Rimstalker's timeline, had led them to a natural lynk that connected directly with the grotto where the static-generator sat.

Pahang hugged Nila, whispered his fidelity, and then, as arranged earlier, went through first so that his temporal torque would not affect the others. As soon as he disappeared, the others followed and found him waiting for them in a hexagonal tunnel whose walls were bossed with faintly glowing Tryl arabesques. The residual torque that Pahang had acquired from his travels with Ned had apparently already exhausted itself. He and Nila embraced, and Chan-ti looked away, wanting no nostalgia to weaken her intent.

Buie, Pahang, and Chan-ti took out their pistols, and everyone peered down the tunnel. A broken smell rode a faint breeze. Far ahead, a sharp hissing echoed, muted by distance. The sibilance mounted gradually as they walked, becoming a grating roar after they had turned several bends. When the tunnel finally ended, the air boomed with blaring jolts of noise. They crouched in the mouth of the tunnel, feeling the thick heat of the planet's interior and smelling the fearsome scent of a thunderstorm.

Before them was a grotto big as a cathedral lit by the Tryl's coiling lux cables and the brambly lightning from a massive, angular tower made of black plates. The blue arcs of voltage jumped among the plates randomly, jarring their hearing and casting shifting, unpredictable shadows through the cavern of fang-like rock drippings.

A green bolt of light zipped over their heads. Another struck the rock wall beside them and spit chunks of stone. "Zōtl!" Pahang yelled, and the three pistols fired rapidly toward where the laserbolts had come from. A high-pitched whistle shrieked from the dark, piercing the electric roar, and a spidery shape fell in bright rags of flame to the cavern floor.

"They know we're here now!" Chan-ti shouted. "Let's move!"

They scrambled down a gravelly declivity and had gone

only a few paces when the tunnel behind them lit up with laserfire.

The zōtl had been surprised before. Other humans had tried to invade from Saor's Forest, and all had easily been dispatched by neurotox flushed into the tunnel and the cavern. The spiders used their makeshift technology to flood the conduits to the cavern with nerve gas. But Genitrix, who had been waiting silently, detached in her machine aloofness, recognized the beauty of the moment; and at last she asserted her internal processes to reverse the flow of the neurotox and to seal the corridors where the spiders had their stations. The rumbling of avalanches shook the grotto. Dust and pebbles shot from the corridor, where the travelers had entered. The zōtl were trapped in Genitrix's maze and instantly killed by their own death gas.

The four zōtl who remained entered from a redrock dolmen perched high on the cavern wall opposite the sparking static-generator. Laserbolts smashed at the stalagmites behind which the humans cowered. Buie returned fire and lanced a zōtl, kicking it into a small fireball.

The three other zōtl split up. Spidery twitches closed in on the crouching humans from three sides. Their flights were too jerky to allow the humans to pick them off until they got closer—but by then one or more of the zōtl would surely hit them.

"Stay here!" Buie shouted above the electrical roar. He was the best shot of the three, well trained over his long life in the Ordo Vala, and he figured to draw the spiders' fire and use their tracers to mark them. He rolled toward another fang of rock, and laserbolts slashed above him, shearing the tip off the stalagmite where he came to rest. The shattered rock bashed him to the ground, unconscious.

Pahang and Chan-ti fired at where they had seen laserlight, and the zōtl swooped toward them, blasting the pinnacle they hid behind. Pahang stood and fired at the source of the tracer light. A zōtl flared into flames. But the two others trained on him in a crossfire. Nila grabbed for him, pulled him away as the green bolts cut the space where he had stood. The brisance of the smashed rock threw them both to the ground. His pistol spun free of his grip and was struck by a laserbolt that smashed it into a splash of hot metal, searing his hands and hair and glaring him blind. Nila and Worm tugged him back behind the stalagmite.

The two remaining zōtl swooped down, firing. Bolts punched the rock on all sides, kicking rock chips as they narrowed in. Chan-ti darted into the open, firing as fast as she could at the source of the laserbolts. One of her shots struck a zōtl, which cometed to the ground and curled up under a sputtering blaze. The other arced around to avoid Chan-ti's wild fire. It swung erratically and returned fire, making Chan-ti leap back.

She curled up against the stalagmite, and her gaze rested on the directional finder that she wore in the belt-web at her hip, the red microlights showing the direction of her lover's grave. She blinked. Instead of the alphanumeric code for Ned's grave on Sakai, the finder's lights indicated a position at the far side of the grotto. She tapped the finder, figuring it had been damaged by a flying rock chip. Before she could further examine it, the air dazzled with laserfire.

Buie roused in time to see the last zōtl spiraling toward Beppu through the glare of the electric tower. Clutching his pistol in both hands, he took aim from where he lay and fired a rapid burst. The zōtl exploded and dropped in burning shards. Buie heaved himself to his feet and raised his arms to accept Chan-ti's triumphant shout. But the next instant, the whole cavern flared blue, and Buie split apart in a sudden conflagration that shot flames from his eyeballs and mouth and hollowed his torso to a nest of venomous fire. The utility pack at his hip flung free with the impact and ripped apart, sending the pages of his annals winging among the flashing shadows.

Through the redrock dolmen, the angular batwing silhouette of a strohlkraft glided. It swooped gracefully under the stalactites, landing gear lowered, and another blue blast from its laser cannon cleared the ground before it in a concussion of shattered rock. It skidded toward a stop on the grotto floor, the smoke and rubble of its attack roiling around it like thunderheads in the lightning glare from the static-generator.

Chan-ti saw at once that the strohlkraft was swerving to

place them in its line of fire. She grabbed Worm by his shoulder, pointed at the tower of writhing voltage, and shouted, "Run there, boy! Run as close as you can to it! Go now!" Worm looked despairingly to his mother, who was crouched over Pahang. The Malay was dazed, his sight just beginning to return. Chan-ti yelled at them, "We have to run! Come on, Pahang! Now!" She grabbed Pahang's arm and yanked him upright.

They ran in a crouch among the glisteny columns of dripped rock. A laserbolt from the strohlkraft's cannon blew up the column that had covered them, and spinning shards pelted their backs. One chunk hit Chan-ti hard behind her knee, and she fell. Her pistol jumped from her grip and disappeared in the dust coiling around them. She abandoned it and let Worm help her to her feet. Squinting against the glare of the lightning and the flying grit, they dashed after Pahang and Nila into the pounding aura of the static-generator and collapsed under their effort in a tangled sprawl.

The strohlkraft sat silent, watching them with its hidden cannon but not firing. At the controls, the scyldar Neter Col's thumbs were locked above the firing buttons by the zōtl that mastered him. It dared not shoot at the humans, for the blast would damage the static-generator and release the Rimstalker.

In the petrified scyldar, in its human brain, the trapped and tormented teacher, Tully Gunther, exulted at the humans' cleverness that had bought them moments more of life and the chance to continue their fight. The zōtl in its rage was unaware of the hopeful joy of the scyldar's human brain, and Tully almost shouted aloud with pleasure at the zōtl's frustration but was restrained by the doomful certainty of what lay ahead. The scyldar would have to leave the strohlkraft to kill the humans. Infrascan revealed that they were unarmed, and Neter Col unstrapped himself from the sling, flushed with the spider's eagerness to destroy its enemies.

The strohlkraft's hatch lifted, and Neter Col stepped out into the blaring illumination. He brandished a laserbolt pistol but dared not use it except at point-blank range. He strode through the smashed rock and stepped over Buie's smoking corpse.

Buie's ghost watched him, shocked by the sight he had just had of his own body smoldering under him. He had died so swiftly, he had not realized he was dead but thought he was dreaming—until the cold set in. Glacial breath hummed through him, chilling his senses with hyperacuteness. Helpless, hopeless, he watched the scyldar stalk the humans through the lightning sheen along the base of the static-generator. There was no place for them to flee, except between the colossal plates, where the writhing energy would electrocute them.

Buie turned his attention away, afraid to see the actual kill, and noticed other presences lurking in the strobe glare of the electric tower.

Spooner Yegg and Nappy Groff appeared beside him. "Don't be afraid, sojourner," Spooner said to him, *in* him, and the spasm of fear relented. "Surely the Ordo Vala has taught you of the body of light. We feel that in you."

"Freedom is always just a mind's inch away," Nappy said with a smile of astral brightness. "Soon we will go with you out of this focking cold and into the warmth of the fields of light. But for now we need your new strength to anchor ourselves here. We've been too long away from our bodies to hold out much longer—but we can't leave yet."

"Not until we see this through to the end of the worlds," Spooner added.

"But that's a scyldar," Buie moaned. "They can't fight that thing. They have no weapons. It will kill them."

"Well it may," Nappy agreed. "But they are not without a weapon."

"Come with us," Spooner urged. "We'll show you the business of ghosts."

Buie drifted away from his corpse, and the cold sharpened. He trembled so violently, he would have flown apart but that the other ghosts pressed near. "The secret is stillness," Spooner informed him. "Keep your thoughts still. Enter the cold. Be the cold. Then you will endure."

"You will surprise yourself," Nappy agreed.

And Buie was surprised. The cold honed him to a kernel of brilliant alertness almost entirely devoid of thought. He drifted with the other ghosts across the cavern, over the predatory hulk of the strohlkraft, and into the jerking shadows at the far wall. There a shadow bled from the caved-in corridor, sharpened to the figure of a man. In the wavery light, Buie could see he had windcast hair, pale complexion, and an avian profile.

Ned O'Tennis walked into the clearing and hurried for the strohlkraft.

"That is Chan-ti Beppu's mate!" Buie stared and almost dissolved away with surprise. The cold hardened his inner-focus, and he asked, "How? I saw his grave."

"And he lay dead in it," Nappy confirmed.

"As many others have lain dead," Spooner pointed out. "until Genitrix reclaimed them. She grew his body anew, birthed him out of the earth a whole man, no different than before he was killed."

"Because," Nappy concluded, his wraith-face a tremor of happiness, "we kept his body of light whole in the cold, just as we're doing for you."

"And he didn't like it any more than you or any of us—until the warmth of his flesh reclaimed him."

The ghosts followed Ned into the strohlkraft and hovered behind him as he stood at the command console and primed the ship's laser cannon. The visor lit up with targeting cues, sighting the scyldar's black profile in its crosshairs. In a moment, Neter Col would be upon his prey, too close for Ned to fire.

Ned slammed on the strohlkraft's external lights, wanting to distract the scyldar—but in the brilliant strokes from the roaring tower, Neter Col did not notice.

With one thought among them, the ghosts knew what to do. They willed themselves before Neter Col. With trembling effort, they defied the battering cold and forced themselves to materialize in front of the scyldar.

Chan-ti, who had pushed Worm into his mother's arms and had swung herself around Pahang to face into the scyldar's black faceplate, saw Nappy, Spooner, and Buie swirl brilliantly out of the mangling light, waving and hooting like madmen in the smiting cold. The effort cost them. In a moment, their last strength drained into the wintering wind blowing from the end of time. They lingered a moment as retinal shadows, spectral mist, and she even glimpsed a wink from Spooner before they wafted away forever.

Neter Col pulled back reflexively. Tully Gunther recognized his one vindictive chance to avenge his suffering and howled angrily at the zōtl pithing his brain, *Look at the strohlkraft, deadwalker! You're sludge now!* The scyldar noticed the floodlights blazing from the strohlkraft, and the zōtl in its chest winced with alarm.

Ned saw the gap widen between the scyldar and Chan-ti and fired the laser cannon. The bolt struck Neter Col in his chest, punching through his cuirass, engulfing him in fire, and throwing him into the static-generator. The scyldar impacted so hard that his blazing body bashed through an electric plate, and a spray of red sparks gushed in a spiral up the magnetic flux lines. The collision sent a disruptive geyser of electric fire shooting through the tower, flaring luminous jets of lightning. One jet struck the top of the tower, blasting it apart. Others smashed into the grotto ceiling and walls, spinning chunks of rock across the cavern.

Ned leaped from the hatchway of the strohlkraft and ran for Chan-ti and the others, who were huddled together under the disintegrating tower. When Chan-ti saw him in the garish light, her heart almost burst, and she had to peer hard to be sure she was not deceived. She glanced at the directional finder strapped to her hip, saw its microlights pointing hard at him.

"It's Ned!" Worm shouted and ran to him. Nila shouted after her son and hurried to catch him.

Pahang rubbed his eyes, thinking his temporary blindness had maddened him.

"It is Ned," Chan-ti said to herself; she took two slow steps and then burst toward him.

Amid the flying debris, everyone collided. Ned tore himself free and herded the people ahead of him, to the strohlkraft. Chan-ti stopped to snatch at the remnants of Buie's satchel and to grab a sheaf of his pages. Slabs tumbled about them among bullets of shooting rock. Ned lifted Chan-ti upright, and they all scampered across the grotto among the flying debris and entered the strohlkraft.

Clutching each other, drunk with disbelief, they stared through the visor as the static-generator tottered inward toward a hot core of plasma fire. With an enormous roar that blotted all hearing, the tower ripped apart in a blinding dazzle. The glare died swiftly, and darkness stampeded toward them, held off by the strohlkraft's floodlights. Only a few embers lingered where the tower had stood.

The cavern shook and lit with a new light, a rubescent shine. A crevice jagged across the grotto floor, caving in walls and rolling boulders into its chasm. Everyone shouted with fright—but the strohlkraft did not budge. Despite the sundering walls and flying rock, nothing touched the ship.

From inside her Form, Gai watched her visual display brighten and the power readouts come on hotly as full control reverted to her.

"Victory is ours!" a familiar voice shouted in Gai's receptors.

"Genitrix!"

"I'm intact, Gai. I was never wholly compromised. The zōtl cut off our comm-lines, but I—"

"Genitrix—the humans who freed me are in danger."

"Not at all, Gai. I've taken the liberty of projecting a repulsive field about the frail creatures."

"And the gravity-amp?"

"Functional."

"Then let's get out of here."

Gai's Form loomed up through the split open crust of the planet, a titanic structure of spark-crawling silver plates. She seized the strohlkraft in an enormous armature and hoisted it with her. Streaming pulverized rock, they surfaced on Know-Where-to-Go beneath the vortex of the galaxy and the dusky spheres of Chalco-Doror. The Form lowered the strohlkraft to the ground, and the invisible shield protecting them vanished. Cool air whooshed in through the open hatch with the organic smell of night.

Their ears ringing with the blood humming loudly in them, the five humans gazed out of the ship's visor at the mountainous and alien shape of convoluted insectparts and viper coils.

"Scary-looking, isn't it?" a feminine voice said from behind the stunned humans. They whirled about as one and saw Gai in her human guise smiling benignly, her long black hair as wavery as though underwater, her stargleam eyes bright as laserpoints. "Better that we part like this, and you remember me as an alien that learned something of being human." Her smile gleamed like melted silver.

You freed me—and now it is finished. I can return home." he placed her radiant stare on each of them, ending with Ned. "Thank you. Before I leave, I'll see that each of you nds home. I've programmed your ship to follow the lynkanes out of here on a vector that will take you to a terrene vorld, where the Ordo Vala have gone ahead. Those humans who yet remain behind will all be gathered up and vill follow. You may want this to remember these times to our future generations." From the fulgor of Gai's raiment, sheaf of scorched and wrinkled pages appeared. Chan-ti ook them with both hands. "I gathered them as we came hrough," Gai said. "They're a little smudged but legible. ou'll find yourselves favorably represented in them."

"What are they?" Ned asked.

Chan-ti added them to the sheaf she had picked up from eside Buie's body and held the complete manuscript to er chest. "The last legends of Earth."

"Oh, yes," Gai added, the flight-pod lights shining in carlet bloom through her face. "Genitrix has logged into our computer all the technical information you and the thers will need to build a ramstat civilization. In a world vithout zōtl, love will set the limits."

"Live love and learn," Chan-ti quoted from *The Book of Horizons.*

"Love—" Pahang blurted, with the sudden memory of osing his youngest wife to his thief-brother in his first life. Love is tricky. Lah."

"Your species seems good at learning tricks," the alien aid, biting her lower lip with teeth like sparks. "And, as a iniversal saying goes, that's your problem."

Worm squinted fiercely at the hot-eyed phantom. "Who re you?" he asked. Nila put an arm about her boy and ushed him.

Gai laughed, and her features blurred inside a nimbus of lue flame. "Just an old soldier, child—waving goodbye. ou won't see me again. Go proud into the mystery, my riends."

Gai's shape wavered into spectral lines of force, like etrified tree-rings patterned in the air, and she was gone. he hatch closed on its own, and the ramstat cells charged p.

As the strohlkraft disappeared into the mountain fissure

of a natural lynk, the Rimstalker let her telempath
strength go a little way with them. Pahang and Ni
strapped themselves into the same sling with Worm ar
stared with hot amazement at the bright plasm of th
Overworld's teeming: Time-floes, oiled with mirror-su
face whorls, drifted in mute immensity through the gra
ness of infinity. In their own sling, Chan-ti Beppu and Ne
O'Tennis saw only each other. With a touch of their finge
tips and a whisper of shared breath, their loneliness ende

Home in the Nightmare

From inside her Form, Gai pulsed at full power to Lo
In Perdur, Lod's suspended torso then gleamed hotte
incandescing first dull red, then bright crimson, orang
solar yellow, and finally whitehot. Limbs materialized ar
the silhouette of a head in a silvery corona appeared. Th
phanes snapped and shriveled away. Out of the vau
above, laserbolts slashed at the revived plasma shape. Lc
breathed in the energy like a spring breeze. All power w
his now. The last of the zōtl in Chalco-Doror squirted awa
through the darkness, darting for the ghost cave and th
Overworld beyond. Lod burned each of them in midfligh
and their bodies fell in twitching flames and dusted th
ground as cinders.

"Saor!" Lod bellowed. He pointed at the archways
contorted human bodies, and the atrocities glared sui
bright and frittered to ash. He threw flames into the gho
cave, and the darkness blazed like a furnace and collapse
in fiery chunks. Lashing fire like a whip, he struck th
serpentcoil pillars and scorpiontail buttresses, smashir
them to a whirlwind of spinning sparks and dropping th
groined ceiling, which ignited and flared away in veils (
hot vapor. The mammoth rockwalls peeled, flowed in fu
gurant streams of lava, dissolving the vast mirror floor int
bubbling magma. At the center of the holocaust, Lc
pulsed like blood, brightening on the fuel of his anarch
"Saor!"

"Forget Saor," Gai's voice opened tranquilly in him. You are free now, Lod. Come back to your Form. The trigger planet is fast approaching endpoint. Genitrix is ready to collapse us back to the range. All our anguish is over now."

"I want Saor." The conflagration Lod had started reached the core of the Dragon's Shank, and the firehung skeleton of Perdur collapsed in a whirling apocalypse. Lod rose above it and alighted on an adjacent peak overlooking the volcanic turmoil. "I must find Saor."

"Let him go. The lynklanes are closed. He can't escape. The collapse will snuff him out."

"No, Gai. You do not understand. I cannot let him die unknowing. He is not the culprit. The zōtl virus program was never in him. It is in *me*. I have been the passive carrier all along. The program has been radiating from me. He has simply been receiving it."

"That's sadly so, Gai," Genitrix's voice emerged. "I had been trying to purge Saor for a long time before I realized that the virus was not there. It *is* in Lod. All these years in solitude, I hardly—"

"But that doesn't matter now," Gai interrupted. "We're going back to the range now. The virus program you carry will provide useful insights into zōtl strategy."

"The virus is indeed in my Form," Lod said. "That will go back with you and can be studied. But I will not return. My mind—my essence—will stay here. I must find Saor."

"I don't understand," Gai said. "If you stay, the waveform of your mind will be extincted in the collapse."

"I know. But I cannot leave Saor alone. What he did, he did unknowing."

"So why must you die?"

"He is my brother."

The visual display in Gai's Form flashed the requirements of the collapse program: The ship's parts that were to be reunited had to be locked in. Lod's and Saor's Forms were the front and back ends of the ship and had to be secured first. Once they were locked in to the program, the machine minds' plasma bodies would be shut out.

"Bring Saor with you, then," Gai said, impatiently, switching the collapse program to hold. "We'll purge you both on the range."

·"I'll not go," Saor said, speaking from the severe blackness of Mugna's polar night. He separated from the black
sky, where he had been hiding, and appeared as a human
outline in Lod's coronal aura. "I live to sustain the worlds—
worlds without end. I can't leave. I'm the benefactor of the
worlds."

"That's zōtl dogma," Gai said. "Come on, already. We
can argue about it on the range."

"No, Rimstalker. When the zōtl tried to perpetuate
Chalco-Doror, I worked with them. But when they sought
to destroy the planets in vengeance, I defied them and was
overridden. This is my place, here where I have suffered
that life may continue. Here, I am a god. On the range, I
am just a machine."

"I still say that's the zōtl program talking," Gai said,
trying to restrain her petulance. "They're dead now. And
the worlds are empty. All the humans are gone. All the
lynklanes are closed. Come home, Saor. Come home."

"Chalco-Doror is my home."

"Yes," Gai agreed, "and Chalco-Doror is our ship. Return
to your station at once. We're taking our home back to the
range."

"No. My home is here, in the nightmare you abandoned.
I belong in the coldness of space—I belong to the vacuum
that accepts my shape."

"Genitrix—purge them both, now. We've only moments
left."

"Just so, Gai. Only moments remain—not enough time
for a purge here. It'll have to wait till we get home. These
cold-set gel bodies will have to be abandoned."

"Lod, talk to Saor. Hurry. The resonance is peaking!"

"What can I tell him that you have not already said?" He
reached an arm out, and where he touched Saor, where his
energy broke apart in the microfield of the black body, a
rainbow haloed. "Saor, I will not leave you. We will meet
the emptiness together."

"I don't want your sacrifice, Lod. That's stupid. You suffered enough under the zōtl. Go to your reward and leave
me to the void."

"There is no reward for me in knowing you died by a
virus I carried."

Saor was silent. The stars ticked. The planets slid into

place. "Lod, you're a fool," Saor said then. "I've always loathed your obsequious formality, your truckling eagerness to please. And now even my death becomes an occasion for your nobility. Die then. But stop pestering me."

"Lod!" Gai called. "Let's go. It's now or never. Leave Saor."

"Farewell, Gai," Lod said. "Do not jeopardize yourself for us."

"Lod—are you certain?"

"Gai!" Genitrix cried urgently. "I have to initiate the collapse immediately!"

"Lod, I have to know. Do you need . . . this death?"

"This does not diminish your victory, Gai," Lod answered. "We are casualties of a good war. Goodbye."

"I'll remember you," Gai said—but there was no response. Genitrix had shut down Gai's Form, locking it into the collapse program. "Goodbye."

Outside, in the cold of outer space, Lod faced into Saor's blackness. It was empty—truly empty. What he had done closed in on him. "Saor—I am here."

Saor was silent, in his own trance. Lod removed his arm from Saor's shoulder and stepped back a pace, budged by what was happening, what he was doing. *I die.* The thought lanced him with its finality. "Saor—you are not alone," he said. "I could not leave you alone."

But he was alone. They were both alone in the cold and the dark—as all life out here had always been. And by that he knew he was alive.

Saor stood silent and unbowed before the boiling mass of molten rock that had been his palace, under the luminous orbs that had been his kingdom. He was given now to the void, standing alone and proud.

Lod turned away from the black shadow, stunned by Saor's isolation. Fear chilled him. Dazedly, he stared out at the great, vacuous reaches beyond his solitude. This was the abyss. Into this chasm, all life emptied. Here, everything came to nothing.

"Locked into place," Genitrix announced. A small laugh echoed from the chief machine intelligence in Gai's receptors only. "Love is tricky, isn't it?"

In the silver interior of her Form, Gai breathed deeper.
"We're set to go? What about Dreux?"

"That's been compensated for. We'll arrive on the range
minus a few hull panels but otherwise intact. At your command, we can go. The geometrodynamic resonance is at its
peak."

Gai listened to her own bloodbeat throbbing like the
pulse of a flame with the expectation of returning to the
range victorious. She sighed herself free of the fear that
had driven her and the losses that had held her back. A
strange nostalgia for the dark of outer space glimmered in
her.

Genitrix chanted:

> *Time is a changeling in the belly of the void,*
> *a weird child that takes the place of nothing.*
> *Going nowhere with its images, it plays*
> *with itself in the womb and dies being born.*

"Let's go home," Gai whispered.

Genitrix activated the magravity thrusters. In an instant,
the scattered modules of the Rimstalker ship reassembled,
contracting in an invisible, inward-spiraling flash to the
edge of the universe. And where there had been worlds
hung against the splendor of the galaxy, there was nothing.

Author's Postscript

The Last Legends of Earth is the final volume in a series I call the Radix Tetrad. My intention has been to thematically structure each novel around one of the four cardinal dimensions that define us and our world: height, depth, width, and time.

Radix, a novel about stature, employs heightened language to define standing tall, our chief physical distinction among the apes. *In Other Worlds* concerns depth and uses deepening language to plumb the interiority of experience. With *Arc of the Dream* the narrative focus spans the breadth of society in an effort to circumscribe the limits of culture, where the group refracts into individuals. Finally, here, in *The Last Legends of Earth*, language and individual character flatten before the inexorable mystery of change that we call time.

About the Author

A. A. Attanasio lives by his imagination on the world's most remote island chain. *The Last Legends of Earth* is the final volume in the Radix Tetrad, whose other titles include *Radix, In Other Worlds,* and *Arc of the Dream*.

A CREATOR'S GUIDE TO THE RADIX TETRAD

A. A. Attanasio

The Vedantic masters of ancient India claimed that the whole universe is inside us. I wrote the Radix Tetrad from that remarkable point of view, the way storytellers of old did, dramatizing the natural world in human form—only instead of sun gods and moon maidens intriguing with mortals, I wrote about aliens from other worlds confronting human beings. The story's the same: It's the hero's clash with the gods. In our psychological age, that clash is the individual's struggle to create an identity, and thus a destiny, out of the infinite flux we label reality.

The Tetrad retells the stories of the solar king and his journey into the abyss, to the home of the wind, the land of the dragon, where the creative and destructive powers collide. These timeless adventures, recast in modern form, ask the same questions that the myths do: Who are we? Is the infinite expanse of the universe really inside each of us? And, if so, what do we do with infinity?

Scientists agree that the universe itself appears infinite: Black holes collapse to singularities, which are infinitely dense; and light—the fabric of reality—has no rest mass and so is timeless. Yet few of us actually believe that we are infinite. Such a bold conception seems a delusion of grandeur to us, because we refuse to accept the basic Vedantic assumption that waking and dreaming are the same.

Radix, the first volume in the series, is about waking up to this unifying perception. The solar votive hero of the myths is reincarnated in the obese, slovenly form of Sumner Kagan, who lives in a world exposed to the strange light from an open black hole at the center of our galaxy. This naked singularity has transformed Earth into the landscape of the soul, where everything contaminates everything else: Animal and human forms bleed together into distorts, ideas from bizarre alternate universes fuse with flesh and become godminds, starlight rearranges the human genetic code and reconstructs alien sentences called voors. On this haunted Earth, everyone whom Sumner confronts is actually himself, and the world changes around him exactly as he does.

Here is an excerpt from Radix, Attanasio's Nebula Award finalist first novel. It was called "an instant classic" by The Washington Post Book World; "an exhilarating novel" by the Minneapolis Tribune.

The morning was still dark when Sumner left home in his bottle-green car. All his important possessions were wrapped in a torn shirt and thrown in the back. Zelda was fluttery with concern and tried to stop him, first with threats about her poor health and then with food. But it was no good. Sumner's dread far outstripped both his guilt and his hunger. He told Zelda he would be back later in the day, though he had no intention of ever seeing her again.

Though he was fond of his mother, he was glad that he was finally getting away from her. She was always trying to change him, and he was happy as he was. Or as he had once been, he reminded himself. From now on, it was life on the road. Zelda was gone—but then, so was his life as the Sugarat. More than security, he had lost his very identity.

His destination was Jeanlu's cottage, 189 kilometers away, on the far edge of Rigalu Flats. It was a lonely ride—lonelier still knowing that he would never be going back—but the voors had things he wanted.

He smiled, remembering his first journey outside

McClure. How old had he been then? Ten? No. It was just after his first kill. He must have been eleven.

It would be at least an hour before he reached Rigalu Flats, and it was a straight, unbroken road until then. He eased his mind back six years to the memories he had of his first lonely ride into the wilderness—

Hunger had led Sumner to the fish stalls by the river where he had hoped to scrounge a free meal. He watched closely as thick-armed men in blood-grimed aprons whacked off the heads of perch and mullet, shook out their guts, and then tossed the cut pieces onto mounds of flaked ice. He searched diligently for the misaimed chunks of meat that fell along the stalls. But the competition was too tough—large wild cats that had been bred to fend off rats—and soon he wandered out to the empty wharves to wait for the returning ships.

Watching the inky water slap the dock pilings, he thought about barbecued fish. Its imaginary aroma and flaky dark crust were so real that he didn't notice the old man until he spoke: "You want to get laid, kid?"

Sumner spun around; his eyes snapped to the old man's face. It was brown and wrinkled as a crumpled bag, the ears doughy, the hair filthy and tangled.

"What're you talking about, wheeze? I got no money for whores."

The old man stepped closer. "But you have a white card."

Sumner's heart skipped two beats. Just a week before, he had gone for his mandatory medical exam. All children at puberty were required by Massebôth law to have their genes tested. After an exhausting series of scrapings, injections, and embarrassing probes, Sumner was issued a white card—the most highly coveted genetic status. He was one in a thousand with unmangled genes.

Yet—how did this crust of a man know about his

white card? Sumner looked more closely at the old man's face. He had a straight, fierce mouth and incongruously dreamy eyes. Eventually Sumner would learn to recognize a voor by those searchless eyes. At the time, though, he thought the old man was just a river pirate. He was hard enough, with bead-rings in the tops of his ears, a black bandana across his forehead, and strange, smoky scents lufting off his clothes.

"You want to get laid, waddle? Yes or no?"

Sumner stood his ground gamely, hands on his hips, both excited by the mysterious prospect of sex and frightened by this uncanny pirate. "How do you know I have a white card?"

A shadow of a smile crossed the old man's rumpled face and softened it. "I'm a voor, waddle. I know."

Sumner's whole body clenched. Voors could craze you with a glance. They were the most alien of the distorts and known to have deep mind powers. And if those weren't good enough reasons to stay clear of them, there was a long-standing Unnatural Edict posted against them by the Massebôth. People were hanged for talking with voors.

Sumner tried to back away, but the water was behind him and there was no one else down by the wharves. Three hundred meters away the fish stalls were bustling with activity, and he realized too late that no one would hear him if he screamed.

With a whimper he lunged past the old voor and scurried down the wharf. A beat-up scavenger truck suddenly wheeled out from behind a row of tarred bollards and cut him off. A cowled man leaped out of the cab, and Sumner froze. The man's outstretched hands were blueshelled and barbed.

Distort! Sumner silently screamed. He tried to fight, but the hooded voor was eerily swift. He accurately anticipated all of Sumner's blows and cornered him between the truck and the water. Sumner's fear overwhelmed his revulsion and he went for the creature's eyes, but the voor snagged his hand in an icy grip and guided him to the back of the truck, where the old voor opened the thin metal doors. They threw him in and banged the doors shut.

Sumner raged. He had heard that voors cracked open the skulls of their victims and devoured their brains. He swung around in the tight compartment looking for a weapon. But there was nothing in the back except rust stains and dents. Screaming, he threw himself against the doors.

*   *   *

In Other Worlds and *Arc of the Dream* both begin when the solar king, in the guise of the books' two heroes, sees that all is a dream. In the mythology of science, that means facing the weird solipsism of the parallel universe theory. Carl Schirmer, the complaisant hero of *In Other Worlds*, is snatched through a subquantal black hole by alien forces to visit alternate Earths. There he must defeat his complaisance and decide which of the infinite possibilities open to him he will make his own.

I went down to Chinatown today for some dim sum and saw a Kwan Yin temple defaced with graffiti: NO BUDDHA! KILL GOD!

So I went inside and looked around. The place was empty and cluttered with trays of spent incense and shelves of offerings to the Goddess. I sat at an offering table and wrote this poem:

> NO BUDDHA only a statue, gold
> paint, wood, and a visage calm as a face
> in a womb—only incense smoke
> unwrapping in silence, a
> movement between a ghost and nothingness.

Ever try to write a story? Notice how the characters get out of hand almost at once? That's because they partake not only of our imagination but also of our will.

Regrets and expectations. That's all I am when I'm not writing. And when I do write, I am the thing the stories come through. I am less than myself and my characters more than me.

My science fiction novel, *Shards of Time*, did pretty well for a first novel. A lot of people read it. It was nominated for a Nebula Award, and I had chances to talk with large groups about my ideas. But I couldn't get them to believe. My ideas were just ideas. No one really thinks ghost holes are real. Or that a man could fall into one and appear elsewhere, anywhere, even as far away as the end of time. Perhaps I am mad. My idea for skylands is based on a flagrant interpretation of gravitational geometry. I think I answered the meteorology of the World correctly, if my hunch about gravity vacuoles in the cosmic black hole are reasonable. But these are trivialities. To believe that Carl has gone to this place—that is madness.

My insanity is really that I don't know if I am mad or not. Reality is an open mystery, and I've closed myself off too long with my ideas and emotions. If I have to go mad to understand what happened to Carl, I won't regret it. Ignorance is worse than madness.

> Where grief meets hope
> we are all ghosts
> of our blood, limbs of the wind, unknown
> to ourselves.

Just as lines of force end nowhere, my own connections are wider than metrics. I am not imbedded in space. I am not flowing through time. I am spacetime. And more. For spacetime is not faithful to the quantum principle. I won't expound on geometrodynamics here except to say that I belong not to spacetime but to superspace, the reality "below" the Planck distance (10^{-33}cm) that projects the manifest world we live in.

At the level of superspace, the gravitational collapse that began and will end our universe is continuing now, seething everywhere as everything. Lines of force nowhere end, so the Field is here with me. Even in the void between galaxies, virtual pairs of positive and negative electrons, mu mesons, and baryons are continually being created and annihilated. Created by what? By the Field—the pregeometry underlying spacetime. It is here, right here where you are. You are made of it. You are it. The point of departure. The metric elasticity of the vacuum energy. You are nothing becoming everything.

> KILL GOD with the dead of night
> and the wound of dawn
> becomes your wound. Lack leads
> the way in.

I rest my life on the darkness. I lay down my soul. I am nothing.

Last month, I was arrested. I hadn't paid rent or bills for three months, and one day the police came. I was inspelling when they arrived. They thought I was in a coma. So I was taken to a hospital and from there I was brought here to this narrow bed in this empty room. They say I'm crazy. I've tried to explain about inspelling and how the mind is a condensation of the Field. But my explanations do sound like madness.

Look, I tell them—I tell you—there are ghost holes all around us. And *inside* us! They are carrying us down the years. And as we go, anything can happen.

—excerpts from *The Decomposition Notebook*
   by Zeke Zhdarnov

*   *   *

Encountering the central, abstract terror of isolation, which the hero must bear to become an individual, is the task in *Arc of the Dream*. The solar hero this time is an adolescent bully, Dirk Heiser. He confronts the fiery-cold spirit of the inner world in the form of Insideout, an alien from a realm smaller than a quark, a reality of infinite energy. Insideout is the innermost secret teacher, who shows the startled-awake hero that the opposite to singularity is not infinity but love.

> *Here is an excerpt from* Arc of the Dream, *third novel in the Radix Tetrad. Attanasio fan Roger Zelazny called it "a kaleidoscopic adventure. A potent piece of storytelling."*

The land looked evil. Black rocks shaped like knives covered the earth. *Aa lava*, Donnie Lopes said to himself as he carefully stepped onto the frozen torrent. The lava was sharp-toothed as a ripsaw, and Donnie with his gimpy right leg stopped frequently and looked ahead to where the black flow slashed down slopes of scaly pines to the green sea miles away. Hell vents streaked with blistery colors leaked wisps of yellow smoke, and the air stank like a sewer. Above the steamy terrain and the bunsen blue of the ocean's horizon, the sky boiled with clouds. Sunlight splashed in evanescent puddles among the charred hills and the tormented oases of scrub trees. *No wonder the Polynesians thought this land belonged to the gods*, Donnie thought. *No one else would want to live here. Moun-*

taintops, oceanbottoms, lava fields—the gods always get the crappiest real estate.

Donnie was a seventeen-year-old from Honolulu on his high school's senior class trip to Mauna Loa, the biggest volcano in the world. Because of his withered leg, he had to forego the hike along Devastation Trail with his classmates. He was supposed to sit in the ranger station and read about the rare plants and birds of the volcanic range, but after the others had left he had gone out to the back of the wood-slatted station and had found a trail of his own that gashed through the bristly shrubs behind the restrooms and emerged in this scorched landscape.

This trek wasn't as dangerous as it seemed, Donnie reassured himself. If he fell and lost his cane, he could always shout and holler and someone would hear him. He had spent his whole life being left behind because of his deformity, left to read books while others played ball or danced or explored. He had recently come to feel that he'd read too many books, that he knew more about what the world was supposed to be like than what it was.

The toppling clouds swept the black landscape with fiery shadows, and from a scarp beside a ridge of ohelo shrubs as gray and twisted as smoke, something flashed. *Mica*, he thought at first, then immediately corrected himself: *Mica's a silicate, fool. It's found in metamorphic rock, not in an igneous flow like this.* He edged closer to get a better look at it.

The nearer Donnie got, the more careful he had to be, because the land tilted steeply downward. Even someone with two strong legs would have been in jeopardy, and Donnie moved gingerly and with a spry wisdom that he had earned from a lifetime with his cane. On the face of the sheer incline, he tested each step twice with the cane and descended far enough into the pit of sharp rocks to see that the sun-hot glint was not bouncing off broken glass or crumpled foil.

The object looked about the size of a twenty-five-cent piece but oblong and blue-silver, and he was disappointed that it wasn't something he could recognize from this distance, because now he would have to go all the way down.

The brittle lava snapped under his weight, and his bad leg spun free. But his cane lodged firmly in a crevice, and his good leg braced itself on a firm jut of stone. He tottered briefly, the sweat of his strenuous effort flying from his face like chipped glass. He squatted, grateful that he was wearing his scruffy green denim pants, and cautiously crabwalked the rest of the way down.

The bright object was a slender metallic ovoid, cool to his touch and shimmery as a piece of the wind. He picked it up, and the sunlight fanned off it in a spectral smile as he turned it with the fingers of one hand, like a monkey with a strange fruit. It was featureless.

Rainbows angel-haired about it, and a peculiar feeling welled up in Donnie. The feeling suffused all of him at once like the rush of a drug but softer, more like a feeling of weather or time of day. He thought of October in an old forest, the ember scent of dead leaves glowing in the air, the sky amethyst, the day's last window, staring through cold vapors into the pins of the night, the depths that held all the stars, the void that encompassed all the days of every world, gleaming like a jewel. *Weird*.

The alien in his palm was terrified and in great pain. It was a 5-space being exquisitely bound to a precise point within the continuum, and by moving it, Donnie was killing it. Within its iridium shell, its brain was verging on panic.

*　　*　　*

The Last Legends of Earth is the Tetrad's coda, in which the dream of human life is woken again by the alien intelligence billions of years after we have become extinct. Humans find themselves in a realm of drifting planetoids built from the shattered remains of Earth, where they are treated as things, bait for an alien enemy. This is the hero's world, the timeless solitude and weirdness of the individual outside the tribe, outside society, in what the aboriginals call the land of the dead—which is really the lengthened shadow of life beyond good and evil. The animal soul gets confused there. The secret understanding of transformation eludes it. It becomes regressive and depressional. And that's where the villains in the Tetrad come from. Those same villains stalk us in our waking lives—the fear, ignorance and pain of human existence.

Finally, the Tetrad, as an adventure series of heroes and villains, is a celebration of those dark forces that challenge the solar power in each of us. After all, the villains are the ones who call down the spiritual powers. They make necessary that confrontation from which all true vitality emerges, often as healing wisdom—so that what before was merely accidental and ambivalent begins to work profoundly on us, and we inherit the power to find meaning, to invent it, and so create a more valid world.

Here is an excerpt from The Last Legends of Earth, *Attanasio's most ambitious novel to date and an example of world-building on a par with such books as* Dune *and the* Foundation *trilogy.*

This chapter is for those people who remember Earth. The first thing you have to know is that your memories are real. Your certainty that you have lived before in a very different place than where you are now is not a delusion. Earth actually did exist, long ago. The swirl of stars that fills the night sky is the galaxy where we lived. Remember the Sun? It was a star in that galaxy. Two billion years ago, it blew up, and the Earth was blown apart with it. This happened long after human life had become extinct. The exploding Sun shattered the Earth and cast the hot debris into the cold darkness of the void. The rubble floated in the vacuum almost all that time, mixing with the gas clouds of space. A few thousand years ago, an intelligent being from a reality we had never suspected found our dust. For its own alien purposes and by its own strange science, that intelligent being read in our dust the cryptarch of our lives (the fossilized DNA sealed in pebbles of the shattered Earth by the heat of the exploding Sun). From our cryptarch, the alien creates us again. And not just our bodies. You remember Earth because your consciousness, which is in fact a wavepattern of light emitted by your brain, was retrieved from the vacuum, where it had been expanding at the speed of light since you died.

The alien that regenerated you is not God nor even a god. The experience of being reborn in adult form out of the ground, cauled in a birthsack that grew with us in the loam, seems miraculous—but only until you understand that this has been accomplished with sophisticated and impersonal machinery. All the forests and jungles, all the multitudes of animals from every era of life on Earth, all the dinosaur herds, whales, and even bacteria and viruses, are products of a machine. The alien that operates this giant machine is a mortal being, albeit one whose time-span is enormously longer than ours. It is known variously as Gai, the Rimstalker, the World Maker, and the World Eater. By whatever name you call it, this being is an alien, inhuman and indifferent to human affairs. It is not interested in you, though you may think that it is because, as you will find, you do not age as quickly here as you did on Earth or as quickly as your fellow humans who were born of parents in these worlds. This is not because the alien favors you; it is a side effect of the regeneration process. The alien is not a spiritual being. Many lives have been lost disputing this issue. The truth is, this being regenerated you to serve as bait for yet another alien intelligence, its enemy, a species of sapient, winged spiders called zōtl. Zōtl eat people. See "Tactics" under *zōtl* in the index for effective ways of avoiding and defending yourself against these cunningly lethal entities.

Your life belongs to you. You owe no debt to the being that roused you to this second life. Neither must you expect this being to guide you or benefit you in any way. It will not. You must find your own way now. This manual is designed to help you understand and survive any of the fifteen worlds as well as the Overworld itself, wherever you may find yourself.